Prima Donna

Karen Swan lives in Sussex with her husband, three children, two dogs and her car called Meltchet.

Visit Karen's website at www.karenswan.com
or you can find Karen Swan's author page on Facebook
or follow her on Twitter @KarenSwan1

By Karen Swan

Players
Prima Donna
Christmas at Tiffany's
The Perfect Present
Christmas at Claridge's

KAREN
SWAN
Prima
Donna

PAN BOOKS

For Anders
You know why. Don't forget it.

First published 2011 by Pan Books

This edition published 2013 by Pan Books
an imprint of Pan Macmillan
20 New Wharf Road, London N1 9RR
Associated companies throughout the world
www.panmacmillan.com

ISBN 978-1-5098-0728-4

A CIP catalogue record for this book is available from the British Library.

Typeset by Ellipsis Digital Limited, Glasgow
Printed and bound by CPI Group (UK) Ltd, Croydon, CR0 4YY

Visit **www.panmacmillan.com** to read more about all our books
and to buy them. You will also find features, author interviews and
news of any author events, and you can sign up for e-newsletters
so that you're always first to hear about our new releases.

Acknowledgements

My biggest thanks must go to Thalia for her expertise, encouragement and valuable time helping me research this book. Quite what I would have done without a former ballerina on the editing team, I just don't know. She has skilfully led me through the maze of performance technicalities – and given me an A level in French in the process – and if I have managed to create an air of authenticity surrounding both the rigours and beauty of ballet, then it is down to her guidance alone.

To Jenny, too, I am deeply indebted. Her featherlight but precision editing has really whipped this book into shape, and I am just so relieved the quest for a title didn't lead to any resignations!

The entire team at Pan is a dream to work with and so hugely supportive. I really couldn't ask for more.

Amanda, my brilliant agent, who has as fabulous taste in Zara tops as she does in books. Thank you so much for the lunches and moral support.

Last but not least, my love and thanks go out to my parents and parents-in-law, who make countless trips to the park and do the numerous school runs in the cause of giving me precious writing time. I love my children more than anything, but heavens they're noisy!

Prologue

She pulled on the black leotard that had been handed to her when she'd enrolled. It was a size too small and it pulled over the bust, but it didn't matter. She looked like a proper ballerina. She slipped the satin ballet shoes on her feet – they were still warm from the previous girl's audition – and tightened the ribbon for a better fit. It was the first time she'd ever worn ballet shoes and she pointed her toes, admiring how her feet looked in them.

The double doors to the audition room opened and she looked up as another five girls came out. It was like that every ten minutes. Five girls in, five girls out. There were literally thousands of people milling about; she'd overheard someone saying twenty thousand kids had come to audition for the eighty places. She tried not to panic about it. She could never have imagined that so many people would come – that she wasn't the only one looking for a way out to a better life.

Many of the girls were busying themselves with impressive displays of stretching that were intended to psych out their neighbours just as much as to warm their muscles.

She pointed her own toes and admired her feet again. To think – pink satin on her feet! For once, they looked so pretty. They didn't usually look pretty. They usually looked bloodied, blistered and dusty as she desensitized them by standing on river rocks and clambering barefoot over mountain scree.

She looked up and saw her brother walking towards her, back in his Sunday Best. The boys' auditions had been held all morning.

'How did it go?' she asked as he dropped his basket on the floor and slid down the wall, tucking his knees up.

He shrugged. 'I couldn't turn my legs round.'

'You mean your turn out?'

He shrugged again.

'It's okay. You're only eight. They wouldn't expect you to be able to do much technically yet. They're just looking to see whether you've got the right body type and any musicality,' she reassured, squeezing him to her.

The boy rested his chin on his knees and sighed. He missed Mamma already. 'How come you know all these words?'

It was her turn to shrug. 'It's our escape ticket. I need to know as much about it as possible.' She looked around at all the children buzzing up and down the corridor. Anyone wandering in off the streets would think it was an orphanage.

'What will happen if we don't get in?' he asked her, resting his cheek on his knee and looking up at her.

'That's not going to happen. We've prepared for this.' She tried to keep her voice even. She wondered how many others among the children had had only a book illustrating ballet steps from which to learn. He didn't know yet they weren't going back, that if they couldn't make a home in here, they'd have to make it on the streets.

A door opened and strains of Tchaikovsky filtered through.

'Hear that?' she grinned, full of the optimism of youth. 'Our lives are going to be filled only with music and beauty from now on. We're on our way.'

His big limpid eyes blinked. She heard her name called.

'Wish me luck,' she said, leaning over and kissing the top of his head. She breathed in his scent and held him close for a moment. 'Stay here and don't go anywhere. I won't be long.'

She ran to the door and it closed with a sigh behind her. She never saw him again.

Chapter One

'*Da!* Leave me, I'll do it,' she said, her accent thickening with impatience, as the dresser struggled to find the front of the tutu. This one, whisper-pink with real diamonds sewn into the tulle layers, had a thong attached, *carnivale* style, at her specific behest. She stepped into it, completely oblivious to being half naked in front of a roomful of strangers.

She slipped her arms through the ribbon straps for the overscaled tulle wings and jiggled her breasts in the balconette bra. She admired her reflection in the mirror. The audience wouldn't even notice the pink diamonds on the million-dollar bra. No one worked a tutu like Pia Soto.

'Miss Soto, if you're ready . . .' the dresser said nervously, frightened of upsetting the notoriously temperamental diva. She motioned towards the director, who was standing at the top of the steps by the stage, a mic wired to his ear and a clipboard in his hand. His face wore a calm smile, but his fingers were twitching against his thigh and she could see the terror in his eyes. Just ten more feet. Ten more feet, then she'd be on the runway, the finale would be underway and he could run screaming for the Seychelles.

Pia pointed her four-inch stilettoed foot and checked the pink ribbons that were criss-crossed all the way up her thighs, then walked towards the eight-foot-square white glittering box, held together by a giant pink satin ribbon. She looked sensational.

She stepped into it and the director shut the door behind her, as relieved as a prison warder to have his charge behind bars. He placed his hand to his ear and spoke to the DJ. Expertly, seamlessly, the familiar tinkling of the Sugar Plum Fairy began to thread into the funk of 'Superfreak' as the box was mechanically levered up through the trapdoor in the stage.

Inside the box, Pia placed her foot on the taped square, and assumed the position. As the box reached stage level the footplate began to revolve smoothly. Outside, she could hear the scantily clad models lining up on each side of the box, hands on each other's hips as they played tug of war with the ribbon.

She heard the bow give, and the sides of the box fell down, bringing the audience to their feet as they saw the baddest and most brilliant ballerina in the world *pirouette* before them like their very own music-box fairy.

Pia rotated four times, letting them absorb the bombshell body that was usually hidden beneath tights and classical costumes and some inappropriate lover. Although, at five foot five, she wasn't tall, she had a figure that was rarely seen on *pointe*. For a start, most of her sixty-five inches were in her limbs – long slight arms that, with the tiniest movement of her wrist and fingers, could phrase a feeling better than any poet; and lithe lean legs she could famously lift and hold at 180 degrees.

But it was her curves, squeezed closely together on a tiny torso, which so scandalized the purists of the ballet world and had *Sports Illustrated* begging her to do their swimwear cover. Her C cup threatened to spill out of every tutu, something she actively encouraged by insisting on designing her own costumes. And her handspan waist – which the male dancers loved to encircle when lifting her – sat atop an unashamedly high and rounded butt. 'My Brazilian heritage,' she would exclaim, defiantly. 'What do you want me to do about it? Stop dancing so that you don't have to look at it?'

The cheers bounced off the walls as she stepped out of the *pirouette* and stalked ferociously down the Victoria's Secret runway like a tiger in the grass – chin down, glass-green eyes glittering, her mane of tawny hair blowing wildly behind her.

Hands on hips, feet apart, she stood at the end, staring past the white-hot lights she was so used to. The slick Manhattan crowd roared with delight as ticker tapes fell from the ceiling and the other models, as gangly as giraffes by comparison, lined up behind her.

She knew she'd be on every front page tomorrow morning. Just like she knew her artistic director, Monsieur Baudrand, would be on the phone first thing, bawling her out. He'd specifically vetoed this type of event. 'Charity or not, it is no good for the image of the company,' he had shouted, pushed to breaking point by his young star, who acted more like a pop singer than a principal dancer.

There was no doubt she had done more to raise ballet's profile and introduce it to a younger audience than anyone since Rudolf Nureyev. She had single-handedly sexed it up. Performances by the Chicago City Ballet Company (ChiCi) were sold out a year in advance because of her and they were being invited to tour all over the world.

Pia Soto may have been only twenty-four but she was already an international sex symbol, and the face of everything from Chanel Allure Parfum, Chloé and Tod's to Adidas, Patek Philippe and Lancôme. Her airtight contract meant she couldn't endorse anything that undermined ballet's prim image but, even with that restriction in place, what she earned in sponsorship deals dwarfed her dancing salary, giving her financial independence from the company and the power to behave like a brat. The tail was well and truly wagging the dog.

Backstage now, the atmosphere was electric. All the tension that had suffocated the room just minutes earlier had released into laughter and expansive spirits. Champagne corks were going off like party poppers, and boyfriends and journalists trooped backstage for telephone numbers and sound bites.

'You! Keep them away, will you?' Pia ordered the dresser, who had – mistakenly – assumed all the hard work was over. The director was nowhere to be seen, but paparazzi flashbulbs were going off.

Turning her back, Pia untied her shoes' silken bondage straps and shimmied out of the priceless bra and tutu, quickly pulling on the silky body stocking she'd arrived in. She smoothed some black leg warmers all the way up her long legs and stuffed her feet into some battered Uggs, as Sophie dashed over, checking her watch.

'You've got nine minutes,' she said, picking up the diamond-encrusted bra from the floor and handing it to a security guard.

Pia nodded, grabbing a hairbrush and bashing out the backcombing the hairstylist had perfected only ten minutes before. She winced as the brush caught in the tangles.

Sophie took the brush from her, and spritzing some de-tangler onto her hair she began expertly smoothing the thick, wavy, toffee-coloured mane that seemed to colour-match

Pia's skin. With a small, straight nose, sparkling light green eyes and pillowy lips that retained an adolescent pinkness, she wasn't just a precocious talent – she was a notable beauty too. It was little wonder American *Vogue* had just put her on their cover.

In the mirrors, Sophie could see her own copper ringlets bouncing up and down like Bo Peep's. She personally bank-rolled the John Frieda haircare empire with her mass-volume buys of serum, trying to keep her frizz under control, and she knew her pale Irish complexion was only ever going to have the 'interesting' gig going on. Aged twenty-two, she had been a lanky five foot eleven since she was twelve, and still had no bum or bust to speak of. It wasn't that she was unattractive – far from it – but compared to the exotic promise of Pia Soto, Sophie O'Farrell felt as plain as they came.

'You really rocked it out there tonight,' Sophie said as she gradually tamed Pia's hair, pulling it up into a high ponytail. 'The Goldman Sachs table was going bananas.'

Pia rolled her eyes. That figured.

From behind her, there was a discreet cough.

Turning, she found herself staring at an elegantly tailored back belonging to the CEO of Victoria's Secret.

'It's okay. You can turn around, Mr Spence. I'm decent.'

'What a shame,' said another voice, from the far side of a hanging rail. A tall man stepped forward, one arm resting nonchalantly on the rail, the other in his pocket. He was wearing Brooks Brothers' black tie and a self-assured smile. His dark brown hair was worn long on top, and he had deep-set grey eyes and a Roman nose that looked as though it may have been broken once. Judging by the cockiness radiating from him, Pia was quite sure he'd deserved it.

Pia raised an eyebrow and looked at Bryan Spence

questioningly. His dove-white hair was offset by a mahogany Caribbean tan.

'Please. Forgive my companion's insolence,' he said, bemused. 'I hope you don't mind our intrusion backstage. It's just that when Mr Silk here—'

'Will,' the handsome stranger offered, bowing forward like Hamlet.

'When Will heard you weren't staying for the auction, he offered a rather substantial sum to the charity if I would introduce you before you left.' Mr Spence shrugged apologetically.

Pia smiled back at him. 'Well, seeing as it's for the charity . . .' She looked at Will Silk. 'A pleasure,' she said demurely, offering an elegant hand, every inch the poised ballerina.

Will took it and kissed it.

Pia withdrew her hand quickly. 'But I'm afraid I really can't stay.' She turned her head slightly towards Sophie, who checked her watch again.

'Seven minutes,' Sophie said.

Pia shrugged. 'I have to fly.'

'Of course,' Bryan smiled.

'So soon?' Will said, astonished. He looked at Bryan. 'That must have been the most expensive minute of my life.'

'I did tell you.'

'Well, never mind. We shall become better acquainted soon enough,' he said, slipping a casual hand into his trouser pocket as he watched Pia. Sophie was tucking and spraying the last stray tendrils into her bun.

Pia cocked her head, irked by his self-assurance on the matter.

'Will's going to be among the many bidders trying to

win the lot for the private solo and dinner with you, Miss Soto.'

'Trying?' Will retorted. 'You know me better than that, Bryan.'

Bryan Spence nodded his head, laughing. He turned to Pia. 'Will heads up the Black Harbour hedge fund and he's known for his . . . uh, winning streak.'

'It's true. I never lose,' he shrugged.

Pia stared at him, a scowl beginning to form across her pretty features. 'Is that so?' she asked.

'Five minutes,' Sophie whispered, beginning to break into a cold sweat. This was cutting it too close. She held out Pia's voluminous orange quilted parka and helped her into it.

'I'm also a patron of the Royal Ballet in London,' he added, aware that his formidable business renown had failed to impress her. 'Unlike most of the men who'll be trying to win you tonight, I do at least know the difference between a *pirouette* and a profiterole.'

'Win *me* . . .' she echoed quietly, before suddenly shrugging. 'I'm just amazed we've never met before now.' Sarcasm hovered above her words but too lightly to settle.

Will tried to read her eyes but Pia looked away. She grabbed her duffel bag and shook Bryan Spence's hand quickly. 'It's been a pleasure, Bryan,' she smiled, her eyes twinkling.

'The pleasure has been all ours, Pia. We're on course to raise over three-quarters of a million dollars here tonight and in a very large part that is directly due to you. So thank you. You are truly our angel.'

Giving Will the briefest of nods, she ran lightly to the back door, turning to Sophie as she got there. She whispered in her ear and handed her the duffel bag. 'I'll see you back there.'

And then she ran out into the snowy night, a woodland nymph swaddled against the New York winter.

Adam was already back on stage, when she burst in through the Met Opera's stage door ninety seconds later.

'Oh my God! Where the hell have you been? Do you have any idea the worry you've caused? The panic that's been going on?' ranted Raymond, the stage manager, as she sat on the ground and pulled off her snowy boots. Her shoes and costume – a diaphanous white tulle dress – were exactly where she'd asked Sophie to leave them. Quickly, Raymond spoke into his mic. 'It's okay. She's back! She's back! Tell Ingrid she's off the hook, and she's Willi number four again.'

Raymond looked down at Pia. 'Do you have *nothing* to say?' he demanded hissily. 'You walk out during the interval and tell no one where you're going? It's been bedlam back here. We thought you'd been abducted. Old Badlands has practically had a stroke. The orchestra has had to play the overture twice, not that the audience seems to have noticed. Oh but, please God, don't let that bastard critic Bowles be out there tonight.' He rocked his head dramatically in his hands. He could feel one of his migraines coming on. Why did artistes have to be so damned . . . unpredictable?

Pia began tying the ribbons around her ankles, stretching and pointing her feet in the blocks, and resolutely ignoring him. She needed to get her muscles warm again, and immerse herself in solitude and calm. She needed to get back into character. Giselle was weak, broken, and if Pia got into a confrontation now she'd be anything but.

Standing by the podium in the wings, hidden by the thick velvet curtain, she stretched her arms into *port de bras*, slowly unfolding a leg like a flamingo. She extended a leg, in *attitude devant*, her supporting foot flat, before raising herself effortlessly on *pointe*, moving through *la seconde* to *arrière*.

Instantly entranced and silenced, Raymond stepped back out of her orbit. And not just to let her concentrate. Getting in the way of one of her powerful legs would be like being hit in the face with a mallet. He knew better than most the tension at the heart of ballet: brute strength cloaked in delicate fragility.

'Okay. We'll talk about it later, then,' he said quietly. Right now, the show had to go on.

Pia heard the music rise, the first flute beckon, the oboes soar. She didn't need to count the bars. The music was calling her, an irresistible pull tearing her from the shadows, drawing her out into the limelight and back onto the stage, the only home she had ever known.

Only when she was on the stage did she realize she still had the black leg warmers on.

An hour and a half later, and for the second time that night, Pia found herself stealing out of the Met Opera before anyone could notice.

'A secret assignation perhaps?' Will Silk quipped, leaning against a limo.

Pia frowned at him. What was he doing here?

'I decided that for the amount I had paid to meet you, the least Spence could do was tell me where you had escaped to,' he explained, walking towards her. His black cashmere coat was turned up at the collar, his hands stuffed into his pockets. 'Starring at a charity gala midway through a performance, huh? Did your bosses even know?'

'I guess they will tomorrow,' she shrugged, looking down

the street for her car. She needed to get away from here before Baudrand came after her. The leg-warmer gaffe wouldn't be easily forgiven.

'Do you fancy that dinner now?'

'No. I've got a flight to catch.' She stared at him levelly. 'Besides, you didn't win.'

Will shifted, surprised. 'How do you know? You weren't there.'

'I have my spies,' she replied coolly. 'What did it go for in the end anyway?'

Will frowned. 'So you *don't* know.'

'No, I do,' she said tonelessly. 'I just don't know for how much.'

Sophie came jogging up the street, Pia's duffel banging on her shoulder. She hit an icy patch just as she reached the duo, careering past in a flurry of limbs.

Will reached out and hooked an arm gallantly around her waist.

'Careful there,' he grinned.

Sophie blushed. 'Thanks.' She looked quickly at Pia, terrified of being bawled out. 'The car's just coming. Sorry. It was still outside the Mandarin Oriental. Miscommunication on my part.' She dug into one of her pockets and handed Pia a form to sign. 'Here. You just need to sign on the dotted line.'

Pia autographed the form just as the limo purred up to the kerb and the driver got out to open her door.

Pia nodded. 'Two hundred and forty thousand dollars? I thought you never lost, Mr Silk.' She gave the form back to Sophie, who in turn handed over some flight tickets.

Will stared at her, baffled. What was that she had signed? 'Well, to be honest, I thought I could probably persuade you to have dinner with me anyway. I had already paid a similar amount just to get backstage. My accountants would have been very displeased with me if I'd shelled out over half a million dollars just to be introduced and have dinner with you.' He shot her a winning smile.

'So, you assume I can be bought, Mr Silk . . .' Pia said slowly, her tone deliberating. He thought she sounded like a Bond Girl. 'But that I'm only worth a certain price.' She looked at him coldly.

'Well, I wouldn't put it quite like that,' he said, surprised. She was unbelievably prickly. Everything he'd heard about her was true. 'But I apologize if I've caused offence, and insist that you let me make it up to you. What are you doing this weekend? Come to Europe with—'

Pia started walking away. 'I've already told you I'm going away, Mr Silk,' she said, bored by his charm offensive.

'Anywhere nice?' he persevered. He didn't usually have to try this hard.

'Given that I would now define "nice" as anywhere you're not, then yes,' she said rudely, stepping into the car. She just wanted to get into the mountains and ride her raw, poor, wicked lover.

The driver shut her door and walked around the car.

Will Silk stood in the cold night and stared at the car's blacked-out windows, which remained defiantly shut.

'Something tells me we've got off on the wrong foot,' he said with impressive understatement to Sophie, who was standing beside him, utterly mortified.

He turned to face her. 'What is that piece of paper you're holding anyway?' he said, taking it from her hands before the words were out of his mouth.

'Oh no. I really don't think you should . . .'

There was a stunned silence.

'*She* was the winning bidder?' he asked incredulously. 'She bid for herself?' He glared at Sophie furiously and she cowered beneath his gaze. 'Why would she do that?'

'So that . . . you wouldn't . . . win, I think,' she said quietly, not able to meet his eyes.

'She paid two hundred and forty thousand dollars *not* to have dinner with me?'

'Something like that,' Sophie muttered. 'Basically gave her advertising fee back to them.'

Will looked after the car as it slipped into the inky night. A small part of him was impressed. Not much surprised him, but he hadn't seen *that* coming.

'Well, I'm delighted to have made such a strong impression on her,' he said finally, a smile back on his lips. He turned to face Sophie again. 'But tell your boss that she's thrown down the gauntlet and I am obliged to pick it up. I won't allow her to get away from me next time.'

And with that, he strode back to his car, angry, intrigued and smitten. The game was on.

Chapter Two

The plane landed with a satisfying whush, the mighty engines' roar muffled by the snowy Aspen mountains on all sides. Pia looked up at the pistes, still teeming with life as the night-skiers added darkness to gradient for their thrills. She was itching to get up there. Her insurance precluded it of course – day or night – but what they didn't know didn't hurt them, she reckoned. Besides, breaking the rules was almost what she liked best about it. *That* was her sport. Renegade, rebel, bad girl. Getting away with it.

During the flight she'd changed into the clothes Sophie had packed for her. Skinny grey jeans, black crocodile-skin boots and a berry-coloured cashmere roll neck. As the host-esses readied the doors, Pia belted her black Prada ski jacket more tightly and pulled up the fur-lined hood, partly to brace herself against the cold that would come rushing through, partly as cover from the other passengers' excited stares.

She was first off, and stalked straight to the car that was waiting for her on the tarmac. She tried Andy's number again. Where was he? Not on the slopes still, surely? The Winter X Games – the Olympics of extreme snow sports – was finishing tomorrow, and as one of the event's headliners, Andy Connor, defending his Snocross title for the third year running, needed to be resting.

Well, after a fashion anyway. She didn't intend to let him get much sleeping done tonight. After all, she hadn't seen him for twelve days now. She closed her eyes as she thought of him and what they had together. It wasn't love. Nothing like. But they'd been together for four months, and the sex was scorching. She was hooked.

The car drew up outside the Little Nell and a good-looking young porter dashed outside to take her bag.

'Such a pleasure to see you again, Miss Soto,' he beamed. The hotel got more than its fair share of celebrities, but Pia Soto was a class above. She wasn't just famous, she was notorious.

'Andy Connor's in the Paepcke Suite as usual, I take it?' she asked, going straight through the lobby and towards the lifts. There was a pause in the buzz of conversation as the other guests clocked her long legs and stunning deportment.

The lift doors opened and she stepped in. The porter followed, her canvas Marc Jacobs duffel bag on his shoulder, and pressed the button to take them up. He watched Pia in the mirror as she untied her jacket and fluffed up her hair. Ready for action.

'Yuh?' said a deep easy voice, as they knocked on the door. Andy opened it, wrapped in just a towel, his long dirty-blond hair looking – amazingly – like it had just been washed. But the stubble on his chin was reassuringly established and no amount of scrubbing would shift the freaky tan marks on his face from his helmet visor.

'Babe! What're you doing here?' he grinned, as Pia launched herself effortlessly into his arms, knocking off his towel. Andy didn't care. He had no modesty. He just turned around and carried her into the bedroom, his white retreating butt signifying that the porter could leave. 'You said you were in New York.'

The door clicked shut.

Andy threw her down on the vast bed, and grabbed her ankles, pulling off one boot and then the other.

'I know,' she giggled as he pushed up her hips and pulled off her jeans, her knickers sliding down with them. 'But we've got a couple of days off and I figured you might need some moral suppor—'

He clasped her head in his hands and kissed her deeply.

'Damn right,' he grinned again, pulling her jumper over her head. She wasn't wearing a bra. She rarely bothered, what with the amount of changing she had to do.

He dropped his head and took one of her luscious, world-famous breasts in his mouth. They were like her, able to defy gravity magnificently. She tipped her head back and moaned as he used his tongue on her, probing and teasing. She'd been thinking about this all the way over.

He scooped her up again and marched across the room, kissing her as he opened the doors onto the verandah. The shadowy mountains pulled around them like black curtains.

'Aaaaah, let me go,' she squealed as the freezing night air bit at her naked body.

'Not if you're going to carry on doing that,' he laughed, feeling her wriggle against him as he stepped down into the hot tub, steaming and bubbling below.

He felt her body go limp as the hot water warmed her up and eased her muscles, which were always so sore. If he ever thought his sport was tough, he just had to look at what she did for a living. When he'd surprised her coming off stage one night, she'd been more bloodied than a boxer.

She stretched out, away from him, her arms holding on to the other side, her head bobbing as she lay back in the water and looked up at the mountains.

'D'you wanna beer?' he asked.

She shook her head.

'I will, if you don't mind,' he said, cracking open a bottle. Pia floated happily, aware of his eyes on her, on her breasts rising out of the water so tantalizingly. She felt Andy move forward, putting a hand under her butt, pushing her up so that she came out of the water, and then a soft, warm fizzing in her groin. She looked down. He was pouring his beer . . .

She closed her eyes in ecstasy as he began to drink. The man was wild! She bit her lip and held her breath.

The papers called her his Snow Angel. They both knew she was anything but.

It was 9.47 a.m. Aspen time (an hour later in New York) when Pia's mobile rang. Usually she would still be asleep. She didn't like rising before ten, not after a performance (and last night definitely counted as a performance – with three encores), but Andy's event started at ten and he had got up early to work on his bike, doing some last-minute tweaks.

'Hi,' she said in her best sing-song voice, as though she was picking up to a lover, although she already knew who it would be. The only people who ever rang her were Sophie, Andy (for the moment) and Badlands. 'Oh hi, Monsieur Baudrand.'

'What do you have to say for yourself, Pia?' the Frenchman growled down the line.

'About last night? I know. I am *so* furious. I mean, was I the *only* person doing my job?' she sighed wearily. 'Let's face it, everybody knows I'm immersed in the role; leg warmers are the last thing on my mind. I can't even *feel* my legs. I'm just *spirit* by then. But I can't believe no one mentioned anything. Or Raymond! What's he there for – just to raise the curtain up and down? *Must* I do everything myself?' She dropped her voice confidingly. 'You know it's just like the company, *monsieur*. They're always so jealous of me. It's just the kind of petty pleasure they take in trying to humiliate me,' she purred.

'*Non!*' growled Baudrand, exasperated by his protégée's silky attempts to wriggle out of the firing line. '*That* is not why I am calling.'

She heard the flutter of newspapers being swept off the desk and onto the floor.

'Why do you do this?' he said darkly down the line. 'I said to you: *Non. Non.* Not this, Pia. It brings the ballet into disrepute.'

'Oh *that*.' Pia chuckled. 'You don't need to worry, Monsieur Baudrand, they're a lingerie company, not sex traffickers. Headlining the Victoria's Secret show is considered a great accolade.'

'Not in ballet, it's not!' he stabbed. 'I said, *Non*! Why do you never listen? Why must you always push me so? Is not like you need the money.'

'Well, I didn't do it for the money,' she snapped, irritated that he thought that was what motivated her. She'd rather strip for the hell of it than for money.

'Then why? It's bad enough we have headlines all the time of you with that druggie skier.' She heard him exhale impatiently.

'He's not a skier and he doesn't do drugs,' she sighed, checking her nails. 'If you must know, *monsieur*, I did it for the charity they were supporting,' she retorted. 'They're helping homeless kids in Manhat—'

'You? Did it for charity?' he interrupted. Now it was his turn to laugh. 'Tell me, did you waive your fee, then? Or did your rush of generosity only come after a little sweetener?'

Pia's nose flared indignantly. 'I gave it to the charity actually,' she huffed. Only to get rid of the arrogant financier of course, but giving was giving, right?

'You leave me with no choice, Pia,' he said quietly. 'You are in breach of your contract and you knew it when you chose to walk down that catwalk wearing little more than a porn-star tutu and some diamonds. I have already had the Board complain to me, and I have their full support in this. You are suspended for all remaining performances of *Giselle* in New York. You need not bother coming back to Chicago until we begin rehearsals for *Le Corsaire* next month.'

'What? But you can't do that,' Pia shouted, outraged. 'I *am* Giselle. You can't honestly think that . . . that girl . . .' She paused. What was her understudy's name? 'She's not up to the job of filling my shoes. She's not even up to the job of *tying* my shoes.' She'd spent two months in rehearsal for this, damn near busting her lower back perfecting that killing sequence of tiny jumps at the beginning of the second act. Besides, the critics had loved her, lauding her vulnerable naivety and fluidity of line.

'Actually, we're not using your understudy. And her name's *Ingrid*, by the way. *Non*. The tour has become too high-profile now. We need a star, not just a dancer.' He paused for a beat. 'We've asked Ava Petrova to guest.'

'What?' Pia shrieked again, outraged. 'No! You can't be serious.'

'But I am,' he said, quietly delighted to have scored a

victory for once. 'The Bolshoi was happy to accommodate our request when we explained you were indisposed.'

'*Filho da Puta!*' she swore furiously.

Ava Petrova had been her most avowed enemy all through ballet school. If Pia had been the darling of the Escola do Teatro Bolshoi no Brasil, Ava was the uncontested star of the Bolshoi's 'mother' academy in Moscow, and the two girls had been forever pitched against each other in ballet competitions. Usually it was Ava who came out on top. What thrilled audiences left judges cold – not to mention there was a prevailing mood among the ballet world's dignitaries that young Soto needed to be kept in check – and if Pia was the bad girl of ballet, showing off with her gymnastic *ballon* and ethereal grace, Ava was its head girl: tiny, terrifying and technically, clinically brilliant.

'This will come back to bite you on the ass. Everybody's only coming to see *me*. She's like a tin robot compared to me. They'll demand their money back. The ticket office will be so overwhelmed they'll . . . they'll go on strike.'

'Pia, you exaggerate your importance to this ballet and to this company,' Baudrand said solemnly. 'Your flagrant flouting of the rules cannot go on. You may be an exquisitely gifted dancer, but you are still not bigger than this company. I hope you will use this time to reflect and come back wiser and humbler.' He put the phone down to Pia, who was still huffing and puffing like the big bad wolf.

She was right of course. Even with Ava Petrova standing in, Pia Soto's withdrawal from the prestigious New York tour would be a PR fiasco. But the girl had to learn her place. The Board had insisted he take her to account on this. For all the youthful vigour and cool new profile she had brought to ballet's stuffy image, it was still very much a world run by staid traditionalists for whom even a diagonal arm position was considered radical.

Pia stared at the phone in fury. She couldn't believe he was reacting like this. She'd got back in time, hadn't she? She hadn't forfeited her contract with *him*. And what about all the money that had been raised for the charity? She'd helped raise nearly a million dollars for homeless kids! How could he ignore that?

A cheer welled up from the crowd below. She was sitting up in the VIP stands, along with the other competitors' wives and girlfriends, and she looked down at the banks of spectators lined up. Very few of them, it seemed, owned hairbrushes.

The roar from the lined-up machines (like quad bikes on skis) was deafening, as the finalists revved their engines manically, giving voice to the gallons of testosterone pumping through them. The crowd cheered even harder, urging them to bring it on.

Pia covered her ears with her hands as she checked out the line-up. Andy was in the middle, dressed in his favourite 'lucky' black and yellow suit. His helmet was already on but he still had the visor up. He looked up at the stands to wave at her, his hand stalling in mid-air. Pia thought he looked uncharacteristically nervous.

She blew him kisses back, encouragingly, and he nodded at her before slamming his visor down. Her hands flew back up to her ears as the flag came down and the race began. There was a mad scramble for space as the line-up immediately converged into a fiercely contested arrow, everyone clamouring for pole position. Four competitors were off their bikes before the first bend, and as much as she tried to be cool, she couldn't help her hands from flying to her mouth anxiously.

'They'll be okay, you know,' said a voice near her. She looked around. A little blond boy, no more than six, was sitting in the row behind, looking earnestly at her. 'My daddy's down there. He's the best.'

Pia smiled widely, her indignation with Baudrand abated by the boy's cute freckled face. 'Yeah? You must be very proud of him.'

The boy nodded. 'You bet. I don't usually get to see him compete, 'cos I have to go to school an' all. But Mom said this was special 'cos it's the X Games. We drove through the night to get here this morning as a surprise.'

'Really? Where did you drive from?'

'Saskatoon.'

'In Canada? Wow. You must be tired.'

The little boy beamed. 'Nah. I'm too excited.'

'So are you going to be a snocross rider when you grow up?'

'Yeah. Daddy's already teaching me. He got me a scaled-down version of his bike for Christmas.'

'Really?'

'Yeah. It's a Polaris XC120 and it's got the Sno-X running boards fitted already. Plus he got Oakley to make me some smaller stickers specially to put on my bike. They're his sponsors. It looks just like his now.'

Pia nodded, charmed by his enthusiasm. 'It sounds great. Really special.'

The little boy looked back down to the track. 'Yeah, it is.'

'What colour is it?'

He sighed, watching his dad proudly. 'His lucky colours. Black and yellow.'

Chapter Three

Sophie checked the room one last time, like a nervous dinner-party hostess, before she went and opened the door.

'Hi,' she smiled nervously, letting him in.

Adam bent down and kissed her on each cheek. He was fresh – or rather, not so fresh – from class and the smell of dried sweat drifted off him. She closed her eyes, savouring the smell of athleticism. The company's tour along the east coast – and currently concluding in New York – had been gruelling, with a full-on repertoire of *Giselle*, *Sleeping Beauty*, *The Nutcracker* and *The Snow Queen*, and Adam Bridges, as one of the male principals and, most pertinently, Pia Soto's partner of choice, had only one day off performances in every four. Today was that day, coinciding with Pia's brief sojourn to see Andy in Aspen.

'Wow! Nice place,' he beamed, taking in the view of the car park on the next block. 'Pia's really knocked herself out for you this time, hasn't she?'

Sophie giggled. As the stars of the company both Pia and Adam had suites on the top floor, eighteen floors up, with commanding views over Manhattan. 'It doesn't matter,' she shrugged good-naturedly. She had no ego about that sort of thing. She'd spent the first fifteen years of her life chasing through fields in southern Ireland, helping her mother milk the cows and collecting the eggs for breakfast. The tallest thing on her horizon back then had been the six-foot-three-inch sunflower she'd grown for a school competition. Power skylines meant nothing to her. Big city life, whatever its guise – be it in New York or Chicago, the place she now called home – was intoxicating enough to her. And frankly, having grown up with three little sisters in a two-bedroom cottage, she was just happy not to be sharing.

'How was class?' she asked.

'Ugh, don't ask. Badlands was in a particularly foul mood today. And my right hamstring's bothering me a bit,' he said, absent-mindedly rubbing it.

'Well, what are you doing here, then? You should have gone to the physio,' she scolded, feeling panicky at the thought that she might be held responsible for aggravating a possible injury. She knew from Pia's insurance paperwork that her legs were insured for $1.5 million. Adam's must be much the same.

He shrugged. 'Yeah, but if I saw her, I wouldn't be able to see you,' he winked.

'God, you shouldn't be missing Mary just to come and sit for me,' she gasped. 'It's not like it's for an exhibition or anything. I mean, no one will ever even see it and . . .'

'I'm not missing Mary,' he smiled, laying a warm hand on her arm and twisting her words. 'And anyway, it's not bad. I just need to get some ice on it before tomorrow.'

'Well look, there's an ice machine in the hall. One of the *considerable* perks of being on this floor,' she said wryly. 'At least let me get some for you.'

'Thanks, that'd be great,' he said, dropping his kitbag on the floor.

Sophie grabbed the plastic ice bucket and walked out into

the hallway. As the ice machine rumbled into life, she checked her appearance nervously in the glass of the fire cabinet. She'd spent the best part of two hours trying to get her hair sleek and she'd put on a new tinted lip gloss – she checked there was none on her teeth. She felt ridiculously nervous, hardly able to believe that Adam was sitting in her room. He was always so *nice* to her but he'd been her fantasy lover for so long, and every day watching him train and perform with Pia was filled with emotional drama – titillation when he caught her staring and grinned at her; despair when she caught him staring, with the same wistfulness, at Pia.

Everybody knew he was mad about Pia; everybody except Pia, it seemed. She horsed around with him in class and looked lovingly in his eyes during performances, but as soon as the rehearsal was over or the curtain dropped she raced off to be with her latest lover. No one had ever known Pia to stay for a single drink, not for celebration's sake and certainly not to socialize. She didn't need to make friends with the staff. She was the star. And although Adam had the talent to shine as brightly as she did, he lacked the attitude. He was too affable, too approachable, too ready to smile – and so, as far as Pia was concerned, once the work was done he was lumped together with the rest of them.

But only to Pia. To Sophie, he might be a team player but there was nothing pedestrian about him. She sighed as the ice clattered into the bucket. She didn't blame him for not noticing her. She never had stood out – well, not in the ways that counted anyway. She was skinny, not slender; lanky not statuesque; pale but with a ferocious blush on her. She was always popular but never the leader, and she harboured no illusions about one day being the cleverest or the prettiest girl in the room – she moved like Olive Oyl, for starters.

Still, her overall grace and grooming had come on in leaps and bounds in the three years she'd been working for Pia. She knew now that sparkly eyes, glowing skin, glossy hair and a perky walk came from facials at Bliss, olive-oil hair soaks, Bobbi Brown eyeshadow, ice baths and hot sex, and although Pia led the last two by example only, Sophie had absorbed the rest by osmosis.

She trotted back to the room, cheered that he had at least agreed to help her out today. In fact, he'd been really interested when she'd accosted him at the first night after-show party and tipsily asked if she could draw him.

'Here you g—' She trailed off, dropping the bucket.

Adam had stripped down and was walking naked towards the bathroom. He turned and her jaw dropped as deep as a *plié*.

'You don't mind if I take a quick shower, do you?' he asked. 'I stink.'

Sophie shook her head mutely.

'Besides, I figure if you're going to be drawing me in the buff, there's no point in me being coy, is there?'

Sophie shook her head again. Who'd said anything about drawing him nude? He must have just assumed it. Then again, ballet dancers viewed their bodies as the tools of their craft – although Pia was preternaturally aware that hers also doubled as a weapon of mass seduction – and, as such, they didn't share the modesty or vanity of the civilian population. If he wanted to be drawn nude, who was she to stop him?

'There's a bottle of vodka in my bag,' he said. 'Why don't you pour us both a glass and chuck some of that ice into it? It's not that cold, I'm afraid,' he said, disappearing into the bathroom.

Sophie nodded and swallowed hard. She heard the water start running and she tried to galvanize herself into action but her heart felt like it was perilously close to having an attack and she didn't dare move for another minute. Adam Bridges was naked in her room! Christ Almighty!

Oops. She caught herself blaspheming and cowered slightly, as though expecting a finger of lightning to strike her down. Think, Sophie! What would Pia do?

She rolled her eyes. She knew perfectly well what Pia would do. She'd get naked too and that would work because she had the body of a goddess. Adam would come out of the shower and pick her up and make sweet love to her right there. If he came out and found Sophie standing there naked, he'd call 911. Or security. Or his mum to come and take him home.

She was still standing there when she heard the water turn off. Quickly, she ran to the bedside table and grabbed two water tumblers, half-filling them with the vodka. She was picking the ice bucket off the floor as he walked back in, a towel round his waist.

'Here,' she said, dropping a clutch of ice cubes into the tumblers and handing him one.

His eyebrows shot up and he burst out laughing. 'Whoa! You'll have me dancing on a hangover tomorrow!' He looked down at her mischievously, a twist of hair flopping forward. 'You're not trying to get me drunk, are you, Miss O'Farrell?'

Sophie blushed beetroot. 'God, no!' she said, her Irish accent getting stronger with her embarrassment. 'I just thought it might calm your nerves a little.'

'My nerves? But I feel fine.' He paused, intrigued by her fluster. 'Are *you* nervous?'

Sophie swallowed nervously. 'I feel fine,' she croaked.

'Okay, then,' he said, clinking her glass and taking a huge glug. He looked around the small cuboid room. The hotel was a shrine to minimalism, with dark wenge-wood consoles, grey walls and coir-covered floors, and on the more illustrious upper floors that restraint felt chic. But down here, where you could almost stand on the bed and touch the walls, it felt naked and mean. Sophie must just have been grateful to find she had sheets on the bed.

'So how do you want me?' he smiled.

'I was thinking maybe . . .' She tried to think of a suitable pose. 'How about if you sit on that chair?' she said, pulling the chair out from under the desk. 'It'd be good to get some kind of after-class, repose position.'

'Okay,' he said, whipping off his towel and sitting forward on the chair.

Sophie blinked hard. 'Great,' she croaked again. 'Can you, uh . . . yes, rest your elbows on your knees,' she directed. She stepped back to look at him. His muddy-blond hair – wet from the shower – could easily be passed off as sweaty from rehearsal, and his damp, pale gold skin glistened like it always did after sixty minutes of spins and lifts. His eyes were blue and pronounced, his mouth wide, and he had a long, straight nose with flared nostrils, *à la* Nureyev, that added drama and passion to his heroic characterizations and had audiences, if not Pia, swooning.

He looked up at her. 'This okay?'

'It'll do,' she joked, hoping her knees wouldn't buckle as she walked over to where she'd set up her easel, and shifted it into position. A shaft of light from the window fell onto his shoulder and sat there like an angel. 'Can you drop your head? Look exhausted.'

'I can certainly do that,' he sighed.

She picked up her charcoals and began to draw. She didn't need to watch what her hand was doing. She just let her eyes travel over him, absorbing his physique critically, mathematically – the proportion of his neck to his hand, the distance between his jaw and his eyes . . .

Even relaxed, his body was astonishing. The curve of his calves was more sculpted than any mere man could attain from rugby or running, the swell of his thigh harder and more sharply contoured; his shoulders were like boulders, and his forearms – after years of bench-pressing ballerinas – were as big as most men's biceps. His was the body beautiful incarnate – Man as da Vinci sketched; Man as Rodin chiselled; Man as God intended; Man as she dreamt about.

Time passed slowly, but he didn't complain or move or fidget. His body had been trained in the art of being still, as much as it had been trained to move. The more junior the dancers, the longer they had to hold single positions for long periods of time and though Adam's senior status meant he was in a permanently dynamic mould, he had paid his dues and worked his way through the ranks. His body remembered it well.

'So tell me how you met Pia,' he said after a while, keeping his head lowered.

'Just the usual way – through an agency,' she replied. 'She'd been through everyone else on the list and I was the last person they had to put forward. They were getting desperate and I guess she was too.' She shrugged. 'To this day I don't know why she hired me. I can't type for toffee, I'm the most forgetful person you'll ever meet and I don't have a qualification to my name.'

'You don't? But you've always looked overqualified for

the job to me – and incredibly well organized, whatever you might say to the contrary.'

'Well, that's just down to the reign of fear that hangs over me. If I wasn't so damned frightened of losing my job every day, I wouldn't get anything done. This is the only job I've had where I wasn't fired in the first month. I was temping before this and, honestly, some of my bosses couldn't stomach my *coffee*, much less my spelling.' She shook her head, baffled. 'I don't know why she puts up with me really.'

'Funny. It's not how I see you at all.'

You see me? Sophie thought, forgetting to draw.

'So is this what you're doing during rehearsals? Sketching?'

'Yeah. Mainly.'

'I always thought you were making up lists to keep the Pia roadshow rolling forward.'

'Pia does too. But I don't think she cares, so long as I'm on top of everything for her.'

'Well, be careful. She'll get jealous if she thinks she isn't occupying every single waking thought in your head.'

Sophie smiled, rolling her eyes. 'That's for sure.'

Adam watched her. Trailing behind Pia she always seemed so . . . not subdued, but diminished somehow. Shadowy, like she was only there in body, not spirit. But she looked different behind that easel. Stronger, more vibrant, empowered. Beautiful, even.

'So why are you a PA and not an artist, then?' he asked. 'Even just watching you now it's clear this is where you're meant to be.'

'I wish,' she shrugged. 'But there's no money in it.'

'There's no money in ballet either. Not really. Not unless you make the top one per cent—'

'Which you have,' Sophie interrupted.

'Luckily,' he said. 'But I had no guarantees of making it. And I would have done it for nothing anyway. Just getting to spend my days dancing is the privilege. I can't imagine life without it.'

'That's because you've trained all your life to get to where you are now. It's part of your DNA. It's not the same for me.'

'You've never had any formal training? You sure look like you know what you're doing.'

'Well, I was invited to apply for a place at the Slade in London, if that counts for anything—'

'Invited? You mean you didn't take them up?'

'I couldn't. I didn't have the formal qualifications to get in,' she sighed.

'So then why did they invite you?' Adam asked, baffled.

'I was waitressing at the time in this little cafe near the College and one of the professors happened to see me sketching one day in my break. He was just being kind.'

'I doubt it was that,' Adam argued. 'He would have seen straightaway that you had talent. You should have followed it through. You never know, he might have been able to bend the rules for you.'

Sophie's cheeks pinked. 'It wasn't that easy,' she said tightly. 'I had other things going on as well . . .'

Adam narrowed his eyes. 'By which you mean man trouble.'

'No,' she replied.

'Yeah, yeah,' he muttered, his eyes twinkling. 'So how about now? Are you seeing anyone?'

'No. No . . . Not enough time really,' she added lamely. As if that was the real reason.

'Yeah,' he concurred. 'I've got that problem too.'

Sophie busied herself with a detail on his hair. She didn't want to hear about his supposed women problems. He'd slept with at least half the girls in the corps and the other half were just watching and waiting for their turn. The ballet world's gruelling hours, long tours and punishing performances – alien to office workers and commuters – meant they bonded into a tight-knit family and affairs were commonplace. Adam had a reputation for casual flings but he was so committed to his work (and his unrequited love for Pia) and so courteous and disingenuous afterwards that the girls could never hate him; the only perceived slight was in not being seduced in the first place. If he had women problems, it wasn't due to lack of opportunity.

He let an easy silence grow between them as Sophie leant in towards the easel, working on the shadowing across his face.

'So where is Pia at the moment anyway?'

Sophie felt herself deflate at the wholly expected turn of conversation. As ever, all roads led to Pia.

'In Aspen, with Andy.'

'They're still together?' He looked up, surprised.

Sophie nodded.

'It's been a while now. By Pia's standards, at least.'

'Yes.'

'When's she back?'

'She'll be back in time for the show tomorrow night,' she replied factually, like the good PA she was.

Adam dropped his head again.

'How do you think she manages these hot-blooded, full-blown affairs, and we don't?' he asked.

'We?' She stopped drawing and looked back at him, one hand on her hip. 'You're bracketing me in with you? Last time I looked, you were perfectly able to afford to jet round the world to hook up with a lover too. Me, on the other hand? I'd have to take the bus.'

Adam grinned at her sarcasm. He liked it. The girl had fire. He held her gaze for a moment. 'Or just not leave the room.'

'Huh?' she frowned, baffled but feeling the tension between them suddenly build.

'You don't need to take the bus. You just need to take your clothes off.'

Sophie swallowed hard as he got up and walked towards her.

'Why should she have all the fun?' he asked, looking straight into her eyes. Usually she towered over most men and felt anything but girlish in their arms, but Adam, although he was only fractionally taller than her, was twice her size, and as he snaked an arm around her waist and pulled her into him she felt just like one of the sylphs he so ardently chased around the stage each night.

'I mean, if Pia's away till tomorrow night, and I'm not on stage till tomorrow night –' he began sliding a hand up under her jumper – 'that means we've both got twenty-four hours to play with,' he said, kissing her lightly on the lips. 'And you know what? I really want to spend them playing with you.'

Chapter Four

Pia had packed her bags and checked out of the Little Nell – not bothering to pick up the tab like she usually did – before Andy was over the finish line. She took his call on the way back to the airport, but she wasn't interested in his excuse, if you could even call it that.

'It's not what you think,' he said, before she could get in first. 'It's all above board.'

'Oh. So you're not married with a kid, then?' she said, her accent thickening, as it always did when she got emotional.

'Well, yeah. But we have an arrangement, my wife and I.'

'An arrangement?' she bristled, hating hearing the words 'my wife' coming from his mouth.

'When the snow's on the ground and I'm away from home in tournaments, I can – you know . . . play away. As long as I go back during the grass seasons, then it's all cool. You know, "what happens on tour, stays on tour . . ."' She could hear the grin in his voice. As if it was his *wife*'s tacit approval that made it okay. What about hers?

'Listen, babe,' he hushed, as her silence grew, 'I'm sorry. I thought you'd be cool with it. After all, she is, and she's the wife.'

'Well, more fool her,' Pia spat. 'She should have more self-respect. Besides, do you really think I'm going to *share* myself around?'

There was a pause as Andy realized his mistake of playing it easy with the proudest woman he'd ever met. He realized too late that Pia didn't give a damn about his 'arrangement'. He'd been a fool to treat her like all the other groupies.

'Pia, listen, I—'

'Your son idolizes you, do you know that? You're his world.'

'And he's mine.'

'I don't think so.'

'Hey, I'm out there risking my neck to bring money home for th—'

'Don't patronize me,' Pia cut in, rolling the R thickly. 'You're out there because you love it. You love the thrill, the danger, the excitement. And you love the freedom it gives you – away from them, your responsibilities. You love all the women it allows you to have.'

'Well, like I said, *she*'s cool with it,' he said testily, unable to refute her claims. 'I don't see why you have to play the role of the jealous wife.'

'Let's get one thing straight, Andy. I'm beautiful, rich, talented and famous. I can and do have whoever I like in my bed and I don't need some other woman's leftovers, do you understand? Your arrangement might be good enough for you and her, but it's not good enough for me.'

She looked out of the window and saw that the car was pulling onto the tarmac. They were out of time and there was nothing more to be said.

'Look, we had fun together, Andy, but don't ring me again.

It's over,' she said flatly, as the driver got out and opened her door.

With her biggest shades on, she swung her legs out of the car and huddled herself into her usual seat on the plane. She'd managed to get on the first flight to Denver, but there she stalled. Where to now? She had no job to go back to – at least not for another three weeks; no lover to stay in bed with; no family to visit; no friends. She stood at the check-in desk, her trademark defiance conspicuously absent. Tossing her hair over her shoulder, she rang the only person who'd know what to do.

'Sophie, I'm in Denver,' she said crossly, as though it was Sophie's fault.

'What?' Sophie asked, panicked, disentangling herself from Adam's muscular arms. Pia was supposed to be in Aspen for another night.

'I don't want to talk about it,' Pia said curtly. 'Where shall I go?'

Sophie frowned down the line as Adam began kissing the back of her shoulders. She'd never heard her boss sound . . . vulnerable before. Pia always had a game plan. Her movements were booked two years in advance. She couldn't suddenly have *a day and a half* going free. She wouldn't have the first idea what to do with herself.

'Uh . . . uh,' Sophie stalled, panicking again. 'Why don't you come straight back to New York, then? You were due back tomorrow anyway.'

Pia yawned dramatically. 'No matter now. Three weeks off.' She didn't offer any explanations for that either.

Three weeks? Just like that? No Andy, and now no work? She wondered if it was anything to do with the Victoria's Secret show. Perhaps Badlands had come down hard on her, after all. 'Well, uh . . . take a holiday, really rest for a bit. Barbados is good at this time of year.'

'No,' Pia said dismissively. 'I need to keep my fitness up.'

'Okay, well, if you want to perform, the Royal Ballet in London's been on the phone again. They've got a guest spot they want to—'

'As if that's a good idea!' she snorted. 'What would that do to my negotiations with Milan if they found out I was even talking to the Royal, much less dancing for them?'

'It's just that they're very persistent,' Sophie said with understatement. Word had clearly got out to the powers that be in London that Pia was in talks with La Scala Ballet in Milan, one of the most prestigious classical ballet companies in the world, and their fierce rivals. Pia wouldn't even table a meeting with anyone else, and yet Paris Opera and the Royal were still calling with ever higher financial packages and perks every few weeks. Sophie was doing her best to get Pia to at least meet up with them, but she was on a hiding to nothing. Getting to Milan had been Pia's lifelong ambition and a fancy salary, cars or apartments held no sway with her because all she really wanted was a title – that of Prima Ballerina Assoluta – and it was in La Scala's gift to bestow it upon her.

'Whatever,' Pia mumbled down the line, inspecting her nails.

Damn. Sophie racked her brain. She was clutching at straws. This was not what she needed right now. Pia Soto with nowhere to go and no one to do was not a good proposition. In the three years Sophie had worked for her, she had never had to cater for downtime before. If Pia wasn't working, she was seducing. There wasn't anything else. Not even shopping.

'Oh!' Sophie said, sitting bolt upright and just about knocking Adam's teeth out, as a thought came to her. 'What about St Moritz? The snow polo's on. Cartier asked you as a guest of honour. They offered you a suite at the Black, that fabulous new boutique hotel. I turned it down because you were already booked in at Aspen with Andy, and it's slightly dodgy territory being seen with them when you're under contract to Patek Philippe but . . .'

'Hmm,' Pia narrowed her eyes, looking suspiciously around the airport. There were always photographers hanging around here, wanting to catch those celebrities en route to Aspen who didn't fly by private jet – yet. She needed to get out of there. Word would get around quickly about her suspension and she would make headline news again.

'Okay. I'll go to St Moritz,' she said petulantly, as though she was doing Sophie a favour. 'But it has to be discretionary, and they're picking up all costs, and I want private use of the gym and a *barre* put in the suite. Plus all the usual.' She stopped for breath. 'And I want you to come out too.'

She hung up without bothering to say goodbye and walked over to the United Airlines priority check-in desk. She kept her shades on to buy the ticket, and before it was even in her hand a manager had appeared to escort her personally to the first-class lounge. A few photographers, who had taken up almost permanent residence in the airport, clocked the deference around her and began snapping away, their fingers triggering faster and faster as they realized their quarry.

Pia tossed her hair haughtily as she strode past, the crowd around her growing quickly, and airport security anxiously brought over a buggy to whisk her away. In all the excitement, nobody noticed the man who went up to the check-in desk after her and asked for a ticket on the same flight.

Sophie's heart sank as she heard the line go dead. It was her first day off in four months, and she and Adam had just started on their lost weekend together. And now she had to spend it on a transatlantic flight?

She dropped the phone into her bag and looked at Adam, who had got out of bed to inspect his teeth.

'Was that Pia?' he asked into the mirror.

'Who else?' She rested her head on her hand idly, her eyes appraising his naked form, the stupendous physique she'd been trying to encapsulate in charcoal only forty minutes before. The etchings lay scattered like pieces of confetti, forgotten beneath the heap of clothes on the floor. She bit her lip as she scrutinized the carved hollow of his glutes.

'Everything okay?

Sophie hesitated. She didn't want to tell him she thought Pia and Andy had broken up – not yet. She suspected Adam was only here because it was seduction by proxy. After all, she was Pia's closest ally, her keeper, the nearest Pia got to a friend – Sophie might be the closest he could get.

'Yes. Just a change of plans. I've got to meet her in Switzerland tomorrow.'

'Tomorrow?' He whirled round.

She shrugged, knowing his concern was about the performance schedule rather than their curtailed love-in. 'Reading between the lines, I think Baudrand may have suspended her.'

'Oh great,' he said, hands on hips. 'Well, I guess that explains his temper earlier.'

'Yeah,' she muttered disconsolately.

There was a long pause and she fell back on the bed, staring up bleakly at the ceiling.

'Of course, you know what this means, don't you?'

'You'll have to dance with Ingrid.'

He shook his head. 'We'll need to make hay while the sun shines.'

She looked over at him in surprise and giggled, diving back under the sheets as he ran athletically back towards her, a devilish grin on his lips.

Chapter Five

Pia slept for fourteen hours straight when she got to St Moritz, and by the time she awoke her body was stiff with sleep. She didn't function like other people. Her body only seemed to relax under strain.

She called down for black coffee and toast, and lay back on the bed, stretching long, feeling the deep muscle fibres across her stomach reinvigorate themselves. She counted back the days since her last performance. Travelling yesterday, Aspen the day before that, New York the day before that. Coming into the third day, then; no wonder she was seizing up. It was true what they said – one day off class and you notice; two days and your colleagues notice; three days and the audience notices.

She got up and moved into her sitting room to do some *barre* work. She couldn't afford to lose form. Regardless of her suspension from the tour, Dimitri Alvisio, the legendary choreographer, was submitting his new ballet, *The Songbird*, to Baudrand in the next few weeks and she needed to be ready for it. After all, he had written it especially for her – one of the highest accolades to be bestowed upon a ballerina – and that was something even Ava Petrova couldn't boast.

visio was the resident choreographer for La Scala and had written this ballet as a gift to his old friend Jean Baudrand, who was spearheading the ChiCi's centenary with a year-long programme of the company's old favourites and a series of specially commissioned new works.

Pia knew she needed to sparkle and shine like never before in *The Songbird*, not to flatter Baudrand's tribute, but to flatter herself – for this ballet was a test. If she interpreted it to Alvisio's vision, she knew he would bring her to Milan and the end of her rainbow.

La Scala was the birthplace of the Prima Ballerina Assoluta ranking and although a couple of other companies had awarded the title in the past hundred years, it tended to be as recognition for a lengthy and prolific career, and was regarded as an honour rather than an active rank. But Pia had no time for such vaingloriousness. She intended to win her status at the beginning of her career, not the end. For her, the Prima Ballerina Assoluta ranking was alive and *pirouetting*, and to prove she was the very best dancer in the world she had to go there to get it.

Ava Petrova was the only other ballerina of her generation who was ever even suggested as a possible rival in this frame, but for once Pia felt she had the edge. The brilliant execution that usually won Ava first prize in competitions was only a starting point for becoming an Assoluta; the other defining criteria, which were less easy to pin down or possess and which had elevated Pia as the bigger box-office draw – exquisite grace, fluidity of line, ethereal lightness and joyous spirit – were hers in abundance. This was going to be the year she achieved greatness – she just knew it.

There was a knock at the door and the waiter came through, carrying her breakfast. Pia was standing with her back to him, one leg resting gently on the *barre*, her body bent over in a stretch.

'Tell them to close the gym,' she muttered, not bothering to turn around. 'I need a session. And arrange for a masseur back here in two hours.'

'*Oui, madame*,' said the waiter, backing out of the room quickly. She was naked except for a lilac thong, and if she unfolded herself from that position, he wouldn't be capable of carrying trays for a while.

Wolfing down the toast, she pulled out a pale lime leotard, pink footless tights rolled up to her knees, some ragged leg warmers and a cropped cashmere jumper. She pulled her hair into a rough bun and made her way down to the gym, barefoot. She shared the lift with a fur-clad, over-tanned couple in their sixties who held their Shih Tzu that little bit closer and kept their eyes firmly glued to the ceiling, clearly convinced they were sharing space with a vagrant.

The gym had been closed by the time she got there, and a buff gym instructor stepped forward from an adjacent office as she walked past.

'*Bonjour, madame*, I am Monsieur Dillion, the manager of the gym. Is there any way I can be of assistance to you?'

Pia walked into the gym and scrutinized it. Free weights, fixed weights, ergo machines, running machines, bikes, spinners, yoga mats, floor-to-ceiling mirrors. It had the lot. Off to the side was a separate Pilates room with pulleys and tables ready assembled. She nodded appreciatively.

'This looks fine, Monsieur Dillion. Privacy is all I need now. Thank you.' And she walked away from him, grabbing a towel and going straight towards the Pilates room. She started up MTV on the monitors in the gym and sat down at the Reformer – a machine rigged with pulleys and weights that looked like a medieval torture device – and embarked upon an advanced and rigorous stretching and lifting routine. She felt the bass from the TVs vibrate through the glass walls as her muscles began to quickly warm, then burn.

But forty-five minutes later, she was still going, the back of her leotard wet with sweat, her hair hanging damply. She had progressed onto the Cadillac machine and groans of effort escaped her intermittently, but stopping – pausing even – didn't cross her mind. She was still only just getting started.

She opened the door into the gym and felt the blast of music hit her as she came out of the Pilates room. Cups of tea would no doubt be vibrating across the tables in the lobby upstairs, but she didn't turn it down. She moved over to the free weights and began curling, dipping, crunching and pressing, exercising and exhausting the muscles in turn over the course of another hour, until eventually, slowing at last, she lay back on the yoga mats and began to stretch her muscles more deeply.

Lying on her back, eyes shut, her ankle resting placidly by her ear, she felt a blast of air waft over her. She shivered and looked over. The door was swooshing shut.

She lifted her head and saw a man putting his towel on a running machine. He grabbed a remote by the water cooler and turned the volume down on the TVs, switching over to CNN.

Indignant, Pia brought her leg back down and curled up. With her elbows on her knees she tipped her head to the side and stared at him.

'I'm sorry,' she said, clearly not. 'But the gym is closed.'

The man turned around.

Pia started.

'You!'

Will Silk beamed. 'Well, what a surprise,' he said, eyes glittering. 'I didn't expect to see you again *quite* so soon. I didn't realize it was to *here* that you were going.'

'I wasn't.'

'And yet, here you are.' Will paused, hands on hips. '*You're* not stalking *me*, are you?'

'Hardly,' Pia snorted, getting to her feet. Will's eyes fell to her curves. She looked a knockout. He thought of all the high-maintenance women in their designer kit usually populating the gym, and she knocked spots off them wearing a hotchpotch of cast-offs that even Britney Spears wouldn't pull together. What was it with dancers wanting to look like they were homeless?

'You can't be in here,' Pia said imperiously, aware of his eyes like hands on her body. 'I have exclusive use of the gym. You have to go.'

She turned her back to him and dropped into a deep *plié*.

'That's funny. That's what I said to them,' Will murmured, watching her. She was incredible. Even just doing that, he could see her brilliance. It was clear she had more raw talent – and passion – than any other person he'd ever met in his life.

'What?' Pia demanded, springing up and turning back to him. Her eyes were blazing. She wasn't in the mood for riddles.

'Well, I figure one of the upsides of owning the hotel has got to be—'

'You *own* this hotel?' Pia stood there with her hands on her hips. '*You* do?'

Will nodded, enjoying her fury. He could see that she

47

felt put on the back foot at being a guest at his establishment. He tried to keep his eyes from following a bead of sweat that was trickling down her neck and into her cleavage.

'I'm the major investor here. I've got a few hotels actually,' he added. 'I'll send the details through to your pretty PA, just in case you're ever passing.'

'P-passing?' She was incandescent with rage.

'Yes,' he nodded. 'Seeing as we're friends now.'

'Why would you think we're friends? I despise men like you. Bored playboys who think you can buy anything or anyone.'

'Oh don't tell me,' he said teasingly. 'You're going to insist on paying for your room too now?'

'Cartier's picking up the bill for this,' she replied witheringly.

'Ah, right.' Will nodded acquiescingly and turned away from her, stepping onto the running machine. Setting it to the Hills programme, he fell into an easy jog.

Pia watched him for a moment, furious that she couldn't force him to leave. The man was impossible, slippery. He had an answer for everything. She picked up her towel and flounced to the door, something she could achieve with a great deal more grace than most women.

'Please – don't mind me,' Will said, as he watched her in the mirror. 'Don't let me drive you away.'

'Oh you haven't,' she said contemptuously, slamming the door behind her.

'I know,' Will muttered, smiling to himself as he pushed the speed on the machine even higher and finally allowed himself to break into a sweat.

*

Sophie was sitting in the suite by the time Pia got back, reading in the *Daily Mail* the full update on her boss's suspension and arch-rival's appointment.

'Are you okay?' she asked, as Pia burst through the doors, pink and flustered.

'No!' Pia pouted, gliding over to a table with the water jug on it. 'That dreadful man from the Victoria's Secret show. He burst into the gym and just *leered* at me. I had to leave.' Her delicate wrist fluttered with distress.

Sophie nodded sombrely. She was well used to Pia's histrionics. As she recalled, that dreadful man had been pretty gorgeous and had retained his manners, even in the face of Pia's outrageous insults.

'I remember him. The guy was such a jerk,' she said faithfully, folding the newspaper away from sight. 'Anyway, this will cheer you up. I've just made some calls to Dior, Chanel and Dolce & Gabbana. There's a party after the tournament today and there's certainly nothing suitable for you in that bag I packed for Aspen, so they're sending a selection of dresses for you to choose from, plus some jackets for the tournament. Cartier has already sent up some necklaces and earrings for tonight – I've put them in the safe for you. And there're a couple of diamond watches there too.'

'No. I can't go to the tournament,' Pia said dismissively. 'That dreadful man will probably be there. He'll think I'm encouraging him if I go to watch. He owns this hotel, did you know that?'

'No way!' Sophie replied, shocked. She'd assumed he was a banker. 'But . . . well, forget about him. You can't have come all the way here to just sit in a hotel room?' she continued, trying to keep the frustration out of her voice. Look at all this decadence – jewels, furs – being thrown at her, and she was fretting about some guy who had made the mortal mistake of assuming he could buy her dinner! 'And anyway, there will be thousands of people out there. He won't be able to pick you out from among them all.'

She bit her lip at the gaffe. Of course Pia believed she would stand out in a crowd of thousands. She was an uncommon beauty.

Pia pulled off her damp clothes and walked into the bathroom for a shower, with the same nonchalance as Adam the day before. Sophie watched her retreat, that perfect butt without a trace of cellulite or jiggle. Not that she should be jealous. She knew better than anyone what it took to hone a figure like Pia's. Sophie saw how Pia moved like a geriatric in the mornings, how two of her toenails were black and dead-looking, how she gasped with pain as the sports masseuse tried to ease and soothe her bruised muscles, how her bloodied feet meant she got through five pairs of shoes each performance. No, Sophie knew she had no right to be jealous of Pia's stupendous physique. The most she sacrificed her body to pain was the occasional spinning class, trying to pump some volume into her butt. She deserved the droop.

There was a knock at the door. 'Housekeeping.'

The door opened and a stream of women in black skinny trousers and black shirts filed in, carrying towers of pillows and blankets. They were the most glamorous housekeepers she'd ever seen; surely they were spies sent in by Gucci?

'Actually we're fine, thanks,' Sophie said getting up. 'The bed's already been done.'

'Is special request of Monsieur Silk,' the first woman replied, pulling the perfectly plumped and creaseless pillows off the bed with a look of disgust, as though muddy dogs had slept on them rather than the exquisitely perfumed Pia Soto. The other two women took their positions at the bottom corners of the bed and expertly, seamlessly, silently stripped it down, synchronizing their movements and origami folds.

My God, they're like a housekeeping SWAT team, Sophie thought to herself as they speedily redressed the bed in gossamer-fine cashmere blankets finished with hospital corners, fat pillows, and a white fur throw lovingly draped across the foot.

The first housekeeper fished an envelope out of her pocket and laid it gently on the pillow, while another sprinkled white rose petals across the bed. A plate of cupcakes covered in white chocolate curls, and a bottle of Cristal were placed on the bedside table. Then, nodding briefly, the women filed out silently again, leaving behind them a soft and inviting snowy scene. What, no albino reindeer? Sophie wanted to ask, as she sighed at the pristine sight. It would be a damn shame to wreck the perfection by actually *sleeping* in the bed.

The bathroom door opened and Pia emerged from the steamy haze.

'Who was that?' she asked, wrapped in a towel. 'I heard the door.'

'Uh, housekeeping,' Sophie replied.

'Oh.' She saw the envelope on the pillow and picked it up, flinging herself casually onto the bed, completely oblivious to the scene change.

Sophie blanched, just as her boss coloured. 'What's wrong? What does it say?' she asked after a moment.

Pia shrieked indignantly. '*Dah!* That man! How *dare* he speak to me like this? After all his insults and *still* he assumes he will get me? I hate him! Hate him!'

She flung the card to the floor and stalked over to the wardrobe.

Hesitantly, Sophie picked up the card and read it.

*This isn't quite what I had in mind when
I thought about getting you into my bed.*

But it's a start.

WS x

Chapter Six

Pia chose the white belted off-the-shoulder fur-trimmed jacket from Dior in the end. Sophie couldn't see how on earth such a jacket could be worn – off the shoulder? In the snow? – until Pia put it over her black 6-ply polo neck with skinny black jeans. With her hair tumbling out from a matching white fur turban, her green eyes hidden behind enormous smoky shades, and a diamond watch dangling precariously from her thin wrist, she looked glamorous and incredibly famous. There was no chance the 'dreadful man' was going to miss her. Not even in a crowd of eight thousand. Not even from the moon.

Sophie pulled up the hood to her olive-green Fat Face ski jacket and they walked out of the hotel together. The wind was but a tickle today, the sun obliging, and as she stared into the dazzling horizon Sophie realized too late that she had left her sunglasses at home. She didn't need to run up and down the street to know she wouldn't be able to afford anything here . . . or that Pia would ever offer to buy some for her.

Reluctantly, she pushed her hand into her pocket and pulled out her ski goggles. It wasn't like anyone was going to notice *her* anyway.

A horse-drawn sleigh was parked outside the revolving

doors, and Pia clapped her hands with delight, a rare flash of childlike excitement softening her pretty features. Sophie grinned back and they jumped in with all the glee of ten-year-olds, covering their knees with blankets and furs.

'Where would you like to go, *m'moiselles*?' asked the driver, a middle-aged man with a thick beard and sun-burnt cheeks.

'The slow route down to the tournament, please,' replied Sophie immediately. Pia didn't speak to the public.

'Ha!' said the driver to the horse, giving a short tug on the red leather reins, which were threaded with bells.

The two women sat back and enjoyed the view, eyeing up all the glossy pedestrians stomping along the pavements in their moon boots as they slid past the upscale boutiques and the grand old-school palace hotels. The town was heaving with revellers and every other car parked was either a Ferrari or a Lamborghini.

As they jingled down the central boulevard they rounded a corner, and the cosmopolitan spectacle on the frozen lake suddenly hove into view.

Sophie gasped. Pia just nodded appreciatively. It was exactly as she'd hoped. All of Europe's flashiest and trashiest were here – and they were here to party. Champagne, snow and Argentinian boys. It was just what she needed.

The sleigh drew to a gentle, silent stop by the grandstands and Sophie reached in her purse to pay. Pia hopped down, being instantly enfolded in a throng of ardent fans all clamouring for autographs.

The PR for Cartier rushed over, ecstatic to see Pia looking so exotic and so here.

'Miss Soto, we are so delighted you have been able to join us. Please, come through to the VIP area, won't you?'

They were ushered through with great ceremony – even Sophie in her ski goggles – and taken to a roped-off area where a magnificent ice sculpture of a polo player and pony was discreetly and regretfully melting. Glasses of champagne were thrust into their hands and Pia was taken over to air-kiss the MD of Cartier and his wife.

Sophie walked over to the ropes and scanned around to make sure no seasoned enemies were hovering within striking distance. Pia's indiscriminate seductions and outspoken comments over the past few years had not only made her a tabloid target but also precious few friends. The woman really was an island.

A hundred yards away, on the pitch, the packed snow was being swept for the final time; the seats in the bleachers were already full and announcements were being made over the loudspeakers in French, English, Italian and German.

Alongside a corner of the pitch, by the gleaming state-of-the-art horse boxes, Sophie could see the ponies saddled up and tethered, grooms milling about and making final checks, the players strapping on their knee pads and helmets. It was annoying how good they looked in their kits, satisfying the clichés with aplomb.

'Are you a fan?' a thickly accented voice enquired behind her. Russian, she thought.

Sophie turned around. A tiny man in a cravat was staring at her. His hair was thinning on top, and he was holding a walking cane in one hand, a *Glühwein* in the other.

'I don't know,' she shrugged ruefully. 'I've never seen a snow-polo match before. Or a grass one either actually.' She paused. 'I'm not really here. I'm just with—'

The man stared at her. 'Well, you look here to me.'

Sophie smiled politely. 'My name's Sophie O'Farrell.' She held out a hand.

He took it without smiling. 'A pleasure to meet you, Miss O'Farrell. Please, allow me to acquaint you a little with the basic rules of the game, else you will never know what it is you're actually seeing. The first thing you should know about polo – of any variety – is that when a goal is scored, the direction of play switches round . . .'

Sophie tried to keep up, but as he baffled her with chukkas and ROWs she came to the conclusion that polo was a more intricate game than just horseback hockey. Besides, he spoke with a devastating monotone that seemed to be the verbal equivalent of a legal document. Why, oh why, couldn't he be a handsome groom instead, with smouldering eyes and hot hands?

From the corner of her eye, she could see Pia revelling in glory, greeting met-once celebrities like old friends and being feted by some of the teams' patrons, who were standing in a gaggle around her as the photographers snapped away, eager to try to catch her with her next conquest. Word was already out about her split with Andy Connor.

She tried to tune back in to what her companion was saying, but found the short man staring at her.

'I'm sorry – I'm sorry, what did you say?'

'I asked whether you knew the beautiful woman over there. Why is everyone flocking around her?'

Sophie shrugged, amazed to have found someone oblivious to Pia's star. 'That's Pia Soto. Pretty much the most famous ballerina in the world.'

'Then why is she here, and not dancing?'

'She's got a bit of time off, so why not?' she said mildly. She had the feeling he wouldn't be impressed to hear she'd been suspended for running out of a performance to model lingerie at a fashion show.

He was silent for a couple of beats as he continued to stare at Pia.

'She is very beautiful,' he said finally.

'Yes.'

'But a whore.'

Sophie's mouth dropped open. She replayed the conversation in her head. Surely she had misheard? Or he'd misunderstood?

'I'm sorry, *what* did you say?'

'I said she is a money-grabbing whore. She sells herself to the advertisers, does she not? She is not interested in the art of ballet. In its spirit. She's in it for the money.'

Sophie tipped her head to the side, her heart pounding. 'Commercial success doesn't make Pia Soto a *whore*,' she said breathlessly. 'Her brilliance on the stage speaks for itself. Why should her fortunes as a businesswoman undermine her standing as an artist? She has nothing whatever to apologize for.'

The man cracked a tight, joyless smile. 'She is fortunate to have such a loyal ally for her personal assistant,' he said finally.

Sophie sniffed, as offended as if he'd called her a whore. 'And what is it *you* do?' she asked tightly.

The man looked straight at her and blinked slowly. 'I'm a broker,' he said, just as the half-time bell rang loudly. He looked towards the pitch and watched the grooms take the tired ponies back towards the stalls. 'I must go now,' he said. 'But we shall meet again.' And he tipped his head politely before disappearing into the crowd.

With spectators roaring around her, Sophie stared after

57

him, completely shaken. Not by his strange assurance that they would meet again. But because she'd never told him she was Pia's PA.

Sophie pushed through the crowd, trying to stem her rising panic. Pia was so far away now. The fourth chukka had started already and everyone was trying to get near to Pia to monopolize her attention. She could only pinpoint her thanks to the extravagant fur turban that was blocking the view of everyone standing behind her.

'Excuse me, *excusez-moi*,' she mumbled, accidentally treading on toes and knocking drinks. She couldn't see the ghastly little Russian anywhere but, then again, he was so short . . .

She made her way over to Pia, who was standing talking to Sharon Stone.

Pia laughed at the sight of her as she approached. 'You look like Rudolph,' she giggled. Sophie crossed her eyes and saw that the tip of her nose was glowing like a lighthouse beacon. Pia, on the other hand, had developed an appealing pink flush that kissed her cheeks like an orgasmic glow.

'Just came to see how you were getting on,' Sophie smiled, nodding to Ms Stone as she left to find more celebrated company.

'Yes fine,' Pia murmured, raising the binoculars to her eyes and watching the game. 'I think Cartier are angling to sign me.'

'Really?'

'Mmm. But we'll see.'

Sophie nodded, casting her eyes around at the guests in the VIP area. The Russian seemed to have gone. 'So where is he?' she asked, shivering.

'Who?' Pia asked, her own eyes firmly on the players.

'The dreadful man.'

'Tch, I don't know,' she said dismissively, although she could see perfectly well that far from being just another well-heeled supporter, Will Silk was wearing the number three patron's shirt for the Black Harbour team. The winning side.

Sophie chewed on her lip, wondering how to broach the subject of her chilling encounter.

'Look, Pia, there's something I think I should tell you.'

'Mmm?' She was engrossed in the action on the pitch – not the game, the players. And, specifically, the number one Black Harbour player: Argentinian, thighs of steel, and high-goal with a nine handicap.

'There was a strange man here earlier. He was very aggressive about you.'

Pia shrugged carelessly. 'I find the men who are most rude and aggressive are the ones who don't have a cat in hell's chance of sleeping with me.'

'Well, uh, that . . . that *could* explain it . . .' Sophie stammered. Pia's ego always took some negotiating. 'He just made me feel uneasy. Like he targeted me deliberately.'

'Yes. To get to me. A balletomaniac, most likely.'

'A what?'

'You've heard of balletomanes, surely?' Pia said, sweeping the pitch with the binoculars. 'Historically, they were rich men – patrons – who paid for the privilege of backstage access and the opportunity to strike up relationships with the dancers.' She looked at Sophie slyly. 'You can probably imagine that some of them paid for a bit more than that.'

Sophie's eyes widened. 'Really?'

'Oh yeah,' Pia drawled, bringing the binoculars back up

again. 'And they're still alive and well today, I can assure you. There's nothing a rich man loves more than a ballerina in his pocket. God knows, everyone's always trying to buy me,' she said darkly, watching Will Silk score a goal.

Eight thousand people roared at once and Sophie felt the hair on her arms stand on end. And not just because of the crowd's party spirit. This man wasn't even a fan, much less a balletomane.

'I just feel that I didn't meet him randomly,' Sophie persevered. She felt spooked.

Pia lowered the binoculars, her eyes narrowed. 'What do you mean?' she demanded.

Sophie shrugged. 'I can't explain it exactly. It's just that he pretended not to know who you were, but then said something that showed he knew *exactly* who you were. Plus, he knew I was your PA – even though *I* never told him.'

Pia's eyes dimmed and Sophie could tell she was beginning to listen. She had taken her security seriously ever since a fan had broken into her apartment and jerked off on her bed a year previously. She'd got a restraining order, keeping the man from getting within one hundred feet of her, but that hadn't stopped him from continuing to watch her at a distance outside the stage doors. Intimidating her. Harassing her.

The snow was falling thickly now, like feathers in a pillow fight, and Pia's eyelashes were becoming laden with fat flakes. She looked like some knock-kneed space-age Paco Rabanne model in white mascara, but she was oblivious, just staring out into the middle distance as if trying to discern where the earth stopped and the sky began.

Sophie instantly regretted her candour. For all Pia's ruthless independence, beneath it all she was as fragile as glass.

Sophie knew that. What had she been thinking? She should have kept her suspicions to herself. Frightening Pia wasn't going to help her.

'You know, actually – thinking about it – he probably saw us arrive together,' she backtracked. 'I'm overreacting. You're right, it's just another fan.'

She cast her hands in the air and rolled her eyes, the snow bouncing off her curls like water flying off a retriever fresh from the river. But Pia didn't reply. She had begun to shiver.

'Come on,' Sophie said, touching her arm lightly. 'Let's get you back to the hotel. We don't want you getting too cold out here. Besides, it's getting slippery, and please God, don't fall. Badlands would have me shot.'

Pia let herself be led away like a lame racehorse, eyes down, her sparkle extinguished. She wanted to get the hell out of here. Nothing put her out of the party mood like the threat that someone was gunning for her.

Chapter Seven

Still, the red leather boxes stacked up in the safe did a heroic job of putting Pia back in the party spirit again. It was like Aladdin's cave in there, with Cartier's best winking at her, wooing her, seducing her – making her gasp and thrill like a new lover.

Like a baby sister, Sophie sat on the floor and watched as Pia decided to ditch the diamonds and opt for emeralds instead.

'This town's ruled by ice,' she proclaimed grandly, clasping a collar to her neck. 'I *dare* to be different.'

Within fifteen minutes, Cartier had sent up a new selection of pieces for her and she settled on some maharani-style drop earrings and a bracelet to go with the white satin corseted Dolce dress she had chosen. Hand-painted with butterflies the colours of irises and pansies, the dress squeezed her possessively, the skirt puddling extravagantly at her feet.

'You could get married in that dress,' Sophie sighed, her elbows resting on her knees, hands cupping her chin.

'Hrrmph, I don't think so,' Pia snorted.

'What do you mean?' Sophie asked, shocked. 'No to the dress? Or no to marriage?' Sophie already knew in minute detail exactly how her own wedding was going to be. Everything had been decided since the age of seven: her mother's dress, the tiny stone windswept chapel at the top of farmer McGinty's field, sweet peas in her hair, her father . . . She stopped herself. The groom wasn't the only variable in the big day now.

'Both,' Pia said, eyeing herself critically in the mirror. 'This is too long. You need to cut it.'

'What?' Sophie asked, eyes bulging. Oh please no . . .

'Yes! Cut the skirt,' she repeated with conviction.

'But . . . but the dress is only borrowed,' Sophie stammered. 'It's a five-thousand-dollar dress. It came up from the store. They'll need it back tomorrow.'

'They can afford to swallow five grand. The publicity I'll give them in it, they'll recoup it twenty times over. It'll sell out worldwide once the papers show me wearing it.'

Sophie knew she was right – she spent a large part of her day elucidating the fashion press on Pia's latest 'looks' – but that didn't make it okay. Reluctantly, she rang the store and haltingly – not just because of the language barrier – explained what Pia wanted to do.

'They're offering to send up a seamstress to do it for you,' she said, holding the phone to her shoulder. 'She can be here in five minutes.'

Pia shook her head. '*Non*. I want you to do it.'

Sophie swallowed. 'Did you hear that?' she said into the phone to the store manager, ever more mortified. 'Mmm-hmm, mmm-hmm. Yes. *Merci*. Thank you . . .' She turned her back to Pia. 'I'm so sorry . . .' she whispered into the receiver before putting the phone down.

'See? It's all fine. I told you so,' Pia said, climbing onto a stool as Sophie got out the nail scissors (the only ones she had). 'I'm far too young to look so "done",' she pouted, while

63

Sophie crawled around her, cutting three feet of fabric from its masterly seams.

Sophie felt like a butcher as she hacked at the gown. It made her want to weep to be destroying such an object of beauty. And yet . . . she had to admit, once she stood up again, that – amazingly – it worked. The slightly wonky hem, with wispy threads hanging down Pia's thighs, transformed the dress from a banker's wife's couture piece into something much more tantalizingly urchin.

'Perfect,' Pia proclaimed at her reflection. She turned to Sophie, hands on hips. 'And now for you.'

'Me?' Sophie exclaimed. 'But I'm not going.'

'Oh yes, you are,' Pia replied. 'I don't have a date. You don't expect me to walk in there on my own, do you?'

'But it's not like you'll be walking out on your own, is it?' Sophie laughed. 'You'll be mobbed by beautiful men the second you walk in. You always are.'

'I know,' Pia shrugged, fastening her earrings. 'But I still need an escort on the way in.'

Sophie looked around the room. It was the 'my other car's a Porsche' version of her apartment in Chicago, with clothes piled up on the bed, bottles and powders cluttering the work surfaces and mismatched pairs of shoes strewn, hurricane-style, across the floor.

'But there's no time. You're just about ready to go and I've got absolutely nothing to wear,' Sophie wailed.

'Sure you have,' Pia said generously, indicating her tower of cast-offs.

Sophie picked up a silk coffee-coloured Phillip Lim dress. She held it against herself. It didn't even go past her bottom. 'We are *not* the same size,' she said sternly, eyebrows to the ceiling.

'Pah, there'll be something there that fits you,' Pia said breezily, applying more gloss to her already luscious lips.

There was. A silk Prada forties-style cocktail dress in a rust colour that did absolutely nothing for her.

'Okay, it fits me,' she said sulkily. 'But it doesn't *suit* me. I look like a nail.'

'I know,' Pia agreed, laughing and smacking her thighs. She loved Sophie's sulks. 'But it *is* Prada.' She shrugged her shoulders as if that was all that really mattered.

Sophie rolled her eyes and gave up. There was no point in arguing. Pia was going to make her walk in with her one way or the other, and frankly it was either this or her pyjamas. She wondered whether she should turn the dress inside out, so that at least everybody else would know it was Prada.

They took a car over to the Palazzo Hotel where the party was being held. Although it was only a five-hundred-yard stroll from the Black, the ride took a good twenty minutes, as the driver had to wait for the bottleneck of Maybachs and Mercedes-McLarens to be valet-parked.

Once inside, the luxury didn't let up. Installations of Swarovski sculptures glittered from corners and niches, and an elaborate light show flickered across the domed ceilings. The grand red-carpeted staircase had Cavalli-clad model-waiters, laden with trays of Krug, positioned on every other step, and Sophie grabbed them each a glass.

They climbed the stairs slowly, like royalty – it was important that everyone should see Pia and clock her formidable legs. As they crested the top, rows of purple velvet banquettes and low ebony tables were set in the middle of the room, with spotlit resin cocktail bars positioned all around them against the walls, hemming in the guests like Bacchanalian sentries.

Pia and Sophie scanned the room, equally desperate to alight on someone the ballerina knew. The sooner Pia found herself a date, the sooner Sophie could get the hell out of this dress.

Cosima Harlow – Valentino's muse and a top-tier socialite – had set up her court in the centre of the room and was lying out on a banquette like Cleopatra. Pia recognized her fuchsia dress as one she had rejected, and gave a small smile of satisfaction. Cosima, mistaking it for a smile of welcome, gestured for her to come over, but Pia was looking for another familiar face. One in particular.

She was determined to get that Argentinian back to her room. She'd be damned if she was going to spend another night alone. The fact that it would be one in the eye for Will Silk was also an enticing prospect – seducing his infinitely more talented teammate would show him he was out of his league with her. She'd show him once and for all that money and power never came into it when it came to bedding her.

'Talk to me, Sophie,' she commanded as she checked out the room – and the competition. There were a lot of cosmetically modified women in attendance. 'Look interesting. Don't just stand there like a lemon.'

'Oh . . . uh . . .' Sophie stalled. Her command of the English language deserted her. 'I, uh . . .'

They continued to stand in silence.

'Hurry up,' Pia whispered through a gritted smile. 'Say something. Make me laugh. Tell me the time. I don't care. Just something.'

'Uh . . . knock, knock.'

Pia frowned, looking at her like she was crazy. 'What are you doing?'

'Telling you a joke,' Sophie said, swivelling her eyes around shiftily and trying not to move her lips – as though someone might be lip-reading their conversation. 'You say: "Who's there?"' she prompted.

Pia's frown deepened. Sophie nodded encouragingly. 'Who's there?' Pia said finally, and very suspiciously.

'Dwayne.'

Silence.

'Now you say: "Dwayne who?"' Sophie prompted again.

Pia sighed, her eyes narrowed. 'Dwayne who?'

'Dwayne the bathtub, I'm dwowning.'

More silence.

'Now you laugh,' Sophie said, dejected. That was her best joke.

Pia was still staring at her, baffled, when Cosima came over. Clearly, if Mohammad wouldn't go to the mountain . . .

'Pia, you simply must come and sit with us,' she smiled, kissing Pia airily. 'I've got some friends who are *dying* to meet you. Bring your friend too.'

Cosima smiled and offered a slim hand. 'Hi, I'm Cosima.'

Sophie went to take it. 'I'm So—'

'Oh no! Sophie's not my friend,' Pia shrieked, batting Sophie's hand down and laughing shrilly at the mix-up. 'She's just my assistant.'

'Oh,' Cosima said, removing her offer of friendship and straightening up. 'Come on, then. Have you met Luca d'Orsognio? His father's the . . .'

Sophie watched the international beauties drift into the centre of the social universe, her cheeks burning at Pia's tactlessness. She knew that technically Pia was her boss, that theirs was a working relationship. But Sophie also knew that she was closer to Pia than any other person in the world. They spent more time in each other's company than they did with any other person, lovers included; they laughed at the same jokes (well, nearly always); hell, they even shared clothes. Yes, Pia insisted on pulling rank and she was so unbelievably self-centred that she probably didn't know Sophie's birthday, the colour of her eyes or what she was wearing on any given day. But she did need her, and not just to pick up her dry-cleaning. They were both walking wounded, and Sophie had recognized it in Pia instantly. She knew, even if Pia did not, that the only people they had in the world were each other.

Sophie stood like a maypole for a few moments – as people laughed and drank and danced around her – before making a furious beeline for the bar. Well, to hell with her! Pia had made her leave Adam still in her bed to come and stand here in this hideous dress. Why *should* she slink off now? It wasn't like anyone was looking at her anyway. She was entitled to just as good a time as anyone else. And the drink was free.

Blinking back the tears, Sophie ordered a dirty martini, downing it in one.

She ordered another.

She was on her third when a man pulled up a bar stool next to her.

'May I join you?' he asked. 'I couldn't help but notice that you are drinking alone. And a woman like you should never have to do that.'

Sophie smiled sarcastically. He was gorgeous, but it was an embarrassingly cheesy chat-up line. He had to be one of the grooms – shaggy brown hair, tanned, muscular forearms, liquid brown eyes. It looked like her wish at the match had come true.

'I saw you earlier, at the match,' he said, his eyes glittering. 'My name's Alonso. What's yours?'

'Sophie,' she grinned, as though she'd said something really naughty, the alcohol swimming around her bloodstream.

'Sophie,' he repeated, as though hearing the name for the first time. 'A very pretty name for a very pretty girl.'

'Ha!' Sophie snorted, before she could stop herself. It looked like all the clichés really were true.

'But yes,' Alonso frowned. 'You don't think so?' He tucked a ringlet behind her ear so that he could see her more clearly. 'I don't meet many girls who look like you. They're all fake: *fake* blonde, with *fake* tits and *fake* tans,' he said sneeringly. 'You're so tall, so elegant, so mysterious – you look like . . . like you grew up in fields in the rain.'

Sophie spluttered with surprise. 'I did,' she cried earnestly. 'I'm Irish. I spent most of my childhood messing about on my mother's family's dairy farm.'

'See? That is why I am drawn to you. In Argentina, I too grew up on a cattle farm. Cows.' He shrugged. 'We share cows.'

'Cows!' Sophie laughed and held up her glass for a toast. 'To cows, then.'

'To cows.'

Tanner Ludgrove turned the handle and stepped into the shiny black lorry to a fanfare of whinnies and snuffles.

'Hello, you lot,' he said gruffly, as the six ponies all pushed their heads out of their stalls, eager for an apple or a pat. He inhaled the aroma of leather and manure – the best smell in the world – and listened to the sound of their hooves turfing up the fresh hay. The farrier had done his job and they had all been newly shod, the cleated shoes they used in the snow taken off already. They wouldn't be needing those for another year now.

His favourite pony, Amos, bent his head down for a comforting rub. Tanner smiled and put his arm beneath the horse's head, patting the far cheek. They both knew the journey that lay ahead. They had done it together several times over the years now – the thirty-hour drive back to England through the Alps, micro-managed and planned down to the last loo break.

Tanner checked his watch: 11.42 p.m. In four and a half hours, the first convoy of three lorries of ponies would be making its way back to Dorset. The second team would be coming on tomorrow, after the final. He despised the early start but it was the only way to do it if they were going to get through the Vereina tunnel and past Zurich before rush hour.

He yawned, exhausted, shrugging off his arctic expedition-style jacket. He'd be glad when this was over. He hated doing such long journeys with the horses; the prospect of one of them falling lame was a real possibility. Not that Silk cared a damn about the horses' welfare, so long as they won him his trophy and his financial largesse – sorry, sporting prowess – was admired by a crowd of thousands.

Still, it was done now.

A sudden noise – a shuffle – above him stopped him in his tracks and he felt his pulse quicken. He looked at the ponies, who seemed wholly unconcerned by the prospect of an intruder. Aside from the considerable worth of the horses themselves, the kit in the truck was worth tens of thousands. And with the final being held tomorrow, and Black Harbour going in as the favourites, doping was a real threat too.

He grabbed a whip that was propped against the wall and tiptoed across to the fitted ladder that led up to his bunk. He climbed it silently, the whip dangling – at the ready – in his hand.

He knew he was at a disadvantage. Apart from the fact that he was holding the ladder with just one hand, the intruder would have seen him come into the truck. The element of surprise was gone. There was only one thing for it.

'HA!' he cried, warrior-like, springing himself up and over the parapet, so that his head banged hard on the roof. 'Aargh!' he cried, less impressively, unable to rub it.

He dropped the whip in surprise. It had been the last thing he was expecting to see – a mass of bronze curls tumbling over the side of his pillow, long milky limbs entwined with a hard, dusty, mocha-coloured body that didn't even break rhythm.

Tanner's shoulders and heart rate dropped as he took in the all-too-familiar scene. 'Still riding, Alonso?' he said, deadpan. 'I thought that was all done for today.'

'Not for me, *amigo*,' smiled the player, completely unfazed. His nine-goal handicap made him a celebrity back home and the prize asset for any polo patron. He could name his terms and set his own price – and if he wanted to have sex with a pretty girl in the horsebox, absolutely no one was going to try to stop him.

Tanner sighed and climbed back down again. There went any chance of sleep. It wasn't even like he could kip on the floor. It was bad enough the horses having to listen to every last thump and groan. He pulled his jacket back on again and stepped out of the lorry. He may as well get a drink.

In spite of the fact that she was the most tantalizing woman there and was being fawned over by an American thrash rock star – usually just her type – Pia was not having the time of her life. Sophie's early departure had left her stranded with basically a bunch of strangers, and her lusty Argentinian prospect was nowhere in sight. To make things even worse, Will Silk was standing at the opposite end of the room, surrounded by a pack of fine young fillies who were doing all they could to become his number one pick, and he hadn't looked over at Pia once. She wasn't sure he had even seen her.

From under the singer's fedora – which she had coquettishly pinched and alluringly perched on her head, dismantling the gown's formality even further – she watched him as he regaled them all, brandy in hand, with some hilarious story that set their bosoms quivering and exposed their long, smooth necks. Something about him made him look different to the other times she had met him. She squinted intently. It was because he looked undone, less manicured. She liked her men rough and ready but even in the gym today he'd looked coordinated, like he was off for a game of racquetball. But now, Pia noticed how his top button was undone, his tie hanging limply, his shirt scarcely tucked in over his flat stomach. He looked rumpled, like the women were gently mauling him, trying to get at him. From a distance she could see why, although she wasn't going to forgive him any time soon for his conviction that she could be bought.

She looked away hotly and tried to focus on tonight's

suitor, but her gaze kept getting drawn back. He *had* to have seen her. The eyes of every other man in the room were on her. Why should he be the only one who was blind? He'd gone out of his way to go after her only three days ago in New York – paying $200,000 for a minute of her time – and yet now he was flirting with every other woman in the room *but* her.

'Come on, baby, let's go back to my hotel,' mumbled the rock star into her neck. She caught a whiff of his hair. Yes, definitely her type. She closed her eyes and tried to get into the mood. She just felt sleepy and didn't fancy him in the least, but she got up anyway. It was better than sleeping alone again.

She put her drink down and grabbed her bag from the table, blowing insincere kisses to Cosima. 'We'll catch up in Palm Beach at Easter.'

She turned and found a fresh glass of champagne placed into her hand.

'Don't tell me you're actually going to leave with him,' Will said, eyes glittering. He seemed amused.

Pia raised her eyebrows haughtily. 'Of course. Don't you know who he is?'

'I couldn't give a shit,' Will said flatly. 'And neither could you.'

'On the contrary, he's just my type,' she purred.

'You couldn't be less interested in him. You're just using him to run away from me again.'

'Oh. So it's all about you, is it?' she said sarcastically. 'And how exactly could I be running *from* you? I haven't been near you all night. Your silicone security team have seen to that,' she said.

Will smiled, his eyes simmering. 'You know they're nothing.

Just like he's nothing,' he said, looking over at the rocker, who was standing nearby, swaying slightly, waiting for Pia. 'You can go,' Will said, dismissing him like he was a serf. 'She's not going with you.'

Pia glared, outraged, but she didn't contradict him. The rocker shrugged drunkenly – whatever – and swaggered off.

'Well, I'm surprised you even noticed,' she sniffed, watching him go.

'I notice everything about you, Pia Soto,' he said. 'I notice the way you sniff when you're feeling vulnerable, for example. I notice the way your right thumb rubs your palm when you're nervous. I notice the way you wince when you land on your left leg because your right leg is fractionally shorter and it's putting stress on your—'

Pia gasped. 'How do you know about that?'

'I've already told you I'm a benefactor to the Royal Ballet. I make a point of knowing everything there is to know about what I'm investing in. And what the greatest assets are.' He took a sip of his brandy, his eyes never leaving her. 'I also noticed the way you circled Alonso Rodriguez's name in your programme that you left on your seat; and I noticed the way you've been looking for him ever since you got here.'

'I have not,' she protested.

'You want to seduce him to spite me, don't you?' His eyes were amused.

'Don't be ridiculous,' she said, tossing her head, appalled he'd read her so clearly.

He looked around casually. 'It's okay. It takes one to know one,' he said, looking back at her.

'You and I are nothing alike. I – I have great talent for one thing. I am world class.'

'And so's your ego,' he laughed. 'But you get away with it because you're so damned pretty.'

Never had a man spoken to her like this before. Who did he think he was? Clenching her fist, she stamped a foot in anger.

That seemed to set him off even harder. He slapped a hand across his stomach and laughed out loud. 'Did you actually just stamp your foot at me? You really are just a spoilt little girl. I've got a good mind to put you over my knee right now and smack your bottom.'

Pia looked at him, horrified. The man was a maniac.

Slamming her drink on the table, she turned to leave again, knocking Tanner Ludgrove's single malt all over his shirt in the process.

'Oh that's just great!' Tanner said as Pia streaked past, all indignation and legs. 'Thank you!' he boomed after her. 'I see your legendary charms are having the usual desired effect,' he muttered laconically to Will, brushing his shirt.

'Everything's going to plan, if that's what you mean,' Will replied archly, watching her hair billow out like sails. 'That delicious creature's on the cusp of falling passionately in love with me.'

'Yeah! It looks like it,' Tanner drawled sarcastically.

'What are you doing here anyway?' Will asked suspiciously. 'You're supposed to be setting off in a couple of hours.'

'You don't need to remind me,' Tanner replied drily, looking around at all the underdressed women. 'But Alonso's shacked up with his latest woman in my bunk. Perhaps you'd like to see if you can shift him. He's your pet.'

Will frowned. 'Damn right I will. Those are *my* ponies you're driving back. I didn't tell him to crash at yours. I'll give him a ring and tell him the coast's clear.' He got his mobile out of his jacket pocket.

Tanner looked at him. 'You didn't what?' He shook his head. 'What are you? His pimp?'

Will looked casually around the room as the phone rang, one hand in his pocket. It was like the lights had gone out now Pia had left. 'I just asked Alonso to make himself scarce with a girl at the bar, that was all,' he said casually. 'You know what he's like. It's no big deal.'

Tanner shook his head. At bang on six foot, he was well built, with rich hazel eyes and a flushed complexion that came from spending his life outdoors. Although twenty-eight, he looked younger thanks to the thick brown hair that was kept in a schoolboy 'short, back and sides' and his boyish smile. Until he'd met Violet, he'd had no problem pulling girls either, but things were on the rocks between them and his eye was beginning to wander again.

Tanner drained his drink and wiped his mouth with the back of his hand. 'Who was that girl anyway?'

'My new project,' Will smiled and looked over at the grand staircase down which Pia had fled. 'She's the girl who's going to change my life.'

Pia stomped down the stairs haughtily, half-wondering whether Will would chase her. She looked around, but he wasn't there. No. Of course not. He didn't have the nerve to come after her.

A porter got her coat for her while she scanned the lobby for Sophie. She couldn't imagine where she had gone. Back to the hotel? It was unlike her to leave without checking Pia was all right first. They would be having words about this in the morning.

A few stray autograph hunters mobbed Pia as she stepped outside the hotel, but she shooed them away crossly. She was off duty. In the distance she could hear the jingle of a horse-drawn sleigh bobbing down the street. Beyond the hotel steps, out on the frozen lake, she could see an army of workers sweeping and brushing the decimated polo pitch in preparation for tomorrow's final. No doubt the Black Harbour team would win. As Bryan Spence had said, Will Silk wasn't known for his losing streak.

Well, she wouldn't be here to watch him lift the trophy. She wouldn't give him the satisfaction of standing victorious before her. She'd go back to the hotel and pack immediately. Forget the final. She wanted to catch the first flight out of here in the morning.

Her jet-lagged body sagged at the thought of another flight, but she wasn't leaving just to escape Silk again. Even after this morning's workout, she was missing her time in the studio and on the stage. Every day's absence made a difference and she could feel her form slacking off. She needed to get back to Chicago and back to class.

Her break-up with Andy and the suspension had confused her momentarily, thrown her into a vortex away from all her anchors. But she should have known to keep focused on her dancing. It was the only thing that had ever mattered to her, the only thing that had ever loved her back.

In the distance, she heard the familiar jingle of bells again. Such a pretty sound. So much nicer than the Chicago cabs that gurgled outside her apartment day and night.

She stepped into the road. Ahead of her, a door in one of the horseboxes opened and a laughing couple tumbled out. She stopped dead at the sight of them. It couldn't be!

But it was. She watched, frozen, as the man leant down and kissed the woman so lustily that she fell back against the stairs, pulling him down with her – on her.

'*Hai!*' a voice called.

Was that . . . ? It couldn't be! She squinted trying to make out the woman . . .

The jingles were closer. So close.

Too close!

Something, an instinct, broke the reverie and she whirled around. The dappled grey mare instantly tried to step back, pulling into a frightened rear as the blue wooden sleigh continued its slide forward.

Pia gasped with terror – there was no time to scream – as the horse's front legs bucked in front of her. She threw her arms up, but too late – the horse delivered a glancing blow to her cheek that knocked her off her feet and sent her flying against the cars parked by the kerb.

Dazed, she tried to get up, to get away, but her foot slipped on some black ice, kicking the horse's leg sharply with her stiletto, and it reared up again. Pia heard the driver shout, trying to calm the horse, but it was too late – it had had enough. With a defiant dip of its head, the horse cantered up the hill and the crystal calm of the Engadine night was shattered by a scream as the rails of the heavy antique sleigh were drawn over Pia's precious, precocious right foot.

Chapter Eight

Had the morphine not knocked her into delirium, Pia would have been delighted to learn that Will Silk was indeed now chasing her – by helicopter.

The rumours inside the hotel had started quickly – before he'd even finished his drink – and by the time news of her accident reached him, most of the partygoers had emptied onto the street.

It had taken him – the person with the greatest interest in seeing that she was okay– several minutes just to push past all the other people present, and the sight of Pia, so pale and her foot twisted at an obscene angle, had almost poleaxed him.

'Oh my God, oh my God, this can't be happening,' Sophie had been repeating, her hands tearing her hair as Pia was lifted into the air ambulance. 'Wait, please. Don't go yet,' she implored the medics. 'I just need to talk to—' She pressed the speed dial on her mobile again; but, as much as the shock had sobered up her brain, she couldn't get her fingers to work properly and they kept misdialling.

The medics ignored her, slamming shut the door.

'No, please. I'll only be a moment.'

Will pushed forward, his jaw clenched. 'You heard the girl. Just wait!' The medics stared at him. It was clear he wasn't in the mood for diplomacy. 'That woman is a world-class ballerina. *No one* touches her foot,' he ordered.

A stunned silence fell around them.

'Monsieur Baudrand?' Sophie yelled into her phone.

'*Oui?*' whipped a thin voice.

'Oh thank God I've got hold of you. It's Sophie, *monsieur* . . . It's about Pia.' She paused as she suddenly tried to find the words to tell him.

'What now?' Baudrand exhaled, exasperated at the thought of his – suspended – star still causing trouble.

'She's been in an accident, *monsieur*. I'm sorry. There's no easy way to tell you this. Her foot has been broken.'

Four thousand miles away, she could hear him catch his breath.

'How bad?' he managed.

Sophie shook her head. 'It's completely crushed, *monsieur*. I—'

Will grabbed the phone.

'That's enough. Let's leave the hyperbole to the papers, shall we?' he said in a low voice. 'Mr Baudrand? This is William Silk, a friend of Miss Soto's. She's in an air ambulance and I've got a helicopter on standby. Where does she need to go in the world? Who's the best?'

There was a long pause. 'Jeremy Rosen at the Royal National Orthopaedic Hospital, outside London,' he said finally. 'He did Talanov's ankle three years ago. I'll call him now.'

'We're on our way.'

Will handed back her phone and looked at the medic.

'She's going to the Royal National Orthopaedic outside London. A surgical team will meet you there.'

'*Aber nein,*' said the medic, holding up his hands in

refusal. 'We are not authorized. We must take her to the *Klinik* here.'

'No. She needs a specialist.'

The medic shrugged. 'Sorry, *Herr*—'

'Fine. If you won't take her, I'll fly her over myself. Get her out of there.'

'But you are not equipped! There's no way you can possibly . . .'

'I'm not negotiating with you. I'm telling you. She is the very best in the world at what she does, and the only person who's putting her foot back together is the person who's the very best in the world at what he does.'

Sophie stared at him – impressed by his great authority and relieved that someone else was directing the show.

The medic knew there was no point arguing with this man – he was too rich, too powerful and too determined. And they couldn't afford to waste time. They only had enough morphine for three hours.

'Okay, okay,' he said reluctantly. He knew he could lose his job over this, but he recognized his beautiful patient now, and it didn't take a genius to work out that there would be a media storm if her recovery was compromised by mistakes at this end.

Will grabbed his mobile out of his pocket. 'Get the chopper going,' he said into it. 'We're going to London immediately.'

Sophie went to climb into the helicopter with Pia but the medic stopped her.

'Family only.'

'But I'm her PA,' Sophie wailed. The man shrugged and shut the doors. Didn't he realize it was as good as the same thing?

'Come on,' Will said to Sophie, who had started wringing her hands frenziedly. 'You're coming with me.'

They raced over the frozen lake, past the pitch hoardings, past the trailers and horseboxes. Beyond all this, a pilot was sitting in the cockpit of a black helicopter, going through the drill and starting up the blades. Crouching low, they clambered in and fastened themselves into their seats.

'She'll be okay,' he said. 'She's going to the best place, with the best people. They'll take care of her.'

He squeezed Sophie's hand and she looked at him, wondering who he was trying to convince – her or himself.

The drone of the blades suffocated any further conversation and the pilot handed them each some ear protectors, isolating them with their own muffled thoughts as the helicopter rose into the bruised sky and into the slipstream of the air ambulance.

When she awoke, purple clouds still sat fatly below them, giving away nothing of what lay beneath. But Sophie knew they had to be nearly there. She checked her watch. Nearly 5 a.m. They had been flying for almost two and a half hours now.

The helicopter began to lose altitude, and as they dug through the woolly night covers, London's grey hub slowly emerged. This had been her home before she'd started working for Pia, and she hadn't been back in three years. Looking down on it now, from this spectacular and privileged aerial vantage, she still remembered all too clearly why. She remembered every hour of every day. She didn't need to come back here to remember. The problem was trying to forget. She bit her lip anxiously. This was the last place she wanted to be – but Pia needed her. She couldn't let her down.

She watched blankly as the capital's neatly parcelled-up terraces spilt out of their boxes into sprawling suburban gardens, before opening out into large and vast fields which were punctuated by stray ancient copses and hedgerows as unending over the horizon as railway tracks.

In front of them, the air ambulance hovered, then started its steady descent to a long, rolling lawn. She thought of Pia in there, alone with the medics: hooked up, knocked out and broken.

Will and Sophie hung suspended, like a cot mobile, in the sky above her, as they watched the ambulance touch down. They could see the emergency team standing, braced. They looked so tiny, like dolls.

A trolley was pushed forward, the doctors' white coats flying like windsocks behind them, and for a moment Will caught sight of Pia as she was carried out on the stretcher. His breath caught at the sight of her again. Hours earlier she'd been like a tornado, a furious and resplendent life force that sucked the air out of the room in her wake. Now, motionless a hundred feet below, she looked as fragile as parchment, like a dead butterfly. As she was wheeled from sight, a shaft of dawn light hit the majestic colours on her raggedy couture dress, and he found himself wondering – not for the first time – why it was that for all her talent and pride and passion, there always seemed to be something about her that was fraying.

Chapter Nine

It wasn't until they got to Basel, on the Swiss–German border, that Tanner allowed himself to relax. They had made good time, in spite of the delayed start. Some socialite had stepped in front of a horse and broken her foot, and all of a sudden the entire Swiss emergency services were descending upon St Moritz, clogging up the roads and airspace, and making a racket that had left it all but impossible for him to sleep.

They'd had to leave an hour later than planned, but still they had passed through the Engadine valley to Saglians by 7 a.m. and were first onto the motor-rail at the Vereina tunnel, loading up the large 44-ton horseboxes. In theory it would have been easier to just drive along the Julier pass but with a sheer drop on one side for a 25-mile stretch and the roads so narrow, he wasn't taking any chances. His cargo was insured for £2 million and Will Silk would chase him to the gates of hell if anything happened to it.

Once they'd arrived in Klosters and had a quick breakfast, they'd travelled north-west to Zurich, stopping every two hours to feed and water the horses, and turn the hay; then north-westwards again to Basel, where they would now have to endure reams of red tape as they moved the three-lorry, ten-pony convoy from Switzerland back into the EU.

Slowly, Tanner manoeuvred the horsebox into the bay.

He rubbed his eyes with the heels of his hands, exhausted. It was 1.25 p.m. and everyone was tired and hungry. In his wing mirrors, he could see the grooms and stable hands in the trucks behind were beginning to get testy, and Tanner knew they all needed to stretch their legs and crack on with lunch. He hoped they could get through this section quickly.

A Swiss border guard in a navy-blue uniform with bright epaulettes and a navy baseball cap, was approaching the horsebox. Tanner rolled down the window and opened the glove compartment, pulling out a thick wad of official documents.

'*Guten Tag*,' the man said, holding out his hand for the paperwork.

Tanner handed it to him with a weary smile.

The guard flicked his eyes over the sheets for a moment, then stepped back and looked at the other two lorries. 'Thank you, sir. Would you like to come with me?' The guard indicated a wooden hut with an overhanging sloping roof.

'Sure,' Tanner replied. 'Jessy, climb up to my bunk, will you? You'll find some crisps and drinks there. Go and give them to the others. They're probably chewing their fists by now.'

Jessy, his head groom and erstwhile lover, with round brown eyes, a bouncy blonde bob and even bouncier body, laughed her dirty laugh and scrambled into the back.

Tanner followed the guard into the hut and they sat down on hard blue plastic chairs. Meticulously, the guard read through the twelve-page livery inventory – twenty-two saddles; twenty-eight bits; twenty-three numnahs and so on – the copious vet's records and list of veterinary medicines on board, the horses' affiliation to the HPA, pro formas, and the entire crew's passports.

By the end of it all, fifty minutes later, Tanner was so nearly asleep and had put his signature to so many declarations, he couldn't be sure that he hadn't signed himself up to national service, or donating a kidney.

'Thank you. My colleague and I will run through the checks on the lorries, then you can go.'

Tanner nodded, relieved. Jessy could do the next shift of driving, through Strasbourg, Reims and up to Calais. He needed to rest. The guard indicated to another, and the two of them walked with Tanner back to the trucks.

'Okay, everybody out,' Tanner shouted. 'We're nearly done.'

The grooms and stable hands all converged outside the trucks as the two guards moved through the horseboxes, starting at the back.

'Tanner,' Jessy whispered, skittering over and looking slightly wild-eyed.

'Mmm?' Tanner said, not really hearing her. He was scanning the paperwork he'd been given. Satisfied nothing had been forgotten, he stuffed it all into the plastic wallet and tucked it under his arm.

'Tanner. I need to talk to you,' she said in a low voice. 'Urgently.'

'What is it?' he asked, concerned. She wasn't the type to make a fuss.

'This,' she said, pulling up her T-shirt and revealing a small plastic bag filled with white powder in the waistband of her jodhpurs.

His eyes widened with horror. He glanced back down at the guards, who were in the first horsebox, and up towards the office where three more guards had come in and were talking together by the desk.

'Where the hell did you get that?' he hissed, his mouth set in a grim line.

'It's not mine,' she hissed, eyes pleading. 'I found it just now in your bunk when I went to get the snacks.'

'What?' he growled. '*I* didn't put it there. I've not touched the stuff.' Jessy squinted at him. 'Well, not for years anyway.'

'I swear I don't know how this got on board, Tanner,' she promised. 'If I'd so much as seen someone sniff around here, I'd have clouted them.'

There was a brief pause.

'Oh no,' Tanner exhaled, squeezing his eyes shut as the penny dropped.

Alonso.

'Jesus Christ,' he muttered, trying to keep the panic from his face. 'Was there any more?'

The guards progressed to the second horsebox.

Jessy shrugged. 'I don't know. I searched the cabin as much as I could, but I knew they'd be out with you any minute and I didn't want to be found looking like I was *hiding* stuff.' Tears were threatening and her bottom lip wobbled.

Carefully, without attracting the guards' attention, Tanner reached his arm to hers and gently rubbed it. 'It's okay. You've done the right thing. It's okay,' he murmured. 'Don't worry. We'll be fine.'

'But – what should I do about this?' she cast her eyes down to her tummy again. 'What if they search us?'

'There's no reason they should. All our paperwork's in order. Everything's above board.'

The guards were in the final horsebox now, Tanner's truck. Two of the guards in the office came out, and for the first time Tanner could see they had dogs with them.

'Oh my God,' Jessy trembled. 'This is a nightmare.'

'Just keep it together, Jessy,' he urged quietly. 'We'll be through in a couple of minutes now. They're not interested in us. It's all just a formality.'

But the guards were walking directly towards their group, the dogs pulling excitedly, and Jessy stepped back, terrified.

'Okay, I'll deal with this,' Tanner said and he marched forward, meeting them way ahead of the convoy.

'Excuse me,' he said, his smile masking his desperation to keep those dogs away from Jessy. 'But are the dogs going into the trucks? I know you've got your job to do, and I don't mean to be obstructive, but there are already two guards in there and I'm worried the dogs will upset the horses. They're nervy at the best of times, and obviously they are very tired at the moment, what with the tournament and this journey.'

The guards looked at each other, and around Tanner to the huddle of grooms standing on the pavement. They formed a motley crew, all propping each other up, swigging from Coke bottles and smoking Marlboros.

The taller guard jerked his chin towards them. 'It is not permitted to smoke here.'

'Oh . . . right. No smoking. Of course. Absolutely,' Tanner cried, relief flooding his face. 'I'll get them to stop immediately.'

He turned and marched back to them all. 'Everybody, lights out. Come on, quickly. Smoking's not allowed. Hurry up.'

Reluctantly and silently they all dropped their cigarettes to the ground, grinding them beneath their feet. They were desperate to get out of here.

If only they knew, Tanner thought, stealing a glance at Jessy. She still looked jumpy.

The door of the horsebox was slammed shut and the two guards came round, poker-faced, one of them holding a brown paper bag.

Oh shit!

The guard held up the bag. 'Whose is this?'

There was a shuffle of feet. No one said anything. Slowly, Tanner raised a hand. 'It's mine,' he said quietly. He needed to get Jessy and the others out of here.

'This is contraband. Taking it out of Switzerland and into the European Union constitutes a contravention of the CITES quotas as administered by UNEP,' the guard said robotically.

Tanner nodded, although he had no idea what the guard was on about. 'I – I'm sorry. It was for personal use only, though . . . if that makes a difference . . .' His voice trailed away.

The two guards spoke quickly to each other in German. Tanner didn't have a clue what they were saying, but it couldn't be good. Nothing in German ever sounded good.

He looked at Jessy, who looked as though she was going to pass out. He tried to give what he hoped was a reassuring smile.

'We are confiscating this from you.'

'Of course,' Tanner replied, eyes downcast.

There was a pause.

'You can go.'

Tanner's head snapped up. 'Huh?'

'You can go. All the checks are complete now.'

'You're not going . . . to . . . arrest me?'

The guard cracked the faintest of smiles. 'Not unless you want me to.'

Tanner held his hands up in relief. 'No. No. I'm good. Thank you. Thank you very much.'

The guards turned and walked back to the hut, laughing quietly among themselves.

With a look of unadulterated gratitude written all over his face, Tanner swept his arm round for everyone to climb back into the trucks.

'We'll stop for lunch outside Strasbourg, everybody,' he called, as the cab doors opened and shut.

Climbing back into the driver's seat – he felt completely awake now – he shifted the truck into first and slowly pulled away, giving a small salute of thanks as they passed the guards.

'Holy shit! Can you believe we got away with that?' he asked, eyes bright, as they built up speed on the autoroute. 'When they brought that bag out . . .' He gave a low whistle. 'I can't believe they let me go. It must have just come under the personal-usage quota.'

Jessy shook her head slowly.

'I'm so sorry,' she said quietly. 'I know I shouldn't have taken it. It's just . . . I was going to give it to my mother for her birthday next week.'

'What?' Tanner looked at her in disbelief.

Jessy shrugged. 'I figured it was worth a shot. After all, who would really miss it?'

Tanner tried to keep up. 'Jessy, what was in the bag?'

'Some beluga caviar I nicked from the kitchens at the party last night,' she replied in a slow, low voice.

Tanner threw his head back and fell about laughing. 'Caviar? Jesus, Jessy! I thought they'd found a haul of coke!

I thought I was going to be busted for drug smuggling!' he roared.

He looked over at Jessy. She was uncharacteristically quiet.

'Hey. You still worried about that bag of coke? Listen, it's all okay now. You can relax. You did exactly the right thing.' He squeezed her knee lightly. 'I've got a very good idea of who that stash belonged to, and don't you worry – they won't be getting away with it. Here, give it to me – I'll take it for you.'

Jessy looked at him and he was shocked to realize that she was still terrified.

'I can't,' she said, bursting into tears.

'Why not?' he asked, his eyes switching rapidly between her and the road.

'Because I swallowed it.'

Chapter Ten

'Back home in Ireland, we called these "soft days",' Sophie said quietly, mainly to herself. She was sitting on the window sill, her legs tucked under her willowy frame. Her cheek was pressed to the glass as she looked out into the dreary January mizzle. The air was as saturated as it could be without actually raining, which for some reason felt more depressing than if it had rained. She blew hot air onto the window, and the view smudged into oblivion.

Sighing, she turned back to face the room. Will was asleep again in the chair, his head propped up in his hands. His skin was sallow, the hollows of his eyes grey, and even in his sleep he looked exhausted. Exhausted, but still handsome.

Sophie couldn't help but smile as she looked at him. His long legs were splayed in front of him, his shirtsleeves rolled up. He was still in his black tie.

Her heart lurched as she suddenly realized that so was she.

She looked down at the creased Prada dress and her shoulders slumped. It couldn't possibly be returned to the store now. She'd worn it for eighteen hours straight and no amount of dry-cleaning would restore this dress to its former glory – sweat stains had swirled under the arms, and there were grease marks across the lap from where she'd absent-mindedly wiped her fingers after eating a packet of crisps. She chewed her lip, instantly stressed. She couldn't exactly ask Pia to pick up the bill now – it didn't matter that she hadn't wanted to wear it in the first place – but there was no way she could afford it on her salary.

Well, that's if she even had a salary any more. Was she going to be out of a job now? She looked over at Pia – wan and immobile in the bed – her right leg strapped up in plaster all the way to the knee.

She stood up, agitated, knocking over a chair. She needed to get out of here. Get some air. Move about a bit. But the noise had disturbed Will and he sat up, panicked and disoriented.

'What's happened?' he asked, his voice deep with sleep. 'Has she woken up?'

Sophie shook her head. 'No. Not yet. I'm sorry. I didn't mean to wake you. I just thought I'd get some fresh air. I'm going a bit stir-crazy with all this waiting about.'

Will stretched out his arms, yawning. 'Yeah, I know what you mean.' He looked over at Pia, his eyes coming to a rest on her mutilated foot, her bunion and the calloused skin beneath her toes left uncovered by the cast.

Sophie watched his scrutiny, and felt protective of her.

'She hates her feet,' she said quickly. 'She's always wishing she could pretty them up with pedicures. She never wears sandals. But she wouldn't be able to dance with soft skin, you know.'

'I know,' Will said, amused. 'I wasn't judging her by the state of her toenails.'

Sophie smiled, embarrassed to have been such a Rottweiler. 'Sorry.'

'Don't be. It's sweet,' he grinned. 'No, I was looking at

her foot because I was wondering if what we've done is enough.'

'What you've done, you mean,' Sophie corrected. 'If it wasn't for you, her foot could have just been reset any old way, without any consideration for her career.'

He shook his head. 'It's just all happened so fast. One minute, she's standing there, looking like a goddess and frightening the life out of me. The next, she's all crumpled and defenceless.' He took Pia's tiny hand in his and stroked it. 'I can hardly take it in. I've known her less than – what? A week, is it?'

'Five days,' Sophie murmured. Five days since he'd met her too, but, as ever, that wasn't the point.

'Five days,' he repeated, his head cocked to the side as Pia lay in front of him, every inch the Sleeping Beauty. Only Sophie knew this Prince Charming's kiss wasn't going to be enough for a Happy Ever After. Not by a long shot.

'Look, Will,' Sophie said slowly. 'I don't want to . . . uh, put a dampener on things. But you should probably . . . um . . . brace yourself for a rocky response when she wakes up.'

Will squinted at her. 'What do you mean?'

'Well, she's been unconscious since they gave her the morphine in St Moritz. She doesn't even know she's in England yet, much less in hospital. It's all going to be a big shock for her when she comes round. And then the doctor will hit her with the prognosis and God only knows what that's going to be. Even if she can ever dance again, the surgery means she's going to be out of action for a couple of months at least, and she's going to be an absolute *nightmare* when she hears that. You have no idea,' Sophie muttered, shaking her head.

'I understand all that. But why would she take it out on me?'

'Because she's going to have a lot to thank *you* for,' Sophie shrugged. 'And Pia doesn't like being beholden to anyone. Not even for career-saving surgery.'

There was a rap at the door, and a nurse came in.

'I've just come to do Miss Soto's obs,' she smiled, walking over to the screen and writing down the blood pressure and pulse figures on her chart.

Mr Rosen came in after her, and smiled at them both.

'Has the patient woken up yet?' he asked, going straight over to Pia, who was still very obviously unconscious.

Sophie shook her head and sat back down on the window ledge again.

Mr Rosen picked up Pia's hand and squeezed it. 'Pia, can you hear me?'

Nothing.

'Can you hear me, Pia? Try to wake up.'

There was nothing for a long moment; then, softly, Pia groaned.

'Good girl, Pia, that's it,' Mr Rosen urged. 'Wake up now. You're okay.'

Pia's eyelids fluttered, her head moved to the side, away from Will, away from the flat light that now seemed to stream through the window. Slowly, she opened her eyes.

There was a long silence as her eyes tried to focus, as her mind tried to remember. 'Where am I?' she asked finally.

'You're in hospital, Pia. You had an accident in Switzerland. Do you remember?'

Pia squinted, confused.

'You're in England now. My name's Mr Rosen. Your director, Mr Baudrand, asked me to look after you.'

'Baudrand . . .' Pia repeated, more awake now, her eyes focusing. She looked at the doctor and Sophie saw the terror in her eyes.

'It's okay, it's okay now,' he soothed. 'There's nothing to be frightened of, Pia. You came in with a severe crush injury to your right foot. There were fractures to the first, second and fifth metatarsal bones, with what we call a Lisfranc dislocation of the first metatarsal.'

'A what?' Pia looked around, distressed, for Sophie. She saw Will first.

'It's okay, Pia, I'm here,' Sophie said, springing forward.

'What . . . why is he here?' Pia asked her. Sophie knew she meant Will.

'He helped you, Pia. He made sure you were treated by the best. He looked after you.'

Tears welled up in Pia's eyes but she didn't look at him.

'I know this is a big shock, Pia,' Mr Rosen said, bringing her attention back to him again. 'And I don't want to overload you with information. Let me just say that we have stabilized the bones in your foot with K wires, which we should be able to remove in a few weeks. Usually, I would have put in a formal fixation plate, but Mr Baudrand left me in no doubt as to the scale of your talent, and that would have left you unable to dance professionally again.'

Pia squeezed her eyes shut in horror at his words, trying to blank them out. But they kept on coming.

'So, I have put the K wires in, on the condition that you remain completely off your feet for four weeks.' He patted Pia's hand. 'If you want to dance at the elite level again, it's vital you don't put any load on your foot before then. After that, all being well, that cast can come off, and we'll fit you with a rigid arch support and a weight-bearing plaster. The

K wires can come out six weeks after that but I'm afraid we're looking at four months before you'll be able to start dancing again, and we won't know until then whether or not you can make a full return to the international stage.'

Pia kept her eyes squeezed shut. It was her worst nightmare come true. The very worst thing that could have happened to her. Well, the second worst. The very worst had already happened.

'Now, how's the pain, Pia?' Mr Rosen asked, seeing her wince. She was blanched with pain. 'Is it bad?'

Pia nodded.

'Can you rate it on a scale of one to ten?'

'Eight,' she managed. Mr Rosen nodded. It must be bad. In his experience, ballerinas had a higher pain threshold than any other group of athletes he worked with, often dancing with injury for weeks before seeking help.

'Nurse, plenty of fluids and Perocet every four hours, please.'

The nurse nodded and attached a new saline bag to Pia's drip.

'I'll be back to see you later, okay?' Mr Rosen smiled, squeezing her hand again. 'Everything's going to be okay. Your friends did a fantastic job getting you over here.'

Pia watched him leave. Then she looked back at Sophie.

'What is it?' Sophie whispered. 'What can I get you?'

Pia murmured something, but she couldn't hear. All the drugs were making Pia's speech slurred.

'What? I didn't catch that,' Sophie said, leaning in.

Pia drew herself up as much as she possibly could.

'I said get out of here,' she hissed. 'You're fired.'

Chapter Eleven

'Pia! Pia! It's okay. You're okay,' a voice said, so close it tickled her ear. She felt weight on her arms, holding her down. She tried to move them but the pressure increased and she couldn't. It was too much, too strong.

'Pia, don't! Stop it! You're hurt. It'll make things worse.'

But she resisted, thrashing, trying to get free. She wouldn't let this happen. She had to . . .

'You're safe now.'

Safe? The word stopped her like a bullet. Safe. Her body went limp. It was defeated. Exhausted. Lame.

'It's me, Pia. Look at me. Open your eyes and look at me, Pia.' The voice was calm. Kind.

Pia opened her eyes slowly. Pale grey eyes, like a cat's, stared back at her. She flinched at their inquisitiveness. So sharp. But the voice had been so soft.

'Do you remember where you are, Pia?' Will asked.

She slid her eyes around the room – the peach walls, the grey louvered blinds, the smell of sanitized oblivion. She nodded.

'Do you remember why you're here?'

She nodded again, her eyes filling like pools. She felt her hand squeezed.

'And do you remember me?'

She looked back at him. He was in a fresh shirt but there were red rims around his eyes and shadow on his jaw. The images came swiftly and steadily. Yes, she remembered him – his cocksure grin, those knowing eyes, the polo groupies, the open wallet. She looked away again.

'Where's Sophie?' she mumbled.

There was a brief pause. 'She's gone. Like you asked,' he added diplomatically. He didn't mention the poor girl's tears in the corridor after Pia had slipped into unconsciousness again. 'Would you like me to get her back for you?' he asked.

She shook her head slowly. She remembered all of that too. It felt like an age ago.

'How long . . .' she whispered croakily. She felt so damned weak.

'They've been keeping you heavily sedated to minimize movement of your foot. It's vital everything knits well in the first week. You've been sleeping almost constantly for the past two days.'

She jerked her head towards him. Two days?

'Just try to relax. You're in good hands.'

He pulled the sheet up smoothly and tucked it under her arms. She looked up at him.

'Mr Rosen is very pleased with your progress. He's said you can be discharged in a few days. I've made arrangements for you to be taken to my house in the country for your convalescence.'

'No,' she muttered. 'Home.'

Will shook his head. 'They've said you're not to fly for at least a month. And *ideally* not at all until they can take the wires out.' He squeezed her tiny hand again. 'Anyway, you're going to need a lot of support. You can't be on your own at a time like this. Monsieur Baudrand and Mr Rosen and I have already discussed your rehabilitation programme. They've given me the name of an excellent physiotherapist, Evie Grainger. Do you know her?'

Pia nodded. Evie had been a principal dancer at the New York City Ballet but had retrained as a ballet-specialized physiotherapist after an injury cut short her dancing career. She was a big character who charged even bigger fees but everybody paid them because her own experience as a former principal meant she knew exactly the strains each individual ballet placed on the dancers' bodies: *Giselle* was a nightmare for producing twisted knees; *Swan Lake* for lower back pain; *Manon* for sheer full-body strain . . .

'She's in Japan touring with the Maryinsky at the moment, but don't worry – her contract won't stand up to much once my lawyers have been set to work on it. We'll get her to bring you back to fitness before you know it.'

Pia looked away. She didn't share his confidence. Technically, yes, she knew Evie and the doctors may well be able to get her back on *pointe*, extending, twirling and leaping. But to be part of the elite, a principal needed *ballon*, and that's something that can't possibly be conveyed with a robotic foot held together by wire. She felt a black chasm of despair open up inside her and she clamped her eyes shut, desperate not to show him her terror.

Will coughed awkwardly, unsure of where to stand or what to do with his hands. The silence between them grew and he paced back to the window.

'Of course, I recognize that all this is my fault,' he said finally.

Pia swivelled her eyes towards him.

'I mean, after you paid such a lot of money not to have dinner with me, I guess I should have known you'd go to extraordinary lengths not to sleep in my bed either. Personally I think this is a bit much but . . .' He shrugged. 'Well, I should have known seducing you would require passing international tests of valour.'

A ghost of a smile hovered on her lips.

'Look,' she said in a quiet voice. 'You have been very kind to me and I am grateful for what you have done, but I can't let you take over my recovery.'

'Why not?'

She sighed. 'Because I don't know you.'

'Yes, you do,' he countered. 'You wouldn't have had so much fun insulting a complete stranger as you have had insulting me.' He took her hand in his. 'And I've had more fun with you snubbing me than I had that time with two supermodels in a Jacuzzi.'

Her eyes widened; his glittered.

'What do you say? Let me whisk you off to darkest Dorset for phase two of our courtly romance. I'll hide you in a tower so that all those hideous press men can't find you and we'll breed goats and live happily ever after while you grow a new foot.'

Pia shook her head, fractionally, at his jokes. He was as bad as Sophie.

'And if you're worrying about your virtue, then don't. You heard what the doctor said. You've got a ten-week chastity zone to protect you and absolutely nothing you can do will make me break it.'

She cracked a weary smile, but still shook her head.

'Ah-ah-ah!' he said, contradicting her refusal. 'You smiled. That means yes,' he said.

Pia tried to sit up to protest, but he gently pushed her back down again, pulling the sheets further up, under her chin. 'Now go back to sleep. I'm going to find Mr Rosen and make the arrangements to get you out of here.'

She closed her eyes, too tired to argue further, surrendering to unconsciousness almost immediately. Will watched as all her arrogance and defences lifted off her in her sleep. She looked like an angel, and he saw what a bundle of paradoxes she really was – ferocious but vulnerable; adored but alone; brilliant but tortured; fit but broken.

He looked down at her mutilated foot – of which Sophie had been so protective – and hoped, for all their sakes, that she was going to make it back from this.

Chapter Twelve

'Hey, good to see you again. It's been a while,' boomed a voice from across the street, as Sophie fumbled with her keys. 'I was beginning to wonder whether I should come over and start sniffing in the hallway.'

Sophie looked up and smiled wanly at Greg, her too-friendly neighbour. 'Ha! No. I'm fine, really. Thanks, though, for the thought,' she smiled, turning away. 'I really appreciate that thought about my dead and rotting body,' she muttered under her breath.

'You've been travelling with your foxy ballerina again?'

'Yeah, something like that,' Sophie replied, getting the key in the lock. She opened the door and picked up her bags. 'I'm beat. I'll catch you later, Greg,' she said, half over her shoulder.

She tramped up the eight flights of stairs to the top floor, wishing for the umpteenth time she'd chosen an apartment block with lifts. Letting herself in, she dropped her bags with a thud on the whitewashed floor and leant against the wall.

Home Sweet Home.

She looked around. Well, kind of.

In truth, the open-plan space looked more like the scene of a crime. Anyone else walking in – most especially her mother – would think the place had been ransacked. But Sophie wasn't alarmed, just defeated. More mess to clean up. Housekeeping wasn't her strong point, and there were old newspapers scattered on the coffee table, piles of un-ironed laundry in a wicker basket, stone-cold half-drunk mugs of tea growing penicillin on the worktops, the bed still unmade . . .

Oh Adam! The memory of him lying back on her pillows rushed back at her and her stomach lurched at the thought of what she'd done with Alonso – just hours after leaving Adam in her bed. To think she'd waited for him so long and then, just as her skin smelt of his and her muscles still ached from his acrobatics – it wasn't easy keeping up with a dancer in bed! – she'd stuffed it up.

Not that it was her fault. It was Pia's. If she'd been able to curb her rampant ego a little bit, Sophie wouldn't have been forced to drink the bar dry in revenge.

She slid down the wall. It probably wasn't going to make any difference anyway. Adam was notorious for his one-time flings . . . She knew that it had just been some fun, his way to while away the time together until Pia came back and dominated both their lives again.

Besides, now that Pia had fired her, she wasn't going to be at the studios, watching him day in and day out, as she had done. In fact, she might never even see him again. They'd never swapped mobile numbers – there had been no need – and short of loitering with intent, why would their paths cross? Chicago was a big city.

She hugged herself dejectedly at the bleak prospect and shivered. The apartment was freezing and she remembered she'd turned the heating down before leaving for the tour. The weather had been wet and mild in England, but back here in Chicago the February snow was still several inches thick and not remotely done yet.

She ransacked through her hanging travel wardrobe (she couldn't afford proper furniture on the salary Pia had paid her) and pulled out a chunky sage-green jumper with funnel neck and floppy sleeves. She swapped her skinny jeans for some grey ribbed leggings and pulled out her sheepskin slipper boots. As she eased into her soft clean clothes, she felt the tension lift off her a little. In spite of the mess, it felt good to be back.

She padded into the kitchenette, turning on the hot water and heating, and made herself a mug of black Assam tea and, grabbing a loaf from the freezer, a toasted marmite sandwich.

She switched on the radio and sat on the arm of her battered sky-blue linen sofa, munching mindlessly. What to do now? It occurred to her that without a job to go to, she had absolutely nothing at all to do and no one to see in the whole city. Being on call to Pia twenty-four hours a day had made it all but impossible to get friendships off the ground.

She closed her eyes for a moment and thought of her family, back in Ireland. It had been so long since she'd been home. She missed them. Missed her mum. Missed her sisters. It would be so lovely to see them again, to go back. Maybe now . . . now that she'd been fired . . . maybe now was the time to return? There wasn't anything to stay for, particularly. Enough time had passed, surely?

Sophie shook her head violently and she nearly choked on a crust. What the hell was she thinking? Who was she trying to kid? She could *never* go back. In her father's eyes, what she had done was unforgivable. Had she not run away first, there was no doubt he would have cast her out. His back was turned to her, she knew, whether she was there to stare at it or not, and seven hundred years' penance wouldn't make it up to him, much less seven.

She took a large, deliberate gulp of too-hot tea. Distraction. Distraction. She stood up and marched over to the small orangery on the terrace, which she used as her studio – the very reason she had rented this flat and forgone an apartment block with lifts. The roof blinds were pulled over the glass roof, diffusing the cold blue winter light into a softer opalescence. Canvases were stacked eight deep against the walls so that there was scarcely any floor space left; several were still sitting on the easels, unfinished.

Instantly diverted from her emotional maelstrom, mug in hand, she appraised them coolly. She'd been experimenting with various different forms – black chalk, pastels, oil, gouache – but all the subject matter was a variation on a theme: Pia Soto – in *arabesque*, in *pirouette*, at the *barre*, in flight, resting, in her dressing room, in practice . . . There were etchings of Adam too (now including the nude that had got her into such delicious trouble last week) and some of the other principals, a few of the corps rehearsing and waiting in the wings, ready to go on stage. Mainly, though, they were about Pia.

'Isn't everything always?' she mumbled to herself.

The smaller charcoals Sellotaped to the walls were details – a foot on *pointe*, an extended arm, a raised chin, a long neck, a turned-out knee. But the canvases were formal narratives. She picked up one of the finished oil compositions. Pia was in profile, the curtain down, moments before a performance. She'd been wearing her puffa jacket when Sophie had sketched the pose in pen, but when she applied it to canvas here in the studio she'd put her in the billowy

Pavlova-tutu with the navy sash which she'd worn in *Romeo and Juliet*. It was old school and Romantic, Pia's still, tense body suffused with grace even in repose.

But it disappointed Sophie. She hadn't captured what she'd been after. She could never get what happened to Pia in those final moments, just before the curtain lifted. When the orchestra was tuning up and the company warming up, Pia froze – quite literally. She turned into a statue, retreating into herself so deeply that nothing, other than the sound of applause when the conductor came out, could break the spell. Then, she would turn and run to the wings where Sophie would hand her a bowl to throw up in and some mints. It was a well-rehearsed drill, always the same. The nearest Sophie ever got to a *pas de deux*.

It wasn't nerves, she knew that much. Pia never doubted her own brilliance or her ability to perform. With the other dancers, Sophie could almost see their dancing characters settle upon them like shrouds, overwriting their own personalities and desires. But Pia . . . ?

With Pia it was almost the opposite. She didn't become Odette or Giselle or Manon by subjugating her own self; she didn't become less herself in those quiet moments, she became *more*. She tapped into something at her core, something which filled her with fire and rage, but also joy and the sweetest tenderness. *That* was what set her apart from technicians like Ava Petrova, not her turn out or the flexion of her back. Whatever she locked into, deep within herself, it released a range of emotion and empathy that elevated her from athlete to artiste. She was compelled by something. But what?

The phone rang and, still frowning, Sophie went to pick it up.

'Hello?' she asked blankly, her eyes appraising her own short stubby brushstrokes.

'Sophie? It's Luce.'

'Oh hi, Lucy.' She'd always got on well with Baudrand's assistant. She had to. They spent a lot of time smoothing out the ructions between their respective bosses. 'What's up?'

'I was just calling to see if you were back actually. I've been worried about you. No one knew where you were.'

'Yeah, well, I've had a bit of a nightmare. I managed to leave Switzerland in a private helicopter with no passport, so you do *not* want to know how long I spent at the Irish Embassy in London trying to get a temporary passport and visa.'

'Nightmare!' Lucy said sympathetically. There was a brief pause. 'Look, I heard Pia fired you. I'm sorry.'

'Yeah, well. Her prerogative, I guess.'

'Don't be daft. She must have hit her head as well as her foot. Everybody knows she's completely reliant on you to keep all the balls up in the air for her. You totally run her life. She can't do a thing without you. Honestly, the crazy cow's lost it this time.'

Sophie smiled, grateful for the support. 'Mmm, well, we'll see.'

'What's it all about anyway?'

'Search me. I'm as much in the dark as anyone.' She took another bite of her sandwich.

'Seriously? She didn't give you a reason?' She lowered her voice to an excited whisper. 'You could take her to a tribunal, then, couldn't you? Unfair dismissal, or something?'

Sophie shrugged. 'Oh I can't be bothered. Can you just imagine the hassle?' she asked, munching loudly. 'Taking Pia to court would be like going to war. And I know which of those two I'd prefer.'

'Hmm. Well, d'you fancy coming in for lunch? Let's catch up properly over a beer and plot a dastardly revenge.'

Sophie laughed – for the first time in days. 'Yeah, I'd love to. When's good for you?'

'One? It'll have to be on the dot though. Baudrand's back from New York for the day with Ava, dealing with the paperwork for her visa, and I've got a meeting with him at two.'

She checked her watch. It was 11.30 a.m.

'Okay, great. I'll come into the office to get you. There are a few things I need to pick up anyway.'

Sophie was ten minutes early and Lucy was on a call when she popped her head round the door. 'I'll just pop to the changing rooms,' she mouthed. 'Back in a sec.'

She ambled down the familiar corridors, stopping to stare in through the windows and watch the rehearsals. Even without a note on the door, much less a programme, she was able to identify the ballets being rehearsed. She realized she'd become a connoisseur.

She stopped outside Studio Four, Pia's favourite – she always said the mirrors were most flattering in there. José Cabrera, Adam's number two, was standing there, hands on hips, talking animatedly with someone. Sophie leant forward, pressing her nose against the glass in the door to see who was partnering him. She could see a pair of black satin *pointe* shoes crossed at the ankle, but nothing more.

She watched him for a few moments more, music from the other studios drifting down the hall, and became increasingly aware of a sadness rising up inside her. She would miss this. She had come to know and love the company so well

– no, to know and love ballet so well – which was funny because she'd known nothing at all about it before coming to work for Pia.

She'd taken the job simply because the idea of all the travel corresponded with her need to keep moving, but little by little she'd been drawn into this closed world – seeing at first hand its rituals and preparations, marvelling at the pomp and ceremony of the performances and galas. But what had really captured her heart were these closed-door moments: the rehearsals, the buzz in the dressing rooms, the flurry of activity in the wings as dancers changed costumes and shoes. It had inspired her again, motivated her to pick up a brush after years of feeling so empty she'd genuinely never believed she would be able to feel anything ever again.

Tearing herself away, she glued her eyes to the floor and walked past the other studios without looking in. There was no point in tormenting herself. She made a beeline for the changing rooms and unlocked her battered wooden locker. It was covered with the initials of all the dancers who'd used it before her. She briefly considered adding her own but thought better of it. She had no right. She hadn't grafted for fifteen years day in, day out in the pursuit of artistic perfection. She was just admin staff, given a locker because she didn't have an office.

She took out her beloved sketch pads, specially chosen for the rose-beige wove paper she preferred, and flicked through the pages. They were just some more line drawings, sketches she'd been working on – most recently of Pia's neckline and upper-back poise – and hadn't yet taken back to the studio to refine and perfect.

One in particular caught her eye. She tipped her head to

the side and held it up to the light. It was good, beautifully balanced, lifted. She could really use this.

Just then the door to the changing rooms opened. Instinctively, she snapped the book shut. Her drawings had always been private and she hadn't shown them to anyone, not even to Lucy.

Hurriedly, she jammed the sketchbook in her bag, but it was a large A1 format and it caught on the zip as she pushed it down, forcing the pages to bow open and scatter across the floor like a deck of cards.

'Jeez . . .' Sophie muttered, clambering to pick them up as they wafted around. She grabbed them all in a messy clutch and stood up again. A stray sheet beneath the bench caught her eye.

She shot back down awkwardly on all fours – well, when you're five foot eleven it's hard to do it any other way – and reached her arm under the bench. Her hand felt something smooth but it wasn't paper. She withdrew her arm and pressing herself further downwards, looked beneath the seat.

A pair of black satin *pointe* shoes were facing her.

'Are you looking for this?' a heavily accented voice above the bench enquired.

Sophie looked up. Two glacial-blue almond-shaped eyes blinked at her, a pursed, sweetheart mouth betrayed no trace of a smile, mouse-brown hair was scraped back into a face-tightening bun, and tiny hands the size of rabbit paws were holding the sketch.

'Miss Petrova!' Sophie exclaimed, recognizing her immediately. 'It's such a pleasure to meet you. An honour actually,' she gushed, wincing as she heard herself. An honour?

Ava Petrova nodded in agreement. She knew it was. Sophie tried to gather her limbs about her and get to her feet. When she did, she saw Ava came up to her armpits. She instantly slouched down and began trying to smooth her curls.

'I heard you were coming to guest with us this season.'

Ava nodded but didn't reply. She was staring at the etching she still held in her hands.

Sophie swallowed nervously. Of all the people . . .

'It's just so wonderful . . . we're all so excited.' She was babbling but she couldn't stop herself, even though Pia would consider such flattery to her sworn enemy nothing less than high treason.

Ava looked up.

'All?'

Sophie knew instantly who she was referring to. Talk about the rock and the hard place.

Ava tipped her head to one side. 'And what do you do here? You're clearly not a dancer.'

'No, I . . . I uh . . .' Sophie stammered, offended by the dig.

'You are too tall,' Ava said, smiling suddenly and fixing her ice-blues on Sophie with instant, intense friendliness.

'Oh yes, that's right. I am,' Sophie shrugged, as though that was the only reason she wasn't part of the company. Nothing to do with the fact that she'd never taken a dance class in her entire life and had all the rhythm of a limpet.

Ava's eyes narrowed again as she glanced back at the sketch of Pia. 'Anyway, it's clear you are an artist.'

Sophie gasped with astonishment. 'Who, me? Oh no. No, no! I'm no way good enough to . . . I mean these are—' She motioned towards the sketch. 'They're nothing. Just scribbles. Doodles, really.'

There was a pause.

'Doodles?'

'Yes, uh – it means—'

'I know what it means,' Ava clipped. She waved the sheet in her hand. '*This* is not a doodle.'

And she turned on her heel.

'Wait! Oh my God, please don't go off with that. Please give it back to me, Miss Petrova, please . . .' But Ava was out of the room and marching down the corridor, peculiarly flat-footed in her *pointe* shoes, the blocks knocking on the floor as she went.

Sophie chased after her – but what the heck was she supposed to do? Rugby tackle Ava Petrova to a halt?

'Wait, please!' she cried, skittering after Ava, much to the amusement of the class in Studio Two, who had broken for lunch and were milling about in the corridor.

Despite such short legs, Ava displayed impressive speed and she reached Monsieur Baudrand's office in record time. Without bothering to stop at Lucy's desk – or indeed even acknowledge Lucy at all – she strode straight through to Baudrand's inner office.

Sophie arrived two seconds later, panic written all over her face.

'Please,' she panted, holding on to the door frame. 'Say she didn't just go in there.'

'She *did* just go in there,' Lucy replied, her pretty pink face scrunched up indignantly.

Sophie bent double, her hands on her knees.

'Then please,' she panted. 'Tell me Baudrand's not in there.'

'He *is* in there,' Lucy replied. She threw her hands out in amazement at the farcical scene. 'What on earth is going on?' she cried, her long blonde ponytail bouncing excitedly behind her.

'Oh God,' Sophie wailed, collapsing into a chair and dropping her head in her elbows. 'I want to die.' She shook her head mournfully. 'Could somebody just give me a break, *please*? For once?'

Lucy twitched her lips and sat back down. Whatever was happening inside Baudrand's office, she'd know the upshot of it sooner rather than later. God, she loved her job.

'Mint?' she asked, deciding to let Ava Petrova's blatant disregard for protocol slide this time.

Sophie sat back up and leant her head against the wall. 'No. I shouldn't even be here. I've been sacked, remember? Officially I have no business being here. I am technically trespassing.' She narrowed her eyes at Lucy. 'This is all your fault.'

'Clearly,' Lucy replied, sucking vigorously on the mint. 'But we'll still go for lunch after this, right? You're going to have even more to tell me once this is all done and dusted.'

The phone on Lucy's desk buzzed.

Sophie shot her hand out to stop her. 'Don't answer it,' she ordered dramatically.

Lucy raised her perfectly tweezered eyebrows and picked it up. 'Yes, *monsieur*?'

There was a pause.

'Yes, *monsieur*.'

She put the phone down and looked at Sophie.

'They want you to go in.'

Sophie shook her head, rooted to the spot.

Lucy got up from behind her desk.

'Go on,' she said, pulling Sophie up by the elbow. 'It'll all be fine.'

She opened the door and pushed Sophie through.

'Aaah, Sophie,' Monsieur Baudrand said in his distinct-ive way. She had always liked the way he said her name. So-phee. But not today.

Ava was sitting on his desk, her legs swinging. He was sitting behind it, his five-foot-six frame practically hidden from view, although what he lacked in height, he made up for in width. He was in his late sixties and still impressively muscular, with a drum-like torso, stocky legs and large, hairy hands. He was almost entirely bald except for a narrow white curtain of hair that swept from the midline of his skull around and over his ears, tapering down into sideburns and finishing with a flourish in a pointy goatee. Unlike the dancers of his company, who liked their clothes distressed, Baudrand preferred to dress like an architect, favouring turtlenecks and Yohji Yamamoto trousers in various shades of grey, accessorized with black-rimmed tinted John Lennon glasses, which did a heroic job of minimizing his bulging, goitrous eyes.

'Monsieur Baudrand, I can explain . . .' Sophie said hurriedly. 'Those aren't what they look like. Honestly. They're just private sketches. Doodles.' She cast a furtive glance at Ava, who had raised an eyebrow again. 'I was never going to sell them or show them to anyone, I promise. I know I never had "official access" and I would never betray Pia or the company's privacy.'

There was a brief pause as Monsieur Baudrand tried to swallow down a smile.

'*Au contraire, ma cherie*. I think that's precisely what you *should* do.'

Sophie's heart skipped a beat.

'Huh?'

'This is excellent, Sophie,' he said, waving the sketch of

Pia. 'Intimate, charming, elegant. You have perfectly captured and communicated an entire mood, not just a pose. I assume it is not the only one?'

His eyes moved pointedly to her bag and the wad of papers clearly sticking out.

'I – uh . . . No,' she said finally, her shoulders sagging. There was no point in lying.

'May I see?' He held out a hand.

Sophie handed them over, and watched as he and Ava fell upon them, scrutinizing, analysing and adoring.

'Ava is right,' he said. 'We have been missing a trick. Thank God Pia fired you.'

'Oh yes! Thank God,' Sophie echoed sarcastically.

'Why yes! Can you imagine what she would have been like if we'd told her we wanted to poach her personal assistant as the company's resident artist?' He shook his head, tutting. '*Non, non, non, non*. I think we all know what a little madam she would have been about letting you go for the greater good.'

Sophie gasped, looking from him to Ava and back again. 'The resident . . . You can't be serious.'

'But I am.' He smiled at her. 'Did you have a formal training? It seems to me you must have.'

'Not really. I was invited to apply to the Slade in London, but—'

'The Slade! I thought so. It is clear as day that you have superb talent; and what luck, *non*, that we should discover you in this, our centenary? We shall hold a series of grand exhibitions throughout the year; your work can showcase the behind-the-scenes aspects of the company as well as the public performances. We shall set you to work immediately. It goes without saying that we shall need a series of drawings of Ava, now that she is our guest artist for the spring repertoire. And we must capitalize fully on her talent and fame while it is ours to boast about.' He looked adoringly at Ava, who smiled back triumphantly. 'You will go back to New York and shadow her for the rest of the tour, with immediate effect.'

Sophie shot a nervous glance at Ava. Living in the pocket of Pia Soto, and now shadowing Ava Petrova. Frying pan to fire, surely?

'I shall ask Lucy to arrange the first exhibition for all your work, which we shall host at the next charity gala, and we'll get on with organizing prints, greeting cards, posters – that sort of thing.'

He stood up and walked around the desk to her. He reached up and she bent her knees so that he could kiss her on both cheeks.

'Congratulations, So-phee. It seems Pia Soto is not going to be our only claim to fame. Just think – all this time and we never knew we had our very own Edgar Degas, hiding in plain sight.'

Chapter Thirteen

The car swept down the drive and Will looked over at Pia. She had been furious when the doctors had discharged her into his care and she hadn't looked at him, nor said a word since they'd left the hospital. As if the past few days hadn't been tricky enough anyway. Her wound had become infected – practically giving him a stroke as they waited to find out whether she'd been exposed to MRSA – and Evie Grainger was refusing to break her contract to come back to treat Pia. Will had tried upping her money, even going up to double her fee, but she was adamant she didn't want to come within a fifty-mile radius of Pia – something about a rumour Pia had once planted and which had swept the ballet world about her manipulating more than just stiff arms and legs on her physiotherapy table.

Will looked back out of the window. He hadn't told her about the short-term replacement he'd got lined up for her yet. He had a feeling she wasn't going to take the news too well.

As the car approached the house, he saw that his housekeeper and the groundsmen were waiting outside on the steps, like Victorian serving staff, as per his instructions. The driver opened the door for Will and he jumped out, going round to Pia's side.

'I can't get a wheelchair over this gravel,' Will said. 'I'm going to have to carry you into the house myself.'

Pia shrugged, she was used to being lifted.

Will lifted her easily, taking extra care not to catch her plastered leg in the door jamb, pausing for a moment for her to take in the impressive sight that awaited her.

'Your new home,' he said grandly.

'My nursing home, you mean,' she replied curtly, her eyes sweeping casually over the Regency period curves, smooth putty-coloured render, the run of arched sash windows and the stone verandah that stretched across the entire first floor. It was a beautiful house but she'd rather die than admit it. Even the roof – pitched and slate-tiled – was pretty, punctuated with three crescent-topped dormers and a medley of chimney stacks, two of which were already puffing. She may be a foreigner to these shores, but she'd hobnobbed with its upper classes long enough to know that this was the epitome of English country living.

Will clenched his jaw at her snippiness and carried her forward. It wasn't quite the response he'd been hoping for.

'Pia, I want you to meet Mrs Bremar, my housekeeper,' he said, introducing a short plump woman with grey curled hair. 'Besides the fact that she's the best housekeeper in the county – and I know this because the Duke of Lamington keeps trying to poach her from me,' he boasted, 'she was also formerly the matron at the cottage hospital down the road and will be supervising your nursing care in the next few days as well; just until we're sure the infection has completely disappeared and your blood pressure's behaving itself.'

'Welcome to Plumbridge,' Mrs Bremar said with a friendly smile. Pia nodded back, a hint of a smile actually softening her features.

He moved up a step to a striking-looking woman with almost-black hair that fell down her back; her shoulders cut a strong line, wider than her hips, and she had a long torso with a hard flat stomach that came from good genes, not sit-ups. Her face was handsome, rather than pretty, with a defiant jawline and generous mouth but she had the thickest lashes Pia had ever seen and extraordinary eyes, in honour of which she had clearly been named.

'And this is Violet,' he said. 'She's going to do all the preliminary physio work with you until we can get Evie back for the more specialized rehabilitation.'

'Preliminary? What does that mean?' Pia looked at her, embarrassed and resentful of the indignity of being held like a baby in front of this magnificent woman. 'Have you ever worked with a dancer before?' she asked.

Violet shook her head. She seemed to be fighting back a smile. 'No,' she said simply.

'Athletes?'

'After a fashion,' she shrugged.

Pia looked at her suspiciously.

'What does that mean?'

Violet shot a look at Will and he coughed. 'There'll be enough time for chatting later,' he said. 'It's cold out here and we need to get you indoors.'

He went to move but Pia kicked her leg out like a brake. 'No,' she said. 'Let her answer the question.' She knew when she was being lied to.

Violet looked back at Will again. He shrugged. She had to find out sooner or later.

'I'm an equine physiotherapist,' she said.

Pia's jaw dropped. She glared at Will. 'Are you fucking kidding me? You practically kidnap me and then tell me I'm going to have some . . . gypsy working on me like I'm a shire horse. What the hell is this? Have you forgotten who I am?'

A low murmur of amusement washed through the crescent of staff and Violet's eyes flashed at the insult. 'Actually, I'm—'

'Spare it,' Pia snapped. 'You can go back to your caravan. You're not needed here.'

Violet gasped, looking to Will for back-up, but he just shook his head. 'Later,' he mouthed, whisking Pia briskly through the front door.

He didn't give her time to admire the impressive hallway as he climbed the stairs, depositing her angrily upon a vast emperor-sized bed. She had just humiliated him in front of his staff and God only knew what it was going to take to get Violet to treat her now.

'I want to go back to the hospital *now*,' she demanded.

'No,' he snapped.

'What do you mean, no?' she cried. 'You can't keep me here against my will, you know.'

'Well, unless you intend to get out of this bed and drive yourself there, then, yes . . . I think I can.'

Pia glared at him, outraged. Her mobile was out of charge now – Sophie usually did that for her – and there was no telephone in the room.

Will looked down at her. She looked like a doll in the huge bed, with hot cheeks and silky hair. He took a deep breath and sat down by her feet.

'Look,' he said, in a more placatory tone. 'I'm just trying to do the best thing for you. I think you've lost sight of how important that foot is to your career. If you leave here now, who's going to look after you?'

Pia didn't reply.

'For all the flowers and get-well cards you've received from your fans, no one has come forward to look after you.'

She flashed him a murderous look. Like she needed reminding.

'And for reasons best known to yourself, you've already fired the one person who did. So from what I can see, it's down to me.'

She stared at him, incredulous. 'How do you do that? How do you manage to make it sound like I'm imposing upon you? I don't want to be here!'

'I'm the only person who's liaised with your doctors and spoken with your dance director since the accident happened, and I know exactly what it is you need,' he reasoned.

'Which is someone from the goddam pony club, is it?' Pia hissed, through teary eyes.

'Violet's excellent at her job and she's only going to be doing very basic exercises with you anyway. I'm trying to secure Evie for you, but it seems you've really pulled a number on her in the past and she's not having any of it at the moment.'

Again, he made it sound like it was all her fault and she was imposing upon him.

'But I'm confident we'll get her. No one can resist me for long,' he winked.

'I think you'll find I can,' she said petulantly, throwing her head back on her pillows and staring up at the ceiling. His double entendres weren't going to raise any laughs from her. She wished for the millionth time that she hadn't been so rash with Sophie. She'd do anything to see her open, friendly face right now.

Will looked at her for a long moment – he imagined this

was what it was like having a toddler – but Mr Rosen had warned him that her ominous silences and sneering rebuttals were classic signs of fear and depression. 'You'll need to take it on the chin,' he'd warned. 'It's a necessary part of her processing what's happened and what she's still got to go through. Don't take it personally.'

He walked to the door. 'Mrs Bremar will be up with your dinner tray in an hour,' he said as the grandfather clock chimed downstairs. 'And there's a bell next to the bed. Ring it if you need anything.'

'A bell? My God, where have you brought me? Do you even have running water here or will you be getting that in a bucket from a well?'

He ignored her sarcasm and shut the door softly behind him, leaving Pia alone with her temper in the plush bedroom. She looked around hatefully at the yellow silk curtains and the beautiful grey de Gournay prints on the walls; then, convinced she was alone at last, she finally let herself cry.

When, an hour later, the door opened again, the tears had dried but their tracks remained.

'Here you are, dear,' Mrs Bremar said kindly, clocking Pia's damp skin as she placed a bed tray over her lap. A bowl of steaming chicken soup and a golden-baked baguette had been arranged on bone-china plates. 'I wasn't sure of your appetite yet,' she said, opening out the napkin for Pia. 'There's not much on you. You look like you don't eat much.'

Pia said nothing. She was used to suspicion about her frame. 'This looks fine, thank you,' she muttered.

Mrs Bremar walked across the room and put on the side

lamps. 'Can I do anything for you while I'm here?' she asked.

'How about arranging a police escort to get me the hell out of here?' Pia said quietly, eyeing the soup.

The housekeeper smiled. 'You know, he's only trying to look after you,' she said, her head tipped to the side.

'But why? He hardly knows me.'

'He must like you,' Mrs Bremar shrugged.

'That just goes to show he hardly knows me. I'm not likeable.'

'I think its romantic,' she persevered.

'I think it's creepy.'

Mrs Bremar gave a chuckle and shook her head. There was nothing more to be said. 'Well, I'll come back for your dishes in a wee while,' she said, shutting the door and leaving Pia alone again.

Pia awoke the next morning to find Will sitting at the edge of the bed and Mrs Bremar arranging the breakfast things.

'Like I said . . . creepy,' Pia muttered to Mrs Bremar.

Will looked quizzically between the two women. The housekeeper suppressed a smile as she handed over a plate of bacon and eggs.

'I'm not hungry,' Pia said sullenly, looking away.

Will raised his eyebrows sternly. 'Eat. Or I'll feed you myself.'

Pia stared at him, hating him, but she knew she wouldn't win here. She cut a minuscule morsel of egg white and chewed it exaggeratedly.

Will resisted the urge to roll his eyes. He knew that was the reaction she wanted. 'How did you sleep?' he asked.

'Terribly,' she lied. 'I'd have been better off sleeping on the floor. What have you hidden in the mattress anyway? Your fortune in gold coins?'

'That's a Halsten bed,' he said wryly, amused by her spikiness. 'Cost ten grand.'

Pia shrugged. 'What can I say?'

'The less the better, I think. Anyway, I've spoken to Violet, and I've convinced her to come in to assess you and start you off on your rehabilitation programme.'

Pia dropped her fork. 'No—'

'Whatever you have to say about it, I don't care,' Will said, holding his hand up. 'She's not some hick doctor who's going to damage you further. She's brilliant—'

'With anything that whinnies maybe!'

'It's bones and muscles, Pia. And it's just until we sign Evie. But she's only coming back on the condition that you apologize to her. She was enormously offended by your comments. You humiliated her in front of everyone.'

'Over my dead body!' Pia sneered.

Will stared at her. 'You *have* to get on with your rehabilitation programme. The more you let slip now, the harder it's going to be to get back. Violet's on your side.'

'I sincerely doubt that.'

'Apologize and you'll have an ally in her, you'll see,' he said, getting up from the bed. 'I've got to fly to Zurich and then on to New York for a few days, but Mrs Bremar will see to everything you need.'

Pia stared at him, aghast. He was *leaving* her?

He stood over her and hesitated, seemingly at a loss as to how to say goodbye. Finally, he picked up her hand and squeezed it like a fond uncle. Pia tried to ask him to stay, not to leave her alone here, stranded in a house full of strangers, but the words wouldn't rise and a strange croak left her throat instead.

Will passed her a glass of water. 'And remember to keep your fluids up,' he said, crossing the room and shutting the door behind him.

Pia stared at the ceiling, the intricate ornamental plaster-work creeping over it in white trellises, like fanciful lacework. She stared as the teardrop corbels hanging down began to slowly blush pink in the late slanting light, the pigment oozing like syrup over the *treillage* until it made its sleepy way down the walls heading, like her, for bed. Day five was nearly over.

It had been four days now since Will had left and she'd seen not a soul apart from Mrs Bremar, who came in at regular intervals to strip the bed, administer medicines and change her position with strategically placed pillows. She had no idea when Will was due back and, contrary to his message, Violet hadn't turned up to start treating her. The days were beginning to rack up and her panic at her visibly shrivelling, deteriorating body – which was moving further and further away from the primed tool she had spent a lifetime honing – was being steadily replaced by a defeated bleakness. Her appetite was almost completely suppressed and she was eating barely a meal a day. She'd never been so still or quiet in her life. She felt like a hibernating mouse – existing, but not living.

As she watched another day die, the tears making their silent, secret pilgrimage to her pillow, her hands periodically balled into fists and her legs twitched frustratedly, the urge to kick almost overwhelming. She knew these nervous tics were her body's way of crying out for movement, stimulation and touch. Being kept immobile and isolated was like sensory deprivation for her and she felt like she was being tortured. How long did she have to endure this for? Every minute was like an hour, every hour like a day. Time was observed only through Mrs Bremar's routine, and she was the sun now, around which Pia's day revolved.

Her fingers rustled against the newspaper that Mrs Bremar had brought in with lunch and which lay as untouched as the food. She picked it up slowly, as though suspicious of the intrusion it would bring of the outside world.

It didn't start well. Harry Hunter, the playboy novelist, was splashed all across the gossip pages as usual. She stared at his photograph – reading the text felt too exhausting – and felt herself leave her prison as she remembered their brief, lost weekend in Venice. She closed her eyes at the memory. He'd been there for the film festival; she'd been performing in *La Bayadère* and *Apollo*. She remembered the foppish mop of blond curls that she'd twisted round her fingers in bed, the Eros mouth that had brought her such pleasure, the six-foot-three-frame that had been such fun climbing on, the pale green eyes that were impossible to look away from . . .

And yet somehow, come the Monday, look away she had, and she'd never regretted it. She opened her eyes again and looked back at his photo. For all the fun they'd had he was too much like her to ever make her happy – every bit as hungry for success, and just as ruthless and selfish as she. And as much as she knew her happy ending had nothing to do with finding Mr Right, she did know that what made for searing passion in bed made for wearisome conflict out of it. And she had enough of that to contend with as it was.

She flicked her eyes down and was momentarily surprised

to see her own self laughing back at her. For a second she didn't recognize who she was with, and couldn't remember where the photograph had been taken. Then she saw the jewels and felt herself start. Something was wrong. She pulled herself further up the pillows and started reading properly.

Beautiful Pia Soto's luck appears to be going from bad to worse as yet more disaster follows her from her recent ill-fated trip to St Moritz, where she was badly injured. In the wake of these photographs, which show her enjoying the full hospitality of luxury jewellers Cartier, rival firm Patek Philippe have announced they will not be renewing her lucrative $1 million contract when it expires later this year . . .

She scrutinized the photograph showing her dripping in Cartier and laughing with the MD. Next to it was a shot of her hotel suite at the Black.

. . . But there is some light on the horizon for ballet's bad girl, as she puts her failed affair with married Andy Connor behind her and enjoys a torrid new romance with financier Will Silk. Silk, who is the major investor in the chic Black hotel group, where Cartier put her up, all expenses paid, in the penthouse, is understood to be overseeing her convalescence at his mansion in the country . . .

Pia let the paper drop from her hands. She'd been sabotaged, of that much she was certain. Someone had betrayed her. Someone had tipped off Patek Philippe that she was Cartier's guest and they were picking up her bill. But who? Who would have access to that kind of information? Who would want to betray her? Sophie – exacting a kind of revenge? It seemed hard to believe.

Before the accident, it would have been inconsequential anyway. Just a paperwork bore. Cartier was desperate to sign her and she would simply have swapped one for the other. But now, with her foot in plaster and her international career – and therefore profile – hanging in the balance, she wasn't such a good bet. And if she didn't get back to the world stage, all her other contracts would probably lapse too.

It wasn't like she needed the money any more. She was already rich enough to never have to work again and still live like an empress, but if her career ended now – at the precocious age of twenty-four – well, what was she supposed to do with the rest of her life? How could she *justify* herself? She'd only just begun. She couldn't be looking at the finish line already. She just couldn't.

She felt the tears bubble up again. As much as she tried to keep them hidden they were never more than two blinks away, and the outer edges of her eyes were red raw from the permanent dampness.

There was a brief rap at the door and Violet breezed in looking like Jayne Russell in *The Outlaw*.

Pia instantly bit her lip hard. Why did she have to arrive now, moments after Pia'd learnt she'd just lost a million dollars from her annual earnings? She sniffed lightly and composed her features back into a scowl.

'Finally!' she said scornfully.

Violet didn't respond. She clearly felt no need to explain her protracted absence. After all, it wasn't like Pia was going anywhere.

Pia swivelled her silky head and watched her cross the room. There was something about Violet that commanded attention. She seemed stately, luscious and barely tamed, like a goddess of fertility. Physically, she was Pia's opposite – an Amazon to her nubile nymph.

'Where have you been?' Pia asked tetchily, feeling like a rusty old dowager confined to her bed. 'I was expecting you *days* ago.'

'I got held up,' Violet replied breezily, taking up a position at the foot of the bed.

'At gunpoint, I hope,' Pia muttered.

Violet raised an eyebrow. She was going to enjoy this. There was a stiff silence. 'What?' Pia snapped.

Violet tipped her head. 'Anything to say?'

Pia looked at her through slitted eyes. 'No.'

Violet paused. 'Okay,' she shrugged casually, walking back towards the door. 'I'll leave you, then. You look like you're withering nicely.'

'Where are you going?' Pia demanded. 'You've only just got here.'

'You knew the terms,' she said, opening the door and stepping into the hallway.

Pia watched it shut. Again. Leaving her alone. Again.

'Oh for Chrissakes! I freaking apologize!' she screamed at it, feeling hot tears of frustration fall.

Violet opened it slowly. 'Hardly the most gracious apology I've ever heard,' she drawled, one hand on her hip.

'I never promised it would be gracious,' Pia snarled, trembling from head to foot with nervy agitation, a frightened aggression that made her look like a cornered animal. Violet almost felt sorry for her. Almost.

'That's okay. Your tears will suffice,' she said, smiling victoriously as she walked past the bed and pulled a yellow silk curtain across one half of the window to keep the low sun from dazzling Pia. A shaft of sunlight was edging across the bed and would, within a few minutes, be at her eye level. She looked back at Pia as though pleased by this random act of consideration. 'There. Now isn't that better?'

She walked back across the room and stood by Pia's feet. Mrs Bremar walked past Pia's room, carrying a pile of laundry, and Violet drew herself up.

'And how are you feeling?' she asked brightly – and clearly for the housekeeper's benefit.

Pia glared at her. 'How do you think?'

Violet ignored her fury and looked down, examining Pia's foot. 'The swelling's gone down a bit, which is good, and the colour's nice and pink,' she murmured. 'Can you feel your toes?'

Pia nodded sulkily.

'Do you feel any tightness or soreness in the cast? Does it feel like one area's rubbing more than anywhere else?'

Pia shook her head.

'Excellent. You're doing very well.'

Pia snorted in derision at Violet's low bar. 'Very well? Hrrmph. I appreciate perfection isn't something *you* strive to achieve on a daily basis, but how exactly can the cast not rubbing be considered progress? It's just *nothing*.'

Violet smiled at her with a saintly patience that didn't match the contempt in her eyes. 'On the contrary, Pia,' she said in a patronizing tone. 'At this point in your recovery, it's exactly what we want to see. Clear, fresh, pink tissue, minimal swelling. It all indicates everything's healing nicely inside at the musculoskeletal level,' she said, keeping her voice that bit too sweet. 'Now, we'll just do a few proprioceptive exercises before supper to boost your circulation and keep up muscle memory. It'll stop you getting restless as well. Now that all the surgical drugs have left your system and you're fully alert again, you might find yourself becoming more restless and sleeping gets harder. This will just help fatigue the muscles a bit, and minimize atrophy.'

She lifted Pia's leg at the knee, supporting the cast with both hands, and – being careful not to manipulate or rotate the foot – gently levered it in towards her body.

Pia sighed reflexively. It felt so good to move. For someone who defined herself through movement, physical confinement felt akin to torture. She closed her eyes and let herself be bent and stretched and pushed and pulled. First one leg, then the other. She was used to working with physiotherapists at the company – although *they* were specialists.

'How does that feel?' Violet asked, as she swapped Pia's legs over again.

'It'll do until the proper physio gets here,' she said curtly. 'When's she arriving anyway?'

'In a few days, hopefully.'

'That's just great. And in the meantime I'm stuck with – I don't know, what are you? A horse whisperer?'

Violet flicked her eyes up at Pia, amused rather than tormented. 'I wish,' she chuckled. 'It would make my life a lot easier. Rest assured, I'm just an equine physiotherapist.'

'And how do you become one of those?' Pia asked disdainfully. 'A subscription to *Horse & Hound* and a massage certificate?'

Violet laughed again. 'You've got a quick wit for a dancer,' she quipped, equally cruelly. 'No, not quite. I've got a degree in human physiotherapy and I'm a chartered physiotherapist. I practised for seven years as a human physio before switching over to equine work. You have to have a minimum of two years' human experience before you're accepted on the course, so I guess you might say I'm actually overqualified to be working on *you*.' Like Will, she made it sound like she was doing Pia the favour, dragging herself down from the lofty heights of horse anatomy to deal with a mere human.

Violet rested her leg back on the bed and looked up at Pia, a satisfied glow in her eyes. 'Right, well, that's you done for now. Those exercises should tire you out nicely for tonight, and we'll do some more work in the morning. Little and often is the key. Is there anything else I can do for you while I'm here?'

'Send Mrs Bremar in,' Pia instructed. 'I need to go to the bathroom.'

'I wish I could, but Mrs Bremar's gone to the shops.' She narrowed her eyes.

'No, she hasn't. She just walked past. I saw her.'

Violet tipped her head to the side, sympathetically. 'You must be imagining things. You're still on a lot of meds. I'll take you.'

Pia couldn't think of anything much worse. 'Don't bother. I'll wait for her to get back.'

'Ah, but she won't be back for hours yet,' Violet smiled. 'And I'm so glad to be of assistance,' she said sarcastically, lifting Pia's tiny frame and shifting her from the bed to the wheelchair before she could protest.

She pushed Pia across the snow-white carpet into the vast en suite.

'Here, let me help you,' she said in a bullying tone. Pia was struggling to hold her foot up off the floor because, even with her incredible balance, the weighty cast threw her off. Violet pulled up Pia's nightie, eased her knickers down and carefully lowered her onto the loo.

Pia's jaw clenched furiously at the indignity of relying on

this uppish woman's help. Eleven years of competing in ballet – in the training school and then in the company – had taught her there was no solidarity among women, and she felt that more than ever right here and now, when she was weak and broken. This woman was supposed to be a nursing figure, but she behaved like a competitor, a rival, like they were two chess queens going into battle.

'Well, you don't need to stand there and listen. Go out,' Pia ordered abruptly.

Violet, a vicious smile on her face, sailed out just as a shower of gravel scattered against the windows, startling both women. A car careered to an abrupt halt outside.

A door slammed shut and they heard the bell start ringing insistently downstairs in the hall.

'What on earth is going on?' Violet exclaimed, running across the bedroom to the window. She pulled the sunny curtain back and heaved the sash window open.

Pia watched her from the loo, as she leant out and looked onto the drive.

'Holy crap!' Violet muttered.

'What? What is it?' Pia called from the bathroom, desperate to see for herself.

The bell stopped ringing suddenly and Pia heard another door slam. Voices raised.

'What the bloody hell do you think you're playing at?' shouted one male voice. Will's? There was a pause, but she could still hear movement, muffled, like something being thrown across the gravel. 'Are you out of your fucking mind?'

'She nearly died! Because of you! She nearly died!'

'*Who* did?'

'Jessy!'

'I don't know what the fuck you're talking about!' Scorn.

'She found the drugs your little pet left behind. Just as we were crossing back into the EU. She swallowed them. She had to bloody swallow them. Because of you!' There was a pause in the shouting, but still a noise, like scuffling.

Pia was nearly falling off the loo trying to hear.

'You can stick your job! I'll have nothing more to do with you. You can take this as formal notice for termination of our contract. You've got three months to get your horses out of my stables and, if you know what's good for you, you'll stay the hell away from me!'

A car door opened.

'Oh! And while we were trying to save Jessy's life, the horsebox was nicked – with the horses still in the back.'

'What?'

'I'll leave you to explain that to the insurers, shall I?'

Pia heard the car door slam shut and gravel pepper the windows again as the car sped back down the long carriage drive.

'Tanner! Wait!' Violet shouted, waving after the disappearing car. 'Come back!' And she raced across the room, her long skirt flying about her endless thighs.

'Violet! Wait!' Pia echoed as Violet flashed past. 'Help me back into the chair. You can't leave me here.'

Violet braked sharply and stared at her patient for a moment. 'Oh, you'll keep.' She winked, before disappearing out of sight, after him.

Chapter Fourteen

Tanner was sitting in his favourite threadbare armchair by the Aga when Violet walked into the kitchen. He was propping his head up with one hand, a whisky in the other; Biscuit, his working retriever, lying blissfully across his feet.

'What on earth came over you?' she asked bluntly, without any preamble. 'You *assaulted* him.'

'Nothing he didn't deserve,' Tanner mumbled darkly, keeping his eyes on the amber in his glass.

'Oh I see. Beating up your boss and jacking in your job is all in a day's work, is it?'

'I haven't jacked in my job. I'm just not working for *him* any more. I don't need him. He was only ever the easy option anyway. I'll build the business away from him.'

Violet stood against the door jamb and absorbed his defiance and defensive body language. Whether he would admit it or not, Plumbridge Stud's fortunes relied almost entirely on Will Silk's patronage and finding a new breeder and player with Silk's deep pockets would be easier said than done. She couldn't imagine what could be so bad that he'd beat up his boss and dump his business.

'You're cutting your nose off to spite your face,' she said, not frightened of contradicting him. Her session with Pia had left her in a buoyant and feisty mood.

'I'm happy to do it if it gets him out of our lives,' he shrugged nonchalantly.

'You're a damned fool,' she said, shaking her head and crossing her arms over her ample chest. 'Just tell me what happened. Maybe the situation isn't beyond repair.'

'I don't *want* it to be repaired,' Tanner countered furiously, his eyes blazing. 'And I don't need *you* to sort it out. You're my partner, not my mother.'

Partner? Not girlfriend; not lover. Partner, as though they were business associates.

'Well, as my *partner*,' she said in a quiet voice, 'perhaps you'd like to tell me where you've been for the past ten days. The tournament finished a week and a half ago.'

He guessed from the tone of her voice that she had found his absence suspicious. If only.

'Jessy got sick,' he said flatly. 'Rob and I had to look after her.'

'Rob's a vet,' she said, pointing out the obvious. 'And while I'm sure there are those who would argue Jessy has an arse the size of a horse . . .'

'Rob was the best option available to me – the only option, in fact.'

'Right. After all, why use a French hospital when you've got a *vet* onside?' she drawled.

'We couldn't afford to get the authorities involved,' he muttered, ignoring her sarcasm.

Violet paused. 'Why?'

Tanner looked at her. He didn't want to be repeating all this. The experience had been shattering. Jessy had suffered heart failure and he wasn't sure Rob was ever going to forgive him for forcing him to treat her in a motel room with only the drugs in his vet's bag.

'Alonso left a stash of coke in the truck. Jessy found it at the EU border and swallowed it,' he said simply.

Violet paled. 'My God – is she okay?'

'She will be.' He drained his glass.

'Are you?' she asked, in a gentler voice.

'I will be, now that Silk and his acolytes are out of our lives.'

She leant against the worktop and watched him thought-fully. There was no point banging on about forgiving Will tonight. It was better to give him some time. He'd see sense as soon as the next lot of bills arrived.

'Well . . . it appears we're all working outside our job descriptions at the moment, then.'

'What do you mean?'

'Silk's hired me to work on his new girlfriend. She's a dancer – got a broken foot.'

Tanner's colour rose. 'I hope you didn't accept! We're having nothing more to do with him,' he ordered.

'Of course I did. How was I supposed to know what was going on between the two of you in Switzerland? You didn't call,' she said pointedly.

'It was hardly the time for chit-chats,' he muttered.

'Besides, he's paying me double for the privilege.'

'Double?' he said, looking at her suspiciously.

'Yes, that's what I thought when he first approached me. "Why double?" Of course, now I've met her it's clear why.'

'What does that mean?'

'It's compensation. She's a complete bitch and without

question the rudest, most spoilt person I've ever met in my life. It's actually quite staggering.'

'It is, coming from you,' he quipped. 'I can't imagine you putting up with that kind of behaviour.'

'Oh I didn't,' Violet said, eyes narrowed, savouring the memory of Pia's humiliation. 'I put her firmly in her place. She won't give me any more trouble from now on, I can tell you. She knows who's boss now.'

Chapter Fifteen

Pia had woken at six. It was still dark outside but a few lone thrushes and blackbirds were trying to get the day moving. She lay in the gloom listening to them, having absolutely no idea what they were – she'd grown up listening to yellow-beetle parakeets and Guianan cock-of-the-rocks – and with every trill they reminded her how foreign she felt here, injured and far from home, forced to accept help from strangers.

Pia felt the tension steal back into her. She'd slept badly all night, in spite of the luxurious mattress beneath her. Violet's abandonment of her had been as humiliating an insult as she could have hoped to deliver. If it hadn't been for Mrs Bremar eventually coming to her rescue she'd have spent the night on the loo.

She felt the resentment surge up in her. Everyone else – Will, Violet, Sophie – was getting on with their life while she slowly rotted – no, what was it Violet had said? Withered? – while she withered in this deluxe prison. Because that is what it was, no matter how beautifully it was decorated.

She looked at the clock: 7.20 a.m. Mrs Bremar had told her last night that Violet would be arriving in just over an hour.

She fidgeted roughly, tensing her leg muscles till they were like rocks. She couldn't bear it. Couldn't bear to see the smile that she'd be wearing when she came in, desperate to find out how long Pia'd been stranded and who had come to her rescue.

Pia knew what was really going on here. She knew Violet hadn't really been offended by her remarks on the steps. She could hardly have been surprised by Pia's incredulity, after all – there were precious few world-famous dancers with a career-threatening injury who would take being treated by an equine physio in a calm and understanding spirit. In fact, the thought of what Ava's reaction would have been made her laugh out loud! That really would have been something to see.

No, this was about ego and their clash would have happened even if Pia had been sweetness itself, because Violet was used to ruling the roost. She was a highly attractive woman operating in an arena populated by men and Pia had known the second she'd seen her that she encouraged and manipulated their lust for her; she would like the feel of their eyes upon her – Pia wondered briefly whether Will's followed her – and the fact that she was intelligent and strong-willed made her a tempestuous and tantalizing proposition. Pia understood the package because it was precisely why men lusted after her.

The difference was that Pia had millions in the bank and her arena was global. Violet may be Plumbridge's queen bee, but compared to Pia she was a mere drone, and Pia already knew how this was going to play out between them: a series of small petty victories in a war of attrition. Violet wasn't the first – or the last – who would try to trump her.

Pia looked out of the window at the burnt-orange sky. She was used to it. She had been extraordinary for a long time now. Her beauty and talent had marked her out, but they hadn't made her any friends. Other women didn't like it – they thought she had too much, that she was too lucky, that she'd been blessed in all departments. That just went to show how much they knew, of course. She'd lost more than anyone else she'd ever met but she wasn't going to play the victim about it. She had a responsibility to make her life count, to be remarkable, and if that meant she didn't have shoulders to cry on, so be it. There was always a willing head to share her pillow. That could be enough.

She watched the cold February sun inch upwards, and felt her customary loneliness lie upon her, like a dog resting its head on her lap. Day Six here. She was dreading it already, willing it to be night-time again, when she wouldn't have to endure people telling her what she should eat, when she should sleep, how she should move . . .

This situation was everything she had always tried to protect herself against. She had always made a point of making sure she was in charge of her destiny. She didn't use an agent, a manager, a nutritionist, a publicist, a stylist or . . . or an anything. Just Sophie to organize the admin and manage her schedule. But every decision that needed to be made was made by her and her alone. She was the only one who knew what was best for her future because she was the only one who knew the worst of her past. She'd endured everything else alone. She'd survive this.

A sudden bubble of indignation rushed up inside her, and throwing the covers off, she bottom-shuffled herself into the wheelchair beside the bed and went over to the wardrobe. Emma, Will's London PA, had shown typical initiative, ringing the wardrobe department at the ChiCi for Pia's measurements and ordering an impressive collection of clothes that – while not to her taste – fitted like a glove. She chose a navy polo neck and a khaki printed wrap dress that Emma had cleverly realized wouldn't interfere with Pia's leg, making dressing easy.

As quickly as she could, before anyone was around, she wheeled herself onto the galleried landing and looked down the oval John Soane staircase, which wound its way elliptically down to the hall. Leaving the wheelchair by the top step, she bumped down the stairs on her bottom with her plastered leg up by her nose – a ballerina's advantage in times like these. It wasn't elegant, but hell – it worked.

A second wheelchair, unused as yet, was parked by the bottom step. The staircase was far too long to be hoicking wheelchairs up and down it each day.

Pia settled down in it, resting her foot on the elevated support board in front of her. She closed her eyes for a moment, feeling weary already. It was the most exercise she'd had in nearly a fortnight and her muscles felt drained.

The bustle and bangs coming from the other side of a door at the far end of the hall suggested Mrs Bremar was preparing breakfast in the kitchen. She couldn't hang about, and yet . . . she'd seen nothing of her jail.

Pia looked at all the doors leading off the hallway, and curiosity got the better of her. She wheeled silently to the room opposite and nudged open the double doors. It was the drawing room, lined with oyster linen walls and black-framed contemporary art. Vast cream suede sofas bore down on a stone fireplace. Oversized burgundy glass lamps were positioned at either end of a console table. A teal-coloured rug blanketed the floor. The room had a masculine, rich look and clearly no one under the age of twelve had ever set foot inside it.

Pivoting herself away, she wheeled slowly to the next room. The door was ajar and she rolled into the dining room. Midnight-blue silk-covered walls bracketed a triptych of floor-to-ceiling windows; a modernist mahogany table on cubed steel legs, which could easily accommodate eighteen guests, ran across the middle of the room. She raised her eyes, unimpressed. She seriously doubted anyone had ever danced or had sex on that table. It was a collector's piece – for showing, not living.

Going back into the corridor, she tried the other side of the hall. There was a downstairs loo, then a cloakroom lined with welly racks and polo boots, tweed jackets, stalking caps, shooting sticks and riding crops – everything brand new and unmuddied. At the far end, a locked glazed cabinet boasted a full arsenal of shotguns. Pia shivered at the sight of them. She'd always despised guns, ever since childhood. They weren't sport to her. Far from it.

Pia reversed out quickly. Only one other door remained. She rolled forward, but she could hear a low voice coming from behind it. She picked up the clipped tones and lack of deference. Will. She already knew he was back. It had been his voice she'd heard yesterday, but he hadn't been up to see her yet. Or, if he had, he'd waited until she was asleep. She bristled at his arrogance in treating her presence here so dismissively.

She turned on her wheel and made for the front door. Sunshine was streaming through the sidelights and pooling in puddles on the stone floor. She felt eager to get out and feel fresh air on her face.

Opening the door – with a great deal of forward-reverse manoeuvring to get the wheels out of the way – she eyed a ramp which had been put up to bypass the three steps alongside. To her novice eye it looked steep, but then so would a speed bump right now.

Warily, she positioned herself at the top of the ramp and, gripping the wheels as tightly as she could, she prepared to lower herself down. For a moment, the wheels held, but the second she released her grip to inch them forward they suddenly ran away with her, and she was shooting down the short drop as though she were on a rollercoaster, too shocked even to scream.

She came to a just-as-sudden halt as the wheels sank into the thick gravel, and the jolt knocked her so far forward on her seat that she had to grip the armrests to keep herself from falling out altogether.

She sat there for a moment, her heart racing at the near-accident and what it could have meant for her recovery, before becoming aware of a searing heat in her hand. Wincing, she looked at her left palm. The smooth tyre, skidding out of her grasp, had branded a red weal across it. She held it tenderly, like a flower fairy with a buttercup.

'You all right, miss?' enquired a man, running over. From the way he was dressed, she guessed he was a gardener, or groundsman. 'You went down there fair lickety-split.'

Pia had no idea what he was talking about. Her hand was throbbing.

The man knew who she was of course. Everybody did. Mr Silk's new fancy woman. 'Are you supposed to be up and about so early, miss? It's pretty parky out here.'

'I may need to be off my feet, but it doesn't mean I have to lie about in bed all day,' she muttered, looking around him. She could see a path that ran along the top of the lawn towards the terrace at the side of the house. 'Could you just wheel me over there?' she said, remembering to add, 'Please.'

'Well . . . if you're sure, miss,' the man said, unconvinced.

With a resigned shrug of his shoulders, he turned the wheelchair around and, tipping Pia backwards, like a baby in a pushchair, managed to get the wheels out of the gravel trench they'd created.

'Thank you,' Pia said as he positioned her on a compacted footpath. She watched him crunch back over the gravel.

A cool breeze pushed past her, and she shivered in her dress. The tempting sunshine had made her completely forget about wrapping up, and though the British winter was nowhere near as harsh as Chicago's it could still be only four or five degrees.

But she couldn't go back in the house for a coat now. It was breakfast time and if Mrs Bremar caught her up she'd herd her straight back into bed. Violet would be arriving imminently and she had absolutely no intention of being there.

Pia looked around her and noticed that the path she was sitting on crossed the lawn and led away from the house, towards a wooded area. She could hide herself away from them all in there, plus she'd be protected from the wind. She headed straight for it.

There were still no buds on the trees but a bank of snowdrops nodded politely as she glided past, and a few early basking daffodils stretched in the sun. She found a rhythm along the smooth, flat path, moving silently into the shadow of the copse, and covering some fair distance within it as her muscles rejoiced in movement again and her lungs grabbed at the clean air.

She rolled past collapsed heaps of bracken, yellow budding gorse bushes that scratched lightly at her legs, stray brave primroses and enormous badger setts in which she was sure she could set up home herself. Her stealth approach startled a couple of still-sleepy rabbits and they darted back into their warrens. Occasionally, the wheels slowed in the stray leaf mounds that had been left to mulch on the path, but nothing could stop her. She was free again. Her own agent.

She went deeper and deeper into the wood, the trees closing around her – though she could easily see the sky through their wintry nakedness – and the path began to meander and dip. She had to stop often, for her muscles emptied of energy all too quickly, but after a few minutes of resting she was able to dig in again and bury herself further in the trees.

After a while, she came to a wooden bridge – beautifully crafted over a rocky stream. She stopped and stared at it, unsure for a moment after her scare on the ramp. But it was flattish, not humped, and looked well maintained and stable. She crawled over it, keeping accomplished control of the chair as she rolled down the far side and continued along the path. Ahead of her, the level began to run down but it was a gentle gradient, and being able to just glide for a while was easier on her arms.

She covered some more ground, savouring the feeling of being lost. Strangely, she didn't feel as alone out here in the wood as she did in the house. And she didn't feel foreign here – she could be anywhere. Her isolation and friendlessness weren't thrust upon her like they were in that bedroom.

Her idle dreaming was brought to an abrupt halt as she saw that, just ahead, the slope sharpened steeply. She put on the brake.

It was clear she couldn't go any further. The path forked, turning right up a steep slope that she had no chance of getting up, and to the left it deteriorated into an unmade track. She crouched low in the chair, trying to see beyond the tendrils of a weeping willow, and saw that the track led down to a shimmering freshwater lake fed by the stream.

A weathered grey jetty jutted out poetically into the still waters, as though pointing towards the lily pads floating out in the deep, and she could make out a dark green boathouse on the opposite side, with a red-painted rowing boat tethered beneath it.

She gasped in wonder. A secret lake, hidden in an ancient wood? It could have been one of her stage sets – she could just imagine Chopin's score for the fauns and sprites dancing in the mists. Oh, if only she could get up on her feet. That little jetty was like a private stage.

She chewed her lip, her weight forward on her lap as she contemplated getting over to it. There was no way she could do it; although the track to the jetty was short, it was too steep. And even if she did make it down there, she'd never be able to get back up again. Not on her own.

She would have to turn back. For all the freedom she'd bought herself today, she still wouldn't be able to get any closer than this. The fun was over for now. The fun was over for a long time to come.

Dammit! She smacked her hands down on the armrests in frustration. She just wanted life back to the way it had been – dancing *Giselle* on tour in New York and having sex in the snow with Andy.

Taking off the brake, and with an angry backwards spin of the wheels, she pivoted round, only catching sight of an unyielding oak tree as she was spinning. She gasped in horror as her outstretched leg on the support board swung straight towards it. She got her hands back on the wheels, to turn away again, but there was no time. There was too much momentum . . .

The plaster smacked sidelong against the tree and she screamed out wildly, hot tears instantly scalding her cheeks as crashing waves of pain rolled through her. Her foot flinched and clenched instinctively on contact, and she felt the dormant, crushed muscles instantly seize and cramp, compounding her agony.

Pia wrapped her hands around the foot but she couldn't manipulate it beneath the rock-hard plaster. Crying helplessly, she threw her head back, her body rigid and lifted like a board from the seat, her arms pinned down to the armrests as the pain crescendoed through her muscles and ricocheted against her broken bones like a pinball.

She couldn't stop the screams from coming and she sounded as wild as any creature that had ever lived in that wood. Nothing dared go near her. There was nothing *to* go near her. She was in the middle of nowhere. No one knew she was here, and she'd been exploring for at least three-quarters of an hour. God only knew how far away she was.

She cried pitifully – with anger, with pain, with frustration – her hands balled up into fists as she screamed intermittently at the injustice of it all, willing it all to be over.

Long, dragging minutes passed and the initial pain began to ebb, leaving in its place a throbbing, heavy, gangrenous ache. It felt like her foot was dying. Her hands covered her eyes. She couldn't bear to look. Was this it, then? Had she delivered the death blow to her own illustrious career? Had she undone everything Will had done in flying her to England and getting her seen by the best in the bone business? He'd saved her career. No, more than that – he'd saved her life. Dancing was her life and without it she had nothing.

He'd preserved it for her, kept the doors open for her to make a full return . . .

For the first time since waking up in hospital, the realization of what he had actually done for her hit home. He'd saved her when she couldn't save herself. And she'd behaved like an absolute brat.

Peeling her hands from her eyes, Pia tentatively studied her foot. The toes looked purplish, and were already beginning to swell. She had to get back to him.

She looked around her cautiously, her temper gone. The roots of the tree protruded like gnarly claws on the right side of the path and the right wheel was wedged between two that held her in position on the slope, even with the brake off. With a determined effort she gave a little jolt forward to release the chair over the front root, but it was too pronounced for her to get the wheel over it from a standing start, especially as she was now facing uphill.

She realized she'd need to change direction, travel crossways over to the other side of the path where it was smooth, and then face back up the slope. Carefully, with her right hand pushing against the tree, she used her left hand to turn the wheels and steer her to the left. She jerked forward in her seat, using her own weight as ballast to help the chair bunny-hop over the root.

The wheelchair rolled over it easily – too easily – and she oversteered. Facing back downhill again, the wheels found traction on the smooth path and rapidly began to gain momentum down the slope. Pia gave a short scream of fright. The tyres were following the grooves worn into the path and being steered, like a train on rails, straight down the unmade track.

Panicking, she grabbed at the bushes as she skittered past,

trying to hold on to something, anything. It didn't matter if she came out of the chair and damaged her foot all over again – she just couldn't end up in that water. But they were just twigs snapping in the cold as she bumped past, like a novice skier on moguls, unable to slow or avert her course.

Within seconds, the tenor of the crisis changed again as the low whirr of the wheels on the mud path was replaced by the rumble of the boards as the chair mounted the jetty. She was above the water . . .

Pia slammed her hands down on the wheels, but they were going much too fast now and she screamed again as the rubber burnt her reddened palms.

For a long elastic moment, Pia felt the wind in her hair, the sun on her face. And then an almighty smack as the chair hit the green water and she was immediately separated from it. She screamed and she heard her own voice above the thrashing water, animal-like in its screams as she tried to turn, to find a leg of the jetty to hold on to. But the weight of her cast dragged her under immediately and the water was so dark. So, so cold. She couldn't see . . . couldn't feel . . . couldn't break the surface . . .

She sank silently down, only the gently lapping ripples on the surface betraying that she had ever been there.

It was Biscuit who'd heard the girl first, defying her master's whistle to race away from the path and down to the water's edge. They'd been coming back from the boathouse when they'd heard her first screams as the cramps took hold, and they'd watched – aghast – as she'd struggled, trying to dislodge the chair from the tree roots. The path dropped steeply right behind her and it was clear that unless she could get the wheels moving with a burst of power, she'd be rolling back down it, towards the water.

Tanner had never moved so fast in his life, racing over the ground like a hare, jumping bushes and ducking branches, trying to get to her before she could free herself. But she was so far away . . .

He and Biscuit heard the splash and knew she was in. He sped on, faster still, the icy morning air burning in his throat as his lungs tried to keep up with his heart, but it was no good. He knew he'd never get to her in time if he followed the path. Just further on, it twisted away from the water's edge, heading deeper into the bushes and up the bank, before emerging again at the top of the steep slope down to the jetty.

Panting hard, he stopped at a tree. He could see the splashes at the end of the jetty from here. Christ! He was out of time. Without thinking, he pulled off his boots and jumper, and dived in. It was only thirty yards as the crow flew – or rather swam – from here. It was the only thing he could do for her.

The water was so cold it almost knocked the breath out of him but his legs propelled him as powerfully as they had on land, and he cut through the water like a blade.

He got to the jetty and duck-dived down, finding her quickly. The water wasn't so deep here – maybe fifteen feet – and the sediment that had been churned up on her entry had started to settle again. She'd been under forty, maybe forty-five seconds, but as he dragged her to the surface she was already unconscious. He hoped to God it was from the cold. It might actually buy her a little time if the shock of the temperature had shut her system down.

Resting her on his chest, he swam quickly on his back, Biscuit barking frantically from the bank, urging him on.

In spite of the wet cast on her leg, the girl was small and only light, and he pulled her easily from the water as his feet found the lake bed. He laid her out on the muddy ground, her legs still floating in the water, and put his ear to her mouth. She wasn't breathing.

'Be quiet, Biscuit! Quiet!' he cried at the dog, who immediately crouched low to the ground as Tanner searched for a pulse. He placed his fingers against her neck and counted against his watch. One, two, three, four . . .

'Okay, got it, Biscuit. Let's pull her up and turn her over,' he said, talking to the dog as though she actually had opposable digits and could do as he asked. She gave a single bark of despair.

Tanner got the girl fully out of the water and shifted her into the recovery position, smacking her back. Eight, nine, ten seconds passed. Oh God, come on. Come on . . .

On sixteen, she started coughing up water, her eyes flickering open with the effort. He kept her in the position for a few minutes, until he was sure there was nothing left in her stomach. She fell back against the ground, her eyes closed. She was conscious, but barely.

'It's okay. You're okay,' he said, reassuring her. 'You're going to be fine. You're safe now.'

Pia remembered those words. Safe now.

She began to shiver uncontrollably. Tanner took in her colour. Her skin and lips had a bluish tinge but the shivering was good. It meant her core temperature hadn't dipped below thirty-two degrees. But he needed to get her warmed up and fast, or hypothermia would set in. He thought quickly. It would take too long to get back to the farm from here.

'We need to get you out of those wet clothes now, okay? It's vital we get you warmed up,' he said, oblivious to the fact that he was shivering incessantly too. 'I'm going to put my jumper on you,' he said, reaching forward slowly to untie her sodden dress, not wanting to alarm her.

'Get it. Fetch, Biscuit,' he said quietly to the biddable dog, jerking his chin towards the path. Biscuit barked happily, delighted to have a role, and raced off. She knew exactly what was needed from her.

Carefully, he unwound the dress from the girl and, pulling her arms above her head, tugged off her thin jumper. She was wearing only panties underneath, and he kept his eyes up, firmly up, even though her silhouette in his peripheral vision was setting off sirens in his brain. Biscuit scampered back with his jumper – now muddied – in her teeth and he quickly slipped it over her head, swamping her tiny frame. The sleeves dangled past her hands, which he noticed had bad burns, and the neck was almost slipping off her shoulders, the hem hanging down to mid-thigh.

He rubbed her hands vigorously in his and blew on them. Her colour had improved a little but she was barely conscious and he quickly needed to get her somewhere warm. He looked at her broken foot. She'd been in a wheelchair when he'd first seen her. She clearly couldn't walk.

'I'm going to pick you up and take you to the nearest house for medical attention, okay?' he said slowly, again wary of alarming her.

The girl gave a tiny groan and he picked her up delicately, worried about hurting her foot further. It looked like she'd had a run of bad luck lately.

He tried to get her to clasp her hands around his neck, but the effort defeated her and her arms hung limply down, her head rocking against Tanner's chest as he stalked barefoot through the wood, knowing intimately every twist and turn and dip of the path. Biscuit ran ahead all the way, tail aloft, before racing back and circling him, herding him along, keeping him going.

He covered the ground in long, loping strides, his jeans clinging to his thighs, and within twenty minutes he had passed the solitary bank of snowdrops. He emerged from the copse dripping and exhausted, and for once happy to see the primly manicured stripes of Will Silk's lawns.

Chapter Sixteen

There was a full-scale panic in the house, even before Will caught sight of Tanner striding up the lawns with Pia, limp and barely conscious, in his arms. He flew out of the drawing room and raced over to them, wresting her away instantly. She felt pitifully light.

'Get the doctor!' he yelled to Mrs Bremar, who was standing at the steps, wringing her hands. 'And run a hot bath!' The woman disappeared inside.

'What happened?' he demanded, the questions pounding around in his head, as he stalked up the grass.

'I saw her down by the lake,' Tanner said. 'She lost control of the wheelchair and went in.'

'The lake! What the fuck was she doing there?' Will shouted.

'How would I know?' Tanner shouted back.

'Well – you're the one who saw her. Was she meeting someone? Having a fucking picnic? Trying to top herself? What was she doing?'

'How would *I* know?' Tanner repeated, furious. 'I don't even know who the hell she is. Do *you* know her?'

'Of course I . . .' Will looked at him and saw for the first time that Tanner – bare-chested and wet in the February morning chill – was in not much better shape than the girl in his arms. 'Christ, you're blue, Tanner. You need to warm up. Get into the house and have a bath. And take some of my clothes. I'll get a fire started.'

'Forget it,' Tanner muttered. If Silk thought playing the charitable saviour was going to change anything that had happened between them, he could think again. 'I'm going home.'

'Don't be an idiot! You'll get sick.'

'You're not my keeper, Silk. I don't take orders from you,' Tanner growled, switching direction and heading back towards the path that led past the terrace and towards the gate in the boundary that divided the two men's estates.

Pia moaned, becoming more alert as the shouts pierced her stupor.

'Sssh. We're home now,' Will said, bringing his attention immediately back to her. 'Let's get you warmed up.'

She opened her eyes and looked up at him. 'You saved me,' she whispered. 'You saved me again.'

Will looked down at her. She was looking up at him through hazy eyes and there was a look on her face he'd never seen before. Gratitude.

She clasped her arms around his neck, letting her head rock against his chest. He felt her curves press against him and he realized that in spite of the dramatic events of the past fortnight, he'd never touched anything more of her than her hand.

He swept into the house, bounding up the grand staircase, two at a time. The bath was already drawn.

'Mrs Bremar,' he said, settling her on the towelling-covered chaise. 'I'll leave you to do the honours of getting Miss Soto in the bath. Just keep her foot up and out of the water, and make sure she doesn't get out until she's as pink as a poodle, okay?'

'A gentleman as well as a hero,' Pia mumbled, trying to chuckle but lacking the energy.

He winked and quickly left the room. He couldn't bear seeing her so weak and listless; he couldn't bear seeing her with blue lips and grey skin; he couldn't bear seeing her pretty much butt-naked in Tanner Ludgrove's jumper.

The doctor arrived within five minutes and arranged for an ambulance to take her down to the cottage hospital. She needed checking out – her temperature was still too low – and they needed to use the X-ray machine to check whether any of the bones in her foot had moved when she'd smacked her leg against the tree. And of course the cast needed to be redone. The original one now looked like a toddler's attempts at pottery.

It was dusk by the time she was returned to Plumbridge House and the fire in her bedroom was roaring, casting out a golden glow that restored the last pigments of colour to her complexion. Mrs Bremar helped her into a fresh nightie, and plumped the pillows on her bed.

'This'll help you sleep,' the older woman said kindly, putting a brandy in Pia's hand.

She sipped the toddy quickly, watching the apple-wood logs crackle and burn. She handed the glass to Mrs Bremar and sank back into the plump pillows. For the first time in God only knew how long, Pia felt at home. She wanted to wait for Will to come up to her, but she was asleep within moments.

Will watched her from the doorway, having left his office two minutes too late.

Two minutes. What if Tanner had been two minutes too late today too? That would have been all it would have taken. Two minutes and it could have been weeks before they'd found her. No one knew she'd gone there. What if . . . what if?

He shuddered at the thought as he watched her sleep. She was dressed in a nightie Emma had chosen and he made a mental note to give his PA a pay rise. It was a gauzy white-dotted virginal number, with cap sleeves, which made Pia's skin looked toffee-coloured and supple next to it, and he marvelled at the way it clung to her curves. God, he'd do the same, given half the chance.

As he swallowed his cognac, his eyes skipped over her – her nipples were clearly visible beneath the flimsy fabric – and his jaw clenched at the sight of her lying there. She could even turn him on in her sleep. It was so strange having this exotic, provocative creature in his house, sleeping in one of his beds yet again. He had pursued her so vigorously, and now she was here and he couldn't act on it. That damned plaster was as effective as any chastity belt and he didn't really know how to behave with her. They weren't friends or lovers, but neither were they strangers. He'd been her saviour, but he couldn't cash in on it. They were together but still apart.

Until today he hadn't been at all certain that she'd ever succumb to him. It wouldn't have surprised him if she'd kept up the defence, just to win the fight. But on the lawn this morning there'd been a look on her face that had suggested a change. She clearly thought he'd saved her from drowning, and there'd been a shift in her demeanour back at the house that suggested he was no longer the enemy.

He finished the last dregs in his glass and shook his head, quite disbelieving that it had taken two rescues just to get *this* far with her. It meant two things were now absolutely certain: the next two months were going to drive him mad; and she could never know it was Tanner Ludgrove who'd pulled her from the water.

Chapter Seventeen

'Mind if I join you?' Will asked, standing in the doorway the next morning. He was standing with a tray in his hands. Pia looked up from her breakfast and smiled.

Will walked in and settled himself down next to her on the bed. He could smell her hair on the pillows as they moved beneath his weight.

'You're hungry, then,' he grinned, taking in the full English that was piled high on her plate.

Pia shrugged as she put a forkful of black pudding and scrambled egg in her mouth. She felt ravenous today, as though her body was trying to recover from yesterday's near-death experience by packing her full of fuel.

'Aren't you meant to be working?' she mumbled, her mouth full.

'I wanted to keep you company,' he replied. 'I've scarcely seen you since you got here.'

Pia thought she heard a note of guilt in his voice and she wondered what Mrs Bremar had reported back to him about the past week.

'Besides, what's the point of keeping a beautiful woman captive in my house if I can't sit and have breakfast with her? Did you sleep well?'

'I don't think I moved.'

'Good. No bad dreams?'

'Uh-uh. No dreams at all. Just oblivion.'

'Excellent.' Will drank some orange juice.

'You?'

Will's hand hovered in mid-air. He looked at her. 'What do you mean?'

'Did you have any bad dreams? At least I didn't know what was going on. But you did.'

'Uh, well, yes, I guess,' he faltered, eyes down. 'I slept okay.'

He felt a small warm hand on his arm. 'Thank you, Will,' Pia said quietly. 'I am in your debt.'

Will looked at her. There was no guile in her face. No teasing. She was just completely . . . open.

'Yeah, well,' he said, breaking out into a wicked grin. 'You'll pay.'

Pia burst out laughing. 'I don't doubt it.'

She clocked the graze and a purple bruise above his cheekbone. He looked shattered. No, more than that – he looked beaten up. She jerked her chin towards the cut. 'What happened?'

Will turned away, embarrassed. 'It's nothing. Just a dis-agreement with one of my staff.'

Pia's eyebrows shot up. Was that what she had heard from the loo? 'And that's how he resolves disputes? By punching you? What is he – a cowboy?'

Will shook his head grimly. 'There's just a lot going on, that's all. Your accident wasn't the only disaster to befall me in St Moritz.'

'It didn't befall *you*,' Pia said quickly, her voice suddenly flat.

'Yes, it did,' he countered, looking straight at her. 'You know exactly how much I care for you . . . how much I want you.'

'Yes. Two hundred grand's worth,' she said sarcastically, instantly reverting to her usual antagonism, and just as quickly regretting it. She didn't want to go back to that.

Will's eyes narrowed. 'When are you going to let that go? You know very well there isn't a price for what I'd do for you. Haven't I shown you that? Aren't I showing you now?'

Will sighed, frustrated, and stared at his plate.

Pia nibbled her lip, feeling small, as she watched him. She knew it was a push too far. It was time to turn the page.

'So tell me about your other disasters, then,' she said in a conciliatory tone.

There was a heavy lull. 'My head groom nearly died on the trip back and my polo manager holds me responsible.'

'But how could he possibly blame you?' Pia retorted angrily, siding with him to show support. 'How can he be so un-reasonable? What is he – deluded as well as incompetent? Surely, looking after the stable hands is *his* job. You weren't even there. You were with me,' she said.

'I know,' he replied, his voice low.

Pia was still for a moment, and then she leant over and kissed his cheek.

Will turned his face to her, astonished. Their first kiss. Okay, so it had been about as sexual as buttering toast, but still – small steps.

'The guy's a loser,' she smiled, feeling better having exerted a little of *her* power for a change. She sat back on her pillows and raised an eyebrow at him as he continued to stare at her. He clearly wanted so much more. 'Do you mind?' she asked, holding her hand out for the *Sunday Times* Culture section.

Will smiled and handed it to her, shaking out the Money supplement for himself, and they settled into a long, easy silence together.

Twenty minutes passed.

'The bastard!' Pia suddenly exclaimed. And then, after a long pause: 'The bitch!'

Will didn't know whether to laugh or not, as Pia gasped and raged her way through the centre-spread article. Best not, he decided, as her language grew bluer and then switched altogether into Portuguese. She put down the newspaper hotly and looked at him, as though he knew what was going on.

'What?' he asked warily – should he commiserate, or run for his life?

'Baudrand's given *The Songbird* to Petrova!' she cried.

'What's *The Songbird*?'

'It's *my* ballet,' Pia wailed. 'Dimitri Alvisio wrote it especially for me. I was going to debut it in March.'

'But you won't be better by March,' he said slowly.

'No!' she said, in a tone that said: 'Yes, I will!'

'So . . . surely, then, Ava has to dance it?' Will replied, worried about saying the wrong thing and inadvertently pitching himself against her. 'She was already filling in for the *Giselle* tour, wasn't she?'

'Yes! But we hadn't even started rehearsals for *The Songbird* yet. Baudrand could have chosen *any* other ballet for her for the spring rep. He didn't *have* to give her mine,' she snarled hatefully.

'I'm sure there's a good reason why he made the decision to debut the ballet without you,' he said, unable to think of one.

'It's my ballet . . . mine! How many principal dancers get their very own ballet written for them? And now he's gone and given it to the very worst person. My arch rival. He *knows* that! And she'll butcher it, you know. Chop it up with her feet. She's about as lyrical as a kick boxer. It'll look like a Jane Fonda workout by the time she's finished with it. How could he? How could he do this to me?'

Her voice was going higher and Will could tell anxiety was beginning to override her shock and anger. She gasped suddenly and the tray on her lap wobbled precariously.

'Oh my God! You know why he's done this, don't you?' she said, her eyes wide, hands cupping her chin.

Will shook his head. There was no point trying to keep up. Her mind was on speed.

'He doesn't think I'm coming back. He's given it to Ava because he doesn't think I'll ever dance it.' Big tears shone in her eyes. 'He thinks I'm finished.'

Chapter Eighteen

Sophie watched, charcoal poised, eyes creased in concentration, as Ava flew through the air, Adam's strong arms outstretched and ready to catch her nimble form. She was dressed in a blood-red unitard, black tutu and her signature glossy black *pointe* shoes. They'd been rehearsing for three hours now but there wasn't a sniff of a sweat patch on her, only wafts of No.5 perfuming the studio.

There was no doubt that Adam and Ava made an incongruous pair. Where Pia's raw sensuality had matched his own ripe looks, Ava looked as pristine as porcelain, and just as frigid.

Sophie watched Adam closely. It was their first day back in Chicago following the end of the tour, and she was desperate for a word or a look or a smile that might mean their affair was back on. Ever since Ava had arrived in New York, Baudrand had been all over his new super-team, and Adam had been whisked from class to performances to press conferences to swanky patron dinners and back again. He hadn't had a moment to himself, much less a moment alone with her, and Sophie wasn't even sure that he had heard about her promotion yet.

She had been hoping that, being back on home turf, things might settle down a bit. The choreographer, Alvisio, had delivered his new ballet, *The Songbird*, and it was to be the jewel in the crown of the spring repertoire. But here in the studio, nerves seemed to be running high. All the smiles Ava had handed out as she ingratiated herself to the company in New York seemed to have gone now, and Adam was looking stressed as he tried to adapt to Ava's bombastic way of rehearsing.

He certainly looked altogether less sleek than his new partner: one leg of his tracksuit bottoms was rolled up past the knee, grey footless tights poking out beneath them and thinning to white over his muscular calves, his black vest rippling over his carved stomach and cut away from his huge shoulders. His cheeks were flushed and a sheen of sweat misted his skin. Sophie wasn't surprised. They were working on *The Songbird* adagio, in which Adam had to perform thirteen lifts over twenty bars. He was exhausted.

The piano playing stopped at the end of the bar. Adam lowered Ava to the ground and she paced away from him restlessly, hands on hips, breathing hard, the blocks of her shoes thumping on the floor.

'That was better,' Baudrand said from his seat at the side, his legs crossed at the ankle but his upper body curiously erect and held away from the chair back. He kept stroking his white goatee as though soothing himself, his bald pate gleaming under the lights.

'Better?' Ava repeated, turning to face him. There was a frosty note in her voice. 'Better' was nowhere near brilliant. She didn't do 'better'.

'Again,' she said imperiously, flicking her arm up into the air, indicating to the piano player to strike up once more.

Sophie looked down at her sketch. Adam was holding Ava in the swallow dive and her arms were pulled back behind her, like a diver's, her neck extended. Sophie frowned at it and rubbed out the breast line. She watched Ava again.

Adam's head dropped, despondently, as the chords sang out. He picked up the bar and stepped into a *glissade*. Ava was across the room, moving towards him in a series of *petit allegro*.

'Lighter, softer, good, yes . . . yes and now up . . .' Baudrand murmured as she advanced, flying into a *grand jeté* and then up into . . .

'*Niet!*' she cried fiercely, stopping the dance abruptly and glaring at Adam. 'Why are you putting your hand there?' she demanded. 'You want me to fall?'

'I've never dropped anyone yet,' he replied. 'Besides, you carry your centre of gravity further forward than Pia—'

'Well, that's hardly a surprise with the size of her ass,' Ava snipped.

Adam paused a beat. Sophie saw the anger flash through his eyes. He couldn't bear to hear Pia criticized.

'I've found that placement to be best for me when lifting dancers, like you, who carry their weight forward,' he said finally. 'It's the way I've always done it.'

'Well, I don't care. *I* like to be held *here*,' she said, and she adjusted his hands further up around her ribs.

Adam looked at her. 'Given that I'm the one doing the lifting, don't you think it's more important that *I* feel secure with the grip?'

But Ava had already turned away and was moving back to her spot across the room. As far as she was concerned, the conversation was over. 'Again!' she said, clicking her fingers at the piano player.

Adam tried to catch Baudrand's eye but the director was watching his new star, rapt. Such passion. Such drive. Such perfectionism. He'd hardly been able to believe it when he'd got the call saying she wanted to be part of the centenary celebrations. And now that she was here, the more he thought about it, the more he realized he'd been handed a golden opportunity in Pia's accident, an opportunity to move the company forward, and up and away from Pia Soto. For too long he'd been blinded by Pia's light, by her unassailable self-confidence that she was the best, and that had allowed her to get away with unforgivable behaviour, behaviour that had made him look a fool. But he'd overlooked one thing: she wasn't the only one who was best. She was joint best. Getting her nemesis on board hit multiple targets at once.

The music started up and Adam slid into the *glissade* again as Ava went through her tiny jumps, coming closer, and higher, and then she was in the air, above him. He reached up, his hands reset to her favoured position, but as he absorbed her weight in the descent, he felt his wrist give and his arm buckled at the elbow.

Ava fell awkwardly to the ground.

'You idiot!' she screamed, from a heap on the floor.

'I'm sorry,' he said, extending a hand to help her up. 'But the balance is wrong. It's too far forward like that. '

'You're too weak, you mean,' she scowled, ignoring his chivalry and getting herself up. She stood glaring at him, her hands on her hips, and her shoes – which look clownishly long when flat-footed – turned out.

Adam's eyes flashed. He prided himself on his strength and stamina, but they'd been practising this sequence for eighty-five minutes straight and the muscles in his arms were empty. Even he couldn't carry on body-pressing seven and a half stone indefinitely.

'Well, maybe if you could get a grip on the choreography, I might actually be able to rest for a moment,' he retorted. 'Pia never took this long to understand what was needed from her.'

Ava gave an outraged, curdled shriek at that. How dare he compare her unfavourably to Pia Soto!

Baudrand jumped up from his chair, keen to avert the contretemps.

'Stop it,' he scolded. 'You are both exhausted. It is my fault. I should have stopped you earlier. One of you will get injured if we carry on any longer.' He pursed his lips and looked at them both. His new super-team.

'It is coming,' he said with a quiet confidence, his head nodding. 'We are getting there. Technically your body knows this now, Ava. That is not where we must concentrate. Your skill is not in doubt. It is simply a matter of feeling the character now, finding her in you and letting her out – just a soft touch. You must remember this ballet was written specifically for Pia. It plays to her strengths – artistry, not technique. To conquer it you must think like she thinks.'

'You mean, dance like she dances, dance *her* way,' Ava sneered, as though the very idea was contemptible.

'*Non*. I want you to dance your way but with her spirit. Don't you see, cherie?' A small smile hovered on his lips. 'Then you will dance *her* ballet even better than she could dance it herself.'

Sophie looked up, shocked, from her sketches. Had she really just heard it? Baudrand pitting Ava directly against Pia? Willing her, encouraging her to outperform his resident protégée?

Ava didn't miss the sycophantic tone in Baudrand's voice, nor had she missed the way Sophie's head had jerked up, or the way Adam had stiffened. She tipped her head in seeming acquiescence.

'And you, Adam,' Baudrand said, his voice becoming hard. 'You need to get back to the gym. Ava's right. You should be able to hold her the way she prefers. Get some strength built up in that wrist, and fast. There're six weeks till opening night but we've got a full programme and five other productions to rehearse.' He dropped his voice ominously low. 'Don't make me regret my decision of choosing you. Just because you were Pia's preferred partner doesn't mean you're necessarily right to dance this with Ava. We'll have to see how we get on.'

Baudrand walked away from them both. 'We'll start again at twelve tomorrow, after class, the Balanchine studio.'

Ava raised her eyebrows at Adam. They both knew she wielded the power. If she decided that Adam wasn't 'right' for her, he'd be off the job.

His jaw clenched, furiously, and she gave a small smile.

'See you tomorrow, then,' she said dismissively, shrugging her petite shoulders and clop-clopping away to pick up her bag.

The piano player nervously rushed past, his folios fluttering under his arm. 'G'night.'

Adam watched Ava go, lost in thought, lost in the threat. When she got to the door – to add insult to injury – she turned off the lights. Only the fading purple notes of dusk coming through the skylight rescued the room from complete darkness.

Sophie gave a small cough, and he turned. She could see he'd quite forgotten she was there. Not that she was surprised. For all her fancy new title, she remained resolutely plain and forgettable.

He came and sat down on the floor with her, pulling off the support rags he tied around his wrists. She crossed her legs and let the oversized sketchbook rest on her lap.

'How you doing?' she asked sympathetically.

Adam shrugged, disconsolate. 'It looks like Pia might not be the only one whose career is put on hold while she recovers,' he mumbled. 'Come back, Miss Soto. All is for-given.' He gave a wry smile but Sophie could see he was gutted.

'Things will settle down,' she said, but even as she said it she wasn't sure they would. Several times in New York, Ava had been spotted deep in conversation with José – who was up for partnering her in *The Rite of Spring* – and rumours were beginning to spread. If Ava wanted to play favourites, things could get bleaker still for Adam. 'And at least she got us through the rest of the tour,' she said quietly.

'I guess.' he shrugged. 'It was odd without Pia though.'

Sophie nodded. 'Yes.'

He sighed. 'Well, it looks like the honeymoon's over. Ava must have been behaving herself in New York. I thought she was unbelievably charming – can you imagine?'

A note of alarm rang in Sophie and she shook her head. She didn't want to imagine. It was bad enough that he was in Pia's thrall.

'But now that Badland's signed her up and she's got her feet under the table it seems I've outlived my usefulness.'

Sophie sighed gratefully. Adam may still be barely aware of her presence, but at least she would be saved the torture of watching him fall in love with his new leading lady.

He fiddled with the unwound bandages. They were wet through and needed a boil wash from the looks of things. They sat in easy silence together in the gathering dark.

He noticed her drawings on her lap.

'I hear things were . . . busy for you too,' he said, shifting slightly to look at her. 'It's great news, by the way.' He leant over and kissed her on the cheek. 'I knew I was onto something with you,' he grinned.

'You did?' she said, brightening up.

'Absolutely. But just remember: I'm the one who started you off, okay? I was your first official model.'

Her shoulders drooped and she nodded.

'I hear Badlands is putting on an exhibition for you? Same night as the gala?'

'Yes.'

'That's so great. At least one of us can look forward to a great time that night,' he joked.

'Don't let her knock your confidence, Adam. You're such a beautiful dancer. She's just trying to mess with your mind.'

'Yeah,' he shrugged. 'So that she can ship in José.'

Sophie looked at him, surprised. Had he heard the rumours too, then?

'It's okay. I know what they're all saying, that she's lining him up as my replacement.'

'Now listen,' she said, suddenly fierce. 'Don't let her do this to you. You've got to come out fighting, Adam. You're a far better dancer than he is. He makes so much noise on stage he might as well wear clogs. There's a very good reason why Pia always chose you, and don't you forget it.'

Adam stared at her, astonished by her lioness instinct, and for a moment he glimpsed the goddess behind the easel again.

'God, I wish I could take you home right now,' he beamed, reaching over and kissing her on the lips.

'You can,' Sophie gasped, instantly forgetting her resolution in the shower that morning to be strong and independent and over him.

He sprang up into standing and began winding the rags back round his wrists.

'Oh Sophie, Sophie. You're a bad influence on me, d'you know that?'

She shook her head, confused. He laughed, suddenly bright. 'But you're absolutely right about Ava. I've got to show her what I can really do. And I've got to listen to Badlands and get down to the gym. The only thing I can pump tonight is iron, more's the pity.'

He picked up his kitbag and walked towards the door.

'Thanks, Soph! You're a star.' And with that, he winked and left.

A sodding star? She sighed as the door banged behind him, cross with herself for having been so eager for him. Why, oh why, was he such a hard habit to break?

The sunlight crept over the bed like a tide, bathing her in its warmth and golden glow. Sophie stretched languidly, still half asleep. It felt so good to wake up naturally – and warm for once. Usually her bedroom was freezing first thing; the sun didn't creep round to her windows until . . .

She gasped and sat bolt upright, grabbing her watch from the bedside table.

Twelve forty-six? Shit!

Leaping out of bed, she pulled on the clothes she'd taken off last night, picked up her bag, which was still unpacked from yesterday's session, and raced out of the door. A second later, she came back through it again and grabbed an easel and a huge, unwieldy portfolio case. The paints and brushes fitted in her bag.

Buying a bagel and coffee from the stall on the corner, she jostled her way down the eleven blocks to the studios, with the bagel held firmly between her teeth, her bags and easel taking out unsuspecting pedestrians with glancing blows to the back of their knees.

'Sorry. Sorry. Wide load coming through . . .' she mumbled through her mouthful of bagel, unable to stop.

She was there in fifteen minutes and used her bottom to burst open the studio door. Adam and Ava were mid-performance and carried on, well used to interruptions during rehearsals. Sophie turned and tried to tiptoe in, but the easel caught sideways in the door jamb and she became stuck fast, the fire door swinging back on its hinges and closing on her.

Instinctively, she closed her eyes on impact; when she opened them again it was to find three pairs of eyes staring at her squashed face in the viewing panel.

They all stared at each other for a long time – well, five seconds, but it felt a lifetime to her; she couldn't move. Her nose was flattened sideways, the cream cheese from the bagel in her mouth was smeared all over the place, and the faces gradually disappeared from sight as her breath misted up the glass.

Adam burst out laughing, and came running over.

'You're a riot,' he said, barely able to get the words out as he gallantly opened the door for her. The squashed bagel broke up and fell to the floor, setting him off even harder. He actually had to hold his sides, she noticed.

She hastily swallowed the bit of bagel that had been in her mouth as she wrestled with the easel's legs, but her outsized portfolio and half-spilt coffee kept getting in the way. Damned bloody hell, she cursed to herself, totally humiliated.

Adam released the easel for her and carried it over to her spot in the corner.

'Thanks, Adam', she muttered, aware that as well as looking like a fool, she also looked a state. Her clothes were crumpled and covered with paint and her eyes were as wild as her hair, which she hadn't had time to tame. She smiled apologetically, and sat down in her chair.

'I'm so sorry. I overslept,' she mumbled. 'I was working late last night . . .' Her voice trailed away.

Adam, who had walked back to Ava, caught her eye and indicated to his mouth. She mirrored him, hesitant, and wiped away a smudge of cream cheese. She nodded bleakly. Of course.

She didn't dare meet Ava's eyes. She could tell from the ballerina's body language that she was furious at the clumsy interruption.

Sophie busied herself with setting up, pulling out her brushes and paint from her bag.

The music started up again and the dancers went back to the piece they were performing. Baudrand's voice was calm and low – as usual – and encouraging rather than critical as they swept through their steps. Over and over and over again they repeated the scene, relentlessly, like a machine adjusting and fine-tuning microscopic flaws that were invisible to everyone but them.

'Good, that's it, yes, higher now . . . not too fast, draw back here . . . take her arm, yes . . . Adam, step back and . . . hold her steady,' Baudrand breathed. 'Now, sweep down, no more . . . yes . . . keep the elbow up . . .' His own arms extended outwards lightly, guiding and pulling them like marionettes, like a conductor with his orchestra.

Sophie watched, rapt. Ava was advancing upon Adam in

pirouettes, her legs a blur of syncopated rhythm, her feet falling and rising on *pointe* as she circled him coquettishly, dazzling him with her bravura display, her eyes catching his . . .

Sophie caught her breath, forgetting even to paint. It was working. They were beginning to gel, the chemistry was forming. Sophie had only ever seen Adam partner Pia. They were an electric partnership and, as such, Sophie had only ever regarded him in the sum of his part with Pia. She would never have thought she could imagine him with anyone else. The fact that he was desperately in love with Pia only brought more resonance to the roles they played, where invariably his characters pursued hers.

But now Sophie saw for the first time that Adam was every bit as versatile as Pia. The difference was that Pia had made herself a star; he – left in her slipstream – had been seen as just the support act by comparison. But maybe . . . maybe that would change now that he was partnering another great name. He was holding his own with Ava, matching her nimble, assured precision with a sleek, brooding magnetism. She was gazelle to his jaguar, and Sophie realized, with rising panic, that they were flashing off the first sparks of a sizzling chemistry all their own.

But not for long. The symphony stopped abruptly.

'*Aaiiee!*' Ava shrieked dramatically. 'You could have broken my foot, you idiot,' she cried angrily at Adam, hobbling away from him.

'I'm sorry,' Adam exhaled loudly, holding his hands up in appeasement. 'I couldn't see where your feet were under the tutu.'

'You shouldn't need to see them, you fool. You should just know. It's called instinct. All great dancers have it.'

'It was an accident. Clearly.' Adam's jaw clenched.

'No, not clearly,' she contradicted. 'I knew that was going to happen. You are standing too close to me, giving me no room to move. You make me feel stifled.' She threw her arms up in the air explosively.

'I was not too close,' Adam retorted. 'I was exactly where I needed to be for the *fouettés*.'

'You are trapping me, making me dance smaller. You want to hog the space for yourself with your big arms and chunky legs.'

Adam looked at her. Chunky legs! He tried to stay calm with her and took a deep breath. 'How do you expect me to hold you in the finger *fouetté* if you're two feet away from me?' he reasoned.

'You figure it out. That's your job. You're the brawn, I'm the ballerina.'

'What?' Adam exploded. 'I'm the *brawn*?'

Ava looked at him through slit-like eyes.

'What do you think I am – a freaking Chippendale?'

She shrugged. 'You dance like one.'

Adam flushed red all over, speechless. He had never been so insulted. He held his hands out to Baudrand. 'Director?' he appealed.

Sophie looked over at Baudrand, who was sitting silently, watching them. He wouldn't let her get away with this, surely?

'Go again,' he said, sounding almost bored.

'What?' Adam shouted.

'Remember who you are speaking to,' Baudrand warned, his eyes narrowing fractionally. 'Now go again.'

'No!' Adam shouted again. 'I can't believe you're going to let her get away with speaking to me like that! I don't need to take this bullshit!' he said, heading for the door, the sprung floor bouncing beneath his angry stomps.

'Get back here, Adam,' Baudrand said, his voice animated now, though he remained seated.

Adam stopped at the door. 'Get someone else to partner her,' he spat. 'I'm sure José will be fool enough to take on the role. I've had enough. I'm out of here.' And he exited the room a good deal more impressively than Sophie had entered it.

Sophie looked after him in astonishment, her charcoal still poised in mid-air.

Baudrand said nothing, and he remained seated, but the whitening of his lips and a bulging vein on his bald head betrayed his anger.

Ava sighed nonchalantly. 'Ah well, he'll cool down,' she said breezily as she mopped her neck with a towel. She dropped it on top of her bag and walked over to Sophie. 'And how have you got on this morning?'

Sophie stared at her, dumbfounded. How could the woman insult Adam like that and then act as though nothing had happened? For all Pia's faults, at least she recognized the other dancers' talents.

Ava stared at the canvas, then at Sophie. Sophie swallowed and looked at the canvas herself. She saw that it was pristine. She hadn't made a mark on the paper in the whole time she'd been there.

Ava tutted and crossed her arms. 'If you're only here to watch, Sophie, we'll have to start charging you entry,' she said coldly.

Sophie looked up at her, willing herself to rise up impressively and tell this witch to stick her grand exhibition up her tutu, before running off to console Adam, preferably naked.

Instead a strange croak came from her throat.

Ava burst out laughing. 'Come,' she said expansively, as though they were great friends. 'Let's go and get some lunch. I think it's time we got to know one another properly, don't you?'

Sophie couldn't reply. She couldn't think of anything worse. But what was she going to do? Refuse? It was clear no one – not even Baudrand – said no to Ava Petrova.

For someone who'd been living in the city for only three weeks, Ava Petrova certainly knew her way around. She took Sophie to a chic little Italian place, hidden down an alleyway. Sophie had passed it thousands of times and never known there was anything there, except for drunks and druggies.

She looked around at the gathered clientele: corporate executives, gallery owners, fashion PRs and socialites, all dressed in furs and suedes and London/Paris/Milan labels. Ava had thrown a pair of black cigarette pants and a Versace silk sweater over her black leotard. With her hair worn up and her gamine frame she looked every bit as immaculate as the other women in the room.

Sophie didn't. She sighed heavily and focused on the menu instead, which was entirely in Italian.

'You must let me order for you,' Ava said, guessing that Sophie didn't speak Italian. 'I know the chef. He always does a special for me.'

Of course he does, Sophie thought to herself. Horse's head, most probably.

'This is nice, no?' Ava said, after she'd placed their orders.

Sophie nodded obediently. 'It's lovely here. How did you find it?'

Ava shrugged. 'Oh you know, just exploring. Trying to find my way around a new city. It's not easy to make it feel like home, you know?'

Sophie took a sip of her water. 'Do you miss home?'

'Moscow?' she sighed. 'Yes, more than you could possibly imagine. It has such history, it is such a beautiful city – majestic! Tragic! Epic!' she enunciated dramatically, sweeping her arms about poetically. You could tell she was a ballerina from that alone. 'Have you ever been there?'

Sophie shook her head.

'You must go,' she said effusively. 'It will take your breath away. This –' she said, indicating Chicago as a whole, and dismissing it with a flick of the wrist – 'it cannot compare.'

There was a brief lull as Sophie tried to think of something to say. She couldn't. Chicago wasn't her home town. She was just a passing resident, rarely ever here. She'd been in the city three years; Ava for three weeks, and Ava probably knew it better than she did.

'Did you always want to be an artist?' Ava asked eventually, rescuing her.

'When I was little, I did,' she replied. 'But I didn't think I'd ever be able to make a living from it.'

'And now you are,' Ava smiled.

'Yes,' Sophie said, looking up. 'Thanks to you,' she added politely.

Ava nodded graciously.

Sophie looked back down at her napkin again as another silence settled upon them. She desperately didn't want to be here. It felt like a betrayal of Adam after the way Ava had treated him this morning. And as for Pia . . .

She caught herself and tried not to think about her former

boss. What did it matter? Pia neither needed nor wanted her loyalty now.

Sophie took another sip of water. She didn't notice Ava watching her intently.

'You are cross about my words with Adam, aren't you?'

Sophie froze. She didn't fancy her chances in a face-to-face confrontation with Ava Petrova.

'He's a good guy,' Sophie said neutrally.

'Yes, he is,' Ava nodded. 'And a great dancer. But he is not focused at the moment. His mind is . . . elsewhere.'

Sophie bit her lip. He'd seemed entirely focused from where she'd been sitting. Exactly how much commitment did Ava expect from her partner? Blood, as well as the sweat and tears? 'I expect he's just trying to adapt to the new way of working with you. He and Pia were . . . I don't know, instinctive. They just seemed to be able to read each other.'

'I see.' Ava ran her finger around the rim of her glass. 'And is that because they were . . . intimate?'

Sophie flinched in surprise. 'No!'

Ava shrugged. 'I'm only asking, not judging. It happens, of course. A lot. It just might explain his mood a bit more. It's good for me to try to understand, don't you think?'

Sophie nodded. Ava had a point. If she could get Ava to see that Adam wasn't clumsy or weak or unfocused it might just get her off his back.

'Well, as far as I know they never got together,' she said quietly. 'But it's an open secret that he's in love with her.'

'He misses her. It makes sense,' Ava replied, just as the waiter came over and reset their cutlery. Sophie was having risotto, Ava the steak. 'Thank you.'

Ava waited for him to leave. 'And you?' she asked casually.

182

'What?' she hiccuped, panicking that Ava had read her feelings about Adam too.

'You miss her also.'

Sophie said nothing.

'It's all right, you know. I know you were her assistant. It is only natural that you should miss her. She is an amazing woman – a *rare* woman. There are not very many like her. I have always had the greatest admiration for her.'

'You have?' Sophie asked, astonished.

'Of course. How could I not?'

'But . . . but . . . I thought you two didn't *get on*?' She was impressed by her rare understatement.

Ava shrugged. 'That was always Pia's decision. She made our professional rivalry personal. Me? I rather like her, though I accept we shall never be friends.' She paused. 'Have you spoken to her since the accident?'

'No,' Sophie mumbled. 'That's when she fired me. And it's best not to hang around if she doesn't want you there.'

'Oh yes, I know that very well,' Ava replied knowingly.

Sophie looked at Ava hesitantly. She was the perfect person to ask. 'Do you think she'll be able to come back from this accident, Ava? I mean, I know the doctors are being optimistic and all that, but do *you* think she will be able to perform at her old level again?'

'I certainly hope so,' Ava said, shaking out her napkin and draping it over her narrow lap. 'I would miss her. I like the fact that there's someone to challenge me. Every champion – whatever his discipline – needs a fierce rival. It's how you come to be considered great. It's not enough to be ahead of the field – or the corps, in our instance. Only by destroying my equal can I claim to be the best. So, me? I enjoy our rivalry. It keeps me on my toes.' She paused. 'So to speak.'

Sophie laughed at the unexpected joke, surprised to find she was enjoying herself. 'Well, I hope you're right. It would be so sad if she couldn't get herself back to the top – for the rest of the world, as well as for you.'

'She's a dancer in her prime, Sophie. She must have had lots of plans in the pipeline that will motivate her to come back.'

'Well, that's for sure,' Sophie said.

'For example, I'm quite sure that me dancing *The Songbird* will make her even more determined to get back to Chicago,' Ava said, eyebrows raised knowingly. 'It is probably making her mad to know that I am here with you and Adam and I have taken her ballet from her.'

'Oh, she'll be mad all right – but not for *those* reasons.'

'What do you mean?'

'Well, Alvisio didn't just write *The Songbird* as a kindness to Baudrand. It was a sort of test for Pia.'

'A test? For what?'

'Going to La Scala.'

'In Milan? But why does she want to go there?' Ava seemed genuinely surprised. 'I heard Paris Opera and the Royal were after her.'

'They are. I don't really get it,' Sophie shrugged. 'She's hung up on getting a particular rank.'

'Etoile? But she can achieve that in those companies.'

'No, higher than that. The once-in-a-generation one.'

There was a short pause, as Ava thought. 'You mean Prima Ballerina Assoluta?'

'That's the one. She says Milan's the only place where she's got a shot at making it. She thinks Alvisio favours her style and he's got the power to appoint her Assoluta if she joins La Scala.'

Ava took a long slow sip of water. 'Well,' she said finally. 'I have to say I'm surprised. I thought she was stalling to up the money.' She shrugged. 'But Pia is incredibly driven, Sophie. If anyone can make it back, she can. I think she has the anger to do it.'

'Anger?' Sophie's eyebrows shot up. Not talent? Determination?

Ava nodded. 'Yes. Anger. I think that is what drives her. Over the years, I have studied her performances and I have come to the conclusion that Pia is a – mmm, how you say? – tormented woman. Off stage she is so much the "Queen of Gesture", *niet*?' she smiled, referencing the Ballet Russes ballerina Ida Rubenstein, who led a python about on a lead and drank champagne from fresh lilies. 'But she is only ever truly at peace when she's on the stage. There's a change in her spirit when she dances that goes way beyond characterization. She's a brilliant dancer but she's not *that* good an actress. If she was, I would say she's in the wrong industry, you know?'

She went on. '*Niet*, I think the Pia we see on stage is the true Pia, not the *brat* we see off duty.' She leant in, waving her fork. 'But I think she is like that because she is haunted by something, and she only ever gets away from it when she dances.'

Haunted. The image of Pia before curtain-up, standing there taut and – yes, Ava was right – tortured, filled Sophie's mind.

It all made a lot of sense. She stared at Ava, impressed by this generous, forgiving and open-minded appraisal of her rival.

'You're right,' Sophie said thoughtfully. 'If she's not dancing, she's running . . . She can't slow down. She has this desperate need to keep moving, keep doing things. It's almost like she's scared to stop.'

'Like a shark,' Ava said.

'Huh?'

'If a shark stops swimming, it drowns, Sophie. She is the same. Pia will make her way back to ballet because she has to. Dancing is the only way she knows how to survive.'

Chapter Nineteen

After the initial wave of Latin histrionics, Pia lapsed into a dejected silence that made the previous weeks' depression look like an adolescent sulk. Will tried talking to her; he tried giving her space. He even abandoned his study and started sitting on the bed and reading to her. But she didn't hear a word.

She wouldn't sit up in bed, she wouldn't allow herself to be washed or moved and she certainly wouldn't eat. She was getting thinner, literally before his eyes, defiantly letting her muscles waste away, as though Baudrand's dismissal of her hopes was the final word on her return to international ballet.

Will could have punched the man. His casual betrayal had done more damage to her chances of recovery than even the second accident. Thankfully, the plaster had done its job in that instance, insulating her foot from the very worst of the impact, and it was only the cast becoming saturated in the lake that had allowed her foot to swell and bruise as much as it had. If there was any delay to her recovery, it would only be by a couple of days. But that seemed irrelevant. Just when she'd seemed to be coming round, she'd lost all hope again and the fire had gone out of her.

Will stood at the doorway and watched her. She was lying

on her side, her back to him, and he couldn't tell if she was asleep. It was two in the afternoon.

It was a week since she'd read about Baudrand's dismissal of her recovery, and she was still wearing the same white nightie that had looked so alluring in the firelight. It was grubby now, and marked with tea and food stains. Her hair – unwashed since the bath after she'd been pulled from the lake – hung limply, and when he got closer to her there was no disguising the fact that she stank.

'Come on. We're going to walk and talk,' he said, marching over to the wardrobe and pulling out a caramel-coloured cashmere tracksuit for her.

'I can't. Remember?' she said flatly, not moving.

'It's okay, you're going to talk, I'm going to walk,' he replied, pushing her onto her back and pulling her up to a sitting position. Her head lolled back pathetically. 'Oh buck up, Pia,' he said sharply. 'You are *not* going to waste away in this room. It's not why I brought you back here.'

'We all know why you brought me back here,' she said spitefully.

Will looked at her and wrinkled his nose. 'You sure of that? Because right now it's not such an appealing prospect from where I'm standing.'

Pia jerked her head up sharply at that. His lust for her was something she absolutely took for granted. It was pretty much one of the only things left she could count on.

'Now, are you going to get yourself dressed, or shall I?'

Pia hunched her shoulders over sullenly. 'I'll do it,' she said quietly. She knew she wasn't going to win this argument. He was in a determined mood and she wasn't anywhere near strong enough to stop him dressing or undressing her. She felt so weak.

'Good. I'll be back in ten minutes,' he said, marching out of the room.

When he came back, he had to bite down his surprise at the sight of her. The tracksuit billowed around her now. She'd added a burnt-orange pashmina round her neck and was sitting in the wheelchair waiting for him, head down, like a patient in a care home.

He carried her down the stairs and placed her in the new spare wheelchair. He'd thrown so many cushions and blankets on it, it was practically a sofa.

For the first time in days, Pia broke a small smile. 'There's no room for me,' she said, wedged between bolsters. 'I tell you what, you take the cushions for some air. I'll stay back here.'

Will looked at her, flustered. 'Well, they'd probably be better company.'

He threw half the cushions on the floor and wheeled her out of the front door. The ramp wasn't nearly so scary with him at the helm, and as he tipped her back to drag the chair over the gravel, the sun shone full on her face, forcing her eyes shut and filling her with warmth.

A sigh escaped her.

They rolled along in silence for a few minutes, Pia taking in the buzz of activity in the world beyond her bedroom. Gardeners were digging in beds, carting barrow-loads of topsoil along the drive, pruning back creepers. A couple of young guys were aerating the lawn, stomping up and down the grass stripes with spiked shoes. Everyone seemed so busy. Everyone but her.

'Where are we going?' she asked finally, as they turned towards the back of the house and went along the terrace.

A pool – covered up for the winter – was situated below it, with a vine-walled tennis court set further back.

'I've got a surprise for you,' Will replied enigmatically.

She looked in the windows as they passed by and caught sight of the kitchen, which she hadn't been in yet. Mrs Bremar was in there chopping vegetables, with her back turned to them.

'Is it far?'

'No. Just far enough for you to tell me what's been running through your head these past few days. I really don't understand why Ava being cast in *The Songbird* means the end of your career.'

It was a reasonable enough statement, but there was a long silence as Pia tried to articulate the politics behind the decision.

'Baudrand knows that I will never play second fiddle to anyone, least of all *her*,' Pia said, struggling. 'Which means he knew when he cast her in my ballet that I would never go back to the ChiCi.'

'But he would never do anything to lose you. You're his top star, *the* top star in ballet,' Will argued, manoeuvring her onto the lawns that ran down and away from the house. 'He can't afford to lose you.'

'He already has. Let's face it: there are no guarantees I'm going to make it back. I may never recover my form,' Pia said, her voice so quiet he could hardly hear her. 'If he waits for me, he risks losing Ava back to Moscow – or, worse, to another company. Everybody knows she's desperate to get out of Russia.' Pia swallowed hard. 'So he weighed up the odds and made his decision. Ava's the sure thing. And I'm on my own.'

'You are *not* alone,' Will said protectively, squeezing the back of her neck.

She smiled, touched by his loyalty, but he'd missed the point. Their relationship – whatever it was, whatever it was going to be – didn't change the fact that she'd been cast adrift from her anchor.

'Yes, I am,' she said. 'Without ChiCi to showcase my return I can't prove I'm performance-fit again.'

'That doesn't matter. Every ballet company in the world will be vying for you once they realize you're available. What about the Royal? I know for a fact that they'd jump at the chance to speak to you.'

Pia shook her head wearily. '*Why* are you so desperate for me to go to the Royal?'

'I'd have thought that was obvious,' he shrugged. 'Because then you'll be near to me. I don't want you disappearing off to the other side of the world. Imagine what it'll cost me in landing fees.'

Pia chuckled. 'Well, I'm sorry to be such a financial burden but if I do get to go anywhere, it'll be to Milan.'

'To La Scala? But why there?'

'To dance under Dimitri Alvisio,' she sighed, not wanting to go into it all. 'Besides, no one's going to sign me, lame, on the strength of how good I *once* was. And to prove to them I'm back I need a stage and a production. And where will I get that now? Nobody's going to want to take a chance on me.'

She realized that Will had brought her to a stop at the bottom of the lawn.

'What's this?' she asked flatly, staring up at a large slate-grey summerhouse, already dreading the extravagant and seductive lunch that would invariably be laid out inside.

'Come see,' he said, scooping her up easily in his arms.

He opened the doors with his foot.

Pia looked around, expecting to see tables covered in linen and grapes, silver champagne buckets, urns full of flowers, and most probably a decadent chaise longue draped in blankets.

But there was nothing in there. Literally nothing. Just mirrored walls, a sprung floor, a piano and a *barre*. A framed poster of her dancing *Sylvia* last year hung next to the door.

'Oh my God!' she gasped, completely taken aback. It wasn't what she'd expected at all. 'You've made me a dance studio,' she whispered.

'Please don't tell me you thought I was going to woo you with some corny lunch,' Will grinned.

'Busted,' she replied quietly, looking around in surprised wonder.

'I'm not going to let you give up, Pia,' he said determinedly. 'Evie Grainger's flying back as we speak and she'll be starting with you the day after tomorrow. You've got six weeks before they take the wires out again, then you're fully back on your feet. After that, it's all down to how much you want it. London, New York – wherever – will be yours for the taking. As far as I'm aware no one's ever said no to you and lived to tell the tale, have they?'

She smiled hesitantly, nowhere near as confident as he was, but just being back in a studio was bringing all her old feelings rushing to the surface. This didn't have the right smells yet – no rosin powder on the floor, no sweat on the mirrors – but with Evie Grainger on her side, it would only be a matter of days before it was broken in.

'Stay there,' Will said, sitting her down on the floor and

running back out to the wheelchair. He returned with the blankets and cushions and spread them all out on the floor.

Pia lay down gingerly, looking up at the ceiling, trying to control the rush of emotions that were breaking upon her. Will turned on a sound system and *Swan Lake* started up. He lay down beside her.

'Is it okay, then?' he asked, looking up at the lights.

Pia turned her head towards him, alarmed by this sudden intimacy. 'I don't know what to say,' she replied, her voice shaky. She felt him slide his hand into hers and she had to suppress the urge to pull it away. He was being kind, she knew, but it felt . . . smothering to her. It really was all she could do to accept his medical care. Any amorous intentions he had were going to have to wait until she was back on her feet and calling the shots again. Only then would she decide whether or not to sleep with him. She was used to looking after herself, it was her primal need, and she abhorred – to a degree that he would never be able to understand – this loss of control over her own life. She might be forced to let him mastermind her recovery, but she'd be damned if she was going to let him dictate *everything* that happened to her. She wasn't a victim.

He mistook the flicker of determination that lit up behind her eyes and gave a small smile. 'That's my girl,' he said, stroking her limp hand with his thumb. 'It's time to fight back. Ava Petrova's not going to know what's hit her.'

It was growing dark by the time they left the studio, and the smell of the coal fires burning in the house wafted down enticingly. Pia inhaled deeply, exhausted. She needed to go to bed. She had all the stamina of a fairy at the moment.

A heavy dew had settled on the grass and as Will went to push her back up the lawn the wheels spun on the slope. He wouldn't be able to get traction without creating deep muddy tracks in his striped lawn.

'We'll follow the path back to the house this way,' Will said, taking her alongside a wall that divided the lawn from a wood.

Pia looked into the trees. 'Is that where—'

'Yes,' Will said quickly, not wanting her to get upset. 'It's in there. Quite far off, though. You really covered some distance. You must have been fairly determined to get away from me.'

'Away from Violet, you mean.'

'Why Violet?' he asked, relieved. He'd been sure she'd been fleeing from him. 'Didn't she look after you properly?'

Pia shrugged, not wanting to go into details. She didn't want him to find out about the loo-stranding incident. 'Technically, I guess she did. She just . . . isn't a girl's girl.'

'Neither are you,' he grinned. He could well imagine their battle of egos.

'Well, thank God Evie's coming now. At least she knows how to deal with me.'

'I didn't know there was anybody who knew that,' Will replied, and she could hear the grin in his voice. 'I thought nobody could pin you down.'

'Well, you have,' she countered, and the image of her pinned down swam before his eyes. 'For the moment anyway,' she added archly, a flash of her old fire flickering up.

They rounded a corner, just as a streak of nutmeg dashed past. A fox?

Pia shrieked as it came back, circling her, barking excitedly.

'Get away! Get back!' she cried, hiding her face and shrinking down, frightened of anything further happening to her leg.

'Sit, Biscuit,' Will said calmly, coming to stand in front of Pia. The dog instantly sat on the ground, panting.

Pia peered between her fingers at the tame dog, and felt instantly ridiculous.

'Oh! It's you,' said a brusque male voice over the wall. Pia couldn't see over it but she could tell from the way Will stiffened that he wasn't happy to see the man.

'How are you?' Will asked tightly.

'Same as before, if that's what you mean. Nothing's changed. You've got until the end of April to get your horses out of my stables, or I'm putting them into auction.'

'Don't threaten me, Ludgrove,' Will said quietly. 'I can't get the livery of twenty horses sorted in that space of time. The insurance for the stolen horses alone is taking an age. Besides, don't you think this is all just an overreaction? We need to sit down and discuss things.'

'I thought I made myself very clear the other day.'

Pia gasped. 'Is he the thug who hit you?' she cried, outraged, to Will.

Will turned to quiet her, but Pia saw her opportunity to show him some loyalty for once.

'What kind of animal are you?' she demanded, her accent thickening. 'Using your fists instead of your brain like some kind of . . . gorilla! And now, now you threaten him again when he's trying to be reasonable with you . . .'

Tanner looked at Will, puzzled and somewhat bemused by the furious disembodied voice. Who the hell was that? 'I see you've got your very own poison dwarf,' he muttered drily to Will.

'Will has told me everything that happened,' Pia continued, ranting to the wall. 'You are a damned fool to hold him responsible. Whatever happened to your staff, it was your mistake. You were in charge, you were there. He was *not* there,' Pia blustered angrily. 'You are no man. You have no honour. You are a *tolo*. A *burro* – what do you call it? A donkey. You are lucky he did not fire you the first time.'

Flicking her hands up disgustedly, and with nothing more to say, Pia sat back in the chair.

Tanner, hearing the cease-fire, peered smiling over the wall. But the smile immediately slid off as he clocked the cast. He looked down at her, astonished. Her skin was glowing, her eyes flashing . . . had it not been for that plaster on her leg he'd never have recognized her as the girl he'd dragged from the water. He could scarcely marry the memory of the limp girl with this furious, hot-headed impetuous little tour-de-force. Of all the ungrateful . . .

He looked back, disgusted, at Will. 'Well,' he said finally. 'I rather wish I hadn't bothered,' he said darkly.

Pia's eyes narrowed. Bothered with what?

Will stepped forward menacingly. 'What did you ju—'

'And Violet's well shot of her,' he continued, speaking over him. 'I see she wasn't exaggerating when she said what an ungrateful brat she had to put up with. You did her a favour giving her the boot.' He slapped his thigh and Biscuit came round and sat next to him. 'I won't tell you again, Silk – get your horses out of my stables or they're going to auction.'

Will bridled at the threat, but he said nothing. It was just better to get away from him as quickly as possible.

Tanner glared down at Pia, who was staring back equally

hatefully, before he turned away and disappeared into the wood alongside them, Biscuit at his heel.

'Thank God you're rid of him. You can't possibly have someone like him on your staff,' Pia said, watching him go.

'Strictly speaking, he's not on my staff,' Will muttered, scarcely able to believe the entire encounter had passed without fuller reference to Pia's fall in the lake. He walked back behind her wheelchair and started pushing it along the path, back towards the house.

'But it would be better if you didn't antagonize him, Pia. He's a rough sort. Tanner Ludgrove is nothing but trouble. He's not to be trusted at all.'

Chapter Twenty

'So, darling, let's see what you can do,' Evie growled in her throaty smoker's voice, her hennaed red hair and pallid white complexion ever-ready for Halloween. 'Come sit on this stool.'

She pulled a tall bar stool over to the mirror. Pia wheeled herself over and Evie hoisted her up onto it. It was so high that Pia was able to sit on it with her legs almost completely straightened on the ground. She was wearing black cropped leggings and a red racer-back leotard – the kind of thing someone might wear to a spinning class. It certainly wasn't what Pia considered to be ballet kit, but it was all she had here.

'Now, let's move through a *port de bras*. I want to see your arms and shoulders.'

'It's my foot that's broken, Evie,' Pia said, rolling her eyes. 'My arms are fine.'

'Not from where I'm sitting, sweetie. You look like you're going to snap.' She held Pia's upper arm between her fingers, like she'd picked up something nasty. She shook the thin arm lightly. 'Tch, how could you let this happen?'

She pressed a button on the remote and Delibes filtered through the room.

Pia sighed and placed her arms in first position.

Evie stood at the side watching her, all Pia's sinews and bones clearly visible through her thin skin. She hadn't had much fat on her to begin with, but this . . . well, she just looked ill.

Pia moved her arms through a sequence she'd known since she was twelve, the memory alone putting her limbs through their paces. Evie could see the rhomboid muscles on either side of her spine trembling as she kept her ribcage lifted – that meant her core strength was diminished for starters . . . and her right shoulder looked stiff in fifth . . . her elbow was dropping through *fourth* . . . She ran through twice.

'Okay, okay, enough. I can't bear to see any more.'

Pia frowned.

'Let's do some stretching at the *barre*. Stand on your good leg.'

Pia slid her bottom off the stool and stood on her left leg as Evie lifted her right foot and gently placed the cast over the *barre*, resting it directly against the mirror.

'How does that feel? Does it feel like it's going to slip off?'

Pia shook her head.

'Okay. Show me a *plié* and then a stretch towards your right leg.'

Pia turned out her left foot, stretched up through her spine, then bent her left leg deeply. She swore she could hear the bones creak as she swept down, rising back up and stretching over her waist to the dead leg on the *barre*. Five, six, seven times she repeated it, before the shaking in her thigh became too much.

'Okay, and stop,' Evie said, a pitying tone in her voice.

Pia sat back down on the stool, rubbing her thigh soothingly.

She knew what Evie was thinking. She herself hadn't realized how far she'd deteriorated. It had been only a few weeks since the accident but with the dramatic weight loss and prolonged confinement to bed, her muscles had wasted quickly.

'Well, it's not just your foot we have to treat, is it?' said Evie rhetorically.

Pia shook her head, staring down at the ground. 'I think we're too late, Evie.'

Evie narrowed her eyes in contemplation. She'd had absolutely no intention of coming back to work with Pia. No thank you. She'd been there and done that. She remembered only too clearly the precocious madam she'd had the misfortune of dealing with three years previously when Pia'd first come into the ChiCi as a *sujet*, straight from ballet school.

She'd thought she'd known it all then, strutting around in her ragged leotards, disregarding her superiors, ignoring etiquette, sleeping with all the boys who weren't sleeping with each other – in short, doing everything she wasn't supposed to – and *still* she had raced up the ranks to soloist and then principal dancer, in three short years.

She had never suffered any type of injury before – much less a career-threatening one – and Evie had expected that if anyone had the arrogance to assume she'd bounce straight back it would have been Pia Soto. She'd tripled her usual fee – which Silk's lawyers had gratefully accepted – regarding it as 'danger money' for the hassle of getting up close and personal with Pia Soto again. So who was *this* girl in front of her? All defeated and weak and compliant.

The lawyers had said she needed a 'maintenance' programme to keep her fitness up while her foot healed.

Well, Pia was right about one thing: they were too late for that.

'On the basis of what you've just shown me, you've lost about sixty per cent of your performance strength,' she said coolly, watching Pia's reaction.

Just as she thought. No surprise at all.

'If you were a car, I'd say you were a write-off.'

Pia nodded.

'You need completely rebuilding from the inside out,' Evie said, shrugging as though that was hardly possible. 'What am I – a miracle worker?'

There was a quick rap at the door, and Will peered in.

'How's it going?' he asked.

Evie looked over at Pia. 'Do you want to tell him or shall I?' she drawled.

Pia shrugged, indicating for Evie to do the talking. She wasn't sure she'd actually be able to get those words out. Write-off. Finished. Over.

'Well, she's a mess,' Evie said, like she was talking about a toddler's playroom. 'Thinks it's too late. Doesn't believe in herself. Weak. Surrendered. Pathetic. Basically everything she wasn't.'

Pia didn't protest. Will looked at her in alarm. She didn't dare meet his eyes.

'So that's where we are now,' Evie said laconically, nodding.

'Can you get her ready in time?' Will asked, a gleam of panic in his eyes.

'The gala's – what? End of April . . .' She sucked on her cheeks, before blowing out hard. 'Yes, I reckon I'll have her ready by then.'

Pia's head jerked up. Gala? She looked between Evie and Will.

Will leant against the door frame, one leg wedged up on the jamb.

'I thought I'd host a charity gala for your comeback,' he replied nonchalantly, but unable to keep a smile down. He'd been planning it almost since Rosen's prognosis and had been waiting for Evie's assessment before telling her. He had feared it would have to be cancelled after Baudrand's snub knocked the spirit out of her, but it was all for the best now. He'd got bigger and better lined up for Pia Soto.

'We're going to hold it here. I'm having a stage built on the lawns. And I'm inviting *everyone*. It's going to be the social ticket of the season.'

'But . . . but . . . but . . .' she blustered, panic all over her face. 'I'll never be ready in time.'

'Oh you will, sweetie, trust me,' Evie winked.

'Well . . . what am I supposed to be dancing?' she asked finally. This couldn't be happening. It was too soon.

'Why, *The Songbird*, of course.'

Pia gasped at the title of her own ballet. 'But how? Ava's dancing it.'

'Yes, with the ChiCi in the States. You're going to be dancing it over here.'

'But . . . I've no one to dance with.' Her mind was a blur. This didn't make sense.

'The Royal Ballet is dancing it with you.'

Pia gasped even harder.

'How did you manage that?' she whispered.

'Well, I've given them nearly six million pounds in the past five years. I figured I could call in a favour. Besides, the fund-raising side of the event is for them, and they're absolutely desperate to collaborate with you. Didn't I tell you so? And, just *entre nous*, I think they're hoping it might lead to something more permanent.' He walked towards her and held her hand in his. 'The English style suits you. And you'd be perfect for their repertoire – Ashton, Macmillan. In fact, Lord Everleigh is a good friend of mine . . . why don't I schedule a lunch, just something informal, see how you all get along?'

Pia shook her head. This was all happening too fast. 'But it's Milan I need . . .'

He dropped her hand, frustrated at her stubbornness. 'I don't see Milan showing any interest right now, do you, Pia? You might have to consider that maybe they don't want you.'

Tears sprang into her eyes.

His voice softened. 'Look, nothing's set in stone. You're just a guest artist for this. You're not going to be tied in to anything. And look at it this way – a collaboration with the Royal will at least show everyone else what you can do.'

Pia's mind was racing. She was feeling bulldozed, bullied.

She shook her head, still baffled. 'I don't understand why Baudrand would agree to let you use the ballet when he hasn't debuted it himself yet. It's going to be the highlight of the spring rep.'

Will put her hands in his. 'Well, strictly speaking, the copyright remains with Alvisio. Baudrand has got the rights for the American production. So I bought the European rights.'

'You did what?'

Will shrugged. 'You were right about Baudrand. I spoke to him. He doesn't think you're going to make it back.' He squeezed her hands tightly as she paled. 'Which is why I decided to use that against him. *I* know you're going to make it back; so does Evie and so does the Royal.' He took a deep breath, excited. 'So we're going head-to-head.'

Pia felt her blood chill. 'What do you mean?'

'Well, just imagine it,' he said, growing more animated by the second. 'The ChiCi going up against the Royal, you against Ava, both companies debuting the same ballet. On the same night. It's a dance-off!'

He started striding around the room, arms outstretched. 'The publicity is going to be huge! We're already collaborating with Ticketmaster to put together a tour package for people to see both productions. Virgin are offering us a discounted rate so that people can fly between Chicago and London and we've got a deal for first-class travel from Paddington to Sherborne. We've block-booked every five-star hotel in a fifteen-mile radius. The BBC is going to televise it – live! They're going to need to interview you of course – and there's going to be a public vote over the radio,' he said, not pausing for breath. 'I've got interviews lined up with every broadsheet on both sides of the Atlantic and we're going to whip everybody up with Tweets – you'll need to issue at least four a day, going up to hourly the day before the performance.'

Pia stared at him. Even just listening to him was exhausting. How long had he been planning this for? She'd not even known him a month.

Will clocked her expression and stopped pacing. He stood and faced her, hands on his hips. He was almost breathless. 'Don't you see? I've turned Baudrand's pessimism about you into your greatest advantage. It's *great* that he doesn't think you'll be ready in time. It's perfect! He's convinced you'll fail and that everybody will judge his production to be the winner. The ChiCi's celebrating its hundred-year anniversary this year so he's desperate for the coverage, and just imagine what it would do for the ChiCi's international profile to trump the Royal *and* you.' He shook his head, delightedly.

'But what if he *is* right?' Pia argued. This thought clearly hadn't crossed his mind at all. 'If his *is* better, my career will be over, Will – for good. It's too high a risk. I could never come back from such a high-profile failure as that.'

Will shrugged. 'But that's not going to happen. Is it, Evie?'

'Not on my watch, darling.' She handed Pia the pristine, as-yet undanced score. 'Here, you'd better start learning this.'

'But you just said I was broken . . . a write-off . . . that . . . that I need complete rebuilding.'

'And you do. But all the components are already there, sweetie. You know, I always say there are three steps to becoming a professional dancer, Pia: learning to dance, learning to perform and learning to cope with injury. This is your final lesson. I'm going to put you back together again, and by the time you get up on that stage you'll be ahead of Petrova in every way.' She grinned. 'You'll be even *better* than you were before.'

There was a long pause as Pia looked between them. 'Is that even possible?' she whispered.

Will burst out laughing, throwing his arms around her and squeezing her tightly. 'You see, Evie? What did I tell you? The old Pia's coming back to us already!'

Chapter Twenty-one

Tanner stood at the office window, the international dial tone beeping through the phone by his ear, his fingers winding themselves in the coiled wire. He watched Violet laughing with Rob by the stables. Matchstick, Will's black stallion, kept nodding his head between them, and they absent-mindedly patted his muzzle as they chatted.

Jessy was coming out of the tack room at the far end of the yard, holding a saddle and numnah over one arm and a set of reins slung over her shoulders as she went to saddle up Kermit, Will's bay hunter. It was her first day back today. Rob and Tanner had told everyone she'd come down with swine flu in Switzerland, and none of the rest of the stable crew were any the wiser.

They'd managed to keep the real story under wraps, and it was imperative the truth didn't get out. Tanner needed the yard and all its staff to have a pristine reputation if they were going to draw in a new big-money owner – nobody would touch them if there was even so much as the whiff of suggestion that drugs were being smuggled through with the horses at international events.

Tanner stared at the empty stalls. Even with Silk's patronage they had had nearly twenty stables going free, and if he didn't get a new client in before the polo season opened – the very week Silk's liveries were due to leave – they were likely to remain empty till the grass season closed in September. Nobody would risk unsettling the horses and their training regimes midway through the calendar, but even now, with a three-month lead time, it was a tight schedule to bring everything right. He couldn't deny things looked bleak, especially with Violet throwing it accusingly in his face every day. She was convinced he was running the yard into the ground.

He watched her stalk across to the sand school where one of the grooms, Ricky, was putting the new gelding through its paces. Violet's long legs were tantalizing in chocolate jodhpurs. He remembered the sight of her in those and nothing else as she was getting dressed that morning . . .

Dammit, she always distracted him. He turned away from the window, sitting on the ledge. He wasn't capitulating this time. She could go grovelling back to Silk over his dead body. That man manipulated everyone and everything around him. He'd conned Tanner's father out of their six-generation heritage and then acted as though giving his business to the yard was balm to the wound.

Everyone else may have bought the alliance, but for Tanner it had festered for four long years. He'd taken Silk's business because he'd had no choice. The yard was all that was left of his family's estate and fortune, and even that had almost folded. Neglected by the family as a money-making concern for so long it had been on its knees when he inherited it.

But they were back from the brink now. Silk's business had bought them some time and given them good exposure on the international scene, allowing Tanner to forge relationships while Silk was on the pitch and in the bar. He had the contacts. Now he just needed to convert one into a client.

The dial tone disconnected, unanswered, and Tanner looked at the shortlist of names on the notepad. If he could just make this happen, he knew it would be the break he needed.

The door opened and in burst Rob Butler. He was pulling off some rubber gloves that had bloody smears on them.

'Oh,' he said, seeing Tanner. 'I didn't realize you were in here. I'll come back.'

'No, it's fine. I'm finished,' Tanner said, putting the phone down.

They looked at each other for a moment. 'I was just going to put the kettle on. Fancy a tea?' Tanner asked.

Rob hesitated then shrugged. He'd barely said two words to Tanner since coming back and Tanner had felt the snub acutely. The two men had met at the Royal Agricultural College in Cirencester six years earlier and they'd formed an instant friendship. Five foot ten and slight, with a mop of muddy blond hair and an easy smile, he was Tanner's opposite and rock. Tanner had been studying for his Equine Business Management MBA, Rob for a postgraduate Applied Equine Science MSc, and when the latter pioneered non-surgical equine embryo transfer, Tanner had collared him into working with him in setting up a fledgling stud and bloodstock business. It was early days yet but, alongside the polo management, their successes had helped consolidate the growing reputation of the Ludgrove equine business.

'Jessy's looking well today,' Tanner began, his back to him as he put a tea bag in each cup.

'Yes.'

'Are you checking up on her?'

'Yes,' Rob said again.

Tanner turned and leant against the rickety pine table the old Tefal was sitting on.

'Look, I'm sorry, Rob,' he said awkwardly. 'I know that I put you in a very difficult situation.' He shrugged. 'I panicked. I didn't know it would get that bad with Jessy. Honestly, I didn't. I was just so worried about the police getting involved.'

'And the reputation of the yard,' Rob said bitterly.

There was a stiff silence. 'Yes, and that,' he replied, looking at his feet. 'I've been so desperate to get free from Silk that I put my reputation ahead of yours. I know you would have lost just as much as I would have done had the truth come out.' He sighed wearily. 'I cocked up. I should have just taken her to a hospital in the first place.'

Rob looked at him. Tanner's guilt was written all over his face. He was a proud man, obstinate, demanding, supercilious even. But he was also moral to a fault. He'd made the wrong call but for the right reasons. Rob knew exactly how much he was tortured by his ongoing alliance with Silk.

He shook his head and smiled. 'Let's just forget about it. It all turned out okay in the end.' Tanner passed him a cup of tea and he cracked a cheeky grin. 'In fact, it's turned out better for me than I might have hoped.'

Tanner looked up at him and Rob nodded. He'd been after Jessy for ages.

'It's amazing what saving a girl can do for your sex life,' he chuckled.

Tanner laughed. 'I'm really pleased for you, mate.' He paused. 'It just goes to show there are some girls out there who know how to be rescued. I didn't even get a thank you, much less a shag.'

Rob frowned. 'What – you mean . . .'

'In fact, all I got was a stream of abuse, can you believe? Consider yourself lucky,' he said, shaking his head.

'You should have left her there.'

'I'm considering throwing her back in actually,' Tanner drawled.

They laughed, and Tanner felt relieved that Rob had forgiven him at last. Rob was the only person he'd discuss his troubles at home with, and things were going from bad to worse with Violet, as she kept on at him about keeping Will's business at the yard. She seemed to have no understanding of the self-loathing the association left him with and he was beginning to wonder how well she really knew him at all. The only thing that seemed to keep them together was the sex, and that had kept them together for far too long already. They'd lived together for six years now, but her strength of character, which he'd so admired in their early years, had taken on a bossy, nagging hue and he was fed up with her always throwing her weight around. Where once he would have tolerated it for a quiet life, now he was pitching himself against her in almost every discussion. He was scared he was beginning to hate her, but in his heart he already knew the answer: Silk's wasn't the only relationship he needed to bring to an end.

Chapter Twenty-two

Violet leant back in her chair and watched as her friends Kit and Minky did the conga, flashing their knickers and white thighs at the delighted and equally drunk men in front of them. The hunt ball, held in the Duke of Lamington's ballroom, had been going on for three hours now. Dinner was over, the annual bread fight dispensed with, and everyone was getting down to the serious business of necking their wine, and then each other. It appeared everyone was having a good time apart from her.

Tanner was on the other side of the ballroom, deep in conversation with Rob and his chief groom Ricky. Apart from squiring her on the way in, he'd barely said more than a sentence to her all night and she knew he was in one of his low-grade sulks with her for banging on about Will.

She watched as Jessy – trussed up in a one-shouldered pink tube dress that looked ineffably cheap – skittered up to Rob. His eyes glittered at the sight of her trembling bosom and he squeezed her bottom lustily. He clearly didn't share Violet's opinion that she looked like a sausage. She wondered how long they'd been together. From the looks of things, they were still in the first randy flush.

Violet looked hatefully at Jessy. She knew perfectly well that Jessy had had an affair with Tanner just before she had come onto the scene and, though she'd never had any evidence of it continuing, she was convinced Jessy had been in love with him. Tanner seemed unconcerned by the new relationship though, laughing uproariously with Rob and telling stupid jokes. She looked away. She couldn't put a finger on why but she felt inched out by the little group.

A well-built brunette with an ample bust and tiny ankles flopped down on the chair next to her. 'I am whacked!' she gasped, grabbing a glass – any glass – off the table. 'God, I thought I was fitter than that,' she wheezed.

Violet smiled. 'The conga's not easy to do at the best of times, Minky, much less drunk and in those shoes,' she said, looking down at her friend's vertiginous midnight-blue velvet Miu Miu heels. They had to be at least five inches high.

Minky groaned. She'd already twisted her ankle, but she wore them so that she stood at nearly the same height as Violet – otherwise she came up only to her armpits and Violet hogged all the men. Not tonight, though. She seemed strangely subdued.

'Everything okay, Vi?' she asked, crossing her skinny legs and swinging them temptingly. 'You seem quiet tonight.'

Violet shrugged. 'Tanner's being a bit off. I've annoyed him.'

'What about?'

'Oh he's kicking out Will's horses. Says he wants nothing more to do with him,' she said, rolling her eyes. 'Only he doesn't seem to have thought about what's actually going to happen once the stables are empty. You know what he's like – so bloody stubborn!'

'That I do,' Minky muttered. He'd rebuffed every single one of her advances over the years. 'But I can't say it's a surprise. Everyone knows there's no love lost between those two.'

'No. But they've managed to make it work for the past four years – just. I don't see why it should all suddenly become *so* untenable.'

Minky didn't say anything. She was watching Tanner. He was looking imposing in his dinner suit and laughing easily. He didn't seem especially angst-ridden.

'You know what's happened of course, don't you?' Violet continued. 'Tanner's shot his mouth off and backed himself into a corner and now he can't see how to get out of it without losing face. He'd rather let the yard go under than look a fool.' She shook her head wearily.

A sudden shriek caught their attention and they watched Kit try to jiggle some ice cubes back out of her dress.

'So why don't you sort it out, then?' Minky said. 'Go and talk to Will yourself.'

Violet looked at her. 'What do you mean?'

'Well, if Tanner's only getting rid of Will to make a point, you can step in as the voice of reason. You two are as good as married anyway so Will will listen to you, and Tanner will be grateful to you for sorting it out for him.'

Violet lounged back in the chair and considered the idea. Minky was all bust and no brain, but she'd hit on something this time.

'Hmm, you could be right,' Violet said. It might be just the thing to put them back on track again. Tanner'd got himself so wound up about Silk's deception again recently that he seemed to have lost sight of the fact that they'd managed to settle into a truce, albeit an uneasy one.

'Well, talk of the devil!' Minky said, sitting up excitedly.

'Look who's just walked in. I've been waiting for this all night.'

Violet looked round and saw Will come through the doorway, dashing in his dinner suit as he helped Pia hobble in on her new weight-bearing cast.

Violet's eyes narrowed at the sight of her. She hadn't seen Pia since the day she'd left her stranded on the loo. Pia had nearly drowned the next morning and Will had wasted no time in sending her an email that evening to relieve her of all her further duties.

From across the room, Violet could see she had made progress. She appeared to have built up some muscle mass again and her movements looked clean and fluid, not at all jerky. She handed Will her crutch as she sat down daintily on a gold chair someone had brought forward for her, and he took it gratefully. Violet felt her stomach twist at the sight of Will's obsequiousness. He was so rarely around – the locals saw more of him in the society pages of *Harper's Bazaar* than in the village – and if he was to be seen, it was ostentatiously in his Aston or the helicopter, a sleek blonde on his lap. It was just the kind of behaviour you wanted from the local millionaire. Yet here he was, chumming it up with the duke and playing the dutiful husband to that brat. Violet felt disappointed that he'd been so easily tamed.

'God, she's gorgeous,' Minky moaned at the sight of Pia in a black Balenciaga dress, her hair twisted low at the front. 'And she's got even better ankles than me.'

'Well, she hasn't got your charm, Minks, that's for sure.'

'Hrrmph, like that counts for anything. No one's there for her scintillating conversation, are they? Silk least of all,' she added knowingly.

Violet bristled. She'd always known that Will's eyes

followed her whenever she passed; that he'd only never made a pass at her because his relationship with Tanner was already volatile enough – and it served him too well to have his horses stabled next door, rather than ten miles away or in the next county.

'Come on, let's dance,' Violet said, suddenly animated.

Minky inwardly groaned. Flashing her legs with Kit was one thing. But dancing with Violet was like dancing with Madonna. She'd look like a garden gnome by comparison.

Pia caught sight of her as the throng of fans clamouring for her autograph began to ebb. She felt exhausted already, her foot aching in the newly fitted weight-bearing cast. Will had persuaded her to come to this tonight, saying that most of the villagers would be present and he wanted to take the opportunity to announce the gala to everyone. But Pia privately wondered whether he was just taking the opportunity to show her off. Ever since news of their supposed affair had broken, people had been watching and waiting for sightings of the two of them together, and when – thanks first to her depression, and latterly to her packed physiotherapy schedule – that hadn't happened, whispers began to spread. Perhaps they weren't together, after all? It had been a surprise to find a couple of paparazzi outside the duke's gates, pressing their cameras to the car's windows, and she knew they had to have been tipped off.

She inwardly groaned that they'd caught her coming into this, of all things. It was hardly the Met Institute Gala. She'd managed to get out of coming to the dinner, quoting Evie's rigid rest schedule at Will, but a local hunt ball, for heaven's sake. It seemed so . . . bourgeois.

She looked up at Will and watched as he played the role of protector to a tee, one hand on her shoulder as he answered questions about her recovery, extrapolating on the upcoming gala. The last time she'd been to a party they'd been warring with each other in a prelude to seduction, and yet now the two of them seemed so . . . domestic. She would never have believed she was capable of this dynamic just four short weeks ago.

So much had changed for her: her freedom had been taken away; her God-given ability to dance was now not a given but a question; Will was not a passionate lover but somehow peculiarly central in her life . . . She was trying her hardest to accept her changed circumstances, but her instincts gave her no peace. The whole dance-off idea filled her with dread. She knew Will was doing his best to give her a goal to work towards, and a shot at revenge on her naysayers, but all she really wanted was to just get through it and go back to her day job.

She watched Violet shimmy on the dance floor in a strapless yellow silk dress, a magnetic pulse gradually pulling all the men's eyes to her. All except Tanner's, she noticed.

Pia hadn't made the connection about his relationship with Violet immediately. When she'd first met him by the woods he was just the redneck who'd roughed up Will. Only later, lying in bed, had she remembered Violet calling his name, just seconds before she'd abandoned her. They seemed well suited of course, each as arrogant and abrasive as the other.

She looked around at the ballroom. It wasn't much less ostentatious than the theatre halls she was used to performing in – same baroque gilding on the ceiling, same ornate panelling on the walls. Only the velvet curtain and tiered seats were absent. She watched the revellers dancing badly and wished she could get up and sweep across the floor in a chain of *piqué* turns – use it in the way it was supposed to be used, rather than this drunken horsey set littering it with plump limbs and boorish voices.

Just then, a bugle started blowing and suddenly all the men got up and began arranging themselves in a chaotic line against the far wall. The DJ stopped playing.

'What's going on?' Pia asked Will.

'God, I forgot about this,' he whispered, as a man went around the room brandishing a helmet filled with scraps of paper. 'They hold a pony race. It's a charity thing.'

'What? They're bringing the ponies in here?' Pia gasped, looking at the beautiful parquet. 'But they can't! They'll destroy the floor.'

Will shook his head, laughing. 'No, no. There're no real ponies involved. The men are the mounts; the women are the riders. The men's names are put into a hat and then the women each draw a name at random, until everyone makes up a team. The teams get written up on that board over there,' he said pointing to a white board, which was being covered with scrawl.

'And then what?' Pia asked, amused. What the English did to entertain themselves!

'Then you climb onto your pony's back, the horn sounds and we all have a race through the house. First back gets to nominate the charity that they want the money raised tonight to go to.' He shrugged. 'It's a bit of fun.'

The man reached her and shook the riding helmet at Pia. She looked up at him blankly.

'No,' she said politely, shaking her head and lifting her injured leg. 'I don't think so.'

A murmur of disappointment and a few 'boos' rumbled through the room.

'I can't, really,' she said, astonished by the reaction. They didn't honestly think that she – Pia Soto – would be seen dead participating in anything as ridiculous as this, did they? Broken foot or not. 'I have to protect my foot.'

'Sure you can,' she heard a woman call. She looked up and saw Violet smiling at her, one hand on a narrow hip. 'Nothing's going to happen to it with the cast on. It's as safe as houses with that plaster. Besides, we're all far too worried about the Mings to get too carried away.'

'Yeah! Come on!' voices in the crowd shouted. 'Be a sport! It'll throw the numbers out.'

Pia looked at Will helplessly. He just shrugged. 'I guess the plaster is very thick.'

'Fine,' she said quietly, unable to see any way out of it. She drew a piece of paper from the hat and handed it back to the man.

A buzz of excitement crescendoed around the crowd while they waited for him to open it – the husbands eager, their wives distraught, to discover which man would have Pia Soto riding on his back.

Pia looked up at Will. 'Thanks for the support,' she muttered. 'I can't believe you're letting me be put through this. Honestly, if I'd known for one second that this was what—'

'It's good fun,' Will interrupted. 'And it's for a good cause.'

'Pia Soto and Tanner Ludgrove!' the man called out to the room and a big cheer went up, with Tanner being patted on the back like a decorated war hero. Pia noticed Tanner himself didn't look best pleased about it and it was hard to tell whose face was darker – his or Violet's.

Pia looked up at Will, aghast. 'Oh God, I don't believe it.'

'Don't worry,' he said, squeezing her shoulder but looking grim. 'I'll get them to change it.'

But they were too late.

'Minky de Lisle and William Silk,' the man bellowed across the room.

'Oh great! It just gets better,' he muttered, as Minky shrieked and ran towards him, arms outstretched. 'I'll hardly make pole position with her great weight to cart about.' She descended in a cloud of Arpège. 'Minky, darling,' he purred, kissing her cheeks.

'I have just the spot reserved for us,' she breathed. 'We can't fail to win from there,' she said, pulling him away.

Everyone began to line up in pairs.

Tanner, realizing he couldn't expect Pia to hobble over to him, sloped over like a sulky schoolboy. It really was too much being coerced into this kind of . . . horseplay, just for the sake of charity.

He looked down at her. 'We meet again. I wonder if it'll be as much pleasure as last time,' he drawled sarcastically.

Pia narrowed her eyes. 'Can't they just take a cheque?' she sneered.

'Trust me, I've already asked.'

Pia sniffed huffily.

'Shall we get this over and done with, then?' he asked, shrugging off his jacket and tossing it onto a chair.

'You'd better mind my foot,' she warned.

'You'd better mind your manners,' he warned back, kneeling down with his back in front of her. Pia looked at his broad shoulders. She wasn't sure she'd get round him.

She shuffled to the front of her chair, easing her dress up

her thighs. Slowly she reached her arms up over his shoulders and she felt his hands on her bottom, pushing her up his back.

'Watch where you put your hands!' she snapped.

'Oh don't flatter yourself,' he muttered, walking her across the room and finding a space in the line-up. Will and Minky were four along to their left; Violet and Rob another two. Violet was draping her papaya-scented hair over Rob's face like a forelock, and he was blowing it up and off, hilariously. Jessy, down at the end on the right on Ricky's back, wasn't looking happy about it.

'Can you squeeze me a bit tighter?' Tanner said, turning his face up to Pia. 'Then I can hold your cast across me, rather than letting it flop about loosely.'

Pia tightened her thighs wickedly and Tanner felt his blood pressure drop. Christ, she had some power in those tiny limbs. She was like a boa constrictor. She was nowhere near as delicate as she looked.

'All right, that's enough,' he said, and he heard her chuckle in his ear.

The duke, who was far too old to take part himself any more but had been considered the one to beat in his salad days, picked up the bugle and the men braced themselves, ready for the off.

The horn blew and suddenly everyone burst forward like a gaggle of geese, the women laughing and shrieking and pretending to whip their ponies as the ridiculous spectacle picked up pace.

The leaders pulled away from the rest of the pack very quickly as some riders lost their shoes, or the effects of all the drink made a rising trot suddenly inadvisable.

Tanner had an easy lead. He could scarcely feel Pia's weight and she was able to hold herself high up his back, rather than sagging down like a sack of Marfonas. He felt her tightening her legs around him, squeezing him onwards, as they raced through the hall into the library. All the reading tables and Louis Quinze chairs had been pushed back to create a long corridor and Tanner charged down it, hotly pursued by Rob and Will, who – in spite of the considerable weight disadvantage – was rallying round. He wasn't going to let Tanner win, not with *his* girlfriend on his back.

Tanner got to the end first, taking the corner in a hopping fashion on one leg to avoid slowing too early and letting them catch up. He didn't need to turn around to see where they were. He could hear Minky shrieking behind him excitedly and Violet bossily ordering Rob about like some S&M mistress.

Pia said nothing. He could just feel her breathing, rapidly, in his ear and Tanner understood that, although she might consider this beneath her, when it came to competition – of any kind – she competed to win.

They dashed out of the library and into the salon. Here, the *chaises* had been set up like an obstacle course, forcing Tanner to swerve left then right, negotiating the turns tightly. He saw that Will had caught them up and was right on his tail, no doubt encouraged into acceleration by the excitement of having Minky's enormous knockers bouncing up around his ears.

Tanner put his head down like any good stallion on the gallop. He'd won this every year for three years on the trot. He knew this course. They had to go back into the hall next, up the stairs, around the galleried landing once, through the pink bedroom, then along the corridor and down the staff staircase. He'd need to pull away going up the stairs.

They came out of the salon and Will was right beside him; Rob was two lengths behind.

Pia looked across at Minky, who looked like she was going to give Will a hernia and herself a black eye.

'*Hiiieeeee!*' she called over excitedly, ecstatic to be sharing airspace and eye contact with Pia Soto.

'Hold on,' Tanner said to Pia, holding her legs even tighter, and he started bounding up the wide shallow steps, two at a time. Will tried to match him. He was fit but he couldn't keep that type of energy output going when he was carrying twice the weight.

He dropped back and Rob overtook him, too scared not to as Violet giddied him up between her legs. Tanner circled the landing, and Pia suddenly burst out laughing as she caught sight of the two of them in the massive brass-edged mirrors. If she hadn't been able to envisage herself in a 'domestic' set-up, she had certainly never even conceived of this! It was more fun than she'd had in years.

Tanner laughed too, her sudden smile dazzling him, and it slowed him down as he got to the door of the pink bedroom. Rob was just a length behind. He opened the door as they drew level and the two men charged through with war cries, like little boys playing soldiers, startling a couple who were bonking wildly on the historic bed.

The two men laughed even harder, losing valuable speed, but Pia and Violet just glared at each other.

'Ready to lose again?' Violet asked Pia, before whacking Rob hard on the bottom. He let out a yowl of pain and accelerated away instinctively.

'Hey!' Tanner cried, following him out of the far door,

just as Will and Minky entered the room by the first. The couple on the bed dived under the covers as the main body of the race followed, busting their illicit assignation once and for all.

Rob clattered down the corridor with Violet issuing her battle cries like Boadicea. There was just the staff staircase now, and then the finishing line back in the ballroom. Tanner put on a final burst of speed. He caught up with Rob at the top of the stairs, overtook him at the bottom, racing into the ballroom first.

The duke was standing there, drinking the better-quality brandy he hid from his guests in his hipflask. 'By jove, that was quick!' he exclaimed at the sight of Rob and Violet, and Tanner and Pia cantering towards him. Both men were pink in the cheeks now, their hair flopping over their faces.

'Come on, Rob! Come on!' Violet screamed. 'We can do it. Come on! Let's beat the bitch! Beat her!'

The duke's jaw dropped and Rob pulled up to a sudden halt, stunned by what she'd just said. 'It's for charity,' he said, straightening up so that Violet slid off his back, a look of disgust on his face. 'It's supposed to be good-natured, Vi,' he said.

Will and Minky raced past them, but it was too late. Tanner and Pia had already passed the finish line.

A stiff silence fell upon the podium winners as the rest of the racers barged down the stairs and burst into the ballroom, laughing and screaming and shrieking with hilarity.

Pia slid slowly down Tanner's back, landing gracefully on her left foot. She held on to the back of a chair, keeping her right leg bent at the knee.

'You okay?' Tanner asked, and it wasn't clear if he was referring to her foot or his girlfriend's barbed comments.

Pia nodded. She felt deflated. She'd actually been having such fun until then. The duke blew on the bugle again and the room fell silent.

'I declare the winners of the race – by a furlong – to be Pia Soto and her steed, Tanner Ludgrove.'

A cheer and various wolf whistles went around the room. The duke fished a piece of paper from his pocket and scanned it, then announced that the total amount raised from the night was £18,763. Another cheer erupted. A hunt record. Will's promise to bring Pia tonight meant they'd had to reissue tickets twice to keep up with demand. 'Which charity are you going to give it to?' the duke asked.

Tanner shrugged magnanimously and looked at Pia. 'You choose.'

'Um, well . . .' she hesitated, amazed by his manners. In spite of what Will had said about him, he didn't seem rough. 'Are you sure?'

Tanner nodded.

She shrugged happily and turned to face everyone in the room. 'Well, then I'd really like it to go to Criancas de Rua Abandonadas do Brasil.' She beamed.

The duke looked confused and put his hand to his ear to adjust his hearing aid. 'What did she say?' he shouted.

'It's a charity that gives homes and shelter to street children in Brazil,' Pia explained, looking out over the expectant, somewhat baffled, crowd. 'They were set up in 1992 and they run a number of homes – some for children under six, another one is for pregnant teenage girls and their babies, and they've even got an outreach programme for children still living or working on the streets . . .' She nodded enthusiastically at the sea of blank faces.

There was a heavy silence.

Tanner gave a small, awkward cough. 'Um, well, generally speaking, we try to give the money to a local cause. Like the school, say – it needs a new roof, for example.'

Violet chuckled at Pia's worldly beneficence, sending a titter of amusement scattering through the guests like a Mexican wave. 'Get *her*,' she said sarcastically.

Pia glared at her, then back at Tanner, feeling humiliated and belittled. 'Well, you never specified that,' she hissed, feeling herself colour. 'You said choose a charity, so I chose a charity. It's not my fault if you're . . . you're small-minded and provincial.'

The tittering stopped suddenly, replaced with a collective gasp, and this time Tanner coloured. Pia bit her lip as she felt the mood in the room change against her.

'Oh give it to whoever you want, then,' she said dismissively, anxious to get out of there. 'It's small fry anyway. I spend more than that on my dry-cleaning,' she said defiantly, her chin in the air. 'Will, take me home now. My foot's aching.'

Will smiled apologetically, embarrassed to leave under a cloud like this, but he took her arm and led her slowly away, the crowd parting for them with tangible disdain, the knocking of her cast on the parquet rebounding against their turgid silence.

Chapter Twenty-three

Adam walked over to his kitbag and grabbed his water bottle, draining it angrily. He wasn't thirsty. He just needed some time out. Sophie watched him anxiously. He looked ready to explode.

'Let's try it again, shall we?' Ava said, sounding more like the artistic director than the artist. 'You need to step in to me a beat sooner.'

Adam flung the bottle into the bag and walked back to her. He stood behind her and put his hands lightly on her waist. She was wearing a white leotard, seamed white tights and a practice tutu. The stiff white tulle flexed up against his torso.

'Too close,' she snapped. 'Take a step back.'

Adam took a half step back.

'More,' she ordered. 'I want you to stand back far enough that you don't disrupt the line of the skirt. It looks better.'

'It looks better that you do fourteen *pirouettes* instead of just ten. Get the tutu trimmed if it's so important,' he said. 'My arms aren't long enough to stand that far back and still be able to support you.'

'I don't need your support. You just need to *look* like you're doing something.'

Adam stared at her mutinously. It was a goddam supported *pirouette*; there absolutely was a point in him being there. She couldn't possibly get up to fourteen *pirouettes* without his help, but the experience of the past few weeks had taught him that there was little point in appealing to Baudrand. He took the step back, barely getting his fingertips onto her waist.

The piano started up and Ava rose onto *pointe*.

Come on, Sophie willed him silently. Get her round. Don't give her any ammunition.

Ava began to spin, but with his touch so feather-light she lost speed quickly. Her balance faltered from the strain of trying to turn without momentum and she fell out of the position on the ninth *pirouette*.

'For God's sake,' she hissed, her eyes flashing dangerously. 'Can you do nothing right? I'm the one doing the hard work. All you have to do is stand there and help me turn. Is it so much to ask?'

She walked away, hands on hips, shaking her head. She stopped and looked at Baudrand.

'This isn't working,' she said categorically. 'He's not up to it. He argues with all my suggestions. It's clear he doesn't want to dance with me. He only knows how to dance with Pia. Do you know what I think, *monsieur*?'

Baudrand shook his head.

'I think he resents me for replacing her and he's trying to undermine my performance with mediocrity.'

'That is not true – any of it!' Adam said, shaking his head. 'I've gone out of my way to adapt to your style, but what you're asking just isn't practical.'

'Practical?' Ava said, raising her eyebrows and looking at Baudrand again. 'You see what I'm saying? *We're* trying to create art and he's trying to be practical. Like this is some kind of science experiment.' She looked back at Adam. 'What we're trying to achieve out there is perfection,' she said patronizingly. 'It's not supposed to be easy and it's got to look faultless. You bunching up my tutu doesn't give any purity of line and being *practical* about things is hardly going to make the audience gasp in wonder, now is it?'

Adam glared at her. It was useless trying to argue. She twisted everything against him and since the press conference when Baudrand had announced that the ChiCi was going head-to-head with the Royal and Pia, her tension levels had ratcheted up. Adam couldn't bear it much longer. He was spending every morning in class, every afternoon in rehearsal and every evening either in performance or in the gym. He scarcely had enough time to eat and he only rested overnight before beginning again the next morning. He was exhausted. He didn't see what more he could do. She was determined to get rid of him.

Sophie registered the defeat that came and sat upon Adam's shoulders. He looked pale. She'd not seen him anywhere other than the studio since they'd come back from New York and she had got the message loud and clear that what had happened between them had been a one-time thing.

Baudrand sat quietly for a moment, contemplating Adam's future. 'It's clear that the chemistry between you both isn't working,' he said finally. 'And that's damaging to the chore-ography. There's only just over a month to go till curtain-up and the way things are going I don't think the audience are going to believe in your need and hunger for each other.' He looked at his fingers. 'On the other hand, I'm not convinced José's going to be a better option for you, Ava.'

Adam's eyes widened, as Ava's narrowed. They both knew she'd expected an immediate capitulation. She'd been paving the way for this for weeks.

'We need a good jumper for the male part, Ava, and José's forte is in his turns.' He held out his hands appeasingly. 'I shall consider the matter carefully over the next few days and look at the performance schedules. I'll come back to you both with an answer by the end of the week.'

Sophie looked at Adam but he had already turned and was packing his kitbag. Without a word or look to any of them, he picked it up and left the studio.

'Hey, Sophie! Wait up!'

Sophie rolled her eyes before she turned. The words – so American high school – sounded odd with a Russian accent. Ava had become quite the all-American girl in the past few weeks, acquiring a transatlantic twang and falling into a habit of bringing a tray of Krispy Kreme doughnuts into the studios each morning. But the gift wasn't received in the spirit in which Ava claimed it had been given, and the other girls kept complaining she was trying to make them all put on weight. It had been noticed Ava never touched them herself, and Sophie ended up munching most of them.

Ava was running lightly down the corridor towards her, her hair tied back in its signature bun. She had changed into narrow 7/8th jeans and a black polo neck jumper, and a delicate tennis bracelet glittered around her wrist. She had been unveiled as a new ambassador for Cartier just the week before and was now never seen without at least ten carats hanging off her.

'What's up?' Sophie asked, trying to smile. She was feeling

dejected about Adam's prospects. It wasn't his fault, or even Ava's necessarily. As Baudrand had said, the chemistry just wasn't there.

'How about lunch? My treat,' Ava smiled, all sweetness now the tutus were off.

Sophie shook her head. 'Sorry, I can't,' she said, indicating the thick sheaf of paper under her arm. 'I've got to get back to the studio and get the details from these drawings onto the oils. I'm falling behind and the exhibition's only a few weeks away.'

Ava's face fell. 'Oh.'

'Why? What's wrong?'

'It's my birthday today,' she shrugged.

'Your birthday? Oh Ava!' she exclaimed, leaning down to give her a hug. 'Why didn't you tell me? I haven't got you anything.' Sophie whizzed through her schedule in her head. She guessed she could spare the time for lunch. 'Of course we must go out – but it'll be my treat. No buts.' She wagged a warning finger.

Ava smiled and they walked out together, looking comically mismatched in height. Sophie rolled herself down to hear Ava as they talked, as she'd become used to doing. They walked past the famous Picasso sculpture outside the Daley Center (Sophie still couldn't decide if it was an angel, woman or horse) and across to Michigan Avenue. It was a bright day but the wind was still bitterly cold as it whistled between the skyscrapers. They dodged the besuited office workers with agile ease as they headed automatically for Porto Bello, off Randolph, near the park. They'd been there several times together now since that first bonding meal, and it had become their favourite place for lunch. They didn't need to book – the maître d' always gave Ava the chef's table.

The friendship had moved fast and they quite regularly hung out after rehearsal, going for dinner or catching a film together. It had stopped Sophie from brooding over Adam's below-radar disappearance, even if she noticed that a lot of the other dancers she'd once been friendly with seemed to have taken a step back from her. Still, she'd had a big promotion since Pia's accident and Ava treated her as an equal now. They were bound to feel more intimidated.

'Ooh! Look at those,' Sophie trilled, catching sight of a pair of shoes in a window. They were red silk with an extravagant rose across the front. 'They're beautiful.'

Ava looked at her and smiled. 'Let's go in and try them on, then.'

'Oh no!' Sophie demurred. They were on the 'magnificent mile', the most exclusive shopping street in Chicago. 'I don't think so. Not with the price tags round here.'

Ava disregarded her protests and pushed the door open. Sophie sighed and followed her into the perfectly climate-controlled boutique. The walls were mushroom-coloured and the deep-pile carpet muffled all sound, like snow.

'My friend and I would like to try on the red rose shoes in the window,' Ava said, sending an assistant scurrying away to a back room.

She came back a few moments later with the shoes nestled in their boxes in pink tissue paper.

'They're exquisite,' Sophie exclaimed, cooing over them like they were the baby Jesus in a manger.

She slipped her feet into her size-seven pair – Ava's looked like children's shoes by comparison – and they were a perfect fit. She twisted her foot first one way then the other, checking the profile from the side, then behind, the shape of her instep, the curve of the heel . . .

'See what you've done now?' she said sardonically to Ava. 'You've made me love them!' She looked up at the assistant reluctantly. 'Give me the bad news! How much are they?'

'Four—'

'It's irrelevant,' Ava said, cutting in. 'You're having them anyway. I'm getting them for you.'

Sophie gasped. 'No, Ava! I can't possibly let you—'

'You have to. It's my birthday.'

'Precisely. I should be getting them for you. I've not even got you a card yet.'

Ava put the shoes back in the boxes and handed them to the assistant. 'Ring them up, please.' She looked back at Sophie. 'Let me. I want to. You're my only friend here, the only person who's shown me any kindness. Everyone else hates me and I don't know what I would have done without you these past few weeks.'

Sophie smiled, touched by the recognition of their friendship – Pia had barely ever acknowledged her presence. It felt good. There was balance in this relationship. They both drew something from it, not least a solace from being foreigners together in a big city.

She watched as Ava signed a couple of autographs for some ten-year-old girls, and an idea suddenly came to her. If she and Ava really were such good friends, could she – dare she – use their friendship to make a more direct plea? If she could get Ava to try to see how hard Adam was trying to make their partnership work . . . His neck was on the chopping block now, awaiting Baudrand's verdict, and Sophie had no doubt that if he was dropped from *The Songbird* production he'd leave the company. His pride wouldn't allow him to stay and the thought of that was more than she could bear. She may not be sleeping in his bed, but at least she got to drink him in during rehearsals. It went against her instincts to lay herself down on the line, but the very idea of not seeing him every day appalled her. Maybe, if she told Ava how she felt about him, Ava would try harder to make it work, for *her* sake.

They walked out of the boutique with the matching glossy shell-pink carrier bags tied with exuberant black bows. Pia would never have done this, she thought, as they swung them along, arms linked.

Porto Bello's was so busy that for other patrons there was a forty-minute wait at the bar, but they were ushered to their usual table immediately. They arranged the bags by their feet as their customary bottle of champagne was opened.

Sophie gulped down her first glass. She felt nervous at the prospect of opening up, but she had to help Adam. She couldn't let him be kicked out.

'Are you okay?' Ava asked, noticing her pinched cheeks.

Sophie took a deep breath. 'Well, actually . . . there is something I wanted to talk to you about,' she began.

Ava smiled, resting her elbows on the table. 'Oh yes?' she said, interested.

'It's about Adam . . .'

Chapter Twenty-four

Pia popped her head round the kitchen door and smiled. *The Archers* was on at full blast and Mrs Bremar was standing beside the window, basting the chicken.

Pia watched her for a minute. The Sunday Roast was an English tradition faithfully observed in the manor house, and Pia had fallen in love with it readily. This house was beautiful and impressive, but it was also cold and too quiet. Only the kitchen, which was out of Will's domain, had any warmth or spirit, Mrs Bremar bustling about it with a homely mirth, and Pia had fallen into the habit of passing time in there with her. It had given her the closest feeling she'd had to a sense of home in years.

She had grown increasingly fond of the older woman as the weeks had worn on. Mrs Bremar always had a bath drawn and the towels warmed when Pia came back, sweaty and exhausted, from her long days in the studio with Evie; she had managed to get hold of a recipe for Pia's favourite dish – *moqueca de camarao* – and insisted on serving it up once a week, despite the fact that Will said it looked like 'a parked cat' and he'd rather eat a Pot Noodle.

Besides, he was rarely around, confident that the gala meant Pia wouldn't cut and run as soon as his back was turned. And he was right – Pia wouldn't have had the energy to leave, even if she'd wanted to. Evie was working her hard, the morning physio sessions getting longer and more strenuous each day, and she was always sent back up to the house with strict instructions to do 'absolutely nothing' in the afternoons.

Pia, who was never good with just her own company and unaccustomed to prolonged rest periods, had started reading prolifically, often burning through a book a day, and she was fast becoming expert at the Sudoku section in the daily papers. But more than anything, she had found she enjoyed sitting in the kitchen, her hands clasped around a steaming mug of black coffee, while Mrs Bremar chopped and cooked and cleaned, and chatted about Ireland.

Pia was rapt. Ireland sounded so different to her own homeland, and yet it held a particular fascination for her: it belonged to her too. Her father was Irish, and before the drink had almost entirely soaked him he had shared a few memories about how his mother would hang the meat in the chimney to smoke it, and the time he'd thrown his school bag in the field with the bull and his mother had made him go in to get it . . .

Her green eyes were the only testament to her heritage there – or indeed her relationship with her father – and she made a point of keeping quiet about it in interviews. She made sure her entire persona was built around her Brazilian nationality – her shape, her passion, her temper, her training, her name – and she would never allow him any opportunity to share in her limelight, not after what he'd done and what it had led to.

She hated him with murderous intensity, and yet she was irresistibly drawn to Ireland and the Irish. The cruel irony never failed to astonish her. It was no coincidence that she'd hired Sophie. She was clumsy, perpetually late and her coffees were terrible. But she had a beautiful Irish brogue that several years in London had done nothing to temper, and when she'd turned up for the interview she'd had Pia, quite literally, at 'Hello'.

'Hi, B,' she smiled, hobbling into the kitchen.

'Oh Pia, I was just about to put the kettle on,' Mrs Bremar smiled, putting down the spoons and wiping her hands on her apron.

'I'll do it,' Pia said, filling it up and getting the cups out. Mrs Bremar opened the oven door and slid the chicken back into the range. Pia hopped onto a bar stool, her legs dangling daintily in black footless tights and one white leather ballet shoe. She had thrown on a yellow bandeau bikini and her hair was pulled back – unbrushed as usual – into a messy bun. Mrs Bremar flicked her eyes up and smiled adoringly at today's ensemble. She didn't 'get' Pia's dance get-ups, but she still thought she looked exquisite. A peach of a girl.

'That was a short session. Are you going back down again today?' she asked, as Pia unpeeled a banana.

Pia shrugged. 'No. Evie says I'm to stay out of the studio for the rest of the day. It is Sunday. It's supposed to be a day of rest, after all.' She took a huge bite. 'What time's Will coming back?' she asked, barely comprehensible with her mouth full.

Mrs Bremar tipped her head to the side and pursed her lips. 'You'll not eat your lunch if you fill up on that,' she tutted, matron-like. She looked suspiciously at Pia's frame, which, even though she was curled forward and bursting out of her top, registered barely a ripple on her bare stomach.

God knows, she could do with feeding up. She glanced at the clock. 'They should be back by two.'

Damn. That was another three hours yet, and Pia felt bored and restless. She handed Mrs Bremar the tea – strong and sweet, the way they both liked it – and pondered.

'I think I'll go into the village, then.'

'The village? What d'you want to go there for?' the older woman asked, unfolding an ironing board.

Pia shrugged. 'Why not? I've been here – what, six weeks? – and I've not been there yet,' Pia said. 'In fact, the only time I've left the estate has been to go to hospital and that horrid ball.' She shook her head, amazed that she – the renowned international globetrotter – had endured such a confinement.

'I don't know, Pia,' Mrs Bremar said, a note of concern in her voice. 'Mr Silk won't be happy about it.'

'Well, what's it got to do with him, whether I go to the village or not?' Pia demanded petulantly. 'He's not my jailer. I can come or go as I please. I'll go to India tomorrow if I fancy it.'

Mrs Bremar's eyebrows shot up as she filled the iron with rosewater.

'Which I don't,' she grinned.

The housekeeper chuckled. 'Well, how are you going to get into town? It's not like you can drive,' she said, jerking her chin towards Pia's cast. She grabbed a sheet from the laundry basket.

Pia shrugged her shoulders. 'It's not like I can drive, full stop. I never learnt to drive. I've always just had . . . drivers.'

'Well, John's obviously taken Mr Silk into London today, but I'll ask one of the men to drive you in.'

'No, no. I don't want someone to drive me,' Pia protested.

'But the village is three miles away, Pia.' Mrs Bremar held the sheet to her chest and looked at Pia. Ever since Pia had been fitted with the new weight-bearing cast a fortnight ago, she had been taking baby steps back towards independence, back to freedom, to a life away from Will. 'I'll call you a taxi.'

'No.'

'Devil's child! How d'you think you're going to get there, then? *Pirouette* your way in?'

Pia smiled at her. 'I'll take the bus.'

'The bus?' Mrs Bremar shrieked, bursting out laughing. She couldn't for the life of her imagine a creature like Pia Soto on the bus.

'What's so funny?' Pia frowned. She took planes like they were buses. Why not the bus like it was a bus?

'For a start, dear, there's only one service a day and that's . . .' She checked the clock. 'Oh my goodness. Well, that's in eighteen minutes.'

'Good, I'll just make it, then,' Pia said, hopping off the stool and grabbing her tea, to take it upstairs with her.

'You won't, dear,' Mrs Bremar called out. 'The bus stop's outside the gates and they're nearly a ten-minute walk away, as it is.'

'Get one of the men to drive me to the bus stop, then,' she shouted back.

'But just look at you – you're not fit to go out dressed like that.' She couldn't understand how that tiny bikini had stayed on during rehearsals. It looked as though it might pop off at any moment.

Pia stood on the bottom step and winked. 'If there's

one thing performing taught me, B, it's the art of the quick change.'

Twenty minutes later, dressed in one Ugg, chocolate-brown leggings (she still couldn't get jeans on over her cast), a chestnut 8-ply cashmere roll neck sweater and a tweed flat cap of Will's that she'd grabbed from the boot room, Pia rested her head against the thick glass and watched the unfamiliar English countryside of ancient oaks and wheat fields rumble past her. In the near distance she could see a fine steeple, ever so slightly off plumb, protruding through the copper beeches and silver birches.

She was sitting in an old air-force-blue 1940s bus, which had maroon leather bench seats and a tug bell. There were only four other passengers on board. Pia was so unused to British currency that the driver had had to help her with the fare. She squeezed the small leather purse, which Mrs Bremar used for her housekeeping and had handed to her, along with a short shopping list, as she'd streamed out of the door. The coins jangled intermittently as the elderly driver hit potholes and occasional squirrels, and she realized it had not only been months since she'd left Plumbridge House; it had been months since she had spent any money at all – even on a tiddly little bus fare. Her bank manager would be pleased of course, but something inside her – her old independence, her survival instinct – bristled. As much as she kept telling herself, reminding herself, that Will was being hospitable, it still felt like control.

As they came into the village of Plumbridge the hedgerows were replaced by mossy walls, the limed pointing bright against the ivy that crept and clung to them. The roads were so narrow they were one-way-only, and the bus had to perform an arthritic three-point turn to get round some of the corners.

Pia tinged the bell to get off. The market square couldn't be far from here, but she wanted to do some exploring around the labyrinthine streets. The bus ambled away.

'Oh wait!' she called, remembering suddenly that she hadn't asked the time of his return trip. But the driver couldn't hear her without his hearing aid or over the jocular engine, and he headed out of sight, managing to negotiate the next turn with both ease and grace.

Never mind, she could enquire at the village shop. She looked around her in amazement. She had never seen anywhere so unremittingly *old* before. She was used to visiting grand cities and performing in historic opera houses of course – the Kirov in St Petersburg, the State Opera in Prague, the Teatro dell'Opera in Rome – but they all commemorated times past on an epic scale. Here, where every single building was tiny and rickety, with four-foot-high doors and thatched roofs you could reach up and touch, you could almost imagine the people who had built and lived in them five hundred years ago. Window boxes were planted with vivid geraniums and pansies, stone water troughs were dotted up and down the street, and there were posters stuck up with Blu-tack in various front-room windows, advertising the primary school's Easter fete and the Easter Egg Hunt in the churchyard. She stopped to read one about the point-to-point next weekend at Ellison, the neighbouring village, before she realized she was looking straight in on a man sitting in front of his telly in his armchair, wearing just his Y-fronts. Hastily, Pia clapped a hand over her mouth to keep from laughing and hobbled off around the corner.

She was unprepared for the scene that greeted her. The square was vast, clearly built around ox-and-cart dimensions, with cobbled streets and a large corn exchange in the centre. The village store, white-painted, with Georgian glass panes and a display of fruit, flowers and newspapers outside, was diametrically opposite where she was standing. Next to it was the Hart Inn, and gathered outside, in a clatter of hooves and scarlet coats, was the local hunt.

Pia looked on nervously. It didn't take a genius to work out she'd be *persona non grata* after the ball. A fat man was walking around with a tray full of whisky shots, holding it up to the riders. Most of those on horseback were in black or navy coats; there were just three that she could see in the traditional red jackets. One had a bugle in his hand and was talking animatedly to a woman in a navy velvet riding habit. She was sitting side-saddle and looked fresh out of a Stubbs painting. Pia absent-mindedly appraised the position of the riders' shoulders and their erect forms. Ballet made her hyper-aware of good posture.

The villagers had come out in force and were standing around, leaning on dilapidated old Land Rovers in Barbours and flat caps, eating flapjacks and drinking tea from Thermos flasks.

Pia walked slowly around the square. If she approached it from the left, she'd be able to get into the shop without passing any of them directly. She dropped her eyes to the ground. Her exposed toes felt cold, even with the customary leg warmer pulled on, and she wished she'd brought her sunglasses – although around here, she guessed, shades in mid-March would probably be more a flashing light to her fame than a disguise. Besides, the plaster cast was a dead giveaway to her identity. She was in plain sight of the riders, and unable to speed up, she had nowhere to go but straight towards them.

As she got closer, she pulled the shopping list Mrs Bremar had given her out of her pocket, and scanned it quickly. Plain flour, butter, cheese, leeks, fish sauce . . .

'Well, look who it is,' she heard one voice say in a low voice to another. 'It's Miss Brazil, out to save the world.'

'No, it's Miss World, surely, looking for world peace,' another voice carped.

'Well, it won't be *Mrs* World any time soon – or Mrs Silk come to that. Did you see his face? He was mortified by her.'

'She's such an embarrassment,' a third voice sniped.

'I could have told you that. They never should have let her in in the first place. I mean, she probably can't even ride. I doubt she knows which way is up on a horse.'

'Well, the duke won't let her in again, that's for sure. You know what a stickler he is for—'

Pia opened the shop door and stumbled inside, as desperate for its sanctuary as if she'd been under mortar fire. The bell above the door rang noisily and the shopkeeper – a middle-aged woman in a green polyester housecoat – came through from a back room.

'Mornin'. How can I help you?'

Pia looked at her dumbly, her cheeks stinging with shame, her ears ringing at the women's taunts. Tears pricked her eyes.

The woman looked at her more closely. 'Are you Pia?' she asked.

Pia just nodded.

'Mrs Bremar rang ahead and asked me to put this bag together for you.' She reached under the counter and pulled out an orange string bag full of all the provisions on the shopping list. 'She said it might be disorientating for you finding all the different bits and bobs, seeing as you're foreign,' she said.

Pia nodded, her eyes sliding over to the window at the laughing girls on horseback.

'Right, let's tally this all up, then,' the shopkeeper said, punching numbers into the till.

Pia kept her eyes on the gaggle outside. The heroine who had been sitting side-saddle, and attracting legions of admiring glances, turned out to be none other than Violet, of course. She dismounted, leading her horse away from the main body of the meet and over to an iron bull-ring at the side of the pub. Pia watched her tether the horse and go inside.

'That'll be eighteen pounds fifty-six, then,' the shopkeeper said.

Pia opened the purse and pulled out a twenty-pound note. She held it up questioningly. She was used to only dollars or euros.

'That's the one,' the shopkeeper said, taking it. 'And here's your change.'

Pia pocketed the change and picked up the bag. She went to the door. Then she turned round.

'When is the next bus to Plumbridge House?'

The woman checked her watch. 'It was at nine-thirty this morning.'

Pia frowned at her. 'But there must be another one today.' It was more of a demand than a question.

The shopkeeper shrugged. 'Sunday service. Nine-thirty out of town. Eleven-thirty back in. That's it.' She looked at Pia and at the plaster cast. What was she doing taking the bus with that on her leg anyway? 'Do you want me to ring Mrs Bremar to send someone to collect you?'

Pia shook her head and lifted her chin defiantly. She was fed up with everyone doing everything for her. Even this shopping had been prearranged for her. 'No. I'm fine.'

She went outside and stood for a moment, hidden from the hunt's view by the fruit stand. The coast was clear for now. The girls, in Violet's absence, had disbanded and merged with the rest of the meet, their attention caught by other gossip.

Pia looked around her. She wanted to make a quick getaway before Violet came back out. She knew Violet wouldn't hesitate to start up the ritual humiliation of the village's guesting ballerina on her return.

She looked down the little lane to her side. It meandered to the left. She should be able to get back to where she had come into the village if she just kept turning left.

She started down it, her hand absent-mindedly reaching out to pat the tethered horse as she passed. The horse whick-ered softly, and Pia stopped. It was a black mare, fourteen-three, she estimated.

'*Hey, crianca,*' she whispered. '*Oh, voce esta tao bonito. Tao bonito.*' She ran her hands expertly over the mare's flank and neck, and the horse nodded approvingly. Violet's words – she'd recognized the particularly vicious tone of her voice – tap-danced in her head: '. . . doubt she knows which way is up . . .'

She looked at the side saddle. It was antique and clearly worth a fortune – more than the horse probably. It gave her an idea, something that would give her the last laugh.

She looked around furtively.

'Hey, would you like to run with me? Would you? Would you like that?'

The horse lifted a leg and hoofed the ground.

'I'll take that as a yes,' she whispered.

Checking that she wasn't being observed, she undid the reins from the ring, and easily lifted her left, strongest foot up to waist height and into the stirrup. She had no problems hoisting herself up. She was fast getting back to performance strength and her muscles felt primed. She instinctively placed her right plastered leg around the pommel on the side saddle. It was both rested and protected there.

With a quick click of her tongue, she deftly turned the horse around and walked her down the lane. Nobody noticed the clip-clop of her hooves over the cobbles. There was too much commotion elsewhere. Although there weren't hounds – this was a drag hunt – some of the foot supporters had brought their pet dogs with them, and their barks were adding to the cacophony of yells, whinnies and laughter.

Pia felt a surge of triumph bubble up within her as she rounded the corner and broke into a stylish trot that would have shown Violet she knew a whole lot more about horses than merely which way was up. She half wished she could hang around to watch Violet's face, but in only three turns she was out of the tiny village and back on the road she had come in on, bordered on both sides by open farmland. A gate with rider's access was to her right. She looked at it for a moment and then grinned. What the hell!

Chapter Twenty-five

Violet came back from the loos, a smug smile all over her face, not least because she knew the men in the hunt couldn't take their eyes off her. They'd fall off their horses if they knew she wasn't wearing knickers beneath her habit. She couldn't wait to surprise Tanner later.

She looked around for him. He was in his pink, the ribbons on his black velvet hat sewn up. As field master he was responsible for keeping the hunt in line and was spelling out the nuances of etiquette to some new riders while reining in Conker, his chestnut stallion, who was beginning to move friskily and was clearly impatient to get going. They'd been delayed half an hour as it was, waiting for the master, who was in delicate, last-minute negotiations with an aggrieved farmer who was withholding access to his land because his hedges hadn't been properly restored from the last meet. Violet caught his eye and winked at him as she walked to the side of the pub.

It took a good ten seconds to really register what she was seeing – that Ebony had actually gone. She ran through possible scenarios in her mind – the knot on the reins had been worked loose, Kit and Minky had hidden her as a joke – but nothing seemed to fit.

'Tanner!' she gasped, running over to him. 'Ebony's gone. She's run off.'

'What? What do you mean?' he asked, looking down at her, trying to control Conker, who was now raring to go.

'I left her tied up at the side there while I went to the loo. When I came back, she'd gone.'

'Did anyone see Ebony come back through here?' Tanner demanded in a loud voice. 'Someone must have noticed a loose horse.' But everyone just shook their heads and shrugged.

'Then that means she's gone down there,' Tanner said, heading Conker down the lane. 'I'll try to catch her before she hits the main roads and causes an accident.'

He trotted frustratingly slowly down the village lanes for fear of riding down pedestrians, but as he turned into the open countryside he jumped Conker off the road into the nearest field, and scanned the horizon. Thankfully there wasn't a covert for half a mile or so and he could get a clear view.

He looked first to the left, towards the distant dual carriageway, before swinging round. There she was!

He narrowed his eyes at the sight of her. And she hadn't escaped. She had been stolen. There was someone riding her. A woman, her hair flying behind her as she cantered. No hat on either. 'Jesus Christ!' he fumed, the anger flushing through him. With a jerk of the reins, he gee'd Conker into a gallop and tore after her. With any luck she wouldn't know anything about him giving chase until he was on top of her.

The fields ripped out beneath Conker's feet as he was finally allowed to fly, and in just under four minutes there were only two fields left between them. Tanner clenched his jaw furiously, his eyes piercing the narrow back that was rising and falling gracefully on the sedate canter. Whoever she was, she knew how to ride.

A huge hedge was looming in front of him. The woman had used the gate at the corner of the field, but he didn't have time for that. He knew these fields like the back of his hand. After all, they used to be his. He jumped Conker bullishly over the blackthorn hedge. It was five feet high at least, and nearly as wide, but Conker trusted him and his bandages protected his fetlocks from scratches. He landed well, but neither could have foreseen that he landed only inches away from two pheasants.

They tore into the air in a torrent of squawks and beating wings. Conker, spooked by the commotion, reared up, sending Tanner – who was as startled as his mount – flying back into the hedge.

Pia, hearing them, turned and watched as the man pulled himself out of the hedge. He was shouting and swearing so loudly she could hear him from across the other side of the neighbouring field, but he appeared unharmed. She took in his hunting jacket and realized he was chasing her.

Her heart began to pound, the adrenalin to flash-flood, and her fingers tightened their grip around the reins, getting ready to flee. Ebony flattened her ears down and started walking backwards, unsettled by Conker's antics. Pia soothed her, rubbing her neck calmly. She knew she should get the hell out of there. She watched the man grab Conker's reins and look back at her. He was shouting something at her. She couldn't hear what, but it was pretty obvious he wanted her to stop. She looked at him more closely – she'd know that high colour anywhere. She didn't know whether to laugh or cry.

Tanner recognized Pia at the exact same moment and he

straightened up, knowing instantly he had a battle on his hands. She wasn't going to hand the horse over to him.

Throwing the reins over Conker's head, he jumped back into the saddle, but Pia had already turned and was jumping Ebony over the gate. She was six fields away from Plumbridge House. She'd be damned if she'd let him stop her.

Tanner took after her, riding harder than he'd ever ridden in his life. She was the fox and he was going to hunt her down. She'd never make it. Conker was seventeen hands and in his prime. He could outrun Ebony any day of the week. They raced over one field, then another. Just four more. Come on!

Pia looked under her arm, terrified. He was gaining ground. There was only a field and a half between them. She hadn't ridden this fast for years. She hadn't ridden, *full stop*, for years. She didn't know this horse. She didn't know this land or what was over the next hedge – how wide it was or whether or not there was a ditch on the far side. She'd been using the gates before, but she didn't have that luxury now. She had to get back before he caught her up.

Two more fields to go. Over this one, then just one more hedge, another field and then it was post-and-rail fencing onto Will's land. Would he follow her onto Will's property?

She urged Ebony on, speaking solidly in Portuguese as panic pushed everything other than survival and winning – which were one and the same to her – out of her brain.

The last hedge rose up before her. It was enormous, far bigger than any of the others.

Tanner watched her in disbelief. 'Stop!' he shouted, hardly able to believe she would – could – jump it. 'Stop! You'll kill yourself!' He'd grown this hedge particularly high, out of spite, to block Will's view of the rolling countryside.

But she couldn't stop. She was too close to it, and he was too close to her, only twenty or so strides behind. If she could just get over it, she'd be safe. She could see the house's chimneys already.

She closed her eyes.

Tanner held his breath as he saw Ebony gather herself, tucking her legs up, giving her all for what was undoubtedly the ride of her life. She clipped the far side of it, but she was over. She had made it!

Tanner exhaled – almost laughed – with relief, before sucking his breath in again as it was suddenly his turn to go over. But Conker was that much bigger and he sailed over, whickering with delight at the freedom of this run.

Pia raced over the lush lawns and through the orchard, her arms round Ebony's neck, her head low to avoid the branches.

Ebony had the advantage in the orchard, her smaller frame allowing her a more nimble path, and Pia galloped out of the orchard and across the drive, overtaking a groundsman on his ride-on tractor.

She pulled Ebony to an abrupt halt outside the double doors and patted her heartily on the neck. She felt ecstatic, elated by her adventure. She'd snatched back some freedom and, in that moment, she felt fully herself again.

The groundsman ran over – panicked by the sight of Pia on a runaway horse. He held his arms out and lifted Pia off the saddle. She landed on her good leg and, smiling calmly, handed the reins to the bewildered man.

'Take him back to the Ludgrove Yard, would you?' she smiled.

Pia turned for the steps, but Tanner came to a shuddering stop in front of her, spraying gravel everywhere and blocking her path.

She looked up at him, her eyes glittering and defiant. She had won. He hadn't stopped her, after all. And he couldn't do anything to her here.

Tanner leapt down, landing just inches from her, but he didn't step back. He wanted to intimidate her. He could see the victory in her eyes and it made him want to smack her. Trying to catch his breath, he stared at her contemptuously.

'What is it?' she asked in a deliberately calm voice, as though he was a fan hassling her for an autograph.

There was a brief pause as he absorbed the boredom in her voice.

'What *is* it?' he bellowed. 'Are you for fucking real?'

Pia raised her eyebrows but said nothing. She stared at his jaw – which was where she came up to – trying to hide her fear. She saw the sweat glisten at his hairline beneath his hat, the scratches on his neck he'd endured from his fall in the hedge.

'You steal Violet's horse and then ride like a maniac across country you don't even know? You could have killed yourself ten times over.'

Pia shrugged and looked over his shoulder. He was far closer than she was comfortable with. 'Ride it like you stole it, I always say. Besides, I needed a ride back.'

Tanner couldn't speak. This woman just left him dumbfounded. He'd never met anyone so completely unreasonable in his life. She operated on an entirely different planet to everyone else. 'More importantly, you could have injured Ebony,' he bellowed, pulling at his stock and trying to cool down. Sweat was running down his back. He hadn't had such a ferocious gallop for years.

'Well, if I have, I'll buy her, and you can buy Violet another horse,' she said coolly.

'I don't want to buy Violet another horse,' he snapped. Tanner put his hands on his hips and shook his head. As if throwing money at the problem made everything all right. She was perfectly suited to Silk. 'You are unfuckingbelievable.'

For the first time, Pia raised her head and stared directly at him. He saw himself reflected in her clear green eyes. 'I know,' she replied tossing her hair back and letting the ambiguity hang between them.

Tanner looked at her, taken aback by her sudden change of tone, her change of attack – because that was what it was. A tactic to confuse him. Well, it might work on other men but it wouldn't work on him. Any urge to kiss her was well and truly tempered by the urge to hit her.

'And I suppose you realize that if you'd fallen, you'd have finished your dancing career for good,' he said aggressively, but with his eyes on her lips.

'I know,' she said defiantly, like it didn't matter, but her voice cracked a little at this truth, and the tremor caught his attention. She was beginning to shake as the adrenalin surge seeped away.

Tanner stepped towards her, still breathing hard. She could feel the heat coming off him. She closed her eyes suddenly as his scent drifted up to her. It was so . . . familiar, somehow . . . She looked up at him, confused. Where had she smelt it before?

He blinked down at her once, then walked past her and up the steps, pressing the bell long and hard.

Will opened the door, puzzled to find Tanner – looking resplendent and thoroughly pissed off in his hunting garb – standing in front of Pia, who was flushed and trembling. His heart dropped. Oh God, no. Not again.

'Try to keep your girlfriend under control, Silk,' Tanner said tersely. 'She's been making a bloody nuisance of herself again,' he said dismissively, striding back to Conker and jumping back into the saddle. Pia frowned as he brushed past, confounded that the only reaction she'd elicited from him was that of exasperated parent. 'And make sure that horse is returned to the yard by the time I get back,' he ordered, before cantering back up the drive, leaving both Pia and Will mute in his wake.

Chapter Twenty-six

Tanner had his back to her when she walked in. Everyone had finished for the day and he was going round doing his final checks on the horses. She watched him as he tested the self-regulated plumbing system. Ricky had said there'd been a leak in this stall. He was still wearing his hunting kit, with only his jacket off, and she admired the contours of his long legs, strong waist and powerful shoulders.

She shut the stable door and pulled the bolt over.

Tanner turned at the sound.

'Oh hello,' he said distractedly, turning back to the tap.

'Oh hello yourself,' she replied archly, bemused by his bumbling.

He heard the mirth in her voice. 'What's up?' he asked, over his shoulder.

Violet shrugged. 'Nothing. Just came to see where you were.'

'I'm here.'

'Yes. I see that.'

There was a pause as he struggled with the washer. 'I'm sorry about today. I don't know why I didn't think to go back to the yard to get another horse for you. Ebony practically needed to be wheeled back she was so tired.' He shook his head bitterly and tightened the wrench around the loose nut.

'It's okay,' she said quietly, though in truth it had been anything but. For a start, she'd felt ridiculous driving around with the car supporters, dressed in her habit.

'It's not, though. You should have ridden today. That stupid bloody girl . . . the arrogance of it all . . . Who does she damned well think she is?'

'I said it's fine. She's just playing to type. It doesn't even surprise me,' she said casually, though it had.

'Well . . . she doesn't deserve your understanding.' He finished what he was doing and stood up, wiping his hands on his trousers. 'Anyway, what's for supper?'

Violet shrugged.

Tanner rolled his eyes. 'Fine, we'll get a take-away then.'

'You know, what happened today could just play into our hands,' she said, completely ignoring his new line of conversation.

'What?' he sighed, sensing trouble.

'Well, Will's live-in girlfriend just stole our horse. He's lucky we're not pressing charges. At the very least it should give you leverage against him.'

'What on earth are you talking about?'

'You could agree to keep his horses, but increase the fees by twenty, thirty per cent.'

'Violet! How many times do I have to say it? I'm not taking his business any more. I don't want it. We're moving on without him.'

'But we can't, Tanner.'

Tanner fixed her with a glare. 'Why?'

'We need his money.'

'No, we don't. There are plenty of people out there who want what I can do for them.'

'Name one.' Violet stood there, looking particularly forbidding in her habit.

Tanner couldn't, not yet anyway. Polo patrons were busy men and difficult to pin down, but those that he had were suspicious about why he should be letting the successful Black Harbour stable loose. He'd managed to get one meeting tabled but nothing more than that, and the grass season was just weeks from opening now. The window was fast closing on him and all the big-money teams would be set up till the autumn.

'I just think you're making a big mistake,' Violet said, softening her voice a little.

'No. You just don't have any faith in me,' Tanner said, looking back at her and shaking his head. 'You never have. If I decide to do anything that you don't agree with one hundred per cent then it's always a Big Fucking Mistake. I'm fed up of it, Violet. It's always the same.'

The silence hung heavily between them, and they both recognized the first steps of the conversation that had been delayed, deferred and silenced for too many months now.

He looked at the floor. He hadn't been intending to do this now, but when was the right time? 'Look, Vi . . . we need to talk.' He looked back up at her.

'What are you doing?' he asked, even though it was blatantly clear she was unbuttoning her jacket. 'No, don't do that! Put it back on. We need to talk.'

She threw it on the ground. She wasn't wearing a bra, and she looked unspeakably erotic bare-breasted with just her stock around her neck. She walked towards him, her full breasts swaying slightly, her hair swinging around her shoulders.

'Oh for Christ's sake, Violet, you know this isn't—'

She silenced him with a hungry kiss, reaching for his hands and bringing them up to her breasts. She groaned, pulling her mouth away, as he instinctively caressed them, and she buried her face in his neck, fiddling with his belt.

She yanked his trousers down, her hand straight in his boxers. He was already hard. He'd never once disappointed her. She reached over and unbuttoned her skirt, letting it billow down to her ankles. She stood up, naked apart from the stock, and started walking backwards, her ripe breasts hypnotizing him, beckoning him towards her, forcing every other thought out of his head, except getting his mouth on them.

They lay together for a long while afterwards, dazed and silent, the hay flattened beneath them, horses snuffling and hoofing the floor in the neighbouring stalls. Tanner closed his eyes, frustrated to have been so easily led off course, but his whole body hurt – the fall into the hedge had jarred his back – and he craved some physical comfort. It had been a long day and he didn't have any more fight in him. He closed his eyes, content to skip dinner altogether and just sleep there.

It was getting dark when he awoke, disturbed by a distinctive low beating sound. He sat up, frowning, ears pricked like a spaniel's.

'If Silk's landing his bloody chopper on my land . . .' he growled, pulling on his trousers. Violet watched him. He always seemed so tightly coiled, as though he was perpetually ready to fight. He went outside to check, and she followed him, pulling on his shirt.

She was buttoning it up when she emerged into the yard. A helicopter had landed in the paddock, but it wasn't Silk's. Two figures were jumping out. A man and a woman.

The shirt flapped and lifted in the wake of the rotor blades and Violet quickly batted it down.

'Ay-ay,' shouted one of the figures in a jaunty voice. 'You two living up to the country clichés, then?'

Tanner looked back at Violet, gobsmacked, and she laughed. It had been – what? Two, three years since his brother had been home.

The figures drew nearer, the man breaking into an athletic run, hurdling over the post-and-rail fencing and hurtling into the yard. He and Tanner hugged roundly, smacking each other hard on the back, before crouching low and sparring with each other, laughing all the while.

'A chopper?' Tanner exclaimed, motioning to the helicopter, which was rising back up into the sky.

'It's only chartered.'

'Oh well that's all right then,' Tanner quipped. 'It's good to see you, anyway. Why didn't you say you were coming? We'd have got a meal ready for you.'

'What? And risk missing the chance of catching you two at it? I'm just sorry I stopped to buy that case of fizz on the way over.' He looked at Violet, beguiling as ever. 'And how's the great beauty? I can't believe you're still putting up with him,' the man said, leaning down to kiss her and pulling a twig of straw from her hair.

'How are you, Jonty?' she smiled. He was tall – a good three inches taller than Tanner – and rangy, with black hair and even blacker eyes. 'The Prince of Darkness' Tanner had always called him as a boy, and it was true. The two brothers were like night and day: Tanner's face so open and earthy, always flushed and grubby from his days spent working the horses; Jonty brooding and mysterious, his head always stuck in a book or up a pretty girl's skirt.

'God, I think you're even better-looking than when I last saw you,' Jonty grinned, taking in Violet's dishevelled appearance. Violet flashed him a delighted smile. She knew her eyes looked electric after sex and no man could resist a woman barely dressed in his clothes.

There was a soft cough, and they all looked round. Another figure was standing in the shadows. Jonty bounded over to her, draping a lazy arm over her delicate shoulders.

'Lu – this is Tanner, my rakish brother I've been warning you about, and his pretty-much-wife, Violet, if only he'd ever get his arse in gear and ask her. Guys, I want you to meet Lulie. *My* wife.'

Violet and Tanner's jaws dropped simultaneously.

'Your *wife*?' They looked at the coltish blonde. She was lightly tanned, with clear aquamarine eyes and long tousled sun-bleached hair. She looked like she'd been brushed with gold dust. She was wearing indigo skinny jeans and a black glossy astrakhan coat that made her hair gleam, and she looked just altogether too impossibly glamorous to be standing in this mucky yard. Next to her Violet felt mannish and . . . well, as wild as Pia's proverbial gypsy.

Jonty laughed. 'I thought you might say that. Surprise, huh?'

'Well, you could say that,' Tanner said, not quite able to laugh. 'I can't believe you didn't invite us. I'm supposed to be your best man.'

'It wasn't actually planned, if that makes it any better,' Lulie said. '*We* didn't even know we were going to do it – until we were actually doing it. Maybe we got a bit carried away . . . ?' She looked at Jonty but he was laughing at Tanner.

'Probably like you two in the stable just now, I should imagine,' he said, chuckling again.

Tanner gave him another thump on the arm.

'It was the best bloody decision of my life,' Jonty said, tipping up Lulie's chin with his finger and kissing her lustily. Tanner and Violet shifted awkwardly in front of the newly-weds.

'Anyway, are you two going to invite us inside or what?' Jonty said, breaking for air and looking up. 'If nothing else, you'll both catch your death out here in your smalls.' He smacked Tanner on the back, leading the march into the farmhouse. 'Why you couldn't wait till bedtime instead of scaring the horses, I don't know.'

Chapter Twenty-seven

Stretching broadly as he stumbled into the kitchen, Tanner yawned and headed for the Aga. Biscuit was in her usual place, stretched along the front of it, her tail thumping sleepily on the stone floor at his approach.

'Morning, Bix,' he mumbled, reaching down to stroke her. He put the kettle on the boiling plate and leant against the rail trying to warm up. It was freezing this morning. Although it was still dark outside the brightness coming in from the yard told him – without opening the doors – that there'd been a hard frost.

Pouring cream and a tea bag into each of the two mugs, he made his way over to his favourite armchair while he waited for the kettle to boil. Biscuit sat up expectantly, ready to climb onto his lap.

Tanner gave a start to find Lulie already curled up there, sound asleep. He stared down at her. She was wearing a yellow-striped vest and blue knickers, and the tartan wool blanket, which was covered in moth holes, was half on her legs, half on the floor. Her legs looked brown, skinny and very long. She was stunning. No wonder Jonty had rushed to marry her.

He vaguely wondered what to do. What was she doing down here? He hadn't fostered any expectations of seeing the newly-weds downstairs for breakfast. He and Violet worked on an early schedule at the yard, feeding the horses by 6.30 a.m., and he had thought it more likely he'd have to rouse the glossy couple at lunchtime.

The kettle began to whistle. Hastily, he picked it up and poured the boiling water into the mugs, tiptoeing like a panto burglar back out of the kitchen. She may be his new sister-in-law but she was also a complete stranger. If anyone was going to wake her up in her underwear, it could be Violet. She was too gorgeous by half, and his brother's wife. He was steering well clear.

He went up the creaky staircase, tea sloshing all over the treads. A door opened across the landing, and Jonty stuck his head out. He looked anxious.

'Morning,' Tanner said, clocking his body language. 'You okay?'

'Yuh,' Jonty replied, his voice two octaves deeper with sleep, still looking around.

'Lost something?' Tanner asked.

Jonty scratched his head. He was in a pair of their father's red-and-green-striped pyjama bottoms and they hung low on his hips, showing off an Abercrombie & Fitch washboard stomach.

'Like your wife, maybe?' Tanner prompted, when Jonty failed to reply.

Jonty looked at him. 'Yeah, how'd you know?'

'She's asleep in the kitchen,' Tanner said, jerking his head down the stairs.

'Oh right,' Jonty said, frowning. There was a long pause. He was still addled with sleep. 'I'd better go and get her, then.'

'Probably best. Few women can resist the sight of me in my PJs.'

Jonty chuckled as he shuffled down the stairs.

'Does she do this a lot, then?' Tanner asked.

Jonty stopped and looked back up at him. 'Do what?'

'Sleepwalking.'

'Sleepwalking? Oh yeah, right.' He rubbed his stomach thoughtfully. 'Yeah, yeah she does.'

'Can't say I blame her,' Tanner grinned, pushing open his door. 'I wouldn't sleep next to that face either.'

When Lulie did finally surface – having been settled back into bed – it was indeed knocking on lunchtime. Jonty hadn't bothered going back to sleep. Down in the kitchen, he'd heard the horses in their stables and the chickens pecking about in the yard and they'd instantly reawakened all the boyhood memories of riding at dawn.

He'd pulled on a pair of jeans, a sweater, a puffa and some riding boots and helped Tanner feed and muck out. Then he'd saddled up Matchstick and gone for a run on the steep uphill gallop.

He came back, panting hard, a red flush staining even his swarthy cheeks.

'God, I've missed that,' he said, eyes bright, pouring himself a cup of the tea that was brewing in the pot.

'We've missed *you*,' Violet said, looking up from her charts. 'It's been too long. What's brought you back anyway?'

Jonty leant against the Aga and wiped his mouth with the back of his hand. 'Lulie needed to get away. The press are always all over her – wanting to know what she's wearing and all that crap – and she's been working back to back on movies for over a year. She's burnt out.'

'Lulie's an actress?' Violet said jealously. She'd guessed model. 'What's she been in?'

Jonty shrugged. 'Nothing you'd have heard of yet. She's just done support roles up to now, but Woody Allen spotted her and cast her in his newest title, which is coming out this summer. This is the year she's going to break through.'

'And what are you doing while she's off . . . actressing? Aren't you supposed to be in lectures?' Tanner asked, every inch the big brother.

'It's fine. I don't need to be there *all* the time for an MLitt.'

'Hmm,' Tanner mumbled doubtfully, as he pulled the pie from the oven.

'Anyway, Matchstick's a fine horse, Tan,' Jonty said quickly, changing the subject. Tanner had assumed the paternal role ever since their father died and he was unusually concerned that Jonty should flourish in his postgraduate law career. 'Where'd you get him from?'

'He's Will's,' Violet said, clasping her hands together as she suddenly realized she could have an ally. 'Did you like him?'

Tanner shot her a look.

'Like him? He's the best horse I've ever ridden. You've certainly pulled the yard up by its bootstraps to have a horse of that calibre in your stables.'

'Yes. It's a shame Tanner's kicking him out,' Violet said mildly.

Jonty's eyes popped. 'He's what?'

'Your brother's had a spat with Will and decided he won't work with him any more. They've all got to be gone by the end of next month.'

Jonty stared at his brother, whose jaw was clenched hard.

'What's going on, Tan? That horse has got champion written all over him. The stud fees alone would keep you afloat. You know that.'

Tanner shrugged. 'Of course I do. I bred him myself. But Silk's got to go. I won't work with that bastard a week longer than the contract forces me to.' He shot Violet a warning look. She wasn't to say another word on the matter. Jonty had been sitting his finals in Cambridge when Silk had scammed their father and she knew perfectly well Tanner had made the decision to shield his little brother from Silk's deception, saying that their father had sold up willingly. Jonty was on the brink of a glittering career in law; there was no point both of them living with a feud.

Jonty looked at Violet, who shrugged. What the hell had happened? He knew his brother well enough to know better than try to railroad him. He'd just dig in his heels even deeper. He took the softly-softly approach.

'So who're you getting in instead, then?'

'No one,' Violet said, lips pursed crossly.

'Actually, that's not true,' Tanner shot back, delighted to prove her wrong for once. 'I've got a couple of owners in Dubai and Brazil who want to break into the HPA league.'

Violet stared at him, dumbfounded. 'You never told me that.'

'You never asked.'

'Yes, I did,' she protested.

'No. You've spent the past few weeks telling me I'm making a Big Mistake, and have to go down on my hands and knees to grovel to Silk.'

Jonty watched the exchange. He'd never seen them like

this together before. The hostility coming off Tanner was palpable.

'So how many liveries—'

'Like I said, it's still only interest at this stage,' Tanner said casually. 'I haven't even spoken to one of the guys yet, so nothing's set in stone.'

Violet rolled her eyes dismissively. No signature on the dotted line? Better the devil you know, in her book.

Tanner caught her sceptical look. 'I guess we'll just have to trust that I'm not quite as hopeless as some people think I am.'

Jonty gestured to Violet silently, his hands splayed as if to say 'What's going on?' but Tanner turned to him, catching him out. 'Anyway, if you two have finished playing charades, do you want to bring your child bride downstairs? This pie's ready and I'm starving.'

Chapter Twenty-eight

Will pushed himself further back in his seat, his arms behind his head, his ankles crossed on the leather-topped desk.

'I'm so sorry, Will,' Emma said on the speakerphone. 'The nearest I can find with this amount of notice is Henry Malting's yard in Shropshire. He's got thirty-three stables available from next month.'

'Yes, but he's in *Shropshire*,' Will muttered as though Shropshire was the moon, cursing himself for not having moved on this sooner. He'd been so sure Tanner had been bluffing. 'How am I supposed to keep tabs on things all the way up there? I don't want anyone messing about with Matchstick.'

There was a brief pause. 'I'll keep looking, of course,' Emma said, keeping the resignation out of her voice. 'But with this lead time . . . well, the yards need more notice.'

'Don't we all?' Will said, taking his feet off the desk and sitting up. 'Keep me posted, Emma.'

He pressed disconnect and stared out of the window, brooding over the fix Tanner had put him in. It had been damned convenient stabling his horses next door. He still couldn't believe Ludgrove was sticking to his guns on this. He'd expected a quick capitulation after Tanner had cooled down from his temper tantrum. He was the yard's bread-and-butter business. Tanner was cutting off his nose to spite his face, determined to inconvenience Will, even at the cost of his own business. Well, fine, let him. Even if he did have to stable the horses in Shropshire, it would only be a short-term thing. He'd be able to sort out closer stabling within the next month. But Tanner? Unless he replaced Silk's business sharpish, he probably wouldn't even last till the summer. The man was a damned fool.

Locking the study, he bounded up the stairs to change. Pia's door was open and he glanced in as he jogged past. He stopped dead at the sight of her.

She was lying on her tummy on the bed, reading the choreographer's score for *The Songbird*. The Royal Ballet Orchestra had recorded it for her and she was listening to it on her iPod, her left leg bent at the knee and swinging idly, like a child's, her head nodding to the music.

She was wearing a black vest and a tiny starched tutu that – being flattened at the front – was pushed up vertically behind, showing off her delectable *derrière*. He watched the silky contours of her left hamstring muscle lengthen and shorten, the hollow of her toned buttock. Her skin was like butterscotch, firm and rich and golden. The temptation to walk over and lie on her, to push himself between those legs, was overwhelming. He could have kicked himself for promising her the ten-week chastity period in hospital. It seemed to suit her just fine.

Pia looked up and saw him standing at the door. She turned on her side, her left leg bent in front of her immobile right leg.

'I'm going for a ride,' he said. 'I need some fresh air. Mrs Bremar's downstairs, if you need anything.'

'I'll come with you,' she said brightly, desperate to get out of the house.

'You're not dressed for it,' he said, his eyes running over her again. 'And the light's beginning to fade. I'll just shoot over there myself.'

'No,' Pia said, scooting off the bed and limping over to the wardrobe – she'd become astonishingly nimble in the past few weeks. She grabbed a chunky black jumper and inched some leg warmers up her legs, like stockings. Will took a deep breath for strength, and continued to his own room to change.

They drove over to the yard in one of the estate's burgundy Land Rovers that happened to be parked at the front. Predictably, Tanner stormed straight out of the office as soon as he caught sight of them.

'Saddle him up, please, Jessy,' Will said, ignoring him and walking straight over to Matchstick. He patted his muzzle, admiringly. He really was a handsome animal.

'What are you doing here?' Tanner asked stonily.

'What does it look like? I've come to ride Matchstick.'

'I thought I made myself clear.'

'You have, perfectly. But until the month is out and they are off your property, I fully intend to exercise my right to ride them as and when I bloody well want to.'

Tanner's cheeks flushed with anger, but Will was right. There was nothing he could do about it. He cast a derisory eye over Pia's get-up.

'And are you intending to ride today too, or do you only ride stolen horses?' he asked sarcastically. He was still incandescent over their chase a fortnight earlier.

Pia gave him an equally sarcastic smile in response and he stormed over to the farmhouse, slamming the door behind him.

Jonty was at the kitchen table, doing the crossword.

'What's up with you?' he asked casually, as Tanner threw himself down in his chair, and then just as quickly got back out of it again. He paced the room.

'Nothing,' Tanner muttered, looking out of the window.

Clearly, it wasn't nothing. Jonty got up to see what he was staring at.

'Holy cow!' he spluttered at the sight of Pia on crutches. She was standing in profile to them, the leg warmers acting like beacons, pointing all the way up her long legs to her very visible and very peachy tutu-topped arse. 'Who the hell is *she*?'

'She's Brazilian,' Tanner said darkly, as though that explained everything.

It actually did to Jonty. He'd spent his gap year travelling around South America and had quickly got a handle on Ipanema beach culture. Forget boobs. It was all about the booty down there.

Jonty narrowed his eyes and peered at Pia more closely. 'Oh Jesus – don't tell me that's Pia Soto,' he breathed.

Tanner stared at him. 'How d'you know that?'

Jonty laughed, his palms outstretched. 'Mate! Pia Soto! She's a fox! Oh God, please don't tell me you didn't see her in that Victoria's Secret ad?'

Of course he hadn't. But then he didn't need to have seen that to know what Jonty was talking about. The memory of her curves as she lay by the side of the lake flashed through his mind. He hadn't looked. It hadn't been appropriate. It hadn't been anything *approaching* appropriate to look, and yet the spectre of them had burnt into his peripheral vision and twice now when he'd been with Violet – his hands on her, his eyes closed – his mind had wandered back there.

Not that that meant a thing. It was just lust. Cold male lust. He may as well have seen her in *Playboy*. He didn't give a damn about the fact that he was objectifying her. In fact he liked it. He despised her. He despised her sort – rude to everyone she met, too bloody spoilt to even thank a man for saving her life.

'I'm going out there,' Jonty said, laughing delightedly as he grabbed a coat from the back of the door.

'No don't. She's with Silk.'

'So? She could be with the sodding Godfather and I'd still go out there,' he said, winking cheekily.

'Could I remind you that you're –' the door slammed shut – 'married,' Tanner said quietly.

Jonty strode across the yard, running his hand through his hair. Yes, he knew perfectly well he was married. He wasn't planning to pull her, for God's sake. But come on – Pia Soto! In his yard! In a tutu! He had to be his fourteen-year-old self, dreaming!

'Hi,' he boomed, holding a hand out welcomingly. 'I'm Jonty, Tanner's brother.'

Pia looked at him, ignoring his hand. 'You say that like it's a good thing.'

Jonty grinned. Feisty too. She just got better and better.

'You here to ride?' he asked stupidly, even though it was blindingly obvious she couldn't. 'Course not,' he grinned, slapping his forehead with his palm. 'Where's Will?'

Will was on the mounting block, across the yard. He swung himself easily into the saddle and came over. Pia reached up to Matchstick and tickled his nose affectionately. The horse whickered happily and nuzzled his head down into her body. Pia smiled and put her arm around him.

'I didn't know you like horses,' Will said, amazed.

'There's a lot you don't know about me,' Pia replied mysteriously.

'Hi, Will,' Jonty said easily. Just because his brother had decided to make an enemy of him it didn't mean he had to. 'Long time no see.'

The two men shook hands. Jonty didn't need to reach far, he was so tall.

'It has been,' Will replied warily. 'Still at Law School?'

'Yeah. Final year now. How're things with you?'

'Well, you've probably heard . . .' He indicated towards the farmhouse. Tanner stepped back from the window.

'Yeah, a bit,' Jonty said. He changed the subject. 'So where're you off to?'

'I thought I'd take him down to the dyke and over the straights,' he said, slapping Matchstick on the neck. 'I need to clear my head a bit.'

'Well, what are you going to do while he's riding?' Jonty asked Pia.

'I'll sit in the car.'

'Nonsense,' he said. 'It's freezing out here. Come into the kitchen and keep warm while you wait. That's all right, isn't it?' he asked Will.

'Where's Tanner?' Will asked suspiciously.

'Dunno. I heard the front door slam. He's gone somewhere in a hurry. He'll be ages I expect,' Jonty lied. 'Why? Do you want me to find him for you?'

Will shook his head, inwardly breathing a sigh of relief. He desperately wanted to keep Pia away from here, away from Tanner.

'Well, you probably should wait inside,' Will said gallantly to Pia. The sky was slate-grey and felt full of water. He leant down to kiss Pia, then clicked the horse onwards with his feet and trotted out of the yard. When he got past the gate he broke out into a canter. Pia watched him disappear over the horizon.

Jonty helped her into the kitchen, holding open the door for her and booting Biscuit off the chair. Violet was working at Wilson's farm down the road today, and Lulie was closeted away in the snug, reading a script.

'Now, what can I do you for?' Jonty said, opening the cupboards. 'We've got builders', Earl Grey, Lapsang . . .' He rummaged deeper. 'Or Violet's got some of those lesbian teas: peppermint, camomile, lemon and ging—'

'Coffee. Black,' she interrupted, sitting down in the chair. Biscuit sat next to her, her nose in the air, her tail wagging excitedly.

Pia looked at her – how could she have thought she was ferocious the other week? – and began to stroke her. 'You're sweet, aren't you?' she smiled at the dopey dog.

She looked up and found Tanner glowering at her, as though he half expected her to skin his pet. Her hand dropped.

'I thought you said *he*'d gone?' she said rudely to Jonty, who was busy sniffing the milk in the fridge.

Jonty peered round the door at Tanner. 'Oh you're back,' he said nonchalantly.

Tanner frowned. Back? He hadn't gone anywhere.

'Fancy a cuppa?'

Pia looked around the kitchen, eager to avoid eye contact with Tanner – he was so hostile. It couldn't have been more different to the cool grandeur of Plumbridge House. A large refectory table sat in the middle of the black stone floor. The bald armchair Pia was sitting in was at one end of the table and opposite an ancient old Wedgwood-blue Aga; a small square Persian rug was at her feet. A vast red housekeeper's cupboard dominated the short wall, and a narrow back staircase was nestled in the corner of the room.

Biscuit laid her head on the arm of the chair and Pia began absent-mindedly stroking her again. Jonty set out a plate of Jammie Dodgers and her coffee. Pia took the coffee.

'I guess you have to watch your figure, huh?' Jonty said, sitting down at the table.

'Not really,' Pia purred. 'I have more than enough people doing that for me.'

Jonty laughed. Tanner rolled his eyes – the ego of the woman.

Pia watched the two brothers' reactions. She liked Jonty – how could she not? He was easy-going and affable, everything his brother wasn't. Handsome too. She thought that was probably the only thing they had in common.

'I can't believe no one told me you were living next door,' he continued, undeterred. 'Wait till Lulie hears about this.'

'Who's Lulie?' she asked, taking a sip of coffee.

'My wife, Lulie Rawthorne,' he said proudly. 'She's an actress. We've just got married.'

Pia's eyebrows shot up. She knew perfectly well who Lulie Rawthorne was. Woody Allen had cast her in his newest film and she was being tipped as a name – and face – to watch. But that wasn't why her name rang alarm bells. Patek Philippe had just signed Lulie as her replacement.

Pia wanted to meet her. Now.

'Where is she?' she asked casually.

'In the snug, working. Would you like to meet her?'

Pia nodded, her lean woollen-clad legs stretched out in front of her, the starched tutu frothing over the arms of the chair. She looked a very coquettish queen.

Jonty dashed out of the room, leaving Tanner and Pia in frigid silence.

Pia carried on making a fuss of Biscuit. 'I think she likes me,' she said eventually.

'She's a bloody atrocious judge of character,' Tanner muttered, his hands wrapped round the steaming teacup.

Jonty came back in, pulling Lulie by the sleeve. 'Here she is,' he beamed proudly, leaning against the table.

Lulie sailed into the room and instantly Pia saw why they'd chosen her. Her hair was like vanilla cream, and she was wearing a vintage tea dress with a man's leather belt wrapped twice around her waist, with beige ribbed tights and flat boots.

'Hi,' she beamed, offering her hand, delighted to meet another star in this remote backwater. Everyone she met around here was a farmer.

'Hi, Lulie,' Pia said, shaking her hand lightly. The brothers watched the exchange. It really did seem extraordinary – to both of them – that two such stunning women should be chatting in their shabby old kitchen.

'I am such a massive fan of yours. I saw you in *Sleeping Beauty* at the Royal Albert Hall when you toured Europe a few years ago,' she said. 'You know, the one in the round? I swear there were times when I thought you had to be hooked up to wires. It was almost as though you could just hover in the air. I mean, *how* can you do that? You're like a superhero to me.'

Pia smiled at the deference. They had a lot in common – beauty, international careers, the same age, Patek Philippe of course – but she wasn't going to do anything to dispel the implicit understanding that, of the two, hers was the greater talent. Lulie had been lucky enough to find a director who liked her pretty face. But Pia? She had taken her God-given talent and dedicated her childhood, her adolescence, her life to moulding, honing, chiselling and refining it into shape. Unlike Lulie, she wasn't an overnight sensation. Any glory that came her way had been earned and was hers by right.

She casually lifted her good leg, rolling it out at the hip, as if stretching. 'And I understand you two are newly-weds? Congratulations.'

'Thanks.'

'Was it a big wedding?'

'We eloped,' Jonty said, keeping his eyes away from Tanner's. 'Just walked into Chelsea Registry Office and took the first available slot.'

'Ah, right,' Pia said, sliding her eyes towards Tanner. He was standing with his arms defensively crossed over his chest.

'I'm guessing your families must have been upset not to have been invited to the ceremony,' she said. 'Have you done something to celebrate since you got back?'

Jonty chewed his lip and looked up at Lulie. 'Well, actually – we didn't think of that, did we? We've just been trying to regroup since getting down here . . .' He paused. 'It's an idea, though, isn't it?' he murmured, the thought of it beginning to appeal. 'I mean, it's only right we should give our friends a chance to buy us toasters, and I quite fancy a new Wii.'

Lulie slapped him lightly on the leg.

'So why don't you throw a party here?' Pia remarked casually, knowing full well it would agitate Tanner.

'It's a good idea,' Jonty said, looking over at Tanner. 'And you could make your best-man speech after all, Tan.'

Tanner rolled his eyes again. 'I really don't think now's the time for us to start shelling out on parties.' He didn't want to elaborate in front of Pia on the financial doom that was staring him in the face with the imminent departure of Silk's liveries.

'Oh we'd pick up all the costs,' Jonty said breezily, his attention entirely on Lulie. 'How about it? Shall we start married life properly? You could do the white-dress thing this time.'

Lulie shrugged nonchalantly. 'If it means I get a new dress . . .'

'Great. We'll hold it, um . . . a month next Saturday. What d'you say? That should give most people sufficient notice.'

'A month on Saturday?' Pia said sharply. 'No. That's April 28th. You can't possibly have that date.'

Tanner stared at her, furious. What – she thought she had ownership over the fucking calendar too, did she? 'April 28th it is, then,' he replied bullishly. 'I'll book the clowns and get Violet to make some jelly.'

'That's the night of my gala,' Pia said in a low voice. 'Everybody's coming – Elton, the princes, Elizabeth and Arun, Elle, Harry Hunter . . . I'd strongly advise you not to go head-to-head with me. My RSVPs are already in.' She broke a small smile and turned on the charm. 'Besides, I'd love you to come too. It's my comeback performance. The Royal Ballet is performing with me,' Pia said, nonchalantly pointing her good foot into an unnatural arch.

'Thanks for the offer but there won't be a clash for the guest lists. We don't need rent-a-crowd for our party,' Tanner said decisively, standing up straight and putting down his cup. 'I realize the concept's probably alien to you, but we've got *real* friends.'

Outside, hooves were clopping across the cobbles. Will was back.

'What made you think I was including *you* in the offer?' Pia replied tartly.

Through the window, Tanner saw Will dismount and toss the reins arrogantly to Jessy. He strode into the kitchen like it was his own home, but the sight of Pia sitting with Biscuit – who had practically gone into a coma from Pia's rhythmic strokes – and Tanner leaning against the wall, made him grow pale.

'How was that?' Pia smiled up at him. 'Feeling better?'

'Much,' he nodded, spotting Jonty and the beautiful blonde. Pia followed his gaze.

'Have you met Jonty's wife?' she asked. 'Lulie Rawthorne, the actress.'

He knew who she was. 'A pleasure.'

'Pia's just been telling us about the gala,' Lulie smiled. 'We're so excited to have been invited—'

'Well, no, hang on a sec . . .' Jonty said, interrupting her. 'I – er, *we* – haven't sorted out dates yet. What about our bash?'

Lulie put a hand on his chest, her head to the side beseechingly. 'Let's just host our party the night before, on the Friday. It's crazy to force people to choose between us, and if everyone's coming down for the gala anyway, it saves them having to do two trips.' In truth, she was scarcely on nodding terms with most of Pia's guests, but her PRs were doing a great job of drumming up interest in her and she was savvy enough to realize that piggybacking on Pia's event would be a great boost for her profile.

Jonty smiled at her and sighed. 'Whatever the lady wants, the lady gets,' he said, kissing the top of her head. He knew Tanner would be pissed off with him for not backing him up in front of Pia, but he couldn't resist his wife's pleas. Her rewards were greater than his.

Pia shot a victorious smile at Tanner.

'Well, I'm so glad that's settled,' she crowed. 'The dress code's white tie, by the way.'

'Great. Bagsy I wear Dad's,' Jonty said to Tanner.

Tanner just shrugged. 'You're welcome to it. I'll be damned if I'm going.'

'I'll be damned if you're invited,' Pia shot back.

'So you must be in wall-to-wall rehearsals now,' Lulie said, changing the subject.

'Yes, Pia's been training very hard for it,' Will replied, shifting his weight from foot to foot. He was eager to get Pia out of there. 'The Royal Ballet arrives in three weeks.'

'Exactly how do you train for a ballet performance with a leg in plaster?' Tanner asked drily.

'Slowly,' Pia said, not liking the laughter in his voice. 'The plaster's coming off in two weeks.'

'Right. And then you'll be able to perform barely a fortnight after that, will you?'

'Yes.' Pia blinked nervously. The schedule was a sore point. She scarcely believed it was possible herself. Had it not been for this stupid dance-off and all the media hype, she'd have pushed it back. She was aching to get back on the stage and under the spotlights but, physically, she didn't feel anywhere near ready. Though she knew the ballet by heart now, her confidence was still low and the press, whipped into a frenzy by her rivalry with Ava Petrova, were backing the Russian. Everyone was. Everyone except Will. As the day of the debut was drawing nearer, her instincts were telling her to back out, that it was too soon, but the scale of the project made it impossible now. She felt trapped but she couldn't let him down. Not after everything he'd done.

'Hmm, maybe I should go and watch after all, then. It should be a riot watching you with egg on your face.'

'Egg on my face?' Pia looked baffled.

'It's an English expression. It means—'

'I can guess what it means, thank you,' she snapped. 'You think I'm going to look an idiot. That I'll fail.'

'It certainly sounds too soon,' he said.

'And that's your expert opinion, is it?' Her cheeks had pinked.

'In as much as I train polo ponies for a living and know what it takes to get them to match fitness. Athletes are much the same. Rest and timing are every bit as important as training. A horse simply couldn't come back from injury in the time frame you're working in.'

'I'm sure you're right. Most horses would need another couple of weeks before they got back on *pointe*,' she said sarcastically, and everyone laughed. 'Your argument is flawed. I am nothing like a horse—'

'Well, I agree, it's not a fair comparison to the horse,' Tanner interrupted.

Pia gasped, her hands balled into little fists.

'Don't sink to his level,' Will said calmly, as Pia reddened further. She hated this man. He was chippy, belligerent, aggressive. He just kept on coming at her with his snide remarks and put-downs. How he could share DNA with the amiable Jonty, she didn't know.

Will pulled her up to standing.

'Thanks for the hospitality, Jonty,' he said. 'Good to meet you, Lulie. We look forward to seeing you at the gala.'

'Well, before then, I hope,' Lulie replied. 'You'll come to our wedding reception the night before?'

'It's a date,' Will said. He shot a withering stare at Tanner, before holding the door open for Pia and walking quickly behind her. He didn't want anyone ogling her retreating arse.

They settled into the car and Will leant over to kiss her, but she was rigid with tension.

'Just forget about him,' he said, pulling back to look at her furious little figure. 'He's an idiot. He's probably only being so hideous to you because he fancies you like mad and knows you're mine.'

Pia arched an eyebrow at his assumptive possession of her.

'Okay, well, more mine than his anyway,' he corrected, grinning. He sat back and turned on the ignition. 'Did he behave himself in my absence? Was his derision of you entirely for my benefit?' he asked, shifting the car into gear. He was desperate to know what had been said while he'd been riding.

'Well, he was pretty quiet until you got back. I was mainly chatting with Jonty and Lulie,' Pia said, relaxing back in her seat.

They rolled out of the yard and up the gravel drive. It was worn bare in certain areas now and there were large potholes that required full-on swerving if you weren't to lose a wheel. The whole drive needed to be redone – a costly project. He noticed that the beech hedging was bosky and becoming strangled with bindweed too. Had Tanner also had to cut back on the gardener?

'By the way, what's your dog called?' Pia asked as they zoomed past the dandelion meadows.

'What dog?'

'The dog that was with you when you pulled me out of the lake.'

Will looked at her.

'I remember it barking,' she shrugged. 'Why haven't I seen it at the house?'

There was a long pause as Will racked his brains for an answer.

'Oh, that dog,' he said finally. 'She's . . . she's in kennels at the moment.'

'Why?'

'Well . . . she's in season. I'll end up with every dog in the neighbourhood camped out on the doorstep if I keep her here. She'll be back in a few weeks.'

'Oh,' Pia said, looking out of the window. 'What's her name?'

Pause. 'Custard.'

'Custard? That's not a dog's name.'

'It is to the English,' he shrugged. 'We actively cultivate a sense of the ridiculous.'

'That's for sure,' Pia mumbled.

He roared up his own immaculately maintained drive and turned off the ignition. Mrs Bremar opened the door and helped Pia inside. Will broke off from them in the hall, as Pia bottom-shuffled up the stairs.

'I'll come and see you in a bit,' he said, heading towards the study. 'I just need to pick up some calls.' And he shut the door behind him, speed-dialling Emma and giving her the strangest set of orders yet.

Chapter Twenty-nine

The sudden sound of the buzzer made her jump, and Sophie looked over crossly at the door. Like an obedient pet, it immediately went quiet.

She resumed the flicking brushwork she was using to delineate Ava's shoulder line, the rest of her body absolutely still, her lips pursed in concentration, wisps of her hair fluttering in the breeze coming through the open studio roof.

The buzzer intruded insolently again, and she gave a startled jerk.

'Oh for Chrissakes,' she muttered, throwing down her brush and wiping her hands messily over her white boiler suit. It was made from a strange perforated paper and designed for professional decorators and DIY enthusiasts to pull on over their clothes, though she only ever pulled hers on nude, when she fell out of bed in the mornings. It had cost only $5 at the hardware store, and was so rigid with paint smudges and stains it could practically stand up on its own. 'If that's someone trying to sell me a sodding bible . . .'

'What?' she shouted irritably into the intercom.

'Is that Sophie?'

'Yes,' she snapped.

'It's Russell Lerner.'

'Who?'

'From the *Chicago Tribune* Arts section. We spoke on the phone.'

Sophie was silent for a long moment. O. M. G.

'Miss O'Farrell, are you there?' the voice crackled.

'Uh, yes, yes, I uh . . .' Panicking, she glanced around her apartment – the unmade bed, the mugs stacked up in the sink, the towering pizza boxes, dirty knickers on the floor. She'd completely forgotten about the interview. Baudrand had insisted upon it, delighting in the opportunity to fan the hype further. His campaign to win the battle against the Royal – and most pertinently against Pia – was beginning to assume epic proportions, and he was adamant that Sophie had to play her part. Besides, he'd said, the higher the profile of the gala night, the higher her new profile in the art world. She didn't want Pia eclipsing her from all the way across the Atlantic, did she?

'Come up,' she said, buzzing him in, and sprinting to the bathroom to check her appearance in the mirror.

'Bugger,' she said, trying to wipe black paint off her eye but managing only to spread it further. 'Oh, great, now I look like a panda,' she muttered, abandoning the black eye in favour of pulling the duvet up the bed. She was just hiding the mugs in the washing machine when there was a rap at the door. She was out of time.

'Hi,' she said, smiling apologetically as she opened the door. 'Oh!'

Russell Lerner smiled back at her. She hadn't expected him to be so good-looking. Well, she hadn't expected him at all of course, but . . . well, wow! Her eyes and smile widened. He was tall, really tall, even by her lofty standards. Six foot four at least, and she liked the look of every last inch show-cased in a dark grey suit and pink check open-necked shirt.

He was boasting a five o'clock shadow, even though it was only two in the afternoon, and had light brown wavy hair, brown eyes and an astonishingly pink mouth whose bottom lip protruded, just so, and appealingly. 'No, really, the pleasure's all mine,' she said, offering her hand.

Russell laughed and took it, just as Sophie realized he hadn't yet said it was a pleasure to meet her. She blushed scarlet.

'Well, that's broken the ice. May I come in?' he smiled.

Sophie nodded. 'I have to confess I completely forgot you were coming. I'm so sorry about the state of the apartment. It's just disgusting. And as for the state of me . . . oh God, you're not going to photograph me today, are you?' she said, peering down the corridor for a lurking photographer. She looked down at her shapeless boiler suit. With horror, she saw she could see her bush through the papery fabric. She looked up at him in alarm but Russell's eyes were travelling over the room, not her.

'No. Not today,' he smiled, amused.

'Uh . . . uh . . .' She was desperate for him not to look at her. 'Why don't you just take a seat on the sofa over there and I'll quickly change out of these work clothes?' she said, skittering to the bathroom.

Ripping off the boiler suit – quite literally – she pulled on some clean knickers and wriggled into her skinniest jeans and a fawn-and-white-striped long-sleeved T-shirt draped over the side of the bath. She managed to scrub the paint off her face with make-up remover – although she'd have used turps if she'd had to – and quickly squeezed some juicy gloss onto her lips. She appraised herself in the mirror. The newly clean eye was now red and slightly swollen, like she had a dust allergy, but at least the hair was behaving itself today. It would have to do.

Russell was standing in the studio when she came out, holding a canvas of Ava in *arabesque penchée* in his hands.

'Oh no, no, no, I'm sorry,' she cried, rushing over and grabbing it from him. 'You can't see these yet. They're not finished.' Hurriedly, she grabbed a dust cloth and threw it over the easels, standing with her arms outstretched, rather overdramatically barring his way.

Russell put his hands in his pockets and stared at her, smiling. 'That's a shame. From that brief glimpse, I was going to say they're really good.'

She dropped her arms and shrugged apologetically. 'I . . . I'm not used to people seeing my work. No one's seen these yet. Not even Monsieur Baudrand.'

Russell nodded. 'I understand.'

'Can I get you a drink?'

'Yuh, sure,' he said, as she led him towards the kitchenette, eager to be away from the studio. 'What've you got?'

She opened her single wall cupboard. 'Tea, coffee – only instant, I'm afraid, or uh . . .' She checked the fridge. 'Shit, I'm out of milk,' she muttered. She racked her brain. 'I could make you . . . uh . . . a hot Ribena,' she shrugged.

'Hot Ribena?' he laughed.

Sophie bit her lip. 'It's good on cold days,' she said defensively.

'Well, then, I don't think I'll be able to consider myself to have lived till I've had one.'

'Oh good,' she sighed, relieved. 'I'll join you.'

Sophie bustled around, filling up the kettle and trying to find clean mugs. The only options were an ancient Snoopy mug and a Wonderbra mug Pia had given her from one of her goody bags, in which the hot tea/coffee/Ribena magically made the model's dress disappear and stripped her down to her underwear. Even she despaired.

'You live here on your own?' Russell asked, watching her.

Sophie grimaced. 'Unfortunately. Of course, what I really need is a wife who can take care of this place and feed me at regular intervals while I paint.'

'The pressure must really be on, huh?'

'Oh yeah.'

'Are you nervous?'

'Beyond terrified. I don't know how I got talked into doing this. It wasn't like I even asked for any of this to happen,' she said, pouring the Ribena, before realizing how ungrateful she sounded. 'Not that I'm not completely grateful for the opportunity I've been given,' she corrected. 'I know there are thousands of artists struggling out there for a break like this. It's a dream come true to have been offered a show with such a high profile.'

He smiled patiently at her PR spiel.

'That's for sure. Even when it was just Ava headlining the ballet it was a big deal locally. But with Pia weighing in with her rival production in Europe it's given you an international platform. You must capitalize upon it. The two biggest divas in ballet have done you the most enormous favour.'

Sophie handed him the mug with Snoopy on it and they sat down on the sofa.

He took a sip of the Ribena. 'Mmm, this is good.'

'Really?'

He nodded. Sophie watched him sitting there, so relaxed. He didn't move to take out a notepad or pens. 'Aren't you going to use a tape recorder or something?'

'No need,' Russell smiled. 'It all goes in here,' he said, indicating his head. 'I love your accent, by the way. Is it Scottish?'

'No, Irish. My family are from a small village called Fennor in Eire. It's near Waterford.'

'I've never been to Ireland. I keep meaning to go.'

'Oh you must. It's so lush and beautiful. It's called the Emerald Isle – you've never seen so many shades of green. Honestly, you'd love it,' she sighed.

'It sounds like you miss it.'

Sophie nodded. 'I do.'

'When did you leave?'

'When I was fifteen.'

'Fifteen! Really? That's so young.'

'I stayed with friends,' she shrugged, trying to be casual.

'Why did you leave at that age?'

There was a pause as Sophie checked her story. She'd never had to give her life story before. 'Ireland's a small place,' she said eventually. 'I guess I just felt I'd outgrown it.'

'I see,' he replied, but he didn't sound entirely convinced. 'You must have been a pretty grown-up fifteen-year-old. I was still five foot six and a soprano when I was fifteen.'

Sophie giggled.

'Do you go back often?'

'No, nowhere near enough. I'm completely petal to the medal trying to—'

Russell choked on his drink, laughing.

'What?' she asked. 'What's so funny?'

'I think you meant to say "pedal to the metal"?'

Sophie looked confused. 'What did I say?'

He saw her body tense. She obviously hadn't done this before, and was tripping over herself, worrying about what to say; although he always took the view that it was what the subject *didn't* say that was most revealing.

'No, nothing,' he said, composing himself. 'I shouldn't have interrupted. Go on.'

Sophie shifted position nervously, trying to get back to her official line. 'Well, I'm so busy with getting the show ready at the moment that I've scarcely got time to sleep and eat. And before that I was on twenty-four-hour call with Pia so—'

'With Pia?' Russell repeated, his interest piqued. 'Pia Soto?'

'Yes. I was her assistant,' she answered, suddenly wondering whether she should have kept that under wraps for the time being. It wasn't that it was a secret or anything – how could it be? – but all the attention on the two rival productions was really ascending to a peak, and Baudrand wouldn't be happy if Sophie brought more attention to Pia in this interview than to herself.

'Really? I didn't know that.' He took a long sip of his Ribena. 'How long did you work for her?' It stained his lips red. She tried not to look at them. He was distractingly good-looking.

'Three years or thereabouts.'

'And you left to pursue your artistic career?'

'Well . . . not exactly,' Sophie replied, wondering how to get out of this. She didn't want to tell an outright lie. He was a journalist. It was his job to check facts and find out the truth. 'We . . . uh . . . she fired me, actually,' she sighed.

'*Fired* you? Why?' This was just getting better and better.

Sophie shrugged. 'Your guess is as good as mine.'

'Really?'

'Honestly. I don't know why she did it. It happened right after her accident.'

Russell nodded intently. There was a bigger story here. He could feel it. Forget the niche Arts supplement – eight hundred words and a grainy head shot. If he could get what he needed from Sophie – and just two minutes in, he knew she was hiding stuff – this story could leap to the colour magazine, three thousand words, two double-page spreads . . . the cover, even. He looked at Sophie, all lean and lanky, her incredible red hair backlit by the sun into a blazing halo. He could just imagine them styling her like a Rossetti muse.

He paused for too long. Sophie was watching him now and saw the cogs turning in his mind. They both knew there was blood in the water.

'I don't want to talk about any of that now, though,' she said tersely, pulling herself up and trying to take control. 'It's got nothing to do with my art and the show.'

'Well, strictly speaking, no,' he said. 'But given that your show for the ChiCi is on the same night they're up against Pia and the Royal, there's obviously going to be an interest in the fact that you used to work for . . . well, the enemy, really.'

Sophie went rigid, alarm bells ringing madly. 'I don't see Pia as the enemy. Not at all.'

'But if she fired you, you can't be on friendly terms, can you?'

'We're not on any terms at all but that doesn't mean I don't wish her well.'

'So you don't feel any conflict of interest?'

'Why would I? My loyalty is with the ChiCi. They're my

employers now. They've given me the opportunity to finally pursue the career I've always dreamt of.'

She'd done it. Brought the conversation back to neutral, bland territory.

'Did you always want to be an artist?' he asked.

'Yes, since childhood,' she smiled. 'And my poor mother's still got the wallpaper to prove it,' she cracked.

He gave a laugh. 'So how did your big break happen? How did you go from being the assistant of the company's star dancer to the company's resident artist? Did Pia put in a good word for you, perhaps?'

Pia again? 'No. Not at all. I don't think she even clocked that I used to sketch when she was in rehearsals. I just did it as something to pass the time while I waited for her. No, it was *Ava* who saw my work and showed it to the artistic director. She was the one who championed me.'

Russell nodded slowly, picking up the new allegiance.

'Are you and Ava friends?'

'Of course,' she said proudly. Her talk with Ava at lunch a couple of weeks ago had gone well, and Ava had said that, as a personal favour to Sophie, she'd do her best to get on better with Adam. And it seemed to have done the trick. She'd stopped picking on him in rehearsal, Adam's morale was up and Baudrand was reassured that Adam was the right partner for Ava after all. 'I've been shadowing her every day for the past two months. I consider it a great honour to be allowed such close access to a dancer like Ava.'

'That must be a pretty bitter pill for Pia to swallow, then, seeing you so close to Ava.'

'I sincerely doubt she knows or cares,' Sophie sighed. She wished to God he'd stop going on about Pia.

Russell picked up the defensiveness in her voice. It was

no good. She was on high alert about anything to do with Pia and was clamming up. He put his mug down on the table and fixed her with his eyes.

'Have you eaten?'

'Sorry?' Sophie said, surprised.

'Why don't we go out somewhere and get something to eat?' he shrugged. 'I missed lunch today.'

'Uh . . . no. Thanks for the offer, but I really need to get back to the studio. There's only two weeks left. I'm on the countdown now.'

'Aw, come on. You can stop for an hour, can't you? A girl's gotta eat,' he grinned. 'Come on, let me take you out. We can talk while we eat.'

Sophie looked at him. He really was ridiculously good-looking. Frankly, compared to him, it was Adam *who*? And she hadn't had anything to eat yet today. That tube of fruit pastilles for breakfast didn't count.

'Oh go on, then,' she smiled, standing up. 'But it'll have to be a quick bite. Every hour really does matter at the moment.'

'Of course. Whatever you say,' he winked.

'I'll just get my coat.'

He was leaning against the door when she came back, hair freshly brushed, lips glossed.

'No coat?' he asked, one eyebrow arched.

'Oh! I . . . I forgot that,' Sophie stammered, hating the fact that it was now obvious she'd disappeared to make herself up for him. He must have women falling at his feet.

'You don't need one anyway. It's gorgeous out there.' She looked through the studio windows to the speedwell-blue sky and high-floating clouds. 'In here too,' he said lightly.

'God, you're joking, aren't you?' she said. 'This flat's a

disaster zone. Strictly speaking, you should be wearing a hard hat.'

She seized her bag and rummaged through it, pretending to look for her keys. She was suddenly aware of him staring at her.

'You're very independent,' he said quietly.

'Am I?' she said, keeping her eyes down.

'Sure. Leaving Ireland at fifteen. Living alone here. I'm wondering who looks after you now? Strictly off the record, of course.'

'Looks after me?' she echoed.

'Yes – you're not wearing a wedding ring, so I assume you're not married. Do you have a boyfriend?'

'Uh, no. Not really. Shall we go?' she said, moving over and putting her hand on the latch. Russell didn't move, blocking the exit.

'Not *really*? What does that mean?'

Sophie blushed. 'There's no one in particular, I mean.'

'But there is someone,' he persisted. 'There's someone on the scene.'

'No, no, not really,' she demurred, looking away.

'Is he married?'

'God, no!'

'In the company?'

Sophie blushed. 'No, really, he's not . . . we're not . . . it's not a regular thing. I mean, that's not to say I . . .' She sighed and stared up at him, frustrated by her ineloquence. 'He's in love with someone else. I'm not really on his radar.'

'So he's a damned fool, then,' he said, taking a step closer to her until she could feel his suit brush against her. His face was inches from hers.

There was a hot silence.

'You've got a very unorthodox interview technique, Mr Lerner,' she whispered finally, her heart pounding wildly.

'Actually, I stopped interviewing you quite a while ago,' he replied, framing her face in his hands. 'I was just trying to find out whether anyone was going to break my nose for doing this to you.' And he kissed her softly on the lips.

Sophie pulled back and looked into his golden-brown eyes.

'Rest assured, your nose will be safe,' she whispered, linking her arms around his neck and kissing him back.

Chapter Thirty

Lunch led to drinks, which in turn seeped into dinner and Sophie forgot all about her strict schedule. Yes, she was high on tequila, but more than that she was high on Russell's attention. It felt glorious to be basking in the compliments of a handsome man after weeks of being forgotten and over-looked by Adam.

They were caught in a flash storm on the way back from the Chinese restaurant, four blocks away, and their clothes became so saturated that puddles of water collected at their feet as they stopped and kissed every ten yards.

'Get a room!' a passing taxi driver shouted as they necked on the pavement outside Sophie's apartment block, fat drops of water falling off the yellow-striped rain canopy and down her back. But she didn't care.

'The man's got a point,' Russell grinned, breaking away from her. 'Are you going to let me come up with you?'

Sophie bit her lip and shook her head. 'I've not even known you a day yet,' she protested, as his hands ran up and down her waist.

'I know, but I'm at my best at night anyway.'

'Oh really?' she giggled. 'Tell me, has that line worked for you before?' she said, slapping his arm lightly.

He shrugged. 'This is its debut? What do you think?'

Sophie looked at him grinning down at her, his hair sopping wet, his suit shapeless and clinging to him in the rain. 'I'll tell you what I think . . .' she said, beginning to back away from him. Slowly, she pulled her T-shirt over her head, watching the way his jaw dropped and his eyes widened at the sight of her. She wiggled her hips and shoulders like a couture model, laughing drunkenly as horns tooted frantically at the sight of her in just her jeans and bra. Then suddenly she threw the T-shirt so that it landed on his head, and dashed into the building. 'You can have me if you can catch me!' she shrieked, darting into the building.

Russell was after her like a shot, but her legs were just as long as his, and she maintained the distance between them as they bounded up the stairs, three steps at a time. Screaming with delight, she unhooked her bra at the third floor and dropped it over the banisters onto his head.

'Get back here!' he shouted, laughing helplessly and finding it difficult to run with a lacy bra as goggles and a raging hard-on. But she was already up to the fifth floor now.

'Catch me if you can!' she laughed. 'Or I'm locking you out.'

That did it. With a new purpose, Russell found his sprint mode, locking his arms around Sophie's waist just as she turned onto the landing of the eighth floor, making her squeal with fright, surprise and delight.

'You're a minx,' he laughed, burying his face in the nape of her neck, his hands wandering up to the tight swell of her small, pale and very cold breasts. He felt her tense.

'Adam!'

'Sophie,' he heard a male voice say.

Russell looked up. A dark-blond-haired man was sitting outside her door, holding a bottle of vodka. Even from what he could see of the muscular physique in the jeans and loose-weave grey cashmere jumper, Russell could tell he was a dancer, but the Arts was Russell's beat and he'd have recognized Adam Bridges in a gorilla costume. Instinctively, Russell closed his hands around Sophie's breasts, as much a gesture of possession as chivalry.

'What are you doing here?' Sophie gasped, breathless from the stairwell race.

Adam watched her little bosom heave in the man's hands, her cheeks spotted pink with drink, exercise, passion and embarrassment, her copper curls having turned a sleek burnished Titian in the wet. She looked beautiful, and incredibly sexy.

Feebly, he waved the vodka bottle. 'I'm sorry. I didn't realize you had . . . company,' he said finally.

Oh God, Sophie thought. Why now? He was eight hours too late.

Adam put the vodka bottle on the ground next to the door.

'Sorry to intrude. I'll see you around,' he said.

'No, Adam. Wait. I, uh . . .' Sophie grabbed her T-shirt and wrapped it around her chest, bandeau-style. 'Um, this is Russell Lerner,' she said, desperately wondering why she was bothering with prim manners at a time like this.

Adam's eyebrow lifted fractionally at the mention of his name. The journalist? He was familiar with his byline. 'Pleased to meet you,' he said coolly, as Russell stepped forward, offering his hand and seemingly oblivious to the fact that Sophie's bra was still draped over his head like earmuffs.

'Won't you come in for a drink?' Sophie offered, motioning to the vodka.

'No. I've made enough of a nuisance of myself already.'

'Nonsense,' Russell said expansively.

Adam looked at him. 'Have a nice night,' he said, and walked down the corridor and out of sight.

'Well, that was embarrassing,' Russell said, as Sophie carried on looking after him.

There was a long silence. From the way both of them had reacted, Russell had no doubts Adam Bridges was the man she was involved with. And from the look on his face at seeing Sophie looking so wild and exciting and passionate, if she hadn't been on his radar before tonight, she certainly would be now.

Russell straightened himself up. 'I'd better get going too,' he said quietly.

Sophie snapped out of her daydream and looked at him. 'No. No, don't do that. Stay,' she said, but it was clear that the moment had gone.

'I've got an early start tomorrow, and you've got a big deadline to meet. Get a good night's sleep.' He moved forward and pulled her hands into his, pulling the T-shirt away from her breasts in the process. He looked down at her slender, freckled frame under the strip light. It was so erotic having her standing half-naked in a public place like that. He kissed her hands softly. 'I'll call you tomorrow,' he said. 'I promise.'

She smiled but felt relieved he was going. She'd had the most glorious afternoon and evening with him but she'd been wretchedly drunk, and finding Adam waiting for her had been an abrupt way of sobering up. She had to stop drinking so much – it always got her into trouble. Look at what had happened last time, in St Moritz.

She let herself back into the apartment, dropping her bag and wet T-shirt to the ground. The Ribena bottle was still on the worktop, the mugs where they had left them on the coffee table.

Pulling off her sodden jeans, she padded naked across the apartment to the studio. The white shrouded canvases looked ghostly in the dark, the night lights of Chicago city muted by the rain that had obscured the glass in the floor-to-ceiling windows.

She stepped over the threshold into the little room and recoiled as her foot became wet. Looking down, she saw the floor was covered with water. She gasped in horror. What had happened? A burst pipe? It couldn't be. The rest of the apartment was dry and there was nobody above the studio.

Above . . . Shit! She looked up and straight out into the twinkling night sky. There was no blurred vision from this aspect. She'd left the skylights open. The flash flood.

With a trembling hand, she lifted the dust sheets that were clinging wetly to the easels. Before her eyes, the exquisitely rendered dancers were running and coagulating like hot wax into a bleary, abstract palette.

Numbly, she flicked through them all, but of the seventeen finished canvases only four were salvageable. Baudrand had wanted twenty-five, but as she looked around at the smudged and distorted artworks she knew it was impossible. Quite literally, the sky had fallen in.

Chapter Thirty-one

Pia flung down the towel furiously and the piano player nervously took his hands off the keys, trying to look invisible.

'It's no good!' she cried. 'I can't do it. I can't.'

'Nonsense,' Evie said throatily. 'You're rushing, that's all. Take a break.'

Pia shook her head, raising her hand for the piano player to start up again, but the boy – a local music scholar – took one look at Evie's face, and decided to remain invisible.

'Take a break, and that's an order, my girl,' Evie growled. 'You're exhausted. And I won't have you getting another injury just because you don't know when to stop.'

Pia hobbled over to where Evie stood and sat on the high stool, taking a swig from her water bottle. Evie couldn't help but be heartened by the fact that she looked such a mess again. She had rolled the offensively pristine red leotard down to her waist and knotted a grey T-shirt of Will's, with the sleeves torn off, under her bust. She'd cut the feet off some 10-denier tan tights and was back in her flat ballet shoes.

And she looked great on it. Her curves were coming back and she looked strong again. The stretching and resistance exercises they'd been working on – day in, day out, for weeks

– had built up her muscle mass and Evie felt she was back up to eighty-five per cent of her old fitness. The K wires were coming out tomorrow and the plaster would be off too. She'd technically be free to dance again. As far as text-books went, she was a model patient. But something was still missing: self-belief? Confidence?

Certainly, the commitment was there. Pia never missed a session (well, she couldn't when she lived only up the lawn) and she'd memorized the music and steps of *The Songbird* within a week of being handed the score. Every afternoon – after a morning's physio – she walked through the steps in her weight-bearing cast. She couldn't spring, jump, spin or twirl; and of course she wasn't even allowed up on *demi-pointe* yet. But, step by step, they paced through the ballet, like a horse being walked the course, repeating it over and over and over until Pia's brain swam with mark-ings and cues, and she knew the shape of that ballet better than the contours of her own face.

It had to be that way. The dancers chosen from the Royal Ballet were already in rehearsals in London, but Pia wasn't strong enough to join them and was going to have to wait until they came down the following week to rehearse with them. Evie didn't want her going back on *pointe* until five days before the gala – the latest she could possibly leave it – and anyway, Rudie Bianchi, her chosen partner, had per-formance commitments until the night before. They would only have the dress rehearsal in which to dance her ballet together for the first time.

In all, it meant she would only have seven days in which to rehearse with the (almost) full company, orchestra and costumes for the debut of *her* ballet and the single most important performance of her career – a schedule that, even taking the fact that she was coming back from injury out of the equation, was scarcely possible. Tanner Ludgrove had been right – although she'd die rather than admit it – but what else could they do? Ava had been over in Chicago and in full rehearsal with Adam for several weeks now, and thanks to Will enthusiastically timetabling her return for this global coup, the culture vultures were tearing up the columns in anticipation of the dance-off. Images of the ballerinas were everywhere, with Ava giving interviews left, right and centre. Pia, by contrast – and to Will's huge chagrin – refused to grant a single one, and it was taken as an own-vote of no confidence, but that didn't stop the magazine and newspaper editors rehashing old interviews – anything to justify putting her picture in their publications. Circulations were soaring as a result and the media juggernaut was hitting top speed. Pia couldn't stop it now, even if she wanted to. She just had to keep going, stepping one foot in front of the other.

Evie walked over to her bag and grabbed a bag of marbles, placing them strategically around Pia's feet.

'Don't tell me you want to play?' Pia said drily. 'I should warn you – I was my school's champion.'

Evie shot her an unamused smile. 'Pick them up,' she ordered.

Pia looked at her, perplexed, then reached down. There was no point asking why. The woman's techniques just got odder. Ice massage and wobble boards, okay, Pia could see the point. But marbles? She bent down.

'With your toes, please.'

Pia looked back up at her. 'Seriously?'

Evie watched her as she extended her leg, hovering the cast above the scattered marbles. They looked tiny by comparison. Pia couldn't even see them round the cast. She lowered her foot jerkily, like a toddler on a JCB, and sent them rolling away.

'See, I can't do it,' she said, pulling her leg up. 'It's useless. I can't do anything.'

'Try again,' Evie said calmly. 'It's not supposed to be easy. Once it's easy, it's pointless.'

Pia tried again. 'Uuurgh!' she shrieked, frustrated. 'What's even the point of this? What have I got to do next? Grab a brush between my toes and paint you a landscape?'

Evie paused. 'Well, I guess we don't have to do this,' she said finally. 'If you're happy for Ava to *own* your ballet . . .'

Pia's eyes narrowed contemptuously. 'She'll never own anything of mine.'

'Really?'

'Damned right.'

'People are saying she's already got your ballet company, your roles, your dance partner. Hell, she's even got your old assistant.'

'What?' Pia's heart thumped at the mention of Sophie.

Evie saw the jealousy flare in her. 'Oh didn't you know? It's all very sweet. I think they're even considering getting matching tattoos: "BFF". Apparently Ava discovered she's a talented artist and Baudrand has appointed her resident artist for the ChiCi. He likes the idea of having his own Degas, you know,' she drawled. 'So Sophie's shadowing Ava and they're throwing a big exhibition of her works on the night of the gala.'

Pia bit her lip and looked away. She could just imagine it – Sophie and Ava laughing together, while she was stranded here, trying to pick up goddam marbles with her toes. Her isolation bit at her again. She said nothing but her cheeks had pinched white. She looked down and slowly, precisely, clawed her toes and picked up the smallest marble on the floor.

It took thirty-five minutes to collect all forty marbles. Evie, pleased by her patient's new-found determination, said she could stop after twenty. But Pia ignored her and grimly carried on.

Afterwards, Evie watched her go back up the path to the house on her crutches and she realized that the missing part of the jigsaw had been found now. It wasn't strength or technique or commitment that she'd been lacking. It had been drive. In order to dance, Pia Soto needed anger.

Chapter Thirty-two

Sophie saw him before he saw her, and she looked into the road to see whether she could cross. She couldn't. Four yellow cabs were chuntering down the street and a DHL van was double-parked on the other side, forcing the rest of the traffic into the central reservation.

It was too late anyway. He'd spotted her.

'Hey!' he called. 'Fancy seeing you here. I thought you'd have moved to a swanky new district by now.'

'Hi, Greg,' she said wanly, wondering what he was on about today. It was the first time she'd left the apartment since the sky had fallen in and ruined her paintings.

After two days of mute shock, which had been spent in bed studiously avoiding calls from everyone – including Russell – she'd switched into manic mode and managed to get twelve canvases completed. There was still one week left and she figured she could whip up another six by then, but she was still going to be seven short and she'd have to ring Baudrand this afternoon and give him the bad news.

Lack of courage, food and milk had forced her out of the apartment, and as she wandered aimlessly round the block rehearsing her excuse, fielding Greg's amorous advances was the last thing she wanted to do.

'You'll need to go incognito soon, you know,' he said. 'Dark glasses, wig . . .'

'I don't think so, Greg.'

'Well,' he said, sucking on his teeth. 'If they're gonna keep up this kind of scrutiny on you, you might think differently.'

'What are you talking about?' she sighed wearily. Baudrand had been bigging up her talent and the exhibition, using anything and everything that he thought would give the ChiCi production more press coverage and a higher profile.

He tapped the Sunday papers under his arm.

'Can I see?'

'Sure,' he said, delighted to get a few extra minutes in her company. He unrolled the papers and handed her the Sunday magazine.

She looked at the cover. It showed one image each of Pia and Ava, both performing *Sleeping Beauty*. The picture editor had managed to get matching shots of them in spectacular *attitude croisé devant* from the Rose adagio, and the art department had tattered the edges of the photos, making it seem that they were mirror images. In between them was a picture of Sophie, the one taken for all the exhibition publicity. Sophie hated it. It didn't look like her – they'd tonged her hair and put eyeshadow on her – but that was the least of her worries right now.

She frowned at the implication that she was piggy in the middle between the two primas. She flicked to the centre spread. They had managed to get some paparazzi pictures of her walking along the streets with Ava and Pia. More specifically, the paparazzi had been shooting Ava and Pia and, to the picture editor's delight as he researched the archives for this particular story, he'd found these ones where Sophie was in shot too.

'Mind if I take this, Greg?' she asked, walking away before he could reply.

'Uh, sure,' he said, watching her go. 'So, does this mean you're not up for dinner in the next few days, then?' he called after her.

There was no reply.

'Yeah,' he muttered to himself. 'Best to let things settle a bit.'

Sophie let herself into her apartment and shut the door behind her. Leaning against the door, she studied Russell's head shot. He was wearing the pink shirt he'd worn to their interview and he was looking into the camera like the cat that'd got the cream. She looked away and began to read the opening paragraphs.

The Chicago City (ChiCi) Ballet's debut production of *The Songbird*, which opens next Saturday, seventeen hours ahead of the rival production being hosted by the Royal Ballet in London, will be the climactic finale to a rivalry between the two starring primas, a rivalry that is fiercer than any other since Bachon and Posevina thirty years ago. Ever since they were students at the Bolshoi, Ava Petrova in Russia and Pia Soto in the fledgling academy in Brazil, they have battled for supremacy against each other – wooing audiences, judges, advertisers, sponsors, patrons and ballet companies – in a bid to outgun each other. Their strengths lie in different areas but as the ChiCi prepares to launch the career of its exciting new resident artist, Sophie O'Farrell, on the same night, with a dazzling exhibition of both primas dancing for Chicago in the past year, will their weaknesses rest, for once, in the same place?

The enigmatic Irishwoman (pictured right), who trained briefly at the Slade School of Art in London, finds herself at the heart of the two women's relationship and keeper of each of their secrets. As Soto's former PA, she was well known in the ballet community for being the Brazilian dancer's closest confidante and loyal to a fault. However, in the wake of her career-threatening accident in January this year, Soto fired O'Farrell without explanation. Soon afterwards, confidential information came to light about Soto's luxury break in St Moritz as the guest of jewellers Cartier, and insiders privately began to ask questions about the source of this information, which led to the abrupt termination of Soto's lucrative contract with rival firm Patek Philippe.

It was Petrova's sharp eye and patronage, soon after she arrived in Chicago following her stand-in spell for Soto during the company's East Coast tour, that gave O'Farrell next week's potentially career-defining opportunity. But damaging stories about Petrova's alleged bullying of her new partner, principal Adam Bridges – also O'Farrell's occasional lover – continue to be leaked to the press, and have raised questions about O'Farrell's loyalty to Petrova too.

The fortunes of her career and personal life have rested in the hands of both diminutive giants, and as media scrutiny on both sides of the Atlantic intensifies upon them all in the next six days, it will remain to be seen whether she is an innocent being manipulated by bigger egos or a woman determined to find success by any means possible . . .

Chapter Thirty-three

'No, I want it cut down to here,' Pia said to the seamstress, who, even if her mouth hadn't been full of pins, still couldn't have replied. Pia had demanded changes to every single one of her nine costumes and the wardrobe department were going to have to work through the next three nights to get the changes made in time.

Pia admired her reflection in the mirror. She looked good. The canary-yellow stiffened tutu – which would make anyone else look sallow – made her skin glow, and the extra starch she'd demanded on the tulle had lifted the skirt even higher, so that her butt would be perfectly on show at all times. It was certainly on show at the moment without the tights on. She put her hands on her hips and looked critically at the seed pearl embroidery on the bodice. 'And these aren't strong enough. They'll be lost under the lights,' she said. 'Replace them with rubies.'

'R-r-real rubies?' the seamstress stammered. You never could be sure with Pia Soto.

'Of course not. Paste,' Pia muttered. Who did the silly woman think she was? Elizabeth Taylor? 'Now, my tiara,' she said, moving on to the next set of problems.

There was the sound of boots stomping heavily up the steps and the door was suddenly flung open.

'Oh! *You're* in here,' Tanner said disapprovingly, his eyes flicking up and down the trailer. He was wearing chaps over his jeans and a brown T-shirt; bits of straw were poking out of his hair.

Pia rolled her eyes. The man was a pig. She was still mad about his comments to her in his kitchen. 'Why shouldn't I be in here?' she retorted. 'It is my dressing room.'

Tanner looked at her. She had her full make-up and costume on and looked extraordinarily exotic. Again, he couldn't help but think how many millions of miles away she was from being the limp, grey girl he'd dragged from the water. 'I was looking for Silk. They told me I'd find him in here. It's like a bloody circus out there,' he muttered. 'This is his final invoice.' He waved an envelope at her.

'I'll take it,' Pia replied, chucking it insolently on the sofa. She turned around, placing her back to him. 'You can go.'

Tanner felt his anger rise. He'd had enough of her arrogance. His eyes travelled down her back to the juicy bottom that was peeking out from beneath the tulle, and, instinctively, he lightly flicked his whip over it.

Pia screamed and whirled round furiously to face him. Tanner had to suppress the urge to laugh.

'I've warned you before about your manners,' he said, his eyes glittering, before turning on his heel and stomping back down the steps. 'Be sure the account's settled in full before he leaves next week or the next visit will be from the bailiffs.'

Pia gawped after him in disbelief, and was only roused from her indignation by the seamstress, who was chuckling with a mouth full of pins.

*

'Anyone seen Pia?' Will asked loudly as he strode past the newly erected stage.

Everyone shook their head, baffled. It was obvious when she was about. It was like another sun had risen in the sky.

He strode up onto the terrace, and looked back down at the industry below, pleased by what he saw. They were into the final phase now, with three days to go till the gala, and there must have been two hundred people milling about his lawns: stage crew, dancers, groundsmen, lighting and sound men, caterers and wardrobe mistresses. And that was just for starters. The event planners, publicity people and security were all due in the next two days as well.

Emma, his assistant, came running over, wielding armfuls of paperwork. Her breasts strained beneath her tightly structured suit and she was out of breath when she got to him. Will listened to the sound of her panting. It had been a while since he'd heard it. He'd recently spent so much time down here and away from the office.

'Highgrove needs your signature for this. It's for the princes' security detail on Saturday,' she said.

Will scanned it briefly and signed it. 'You haven't seen Pia, have you?'

'I think she's in the dressing rooms with wardrobe. One mistress has resigned already,' she sighed.

'Well, just as long as you don't,' he said in a low voice, winking at her. Handing back the paperwork, he headed for the trailers, which had been set up behind the stage.

Pia had changed out of her costumes and was on her way down to the studio for a rehearsal of the *grand pas* sequence with Robert Washington, one of the male soloists. Her partner on the night, Rudie, would not be arriving until Saturday and they would have only a couple of hours in

KAREN SWAN

which to rehearse together, but Evie had been adamant that Pia needed to get her confidence back with the lifts. For the past few weeks Pia's energies had been so focused on working up her physical strength and fitness that she suddenly felt besieged by doubt and fear now that the K wires were out and she had been given the all-clear to dance fully again. The doctors had told Pia her body was ready, but the question now was: was her head?

Evie had been able to do only so much – she'd played the male role in their rehearsals so that Pia knew how Rudie's steps correlated to her own – but Pia needed to get back into being thrown and caught in the air again. *The Songbird* featured several tricky, virtuoso lifts that would have the crowd on their feet, but the accident had taken away her nerve as well as her mobility, and she needed to re-establish trust.

Will watched them as Robert said something that made Pia laugh out loud and she put a friendly hand on his arm. It was clear she was relishing the company of dancers again, of being part of a production, part of a team. She was wearing a floaty baby-blue chiffon skirt over a plum-coloured cat suit and he saw that she was back in her *pointe* shoes. The K wires had been out for eleven days now and she was walking without a limp. Will gave a satisfied smile. She was bang on schedule. Everything was going according to plan.

Pia looked up and saw him watching her. She hesitated, then smiled and waved him over.

'Hello,' she said. 'Who's this?'

'Someone who wanted to meet you.'

Pia looked at him curiously as the Labrador pulled her lead out of his grasp and excitedly torpedoed up to her feet. Pia bent down to pat her.

'Oh, she's gorgeous,' Pia beamed, as the dog fell into submissive mode and rolled onto her back. Pia rubbed her tummy. 'When did you get her?'

'Today. I picked her up from the kennels this morning. She's off heat now.'

Pia looked up at him, sharply. 'You mean – you mean this is the dog you had with you when you pulled me out of the water?'

'The very same. I think she remembers you, don't you?' Pia looked down at the daft dog that was lying across her feet.

'*This* is Custard?' she asked.

'Yep. What's wrong with that?'

Pia stood up, bemused. 'Well, nothing, I guess'. She cocked her head to the side. 'Except for the fact that she's black.'

Chapter Thirty-four

Tanner had caught the first train up to London with a sigh of relief. It felt so good to get away. Violet had hit the barn roof when he'd said he was shooting off to London on the day of the party. He didn't know why she was so stressed about it. Jonty and Lulie had booked party planners to deal with everything – from cleaning and decorating the house to sending out the invitations and blowing up balloons. All she had to do was buy a new dress.

He'd not given her any explanation of why he was going up, or why it couldn't be rearranged. She didn't need to know Velasquez was only in town for one night before moving on to Paris. She didn't need to know anything. She could keep her scepticism to herself. The business was his, after all.

He jumped out of the cab at Claridge's and handed the driver a twenty. As he waited for his change he fixed the cufflinks on his blue shirt and looked up at the familiar grand red-brick hotel that stretched along Brook Street. It had been a long time since he'd been here. The memories of his last visit had stayed with him for a long time, too long, interrupting his life.

He'd had to bury them, for sanity's sake, but he let his last glimpse of Veronica surface now. He could see her sitting up in the bed dressed in a scrap of champagne lace, the pillows scented with her Annick Goutal scent – even now, he could detect that perfume in a roomful of thousands – her eyes pleading with him to change his mind.

His eyes hardened with the memories. He hadn't been the one who'd needed persuading. She had been the one getting married. *She* was leaving him. She had made her decision, chosen the guy with the money.

He wondered whether they were still married, whether it had lasted. He'd met Violet soon afterwards and tried to lose himself in her, but Veronica had cast a long shadow over the relationship. She was the one who'd got away.

A courier sped past on his bike, motioning angrily for Tanner to get out of the road, and he stepped onto the pavement, trying to focus. He needed to get his mind on business, not bed. This was no time for sentimentality. The future of the business was on the line. Landing Velasquez as a client would mean a far bigger account than Silk's and would wipe out all his financial problems at once. But if he didn't pull this off he'd have more to worry about than the irritation of Violet saying, 'I told you so'.

Squaring his shoulders and straightening his tie, he walked briskly through the revolving doors. It was like a second home to him, though a lot of the staff had changed and it had had that big revamp back in the noughties. His father had spent much of his twenties living here, and after his wife – the boys' mother – had died, he had brought Tanner and Jonty up here every Christmas as none of them knew how to cook a turkey.

With relaxed familiarity, Tanner walked straight through to the bar and ordered a whisky sour. The place was packed with shoppers and tourists. Tanner saw Vittorio Velasquez was already seated in the Snuggery at the back.

It was reservation-only for twenty or so people. Clearly, he wanted the meeting to remain private. Tanner took his drink and walked over.

'Senhor Velasquez,' he said, holding out his hand. 'It's a pleasure to see you again.'

The man rose from his chair. He was Tanner's physical opposite in every way: short, stocky and darkly tanned. 'Thank you for making the effort to come here to see me, Tanner. I appreciate it.'

'No problem,' Tanner said lightly, putting his drink on the table. 'How are you?'

Velasquez nodded. 'Very well, my friend. Please, sit.'

They settled down in the red leather chairs and Velasquez reached into his crocodile-skin briefcase. He pulled out a leather folder and placed it on the table between them, pushing it towards Tanner.

'Have a look at this. It's my portfolio for the grass season.'

Tanner picked up the folder and flicked through it quickly. Thirty-six ponies, eighteen of which were high-goal; three stallions and four foals – and this was only half his stable. The other half was in Florida for four months for the American season. Tanner raised his eyebrows appreciatively. It was a plum pick.

He studied the photographs. 'What are they? Argentine polos?' he asked, squinting at them all.

'Yes. We find them to be faster. They are athletic and bold, and they turn on a sixpence.'

Tanner nodded, determined not to betray his excitement. The ponies looked like winners, every last one of them, with deep girths, short backs, long necks, and good strong chests and rumps.

'What's the drop of the withers for these ones?' he asked, scanning the page.

Velasquez leant forward and pointed to a table at the bottom.

'Between sixty-one and sixty-two inches.'

Tanner nodded.

'Well, for our part, we've got what you need in terms of facilities, location and expertise,' he said slowly. 'We spent most of last year upgrading our stabling to American barns; we've got three polo pitches, a stick-and-ball field, two horse walkers, a schooling arena and a quarter-mile all-weather canter track. The grooms, physio and vet live on site and are on call twenty-four seven,' he said mildly, flicking through the rest of the pages. 'Who's your high-goaler?'

'My son, Paolo.'

Tanner kept his surprise to himself. Paolo, as the indulged son of the patron, was well known on the circuit for reasons other than his stick-and-ball skills; but although he was a good enough player, he wasn't the obvious choice to lead the team on the field.

'I've never met him but I watched him closely in Florida last summer,' Tanner said, keeping his eyes down. 'He's a great player.'

Velasquez watched Tanner's impassive face. He was impossible to read. 'I heard you've evicted the Black Harbour stable.'

Tanner's eyebrow lifted fractionally. 'Evicted?' He shrugged lightly. 'No. The contract was up. It was time for a change – for both parties.'

Velasquez pursed his lips, unconvinced. 'A brave move. William Silk's got a fine record: winners of the Gold Cup three years running, runners-up at Guards; and he'd probably have won at St Moritz this winter if he hadn't pulled out to rescue that ballerina.' He frowned. 'What was her name?'

Tanner lifted his drink and took a sip. 'Pia Soto,' he mumbled.

'Ah yes, Pia Soto.' Velasquez pressed his hands together and raised his fingers to his lips. 'How could I forget? She's a national icon back in Brazil.'

'Is she?' he muttered. She was a monumental pain in the arse over here.

'Mmm. Very sexy girl. I'd be after her myself, but I'm realistic enough to know that if it's a question of my millions, or Silk's, she'll choose the man thirty years younger.' Velasquez chuckled.

Tanner tried to smile.

'You must know her, of course, if she's living with Silk. You're neighbours, I understand.'

'That's right.'

The older man raised an eyebrow conspiratorially.

'Tell me – is she as luscious in the flesh as she was in the Pirelli calendar?'

The image of her toned buttocks yielding to his whip flashed past Tanner's eyes and he took a deep breath. 'She's too thin for my liking,' he said dismissively. 'And a spoilt brat.'

Velasquez smiled at Tanner's vehemence and sat back in the chair. 'Ah, but brilliance and beauty make bad behaviour permissible, do they not? And when the two are combined?' He threw his hands up in the air delightedly. 'I imagine she's a *devil* woman.' He leant right in, slapping Tanner's leg. 'But worth it, no? Hey?' he laughed. 'These women, they're the ones we need to keep us on our toes. They make our lives exciting.'

Tanner put down the file and gave a short, polite laugh, his mind wandering back to Veronica. His version of 'life' with a woman like Pia Soto would involve prison warders and iron bars. They'd kill each other within a week.

'Where are the horses stabled at the moment?' Tanner asked, bringing the conversation back round to business.

'My estate in Bahia.'

Tanner looked up. 'In Brazil? Still?' The grass season was just about to kick off.

Velasquez watched him. 'I know we are late. We need to get things moving, no? I've been travelling a lot recently and I haven't been able to spend the time I would have liked on the polo.' He sighed. 'If you want the truth, it is my son, Paolo, who has been pushing for me to bring the team over to Europe. He is bored now with the American circuit. He wants us to be global players. So what can I do? If that's what he wants . . .'

Tanner nodded. 'With the greatest respect, you're too late for this year,' Tanner said with his best poker face. He didn't let on this was precisely the scenario he'd been praying for: a lazy patron, a spoilt son and a ready-to-ship team.

'There's time enough,' Velasquez said smoothly. 'I have a plane that's specially outfitted for horse transportation. The arrangements can be organized very quickly, I assure you.'

'It's more the acclimatization that I'm thinking of,' Tanner countered.

'They'll be fine, Tanner. I took them to St Tropez to play on the beach last summer and they loved it. My horses are every bit as well travelled as me.'

'I can well believe it,' Tanner smiled.

'So maybe, then, this is not a matter of timing, but of money, hey?'

Tanner let a beat pass. 'It's more than that, I'm afraid. I've been talking informally with someone in Dubai for the past year. I can't make any decisions today.'

'Of course you can – if I say I'll pay double.'

'Double?' Tanner tried to keep his voice flat.

Velasquez nodded, a smile on his lips. 'Shall I say it?'

A moment passed, then Tanner grinned and shrugged. 'Well, I guess it *is* a very nice word.'

'Double,' Velasquez laughed, leaning forward and offering his hand.

Tanner looked at it for a moment – the key to his freedom – then grasped it and shook it vigorously. For the first time since his father died he would be able to live life on his own terms again. Finally, he was his own man.

Chapter Thirty-five

Pia was just putting the finishing touches to her make-up when there was a knock at the door. Will stepped into the room, smiling. 'He's here,' he said.

'I'm ready.' Pia pouted at her reflection one last time and fluffed her hair, then stood up. She was wearing a black silk sleeveless jumpsuit that plunged at the front and hugged her butt. Her legs looked endless, her torso impossibly lean and strong.

Will whistled. 'How the hell do you manage to make trousers look that sexy?' he said admiringly, pulling a long narrow black box out of his dinner jacket.

Pia shrugged nonchalantly. She'd never lost *that* power, even during the darkest days after the accident.

'Before we go . . .' he said, walking up to her and opening the box. Inside, an emerald lariat winked back at her. Pia looked up at him, surprised.

'You didn't need to do that,' she said, making no move to pick it up.

'How could I not? They match your eyes,' he said, winding it round her neck and letting the loose ends dangle between her breasts.

They both admired her reflection for a moment. 'You like?' she smiled, looking at him in the mirror.

'You have no idea,' he replied confidently – intimately – letting his hand skim down her spine. She slid away. The ten-week chastity zone had passed and her plaster was off, but although he hadn't made a move on her yet, Pia knew that he was building up to it – cocky winks, familiar touches, a general assumption that she was his. She figured he was probably waiting till after the gala, when he would expect sex as the finale to his grandiose, ebullient investment in her.

They went down the stairs together to greet their house guest. Harry Hunter was standing by the fireplace in the drawing room, drinking a brandy. Pia beamed at the sight of him in the flesh. Pictures never truly captured how impossibly good-looking he was – six foot three, with broad shoulders, long legs, laughing eyes and ruby lips. And, in his dinner suit, he cut an especially devastating figure.

'Harry,' she squealed, running over to him delicately. 'You're here! Did you find us okay?'

Harry shrugged as he raked his eyes over her. 'The big H in the lawn was a good clue. How are you, more to the point?' He squeezed her bottom as she reached up to kiss him on the lips. 'It doesn't feel like you've lost any of your form.'

Pia giggled and slapped him lightly on the arm. 'It is good to see you again,' she said. 'I'm so touched you came all the way out here just to see me perform.'

Harry winked at her. 'Well, you know me, darling. I always did enjoy watching you perform.'

Will's jaw clenched at the flirtatious banter between the two former lovers. It was one thing having Harry on the guest list for the gala – the publicity he generated was phenomenal – but it was another matter entirely having him as a house guest, sleeping in the room next to his old flame. Especially when she was still sleeping alone.

'She's the best damned performer I've ever met,' Will said, butting in on the joke and ignoring Pia's narrowed eyes. If anyone was going to feel that three was a crowd, it wasn't going to be him. 'But come on, we'd better shift,' he said, deadpan. 'Traffic will be shocking.'

The party was already in full swing by the time they walked through Tanner's front door, four minutes later. The gravel was practically bouncing off the quarter-mile drive, and vintage Astons and MGFs were parked, askew, on the grass.

Several couples outside were already in the late stages of heavy petting, half-hidden in the thick ivy that covered the entire front of the house like a beard, and there were stacks of empty magnums on the front steps, as though left out for the milkman.

'It's yet to find its mojo, then,' Harry quipped, as a collective shriek came from the female guests catching sight of him standing in the doorway. His signature tumble of golden curls shimmered decadently under the lights and he held himself with all the swagger of someone used to commanding the room. Will watched Pia sidle up to Harry possessively, linking her arm casually through his and warning off the other women.

He looked away, his face grim. In spite of everything he'd done for her these past three months, Pia had never shown anything more than gratitude in return (and often barely even that). All the heat from their interplay in New York and St Moritz seemed to have melted with the snow, and since coming to England after the accident she'd toyed with him as idly as a sleepy cat with a mouse.

KAREN SWAN

But now she was wide awake, and Harry was clearly the one in her sights. Will felt his ego bristle. He wasn't used to being the runner-up – he *wasn't* the runner-up, dammit. They were both alpha males, both top of the tree, with more women falling at their feet than most men would be able to count.

But it wasn't just Pia vying for his attention. Will scanned the room. *All* the women were eyeing up Harry and he knew it came down to one thing: Harry was a celebrity, famous for being famous, and photographed everywhere he went. That was currency in itself these days. He shook his head at their collective stupidity. If those women only knew how his bank account stacked up against Harry's they wouldn't give the pretty boy a second look.

He inflated his chest and nodded to himself. He may not have fame on his side, but he was the top dog here. He had nothing to fear from Harry Hunter, even if Pia was pressing her curves against him. Harry seemed oblivious and it simply proved, loud and clear, that she was back to her old tricks again. She was playing games, trying to inflame his jealousy, just as she had done in Switzerland before their prelude to seduction had been so rudely interrupted.

A small smile twitched across his lips. It all boded well for the plans he had set up for tomorrow night. The timing couldn't have been better.

He went to get himself a drink to celebrate and found Lulie standing by the stairs.

'Hello, Lulie, you're looking radiant tonight,' he smiled, leaning in to kiss her.

'Thanks,' she preened. She knew she made a ravishing bride. Her buttermilk hair was wound up with pale pink roses, and she was wearing a dove-grey tulle ball skirt with an ivory silk shirt that was barely buttoned up. The trace of her nipples was clear through the flimsy material.

'Where are Tanner and Violet?' Will asked, looking round. 'I must thank them – even if Tanner will probably deck me for daring to set foot in his house.' He gave a small grimace of fear.

'Violet's in the drawing room,' Lulie giggled. 'But I don't know where Tanner is. He went into London earlier today. In fact, I'm not even sure he's back yet.'

'London? Really?' Will repeated, joking forgotten. His interest was piqued. 'What for?'

'He was meeting with a potential client, I think,' Lulie replied absently. The ruction between Will and Tanner had never really been explained to her – Jonty knew precious little himself anyway.

A shadow fell across them.

'I'm Harry,' said a cut-glass voice. 'And I just came over to kiss you.'

Lulie's eyes widened – delighted.

Will's narrowed – not.

This house wasn't big enough for the two of them.

'It's tradition, after all,' Harry continued, leaning down and kissing not her cheek, but just below her ear. Lulie shivered and he caught her eye as he pulled away. 'Congratulations.'

Pia was pouting next to him and looking as put out as Will.

Jonty sidled up, and placed a proprietorial arm around Lulie's waist. 'Hello, chaps,' he said, kissing Pia and offering Will a hearty handshake. He looked at Harry. He didn't need an introduction to know who he was. No one did. It was no coincidence that he'd crossed the room in four seconds flat when he saw Harry's eyes radar-locked upon his bride.

'I'm Jonty, officially the luckiest man here,' he grinned. 'And you must be Harry, the second luckiest, if what I'm always reading about you is true.'

'I guess I must be,' Harry drawled, just as a streaker shot past, shouting his name. He drained his glass, nonplussed. ''S okay. That happens a lot,' he said drily, watching the woman's bottom disappear round the corner.

Jonty laughed. He looked at Pia, who was looking luscious but miserable, and very tiny in her flat shoes. 'Pia,' he said, 'let me get you something better to drink than that. You can't drink water at a wedding reception! My reputation will be in tatters if it ever gets out.'

Pia shrugged. 'No choice, I'm afraid. I've got to stay fresh for tomorrow.'

'Oh I don't believe you're ever anything other than perky, Pia,' Harry grinned.

'Ha ha,' she quipped, sulkily.

Will's eyes flashed again.

'Are you nervous about tomorrow?' Jonty asked.

Pia looked quickly at Will. 'Well, of course it's . . . it's the biggest night of my career.' She laughed tightly. 'And, if it doesn't go well, it could be the last night of my career.'

'Rubbish. She's just being modest,' Will interjected, hooking his muscular arm around her and drawing her in possessively. 'I've seen her in rehearsal this week and she's back to her best. None of the other dancers can believe her recovery.'

'And it's all thanks to you, isn't it?' Harry quipped devilishly, watching their body language. He knew Pia well enough to know that her flirtation with him was a cover to hide misgivings in her relationship with Will. She'd barely acknowledged Will's presence since Harry'd arrived. 'From what I understand from my dear friends in the press, you masterminded her surgery and recovery, and now her triumphant return to the international stage. You're quite the hero.'

'Well, I . . . I . . .' Pia stammered, horrified that her encumbrance to Will was being laid out so explicitly.

'What a thing that must be, Will – having Pia Soto in your debt?' Harry winked conspiratorially. 'I do hope you're making her pay.'

Will laughed, suddenly glad of Harry's company, after all, and feeling no compunction to admit that he had yet to cash in his chips on that score.

The streaker shot past again and this time Harry got a good full-frontal look. She was a pretty girl. He raised his eyebrows to the group, speculatively, and gave a heavy sigh.

'Oh what the hell!' he said, tossing his glass into a fern before chasing after her.

Will roared with laughter at his new conspirator's antics, now that Pia was forgotten. Harry's unilateral reign over the opposite sex was quite a sight to behold when you weren't in direct competition.

A small silence fell upon the group as Harry's wattage lit up the other side of the room, leaving them all in subdued darkness.

Lulie smiled stiffly and extricated herself from Jonty's iron grip. His jealousy annoyed her. 'I'm just going to check how they're getting on in the kitchen,' she said. 'I think we could do with some more food out here.'

Tanner stood on the steps by the front door and looked down into the hall. He felt his excitement grow. He'd signed on the dotted line with Velasquez and he was walking back into his own home a free man. He owed no one anything any more. He had extricated the business from Silk's poisonous stranglehold and returned it to profitability, restoring a post-humous pride to his father and raising two fingers to Violet in the process. Damn right, he was up for a party.

He looked around at the hedonistic scene. It was packed with familiar faces – lots from the hunt and the village, but others too from school and university that he hadn't seen in years. Waiters were tentatively making their way through the crowds, holding their trays protectively with both hands and doing their best to get back to the safety of the kitchen.

Over on the stairs, he could see Jonty talking to Will. Bloody traitor. Pia was standing next to them, clearly in a terrific sulk as she looked around the room. Probably beneath her to attend such a non-A-list event.

'Tanner,' he heard a familiar voice call, and he looked towards the drawing room. Violet had spotted him and was motioning for him to come over. She looked incredibly sexy, wearing a slinky lilac dress that was cut low over her breasts. Her long hair was brushed over to one side, held in place by a huge white peony.

Quickly, he stepped down into the crowd, trying to lose himself. He didn't want to deal with her yet.

'Tanner! You made it!' yelled a bloke in a tight-fitting dinner suit, thumping him on the back. 'How are you, mate?'

Tanner looked at him. 'God, Wonky – is that you?'

The man held his arms out wide, a jeroboam of champagne in one hand. 'The very same.'

'And so's that DJ, from the look of things. Isn't that the one you wore at school?'

Wonky looked down at himself. The trousers were an inch too short and the waistband fastened by a safety pin. 'What gave it away?' he laughed. 'Here, have a drink.'

He passed the bottle to Tanner, who emptied the bottle F1-style, letting the drink flow over his mouth and all down his shirt.

'Animal!' shouted Wonky, roaring with laughter and jumping up and down like a pogo stick. 'The Animal's in the house!'

Tanner wiped his mouth and laughed, handing him back the empty bottle. That should help him catch up. 'I'll be back in a minute. Better go and get changed before the missus sees me.'

He walked towards the stairs, pulling off his tie. His shirt was soaked through.

'Where've you been, me old mucker?' Jonty asked as he approached.

'Wheeling and dealing,' he replied drily, unable to stop his eyes travelling up Pia's slinky body. The silky fabric hugged her possessively, clinging for dear life around her pneumatic curves, holding on to her breasts and sinking down to her smooth stomach. She looked sexy as hell in that all-in-one, and it was obvious she was wearing nothing underneath. All the other women in their standard little dresses looked mother-of-the-bride by comparison.

'Tanner,' Will said tightly. It clearly hurt him to be so polite.

Tanner nodded. Ditto. For his brother's sake, he was going to have to put their feud on hold for tonight. Lulie had wanted them here. 'Well, it all looks like it's going well,' he said with characteristic understatement, as a champagne cork arc'd behind him and hit the chandelier.

'You could say that,' Jonty laughed. 'Just as well we decided against the sit-down dinner, don't you think?'

Through the crowd Tanner picked up Violet's voice. He could feel her eyes on his back and ducked down again. Pia raised an eyebrow. He was clearly in trouble.

'I'd better get changed,' he said quickly. 'I take it you're in Dad's DJ,' he muttered to Jonty.

'Course,' he shrugged.

'Course,' Tanner nodded, resigned, and went upstairs.

He went into the moonlit bedroom, shrugging his jacket off. He could feel the booze hitting his bloodstream already, the beat of the music beneath his feet. He walked over to the wardrobe. Violet had left his tux hanging on the door, ready for him. He stripped off his wet suit and shirt, and let them lie in a heap on the floor, unbothered about how much it would annoy her in the morning. His mind wandered back to Veronica as he buttoned up his shirt, wondering idly whether she was still on that old number he had for her. Revisiting the scenes of their passion had unlocked the floodgates and memories had been resurfacing all the way back home.

He was fiddling with his cufflinks when he heard a sound that made him stop. Rustling. Breathing. In the room with him. He turned and looked round. Coats were piled high on the bed, and some had slipped onto the floor.

He saw a pair of shiny leather soles reflecting the moonlight; they led to a pair of tuxedoed legs that disappeared up a voluminous tulle skirt. The girl's face was hidden by her arms.

Christ, not again! It was like being back in St Moritz.

The pleasured girl's breathing began to get faster, and as her back arched away from the bed in ecstasy, her shirt fell open. Tanner watched, transfixed by the sight of her, utterly unable to move.

She circled her hips rhythmically, going slowly at first, getting faster and faster until finally she gasped as she was spirited away on the waves of her orgasm, and then the room fell still and silent. Tanner realized he'd better get out of there. Ignoring his jacket, still on the hanger, he strode out of the room, abandoning his cufflinks altogether and rolling up the sleeves instead.

He closed the door quietly, hearing laughter bubble up just as it clicked shut. He bounded down the stairs and saw with a sinking heart that Violet had joined Jonty and Pia and Will. They made an uneasy group, as Pia and Violet jostled for position against each other.

'Did you hear Harry Hunter's here?' Violet asked him excitedly, forgetting all about her fury at his late arrival.

'Who?' Tanner muttered, fiddling with his sleeves, and hoping no one would notice he was hopelessly turned on from the scene he'd just encountered in the bedroom.

Pia watched him fidget, intrigued. He looked a mess – flushed, half-dressed, wild-eyed and with a severe case of five o'clock shadow. She'd hardly ever seen him look anything other than buttoned up and austere before.

'Oh Tan, don't say you haven't heard of Harry Hunter,' Violet scolded, leaning in coquettishly. Tanner realized she was drunk. 'He's the famous writer. Remember we went to see that film of his at the cinema?'

'No.'

Violet rolled her eyes. 'Yes, you do. He's notoriously naughty, always in the papers for seducing other men's wives.'

Tanner stiffened. 'He sounds charming. So what's he doing here, then?'

'I brought him,' Pia replied insolently. 'He's an old friend of mine.'

Tanner stared at her. He might have known. If there was trouble brewing, she'd be involved somehow. 'And I suppose when you say "old friend" you mean . . .'

'Lover?' she finished for him, flashing a glance at Violet. 'Yes.'

Violet's eyes narrowed jealously. Harry Hunter. Will Silk. How come Pia got the lion's share of the rich and lusty, when she was saddled with a poor posh boy with a chip on his shoulder about his family's lost heritage?

'That figures,' Tanner muttered darkly. 'Well, where is he, then? I can't wait to meet this character.'

'He was last seen chasing a streaker out into the gardens,' Will offered, hoping that would induce Tanner to leave. He preferred looking at Violet when she wasn't hanging off Tanner's arm.

It didn't.

'Where's Lulie, by the way? I haven't seen her yet,' Tanner said, raking his hair back off his face. 'I imagine she's looking stunning.'

'You'd better believe it,' Jonty grinned, scanning the room. 'She went to check on the caterers. Oh! Hang on. Here she is,' he said, looking up the stairs. 'Hello, darling, I thought you were in the kitchen.' He kissed her cheek.

'I was. I went up the back stairs to have a quick lie-down.' She checked her hair which was provocatively tousled. 'Think I had too much to drink,' she smiled, wrinkling her nose. 'Oh hi, Tanner, you made it back to us in time, then.'

'Uh . . . yes,' Tanner croaked, his voice breaking. He leant forward to kiss her, letting his fingers rustle her tulle skirt. 'You look lovely,' he managed.

Lulie smiled.

'I hear you had a successful meeting in London today,' Will said blandly.

'Who told you it was successful?' Tanner countered. He couldn't stop looking at Lulie's skirt. It couldn't have been her. Jonty had been standing on the stairs the whole time he'd been getting changed. And surely she wouldn't . . .

'What meeting?' Violet asked.

'We'll talk about it later,' he mumbled. 'This isn't the time.' He grabbed a half-empty glass off the table and drained it. He needed to get wasted. This couldn't be happening. 'I need to start thinking about my speech.' He looked around the room, scrutinizing the other women's outfits – cocktail dresses, little black dresses, sparkly things. But no other big net skirts.

Jonty slapped his hand to his forehead and groaned. 'Oh no, bro! Don't do it. No one needs to hear it. They're all too lashed anyway.'

'If you think you're wriggling off the hook, you can think again,' he said slowly, looking back at Lulie. She was sipping a drink and scanning the room absent-mindedly. Who was she looking for?

Jonty shook his head. 'I reckon that's why you and Vi haven't got married yet. You're not man enough to square up to what I'll have to say in the best-man's speech.'

Tanner took his eyes off Lulie and looked at his little brother, protectively. 'Tonight's all about you, shandy boy!'

'Harry! You've come back to us,' Pia purred, grabbing a tall, blond man's arm and nestling under it, like a duckling.

'Don't I always, darling?' Harry grinned, letting his fingers lightly brush past her nipples. He watched as they grew hard under the silky fabric. 'I'm your very own boomerang.'

So this was Harry. Tanner took a good look at this handsome newcomer who had Pia almost rolling over to have her tummy rubbed.

'Where've you been anyway?' she sighed, infinitely brighter now that Harry had returned.

'Oh, you know . . . mingling.' A waiter suddenly appeared. Harry took two glasses, and drained one.

'We haven't been introduced,' Tanner said tersely, holding out a stiff hand. He didn't like the cut of this guy's jib. 'I'm Tanner Ludgrove, Jonty's brother. And this is Violet, my partner.'

'The hosts of the evening! Harry Hunter,' he replied, shaking Tanner's hand and kissing Violet. 'Lord, what pretty eyes you have.'

'Why, thank you, Mr Wolf,' Violet flirted, much to Tanner's chagrin. Harry laughed, showing off his Hollywood smile.

'Oh, what's this? Did you need to make a quick getaway or something?' Violet asked, reaching up to him and pulling a sprig of ivy from his hair.

Ivy? Tanner frowned, then looked aghast at Lulie. Nobody had followed Lulie back down the stairs and . . . and the ivy practically fell in through that bedroom window. Surely Hunter hadn't been that much of an idiot that he'd climbed down it?

'Ah, that's my standby prop. I take it everywhere with me, just in case someone forgets to mention the party's fancy dress,' Harry replied jocularly, tucking it in his breast pocket. 'Hate it when that happens.'

'Oh *really*? And what character could you possibly be with that little sprig?' Violet asked slyly.

'Why, Puck,' he shrugged.

Chapter Thirty-six

Sophie sat in the chair as the hairdresser tugged and smoothed her hair into obedient silkiness. She checked her watch. She had been here over two hours now, and desperately needed to get over to the opera house to see her canvases in all their hanging glory. Baudrand had called in one of Chicago's pre-eminent gallerists to curate the show and she'd been meticulous to the point of neurosis, not even allowing Sophie a preview until minutes before curtain-up.

She stared at herself in the mirror. Not bad. You almost couldn't tell that she hadn't slept for the past week. Red Bull and Pro-plus had kept her going, and she'd even taken up smoking. She'd lost a shocking amount of weight but the new make-up she'd bought at Macy's had done a great job of masking her fatigue. She felt so tired she half expected her skin to shed like a snake's. This layer was dead and done. She had nothing left to give.

'*Et voilà*,' the hairdresser said, with a final flourish. He held a mirror up behind her and Sophie admired the back of her own head. Her hair, downlighted into a sophisticated garnet shade and smoothed into submission by a Brazilian perm, looked luxuriant and glossy, billowing down her back in thick non-frizzy waves.

She smiled, tossing her head from side to side and wondering whether Adam would like it. She hadn't seen him since their encounter in the hallway, and certainly not since Russell's article had outed them as lovers. She felt the tears well up and dabbed her eyes quickly.

'You'll knock 'em dead,' the hairdresser declared, proud of the transformation he had wrought. She'd looked like road kill on the way in. Sophie shrugged off the black salon cover-up and pushed her arms into a gold satin cocoon coat. It had cost almost a month's rent but it did a good job of giving her some shape and looked sumptuous against her claret velvet minidress.

She stepped outside and hailed a cab. She couldn't walk more than fifty feet in her shoes and, besides, it was almost dark. The opera house was lit up like a Christmas tree, and as she drew up outside and saw the huge crowds she felt a tingle of excitement. Tickets for the production had sold out within hours, and demand to witness the American leg of this dance-off was such that enormous screens had been erected in the plaza outside. Thousands of people were sitting in plastic chairs, eating hot dogs and drinking coffee beneath huge banners of Ava and Adam.

In earlier meetings, Baudrand had said the banners would be printed from Sophie's best images, highlighting both their new partnership and her exhibition. But as she walked towards the theatre for the first time in weeks, she saw they'd taken a completely different turn. Punning on their names, Adam and Ava had been provocatively shot by Bruce Webber as the First Man and Woman of ballet – another shot in the eye to Pia.

Sophie studied the images, spellbound. Manipulating their majestic bodies to entwine each other, wearing nothing more than the figurative fig leaves, their sizzling chemistry leapt out like flames and the results were titillating, erotic and artistic, all at once. Even under Pia, ballet had never been seen like this before.

Sophie kept on walking, trying to dam the hurt. She could see why the decision had been made. Even passers-by with not the slightest interest in ballet would stop and stare at this. Sex was universal – regardless of whether or not you could do the splits in mid-air.

'Soph-eee!' Baudrand exclaimed. He was standing in the foyer awaiting the night's VIPs as she came through the doors. 'Why! You are a vision.'

Sophie smiled. 'Monsieur Baudrand. How are you feeling?'

Baudrand wrung his hands. 'What can I say? Tonight signifies a new chapter for the Chicago City. For one hundred years we have been a dominant force in American ballet but tonight? Tonight we become a global brand. Everything has come together in the most perfect way.' He lowered his voice. 'Wait until you see Adam and Ava – they dance as one now. Ava said you had a little talk to her about it,' he winked. 'Did you see the banners?'

Sophie nodded. 'Very sexy. Good choice.'

Baudrand shrugged. 'It is the future. We must move forward with the times. And your exhibition, eh? Already security have had to throw out the paparazzi. Everyone is desperate for the exclusive on your prints, especially since that piece last weekend in the *Tribune*.'

Sophie cringed. 'I know . . . I'm so sorry about that, *monsieur*. I had no idea he was going to—'

'Sorry? Do not be sorry, Sophie. You know what they say – all publicity is good publicity. It has generated even more hype for tonight.'

Sophie gave a tight smile. Maybe – but at what cost to *her* reputation? Russell, aggravated by her snubbing silence, had done nothing less than a character assassination and she didn't have anything like the resources to fight it.

She looked up and had to suppress a sudden giggle, her mood instantly lifting again. Lucy was standing behind Baudrand, wrapped around a life-size cut-out of Adam. She had one leg hooked round his waist and was waggling her tongue near his ear.

'I . . . uh . . . I suppose Adam and Ava are backstage?' she spluttered.

'I certainly hope so,' Baudrand chuckled, checking his watch. 'It's only fifteen minutes till curtain-up. Well, I will see you after the performance, So-phee. There is still much to be done.' And he clapped his hands briskly and walked off around the foyer, buoyant on anticipation of the night's success.

Sophie collapsed into a fit of giggles as Lucy ran over.

'You look amazing!' Lucy said as they hugged excitedly. 'My God. You look like a model! Has Adam seen you?'

Sophie shook her glossy head. She was desperate to see him. She wanted to apologize for having letting slip about their tryst, for having her boobs held by another man in a public place, for not having been in touch since – he'd looked terrible that night, no doubt pushed to the edge by Ava's antics, and she hadn't been there for him. She'd been so caught up in her own disasters.

'Not yet. Come on. I was just going to see the gallery first. I want to make sure they've hung everything in the order I asked. Honestly, that gallery woman's a control freak – she made me do everything by email.'

They clip-clopped over the marble floor in their finery,

and walked through to the auditorium, which had been transformed into a gallery for the night. All the furniture had been stripped away and pink lights streamed up the white walls, throwing a soft haze, like tulle, over the canvases.

Lucy gasped. 'It looks fantastic, Soph!' She ran forward to look closer. Sophie's heart leapt. She could never have imagined it would look so . . . professional. If only Lucy had seen the wreckage of the pictures in her studio two weeks ago.

'Look, some have got red dots on already,' Lucy said. 'That means they've sold, doesn't it?'

Sophie peered closer, hardly able to believe people were actually buying her work. She'd spent so long just scribbling in her studio, amusing herself and drawing for her own satisfaction, that even after Baudrand had given her the fancy title, she still hadn't ever truly thought that she could make a living from it.

'Yes. But who can have seen them already? Baudrand was just saying they've tightened security. He doesn't want anyone seeing anything before the official unveiling later.'

Sophie looked up and saw Miriam, the exhibition curator who'd be exhibiting it in her gallery after tonight. She was tweaking the spotlight that fell on a canvas of Adam in *brisé volé*.

Lucy checked her watch. 'Hell, I'd better get back to the front and check whether the VIPs are turning up. Badlands will no doubt be going demented.' She hugged Sophie again. 'I'll catch you afterwards.'

Sophie walked over to Miriam. She couldn't have been anything but a gallery owner – her wiry black curls had been left wild, unlike Sophie's, and her short frame was swamped in asymmetric Issey Miyake.

'Hi, Miriam. I'm here. I'm Sophie.' She held out a hand.

Miriam smiled blankly without turning round, barely registering her artist's arrival. She was oblivious to everything but the walls. 'No, no, it's still not right. What do you think?' she asked Sophie vaguely. 'Do you think that one needs to move over to the right a little? I think it's upsetting the balance between these two.'

Sophie cocked her head, considering. It all looked fine to her. Miriam was operating at a level of detail beyond her scrutiny. 'I think it's great,' she said.

'Hmm . . . No. It needs to move over . . . Paul!' she called, bringing an assistant running. 'We need to move this one over an eighth of an inch to the right.'

'Miriam, I noticed there are some red dots on the paintings. That means they're sold, doesn't it?'

'Yes,' she said, taking the picture off the wall. 'Paid full price, too. There was no question of haggling.'

'Oh. It's just that I thought no one was supposed to see them before the official unveiling.'

'It's okay. Monsieur Baudrand approved it. It was Ava's manager who wanted a preview. He has a greater interest in securing the best images of Ava than anyone, after all.'

'Yes, I guess so.'

The tannoy announced that the performance was due to begin in five minutes.

'Well, would you point him out to me during the private view? I'd like to thank him personally.'

'Absolutely,' Miriam said vaguely, making a microscopic pencil mark on the wall to indicate the precise new hanging location of the canvas.

'Okay. Well, I'd better take my seat. I'll see you afterwards.

This all looks amazing, Miriam,' she said, waving her arms around the space. 'You've done a fantastic job.'

Sophie sat in the dark, eating her tub of ice cream – the first thing she'd had a chance to eat all day – utterly mesmerized by the action on the stage. Baudrand had been right. Ava and Adam moved as one now, like oil on water, one on top of the other and unable to break away from each other.

Her painterly eye followed the cut of Adam's muscles as they gleamed under the lights, his straw-coloured hair the only untamed thing about him. Not a finger was out of line, not a step missed a beat. His eyes never left Ava once – wherever she travelled to on the stage he was chasing her, catching her, spinning and holding her.

Sophie's breath caught at the sight of his classical dominance and she let herself surrender to the memory of how he'd held her in those arms too – pinning her down to the bed, enfolding her in their warmth.

He looked bigger than she remembered and she could tell he'd spent extra hours in the gym, building up the strength to perfect the new hold that Ava had insisted upon. Whatever he'd been through in the past few weeks – making sacrifices, adapting to the changes – it had been worth it. He more than justified his place on that stage with Ava now.

In fact, she thought, licking the spoon and considering their partnership more closely, if anything Adam's performance was adding infinitely more to hers. His simmering passion and sensuality had thawed her usual clinical execution, and she was leaping higher, stepping lighter, with joyful spirit.

Sophie blinked hard, suddenly realizing that the transformation was complete. Ava had done as Baudrand suggested and shed her sterile laser-perfect technique for Pia's whimsical artistry. She was dancing Pia's ballet, with Pia's partner, exactly as Sophie knew Pia would do herself. But she'd done it first. The Royal's production wasn't for another seventeen hours, allowing for the time-zone changes and the need for the international press and VIPs to travel from here to there. The charge that would be levelled at Pia was already clear: she would be copying Ava.

The curtain came down two hours later to rapturous applause, and even the cheers outside in the plaza could be heard in the theatre. It took nine encores before the curtain stayed down for good, and Sophie found herself swept along by the current of people rushing out to the bars.

She was desperate to go backstage and congratulate the dancers but, as she checked her watch, she realized there was no time. Monsieur Baudrand was opening the private view imminently and, for once, her presence was vital.

'Sophie! Soph! Wait up!'

Sophie turned and found Lucy running after her.

'Can you believe that? They'll never beat it. No way,' Lucy gushed, hoping the ChiCi's new fortunes might mean a pay rise.

'I know,' Sophie shrugged. 'It was incredible. The energy between them was just mesmerizing. I can't believe what a change there's been between them. So much has happened in the past few weeks.'

They walked into the auditorium, and Baudrand, who was waiting to start his speech, convivially signified the arrival of the new artist. A wave of applause swept round the room, and Sophie smiled, delighted and awed all at once. All these people were here . . . because of her? She listened meekly to

Baudrand's hyperbole, trying to allow the elation that followed weeks and weeks of tireless work to wash over her, but there was a stubborn regret yawning inside her. Everything felt incomplete – and she knew precisely why. She wanted her family here to witness her success, to see that she'd been right, after all. That there had been a life and career and happiness out here for her.

The sound of more applause roused her and she looked up to see the crowd quickly dispersing to admire the paintings on the walls.

Lucy sauntered over and put a drink in her hand. 'Congrats, Sophie!' she smiled, raising a toast. 'You deserve it.'

They took a large swig.

'What a party!' Lucy said. 'Here, you can't see Badlands can you? I reckon now's the perfect time to ask for a pay rise. He'll be drunk with success for days after this.'

Sophie looked around the room. Baudrand was in the corner, standing in front of the picture of Adam and Ava in the *presage* lift, and was in the middle of an animated conversation with a man even spectacularly shorter than he.

'He's over there,' Sophie nodded. 'But he doesn't look too happy. I'm not sure now's the right time, Luce.'

'Hmm, yes. He does look pissed off,' Lucy murmured. 'Oh well, tomorrow, then. Look, do you mind if I cut and run before he spots me. I'm officially off duty now but I'm not going to have a hope of enjoying all this free champagne when he's in the room. He'll have me gumming envelopes.' She winked. 'Besides, I said I'd meet Jack at the Blue Bar afterwards.'

'Who's Jack?'

'You know, the new sound guy.'

Sophie shook her head. 'No. Never heard of him.'

Lucy put a hand on her arm. 'That's because you've not left your apartment in weeks. We've got a lot of catching up to do.'

'Well, can I come with you? All I had to do was show my face here.'

'Absolutely not. You need to mingle. You're the woman of the hour. This is your moment. Go and bask in the sun. You deserve it,' she smiled, walking off. 'Tomorrow.'

Sophie looked around. People were milling about in clumps, huddled around the paintings, nodding and chatting intently, still high on the back of the performance. Everyone knew they'd witnessed something historic, and buying into the paintings was the perfect way to take a piece of it home with them.

She searched for Adam and Ava but there was no sign of them yet. She looked at her watch and imagined the stream of bouquets and backstage visitors would probably have dried up by now and they'd be taking off the stage make-up and getting changed. They should be here any moment. Secretly she'd been hoping that they'd whisk straight over once the curtain fell, wanting to witness her own moment of glory. Still . . .

Miriam came over. 'It's going well, don't you think?'

'Better than I dared dream,' Sophie smiled, drinking her champagne in gulps.

'We'll be a sell-out within half an hour if it keeps up at this rate. I'll have nothing left to sell.' Miriam turned to face her, her expression intense. 'Tell me, do you have anything else you can give me? Seriously, I'm going to need something to hang on my walls.'

Sophie looked back at Miriam in surprise. 'Well, I've got lots of half-finished canvases, and hundreds of drawings and photos to work from. I guess I can keep supplying you as long as you want.'

'Good girl, that's great,' Miriam smiled, patting her arm. 'We're onto a winner with this. I reckon we'll be able to put them on for another twenty per cent. Nobody's even asking about the prices.'

'By the way,' Sophie said, finishing her drink and taking a canapé. 'Where's Ava's manager?'

'He's, uh . . .' Miriam looked around the room. 'Oh where is he? . . . He was here a moment ago. I saw him chatting to Monsieur Baudrand. Mmm. No, I can't see him . . .' Her eyes suddenly widened excitedly. 'Oh! Juergen Vanderveldt's just walked in. I *must* speak to him. He's a big collector and this is just his thing. I'll catch up with you later.'

Sophie watched her go. The only other person she knew in the room was Baudrand, and from the looks of his body language now, silhouetted against her own giant canvas, he didn't look the life and soul of the party.

'To heck with it,' she muttered to herself, putting down her drink and walking towards the doors. It's not like she really ever expected the mountains to come to Mohammad. The pictures were selling themselves – red dots were popping up everywhere like a virulent case of chicken pox – and she'd have a better time in the dressing rooms with her friends.

She strode happily out of the gallery, the sound of her heels echoing through the near-deserted halls, her long legs flashing like scissors below her coat. Security, not so much recognizing *her*, as recognizing the authority that came from a sophisticated woman in full march, threw open the back-stage doors for her. She walked unhesitatingly through the labyrinth towards Ava's dressing room.

'Hey, Sophie, looking good!' Pete, the lighting prop, called out, walking backwards to have a good look at her. 'Coming for a drink?'

'Yeah, later maybe,' she called back, not breaking stride.

The door was ajar, but she didn't bother to knock. She burst in excitedly, keen to offer her congratulations at last, and was instantly overpowered by the scent of a hundred bouquets covering every surface. She looked around but it was like hacking through a jungle. Where was she?

Ava's tutu was lying frothily in the middle of the floor, as though she'd just stepped out of it. She couldn't be far. Adam's dressing room, probably.

She went to leave the room again when she heard a sound behind the antique embroidered dressing screen. She *was* getting changed.

'Ava!' she said, walking over. 'You'll never guess! It's been a sell-out! The entire exhibition. Can you believe it? And as for you guys! You were *amazing*! A dream-team!'

She rounded the corner and found herself face to face with her friend. Ava met her eyes and smiled – just as Adam came deep inside her.

Chapter Thirty-seven

Tanner creaked down the stairs, a disgusted snarl on his lips and feeling hungover to hell. The last guests hadn't left till five and there were bodies everywhere, crashed out on sofas and under the tables. Looking out in the garden, he saw some people had even pitched tents in the garden, Glasto-style.

He wanted them gone, the lot of them. His head hurt, and not just because of the bottle of whisky he'd polished off, as eager for its amnesiac effect as its deterrence to Violet's overtures. His mind had raced for all of the two hours he'd tried to sleep, the vision of Lulie, bare-breasted and legs spread, swimming in front of him every time he closed his eyes. He felt guilty that it had excited him so much; enraged that this had happened to his brother.

He clattered about angrily in the stables, knocking over feed buckets and upsetting the horses, who instinctively picked up on his mood. He didn't care. He wanted to rage and kick the hell out of things. In the absence of actually having Harry Hunter to beat to a pulp, it was the best he was going to get for the time being.

He tossed the hay furiously, throwing it three feet into the air, moving from one stall to the next, until he came across Jessy and Rob, half naked and snoring, wrapped around each other and clearly sleeping where they had fallen. He stared at them both, still resolutely unconscious and as yet un-troubled by their hangovers.

He walked outside and saddled up Conker. He couldn't risk waking them. He couldn't speak to anyone yet. And certainly not Jonty. He had to get out of here.

He hoisted himself unsteadily into the saddle, pulling back on the reins as Conker took a few steps back. He looked up at Jonty and Lulie's bedroom window. The curtains were firmly drawn.

He shook his head in despair, then dug his heels hard into Conker's sides. The hunter immediately took off in an all-out gallop, Tanner holding on grimly as his adrenalin levels fought to override the alcohol in his bloodstream. He knew it was dangerous to ride in this condition, but it was the only thing he knew for clearing his head.

The smell of bacon and sausages being fried was wafting from the stable door in the kitchen by the time he got back to the yard. It was one in the afternoon, and although all the stragglers had gone, the residents of the house were only just beginning to come to.

He walked sombrely into the kitchen. He knew now what he had to do.

Jonty was standing in his pyjamas, cooking an entire twelve-pack of eggs directly on the simmering plate of the Aga. Tanner raised an eyebrow at his brother's appetite.

'That bad, huh?'

Jonty grinned and poked them with the spoon. 'Munchies like you wouldn't believe. Have one.'

'Oh, one? Really? That's generous.'

Jonty chuckled and poured him a cup of tea from the pot. 'Here, have that. It might put you in a better mood.'

'Nothing's going to improve my mood today,' Tanner said quietly, turning his back. 'Where's Lulie? Still sleeping?'

'No. She's gone off for a walk.'

'A walk? Where?' Tanner asked, instantly suspicious.

Jonty shrugged. 'I dunno. She'd already gone by the time I woke up. You know what a poor sleeper she is.'

Tanner rolled his eyes at that. Lulie's sleepwalking had become the stuff of legend in the Ludgrove household, but he said nothing. At least it meant she wouldn't overhear them.

Jonty grabbed the serving plate of sausages, bacon, tomatoes, black pudding and mushrooms that were keeping warm in the warming oven. 'Here,' he said, putting it on the table. 'Tuck in.'

Both brothers speared the food onto their plates and covered it with hefty doses of brown sauce. They ate in noisy silence for a few minutes, both grateful for the starch that would ease their cravings.

'So,' Jonty said finally, wiping his mouth with the back of his hand and leaning back in the chair. 'Kicking party, huh?'

Tanner smiled. 'It was a big one, all right. Just as well you don't get married too often. The house couldn't take it.'

'*I*'m only ever getting married once,' Jonty grinned. 'You don't let a girl like Lulie slip through your fingers.'

The smile slid off Tanner's face and he stared at his hands. He knew he had to say it. He couldn't let his brother labour under the illusion that his marriage was a good one. She'd cheated on him at their wedding reception. He had to know.

'Look, Jonty,' he said, fiddling with his mug of tea. 'There's something I really have—'

'Morning,' Violet groaned, stumbling into the kitchen in

a T-shirt. She still had the large peony – now very crushed – in her hair, and her mascara had migrated to her cheeks. She ruffled Jonty's hair like a child's as she passed, and checked the teapot.

Tanner looked up at her as she bent down to kiss him but he forgot to purse his lips, and she pulled away, baffled. 'Do you feel as rough as you look?' she asked suspiciously.

'Yes,' Tanner muttered.

'Here, have some tucker,' Jonty said, putting a plate together for her. 'It's still warm.'

'Oh good, 'cos I'm not,' Violet said, shivering. 'It's bloody freezing in here. Why've you left the door open?' She walked over to the door and shut it.

'Needed to blow out the cobwebs, Vi. Best thing for getting rid of a hangover,' Jonty grinned. 'I reckon we should all go for a big ride this afternoon. Whaddya say?'

'I say I want to go back to bed,' Violet groaned, shivering still. 'Where's my cashmere jumper that I saw Lulie walking around in? I want it back.'

'It's in the wardrobe. You can go in and get it. Lulie's not sleeping. She's gone off on one of her walks.'

'Collecting things for the nature table, is she?' Violet quipped, smiling as she disappeared up the back stairs.

Biscuit came and sat by Tanner's knees, and he pulled her ears gently.

'Hey, did you get a chance to talk to Felix last night?' Jonty asked, one eyebrow cocked, as he settled himself into the armchair by the Aga. 'Did you hear he's gone and landed himself a record contract?'

'Felix? What, Felix Shepham? Really?' Tanner raked his mind back through the years, frowning. 'I thought he played the recorder.'

Jonty chuckled. 'Well, yes – aged seven, you tool! He's on drums now with that band he set up with Matt Ashley.'

Tanner put on a look of concentration, trying to pretend he cared about Felix's band. He didn't. He wanted to talk about Lulie, but Violet would be coming back down any moment.

'Look, why don't we go for the ride later – just you and me? The girls aren't going to be up for it,' he said casually. 'You can take Kermit. It's been ages since we went for a hack together and, besides, I need to check on some hedging in Long Field.'

'Okay,' Jonty shrugged. 'Lulie will probably be working anyway. She's got another sackload of scripts to get through.'

Violet appeared at the foot of the stairs. She looked pale.

'Uh-oh! You okay, Violet?' Jonty asked, taking in her pallor. 'Gravity catching up with last night?'

Violet shook her head and walked slowly back into the kitchen. She looked like she was choosing her words. 'Where did you say Lulie had gone?' she asked quietly.

Jonty shrugged. 'Just off on one of her walks. Why?'

Violet looked at Tanner, and then back at him. 'Because she's taken all of her clothes.'

Jonty raced through the house, ransacking the wardrobes like he expected to find his wife hiding behind the shirts at the back. He turned the bedroom upside down but every trace of her had gone. Her laptop, her lingerie, her hairbrush. Only her wedding ring remained on the dressing table, sitting on a crushed receipt that had the single word 'Sorry' scrawled on it.

Tanner stood down below in the kitchen, incandescent

with rage as he heard his brother – as broken as if he'd been kneecapped – sobbing through the floorboards. For hours, he listened to Violet talking to him through the locked door.

'Open the door, Jonty, and let me in,' she said softly. 'I can help.'

But the door remained locked. Biscuit whined from her bed, made anxious by all the unusual frenzy and high drama in the house. Tanner dragged his hands through his hair, conflicted. He was still the only one who knew she must be with Hunter. But what was worse: the fact that she'd left him, or the fact that she'd left him for Hunter?

He paced up and down restlessly, kicking the chairs and slamming shots of whisky. He was desperate for something to do, for someone to blame. Harry fucking Hunter. He hadn't needed to know of his reputation to know, the second he lay eyes on him, that the guy was trouble. Seducing her at her own wedding reception? It was a sick joke. It was . . .

Tanner stood bolt upright and Biscuit's ears pricked up, on full alert.

He suddenly knew exactly who to blame.

Chapter Thirty-eight

Pia was sitting at her dressing table, staring at the card, a thick coffee-coloured card nestled in a cream satin-lined box, with the words engraved in gold leaf: 'Boathouse, 10 p.m.'

She read the words over and over, knowing full well what they implied. This was it. Her summons. Her boat was finally being called in.

She put the tablet down and looked at herself in the mirror. The image that greeted her was the one she'd dreamt of seeing as a child – the dramatic sweep of kohl, the rouged cheeks, her hair oiled back and glistening with a ruby-studded coronet. But she didn't see a classical ballerina reflected back. She saw a chorus girl – gaudy, tacky, cheap, for sale.

Her time was up. He wanted her, and how could she refuse him after all he'd done? He'd been true to his word and played the perfect gentleman at all times, but now he'd done what he'd said he would – he'd put her back together again – and he clearly wanted to pick up where they'd left off.

She shook her head. He didn't get it. He didn't get *her* – he didn't know her any better now than he had when they'd met in the gym in St Moritz. He just didn't understand that the accident had changed the rules. It had enabled him to rescue and trap her and had put everything on his terms, which had been exactly what he'd wanted the very first night they'd met: she may have won that battle, but he'd won the war. Her loss had been his gain and the more time, money and kindness he invested in her, the more beholden to him she became.

But Pia Soto didn't *do* debt. Her independence was her lifeblood and she just couldn't reconcile her obligation to him with her ferocious need for self-determination. Something had to give. They couldn't both win.

Outside, the ambient noise level was ratcheting up the decibels and the orchestra was tunelessly tuning up. She automatically flexed and pointed her foot slowly. It moved beautifully. But she knew it was too soon.

There was a knock and Evie popped her head around the door.

'How you doing, sweetie?' she drawled, throwing a limp posy of carnations onto the dressing table. 'Not the greatest selection in the village,' she apologized, rolling her eyes.

Pia tried to smile, but Evie clocked one look at her and saw her energy was off.

'Ah, like that, is it?' she said, her stomach sinking as she saw the newspapers rolled up on the sofa. 'Oh don't tell me you read the reviews!' she said sharply. They had been evangelical in their praise of Adam and Ava's performance.

Pia shook her head. She hadn't needed to. She'd heard quite enough on the radio as she was having her make-up done.

Evie looked at her star. She was looking far from starry at the moment. 'You're ready for this, Pia.'

Pia cocked an eyebrow disdainfully.

'Yes, you are,' Evie said firmly. 'I wouldn't let you go up on that stage tonight if I didn't think you were. My reputation's on the line here too, don't forget.'

Pia squished her lips together. Yadda, yadda, yadda.

'And you and Rudie? You're a much better fit together. That rehearsal this morning was a dream to watch. I have no concerns. Adam Bridges was always too limp, following you around the stage like a lost puppy. It was embarrassing to watch, frankly.' Evie flicked her hands dismissively 'Rudie's perfect. He's a better height, for a start; you look beautiful together and he's as gay as a lord. He'll show you off beautifully.'

Pia allowed a small smile to break through.

'You need to master technique and then forget about it and be natural. Who said that?'

'You did,' Pia quipped.

Evie narrowed her eyes. 'Who said that, lady?'

Pia sighed. 'Anna Pavlova.'

'That's right. And she knew what she was talking about. You've got the technique, you've got the fitness, you've got the strength and you've got the team. Forget about Ava. Forget about Chicago. This is *your* ballet, Pia. Ava was miming up there. You don't need to think about this. You just need to feel it.'

There was another knock and Mrs Bremar appeared.

'Oh! I'm sorry, dear. I didn't mean to intrude,' she said quickly, seeing Pia in consultation with Evie. 'I'll come back later.'

'No, it's fine. I was just going,' Evie said, taking Pia's hand in hers. She looked back down at her. 'Remember: the only way to do it – is to do it,' she said intensely.

Mrs Bremar edged into the trailer cautiously, worried about knocking over the flowers.

'Do you want me to get rid of some of these for you?' she said, looking around. 'Sure, you can hardly move in here.'

'It's fine,' Pia said quietly, her fingers tracing the letters on the card.

Mrs Bremar peered over and read the words upside down.

'Aah,' she said quietly. There was a long pause. 'Do you want to talk about it?'

Pia shook her head and they sat in silence for a little while.

'Well, it looks wonderful outside with all the flowers and the pretty lights,' Mrs Bremar said brightly. 'And haven't they made the stage set beautiful? It's a real wonderland.'

Pia nodded.

'The seats are filling up already, you know. I managed to get autographs from Prince William and Elton John on the way down here. Everyone looks so grand in all their finery.' She looked at Pia in her yellow costume, the vision before her for once finally correlating with her own expectations of what a ballerina should look like. 'Not as fine as you, though. You look just beautiful.'

'Thanks,' Pia said, smiling wanly, fiddling with her leg warmers. If only B could see what she saw.

'He's done you proud, to be sure.'

'So everyone keeps reminding me.'

'And you'll do him proud tonight up on that stage. You'll get up there and glisten like the star you are. Show the world what a good job he's done of putting you back together again. And then you can relax, knowing you're all square.'

Pia frowned at her. 'All square? What do you mean?'

Mrs Bremar tipped her head to the side, her eyes twinkling knowingly. 'Well, let's be honest, tonight is mainly about his ego, isn't it? You're risking a lot getting back out there so soon. I don't think if this – what are they calling it? – this *dance-off* hadn't been set up, that you'd have chosen to come back so early, would you?'

Pia shook her head. She had been trapped into this from the start. At first, she had thought Will had set it up as an incentive for her, something to focus on after the shock of Baudrand's betrayal, but very quickly it had become apparent that the upsides for him outweighed those for her. From what she could fathom, she was taking on all of the risk, while he was just taking all of the credit.

A flurry of profiles in the financial and social press meant his philanthropy to the Royal Ballet was now well documented, and his dominance on the polo circuit confirmed; *Tatler* had rocketed him to the top spot of their annual *Little Black Book* edition and he must have added £1 million to the value of Plumbridge House with a beautifully shot glossy 'At Home' feature, which showed Will and a very reluctant Pia draped across the sofas and walking hand in hand through the gardens. It all meant that as well as garnering the jealousy of every male in the western world for capturing the delectable Pia, the resulting publicity had been good for the Black Harbour brand too. Recognition of the financial arm of Silk's empire had spread beyond the closed confines of high finance to the man on the street, and bookings were up forty per cent for the string of boutique Black hotels which were popping up like mushrooms in the chicest European cities and resorts.

'Precisely. You're getting up there for him because you feel you owe to it to him for looking after you during your convalescence. But that's all you owe him.' She tapped the card. 'Not yourself. Not if you don't want to. Don't let him pressure you. It's your life, Pia; you need to live it on your terms.'

There was a brief pause as Pia took in her words and the sense behind them. Someone understood!

'Oh B! You're the best!' Pia exclaimed, throwing her arms around the housekeeper's neck. 'Whatever would I have done without you these past months? You've kept me sane. When I thought I was going mad, you were always the person who made everything better again.' A tear rolled down her cheek as she realized that what she'd needed – and found – these long lonely months hadn't been a lover, but a mother.

'There, there now. Don't cry. You'll ruin your face,' she smiled, dabbing beneath Pia's eyes as tears welled in her own. 'I'm so proud of you.'

There was a knock at the door and a stage hand peered in.

'They're ready for you, Miss Soto.'

Pia looked at Mrs Bremar, who smoothed her sleek hair proudly, and nodded. Pia nodded back to the boy, who disappeared to tell the orchestra. She slid off her leg warmers.

They walked to the door together, and the noise outside rushed in like water. Tinkles of laughter and lilting conversation competed with the caterwauls of the orchestra tuning up as violins, flutes, piano and oboes chased each other up and down the scales, like children on stairs.

Pia felt the first wave of adrenalin hit her as she took in the sight. After the morning's full dress rehearsal she'd closeted herself away in the trailer – partly to avoid Will, who was now like a wedding planner on speed, and partly to keep out of sight of the guests, who'd been arriving in a steady stream all afternoon. Will kept banging on about introducing her to the Royal Ballet grandees, but she had insisted upon total seclusion. She knew he was irritated by her 'head down' attitude but this wasn't a social event. Not for her.

She was stunned by the vision before her. The estate had been transformed. She looked at the glow of the flaming torches that had been set up around the lawns, with shrubs spotlit and candlelit chandeliers swinging from the trees. Some guests were still sipping champagne and wandering about the grounds, but most were now seated. Rather than opt for gilt chairs, Will had extravagantly splashed out on two hundred and fifty sofas, all upholstered in William Yeoward jewel-coloured velvets, and huge antique Iranian rugs were spread atop the matting on the grass. As she surveyed the audience – the women in full-length dresses and their best jewellery, the men in white tie – she thought it was like a grand restaging of Renoir's painting, *The Picnic*.

Television crews from NBC and the BBC had set up tracks in front of the stage area, ready to catch her from every angle. In the front row she saw the notorious ballet critics Mary Stoppes-Wade and Spencer Bowles. They were sharing a sofa and talking together intently. They had both travelled overnight from the ChiCi production, and far from being jet-lagged they looked well into their second wind. Pia watched them from the steps of the trailer.

The evening breeze ruffled her tutu like feathers and instinctively she turned her face up to the still-warm red sky. This would be the first time she had danced outside since she was a girl – barefoot on the *cerrados* – and the memory of that freedom stirred within her. If she could do just enough to get through this, she would be free to dance on her terms again. But, more importantly, she'd be free from her debt to Will.

Rudie, spotting her from backstage, ran over. He was wearing thick white tights and a black velvet jacket, his stage make-up transforming his voluptuous features into something more brooding and dramatic. The perfect leading man.

'Ready?' he smiled, taking her hands in his.

Pia nodded, almost shyly.

'Let's dance it off, then,' he grinned, pulling her into a run, eliciting a roar of approval from the crowd as they glimpsed the pair making their way backstage.

The conductor picked up his baton and eased the orchestra into the overture, as Pia began to dance behind the curtain, stretching and sliding her body into warmth. The corps – ready and warmed up for twenty minutes now – stopped their own pre-performance routines to watch, the air around her shimmering like fairy dust. She rose and fell on *pointe* with a sparkling vibrancy that belied the occasional twinges of pain that shot through her foot, and she leapt into the *grand jeté* with a silky elegance that made everybody else's appear clunky by comparison. By the time Rudie lifted her into the dramatic swallow lift she had hidden her terror behind a stage smile, and the backstage company and crew spontaneously burst into applause.

The audience – whipped by now to almost a frenzy of anticipation – heard the dancers backstage and clapped even harder in return, willing her to come out. The dancers fled to their positions in the wings as the stage manager counted down from ten and the green velvet curtain finally rose. And as Pia flickered like a flame back into the spotlight, the audience rose to their feet with encouragement, and she knew the day of judgement was finally upon her.

Chapter Thirty-nine

She burst through the trailer door, flushed and breathing heavily, a beam across her face. She'd done it, she knew she had – she'd shown them all.

She scanned the trailer, surprised to find it almost empty. Where had all the flowers gone? She frowned. The mirror was broken and . . . and why was her make-up swept off the dressing table onto the floor? There were five hundred people sitting outside. She couldn't possibly have been burgled.

And then she saw him, sitting defiantly on the bench by the window, one ankle resting arrogantly across his knee, his arms outstretched behind him.

'Oh. What do *you* want?' she demanded, sliding the coronet out of her hair.

'I thought you'd be pleased to hear that your little plan worked,' Tanner said bitterly.

Pia looked at him, bored. 'What plan?'

'The one to break up my brother's marriage.'

Pia snorted contemptuously. 'I don't know what you're talking about,' she said, reaching down to pick up the make-up from the floor. The last thing she needed was to twist her ankle slipping on a lipstick.

'I find that hard to believe,' Tanner said sarcastically. 'After all, what other possible motive could you have had for inviting Harry Hunter to the party?'

'Harry?' she said, looking up. 'What's he got to do with it?'

Tanner threw his head back and laughed. 'Oh come on! Surely you can guess?'

Pia stared at him blankly. What was he talking about?

'He's gone,' Tanner said finally. 'And taken Lulie with him.'

Lulie? With Harry? So that's where he'd gone. Oh God, poor Jonty! She looked away quickly. She felt like she'd been kicked in the stomach.

Tanner watched her, his anger inflamed just by the sight of her – it had become something of a Pavlovian response now.

'Does Jonty know she's with Harry?' she asked in a tight voice.

Tanner shook his head. 'Not yet. But *you* must have known that he would make a beeline for Lulie,' he demanded. 'What was the problem? Too much competition for you?'

'No!' she said, keeping her eyes away from his, throwing everything into the bin. 'I didn't think of her like that at all.'

'Well, what *did* you think, then?' he asked, jumping up. 'What exactly was going on in that twisted mind of yours to think that bringing a man like that to her *wedding reception* was a good idea?'

Pia stopped moving. 'Well, I didn't think for a minute that anything like this would happen. How could I know that they'd fall in love?'

'Love?' Tanner mocked. 'Who said anything about that? Love wasn't what I saw between them.' He glared at her from the far end of the trailer and for a moment she genuinely wondered whether he would come for her. A half-empty bottle of whisky was sitting on the floor by his feet. She wondered whether he'd even stopped drinking from the party last night. From the stubble on his face and the redness of his eyes, it didn't look like it.

She went and stood by the hanging rails. 'Look, I'm sorry about Jonty. Really I am,' she said, genuinely shocked by the conversation they were having. 'He's a nice guy and he doesn't deserve any of this. But I can't talk about this now. I have to get changed.' She looked at the clock on the dressing table. 'I'm back on stage in ten minutes.'

He stood up angrily and advanced towards her.

'If you think you're getting rid of me that quickly you can think again. I'm not leaving this trailer – and neither are you – until I've had a reasonable explanation. Get dressed if you want to,' he said, turning his back. 'I'm not the least bit interested in looking.'

Pia stared at his back for a moment. There were no screens to change behind in here.

Slowly, she took her next tutu off the hanger and moved behind the rail, trying to hide herself behind the clothes. She wriggled off the yellow costume and stepped into the next, a midnight-blue velvet tutu which she had had altered to sit just an inch above the nipple, the internal corset squeezing and pushing up her breasts so that they trembled with every move. She pushed the separate velvet cuffs up her arms, arranging them just below the shoulders, and slid a paste-diamond tiara into her hair.

She came out from behind the rail and sat down at the dressing table, unwinding the ribbons on her shoes. Tanner, hearing the noises, turned around again and watched her.

He saw the satin on the yellow shoes had worn through. Six other pristine pairs – white, and custom-dyed yellow and navy – were hanging up by their ribbons on the wall.

'I didn't realize it was the Rio Carnival out there,' he sneered, staring down at her and taking in her swollen bosom.

Pia sighed at the insult but didn't reply. She was trying to think of the quickest way to get him out of there. He was completely destroying her calm, tensing her up, and she knew she wouldn't be able to dance if he carried on like this.

She spritzed water into the toe box of one of the new navy satin shoes and began jabbing it with a pestle. Her mind raced as she tried to think of a cover story, but his scrutiny made it hard to concentrate and she came to the conclusion that, if she wanted to get him out of there as quickly as possible, she was going to have to tell him the truth.

'Look. I'll tell you why I invited Harry down,' she said quietly, keeping her eyes on the task in hand. 'But then you have to promise to leave. Agreed?'

'Fine,' Tanner muttered, watching her absorb herself in her routine. It was the first time he'd noticed her grace. It was usually subordinated to her arrogance or anger. And her arse . . . he always noticed that. He saw there was blood on the toes of her tights and her right foot looked swollen.

She began jabbing more vigorously. 'I invited him not because I was hoping he'd make a beeline for Lulie.' She took a deep breath. 'I was hoping he'd make a beeline for me.'

Tanner narrowed his eyes. He should have known she'd talk in riddles. 'Why?'

Pia reached up and switched to the other shoe. 'Because

I thought that if he had me, Will wouldn't want me.' She swallowed hard and looked up at him, feeling as humiliated as she had feared she would. 'That's the truth. It had nothing to do with him and Lulie.' She put the shoes on the dressing table and stood up. 'And now I'd like—'

Tanner grabbed the crook of her elbow and spun her back round. 'No. Wait a minute. That doesn't make sense. Why would you do that? Why didn't you want Will to have you?'

Pia looked up at him. He was holding her arm tightly.

'Tell me!' he said, shaking her.

'Because from the moment we met, he's tried to buy me, to own me. Just look at tonight!' she cried angrily. 'It's cost him a million pounds to put this on – did you know that? So what if I'm terrified of jumping and getting back on my toes? The world's watching, right? How can I possibly refuse anything he asks of me?'

'So you were trying to sabotage your own relationship?'

'Of course! *He* has to reject *me*! I thought hurting his pride would do it, and I . . . I thought I could rely on Harry to seduce me, for old time's sake.'

Tanner shook his head in disbelief at her screwy morality, before realizing he was still holding her arm. He let it go and took a step back, confused. He'd naturally assumed she and Will had been lovers from the start. He'd never thought for a moment that Silk had effectively held her hostage to his chivalry.

Tanner frowned. It didn't ring true. 'This doesn't add up. Why's Silk got you here if you're not sleeping together?'

Pia glared at him. 'Because he's *waiting* for me.'

'I don't think so,' Tanner snorted. 'Silk's no gentleman. He wouldn't go to all this trouble if he wasn't getting any action from you, sweetheart. He must have had another reason for keeping you with him.'

'Oh! Is it really so unbelievable that a man would choose to *wait* for me?' she bridled, tossing her head back proudly and showing off her beautiful face and neck.

Tanner was unmoved. 'Frankly? Yes.'

'You just don't know what it is to do the honourable thing,' she hissed indignantly.

'Oh really?' Tanner replied archly. 'And you're basing that on what, exactly?'

'Well, you always look for others to blame – what do you call them? Scapegoats.'

Tanner put his hands on his hips. He'd had enough of being tarred by her sweeping accusations. 'Go on, then. Give me an example,' he challenged her.

'Okay. What about . . . what about that time you blamed him for what happened in St Moritz? He wasn't even *there* when that girl took the drugs.'

'He didn't need to be,' Tanner shot back. 'He'd already given his orders.'

'Orders? What orders?'

'He wanted his star player off the scene so that his way was clear to some socialite's bed. Will ordered him to seduce another girl instead. Alonso left drugs in the truck afterwards and Jessy nearly died as a result. It's a clear thread of culpability, and yes, I blamed him. Try again.'

But Pia had stopped listening.

Alonso? Sophie and Alonso? The fateful image of the two of them coming out of the trailer floated before her eyes, the one that had paralysed her and stopped her in her tracks in front of the sleigh . . .

Oh God, poor Sophie! Alonso had seduced her on Will's

orders. Then, when Pia had woken up in the hospital after the accident, she hadn't been able to bear what had happened and the implications it had had for the rest of her life. She'd been frightened, and angry, and humiliated that her assistant and friend had won the man she'd desired . . . so she had struck out by firing Sophie.

She closed her eyes in despair at her own appalling behaviour – then suddenly opened them in gratitude at Will's! He had known that she was after Alonso – he'd even said it to her '. . . You want to seduce him to spite me, don't you? . . .' She wasn't blameless in her own tragedy by any means, but it had been *his* actions that had set in motion the chain of events leading to her accident.

If there was anyone to blame, it was him, and everything he'd done since to save her had actually only cancelled out *his* debt. For three months she'd been physically incapacitated and systematically stripped of all her defences – kept in one place for weeks on end and forced to accept kindness from strangers. But it was all over now. It was suddenly all over. She owed him nothing. At last, she'd got what she'd craved. She had her freedom back.

Chapter Forty

The wardrobe mistress knocked on the door again. Please God, don't let there be a wardrobe malfunction, she thought, squeezing her hands together in a little prayer as she waited for it to open. She should have insisted on helping Pia into the costumes herself. They were impossibly tight.

She heard low voices behind her and turned around.

'. . . This is probably the best time to catch her, now that she'll have some of her confidence back. What a first act, Perry!' Will was saying as he led a tall, grey-haired man towards Pia's trailer. 'I think you'll find she's more—' He saw the wardrobe mistress standing at the top of the steps. 'Anything the matter, Mrs Tufnell?'

The woman shrugged. 'She's not answering.'

'Here, let me,' Will said, stepping up and knocking briskly on the door. 'Come on, Pia. The beeb's on a tight programming schedule and I've got someone I want you to meet.'

There was no reply. Will looked around. The audience was back in its seats and the orchestra was waiting to start. 'Tch, women!' he muttered, turning the handle and barging straight in. 'Never ready when . . .'

He saw the broken mirror and the empty dressing table

first. Then the navy tutu puddled on the floor. 'Pia?' he asked, his voice climbing an octave.

But he already knew that she had gone.

Sophie tried to count the different shades of green as the coach trundled along the lanes: moss, emerald, sage, forest, bottle, grass, racing, lime, royal . . . uh, light, dark, blackish . . .

She gave up and opened a bottle of water that she'd grabbed on her sprint through Chicago airport. She'd only just managed to secure a seat on the first flight out and had had to run to make it.

She closed her eyes at the memory of last night. The show had been a sell-out. Not a single painting remained unsold and Miriam was pressing her to get to work on the next set; but, as she looked out of the window, the thought of it made her feel sick – scrutinizing Adam's hands on Ava's waist, his hands on her thighs, their bodies twisted around each other in an expression of the most sublime language the human form had to offer. Why would she put herself through the pain? She didn't want to look at Ava; she didn't want to set eyes on her ever again. Not after what she'd done to her.

She'd been manipulated and played by too many people, for too long. It had been bad enough being tossed away by Pia like some disposable tissue – *she* hadn't even had the decency to tell her why. But now, for it to happen all over again with her replacement, to realize Ava had just used her . . . The friendship had been a lie. Sophie had been nothing more than a patsy, something else for her to steal from Pia – because, as ever, it was always about her. Sophie had simply been a pawn in the middle of their battle for supremacy.

It was clear now that Ava was trying to take over everyone and everything in Pia's life. Her own success wasn't enough. She was a parasite, determined to strip Pia of her reputation, her contracts, her dancing style, her repertoire, her partner, her assistant – even her assistant's lover, just for the hell of it.

Pia had been right all along. Ava couldn't be trusted at all.

Pia. Sophie stared back out of the window, wondering where she was. Her disappearance from the Royal Ballet's production was front-page news. Will Silk had had to go on stage and make a statement saying that she'd become 'indisposed'. The audience had been in uproar, jeering and booing him, and the television companies had had to quickly fill the live coverage with old footage. And within a matter of minutes the worldwide web was abuzz with rumour and conspiracy theories.

Baudrand's fears about Pia eclipsing them from the other side of the Atlantic were on the money – and she'd managed it by not even being there, as the front pages ran 'Where's Pia?' headlines.

The critics, bumped up to the third, fourth and fifth pages, waxed lyrical about the two divas' interpretations and their rival productions. By the end of Pia's first act, it was looking too close to call. Yes, she'd been wary in parts, with a few winces as she landed from the bigger jumps and a slight tremor as she held her beautiful *arabesque effacé*, but allowance had to be made for her very recent injury and everyone was expecting, no, *willing*, a more confident second act as she settled back into performing again.

So the news of her disappearance had been a bitter blow. Every critic, dancer and observer wanted a decisive finale to the Soto–Petrova rivalry but, in the absence of a full perform-ance, Ava was crowned the winner by default.

Everyone felt cheated but it was another point to Camp Petrova, Sophie thought glumly, sighing heavily and misting up her window.

She rubbed it clear and saw the landscape had become familiar again. The coach was entering her neighbouring village, and the houses and fields she'd played in all her early life unfolded before her with comforting sameness. She wiped the window fully with her sleeve and followed the hedgerows with her eyes. She still remembered exactly which farmers they belonged to: O'Brian, Murphy, Fitzgerald, Ryan . . .

Nothing much had really changed in her absence. There were a couple of small housing estates springing up on the outskirts of the villages and there were more road signs than she remembered, but she could see old man Finlay was still dropping his hay all over the road as he took his tractor back from the field to the farm, and he still hadn't got round to patching up the old barn, which now looked like it should be condemned, not repaired.

The coach turned into her village, Fennor, and Sophie found herself suddenly alarmed to be back home. She didn't know why it should startle her so much. After all, she'd taken an eight-hour flight, another hour-long connecting flight and a three-hour coach ride to get here.

She watched as they passed the primary school with its slate peaked roof and all the children playing in the play-ground; the grocer's with its vegetables stacked up in the same old wooden barrows outside; the small square with its war memorial still decked with a few rain-sodden poppy wreaths.

The doors opened with a hiss and she stepped down, taking her bag from the hold underneath. It was fresher here than in the city and she pulled the gold cocoon coat tight, her bare legs already beginning to goosebump in the spring breeze. She knew she looked bizarre standing in evening dress in this tiny Irish village, but she hadn't wanted time to think, much less to change. She had grabbed her passport and her dignity and got the hell out of thére.

She let the coach leave, suddenly not so sure of the next step. The breeze picked up the satiny wisps at the front of her hair and blew them lightly across her face. She went to smooth them back with her hand and found to her surprise that she was crying. She dropped her hand down, preferring to stay hidden away. She didn't know what to do now.

Window-cleaners washing the front of the pharmacy stared at her in the plate-glass reflection; a couple of schoolgirls coming out of the sweet shop openly admired her extravagant coat. She felt ridiculous.

A middle-aged woman with twins on bikes saw her, and came over. 'Are y'all right, dear?' she asked, rummaging in her bag for a tissue. 'Are you lost? Dublin's three hours that way,' she smiled, nodding her head back the way Sophie had come.

Sophie stared at the woman in amazement. She slowly pulled her hair away from her face.

'No, I'm not lost, Mam,' she hiccuped. 'I'm home.'

Chapter Forty-one

Pia looked down from the Principe's grand balcony and watched Milan move through its day in exquisite, controlled synchronicity. The chestnut trees stood rigid against the soft breeze, shiny orange Lamborghinis double-parked around the Vespas, tiny women in huge sunglasses and chic skinny layers of taupe, olive, camel and cream criss-crossed between them, swinging their wait-list bags, hair and hips.

Pia absent-mindedly bit her lip, wishing she could be so free. What it must be to just walk outside in the sun and eat ice creams and sip espressos in street-corner cafes. That was far more of a luxury to her than the unlimited credit on her Amex Black. But she couldn't take the risk of being seen. No one could know she was here.

She turned her back on the city and walked into the suite. She wished she'd chosen somewhere smaller, less ostentatious. The decorator's rule of thumb had clearly been 'if it doesn't move, gild it'. It was grand, yes, opulent and impressive. But it made her feel like a bird in a cage. She felt stifled, trapped. She'd been here for two days now and hadn't left the room once. She couldn't. If the papers had been ecstatic about her return to the stage, they'd been doubly ecstatic about her disappearance again: they could always rely on Pia Soto to make good copy. And it had been nothing short of an international manhunt to find her. Twitter and Facebook were full of supposed sightings, giving locations of where she'd been seen and reports of what she'd been doing and with whom. They were all wide of the mark, of course, but that was okay, just so long as no one knew she was in Milan. She couldn't afford to be spotted and have the rumour mill swing into action before she'd signed on the dotted line.

She smoothed down her pink Chanel skirt anxiously, catching sight of herself in one of the baroque floor-to-ceiling mirrors. She was appalled by what she saw and planted her hands on her hips. Since when had Pia Soto *ever* imagined she'd wear tweed? She shook her head. If only B could see her now. At least she'd approve.

She stared at her reflection and tried to recognize her own face at least, but even that seemed foreign. She took a few deep yogic breaths. It was just because she was nervous and on her own. If Sophie was with her she'd make her laugh with some dreadful – what was it again? – ding-dong joke?

An image of Sophie, all skinny arms and legs and wild hair, looking indignant and just like a rusty nail in the Prada dress, floated into her head. Pia smiled to herself. She missed her, more than she could ever have expected, more than she would ever admit. She hadn't just fired her assistant, she had thrown away a friendship – her only one, in fact – and all in a brattish fit of pique that even morphine hadn't been able to smother.

Not that Sophie cared. She'd wasted no time in cosying up to Ava and, now that she had her own illustrious career to nurture, Pia would be nothing to her. Just the enemy.

Pia exhaled sharply, banishing the regrets. No, she was on

her own now and that was how it was. How she'd always liked it best. It was better to be alone and independent. She didn't need anyone's help. She'd already proved herself up on that stage. In that one short hour in the English dusk, she'd given Alvisio's songbird not just life and spirit, but also immortality. *The Songbird* was not only sold out for the rest of the season but, thirty years from now, people would still remember it as the ballet she and Ava had danced. Their dance-off would go down in the ballet history books and she had put him up there with Stravinsky and Diaghilev.

There was a light rap at the door and she stared at it. She'd done all this for him. Now it was time for her reward. The butler went to open it and Pia turned her back to stare out of the window again.

'*Segualo, prego, signore,*' she heard the butler say in a quiet voice.

Pia counted to five, then turned round, full of grace and poise. 'Signore Alvisio,' she said, gliding forward and offering a delicate hand. 'It is such a pleasure to meet you face to face, at last.'

'*Il piacere e tutta la miniera.* The pleasure, it is all mine,' he said, gesticulating stiffly, taking her hand but kissing her twice on the cheeks.

He was in his seventies, with small dark eyes, his hair and matching beard the colour of anthracite. He was wearing black bagged trousers, à la Cary Grant, and a dark grey-striped crew neck jumper. Pia instantly felt overdressed and wished she was wearing something more . . . her.

'Won't you sit down, *signore*?' she said, gesturing to the bony salon chairs.

'*Grazie.*'

Signore Alvisio studied her openly while the butler served

coffee, and she knew she'd confounded his expectations. She looked nothing like ballet's *sauvage belle* today.

'So this is where you hide,' he smiled. 'Many people trying to find you, no?'

Pia grimaced. 'Yes, I know. It's bad at the moment. I feel as though even Interpol must be after me.'

Alvisio's eyes twinkled. 'Everybody wants a piece of you. And who can blame them?'

Pia drew herself up, pleased by his flattery. She had been right to come here.

He sat back in the chair, hands linked lightly across his lap. 'So you liked what I did for you? *The Songbird* flattered you well, I thought.'

'Oh *signore*, it was . . . such an honour to dance it. If I could have come back to dance only one last ballet, I would have chosen that. I still can't quite believe that you wrote it for *me*,' she said, bringing both hands up to her heart. It didn't hurt to remind him that it was still her ballet, and not Ava's.

Alvisio nodded. 'I wanted to showcase that light jump of yours. It is . . . how you say? *Eccezionale*. You are always like a bird to my head.' He tapped his temple.

'*Grazie, signore*,' Pia said modestly.

'And how is your foot feeling, now that you have danced on it again?'

They both looked down at Pia's tiny ankles. She was wearing two-tone pumps – pumps? – and there was no hint of swelling or bruising to be seen. Pia rotated the foot easily.

'As good as new,' she smiled, lying only a little bit.

'Show me your arch.'

Pia flexed and pointed her foot seamlessly. Evie had done

a fantastic job of ironing out the judder that had made it feel like it was pushing against rubber when the wires first came out.

'No pain? No swelling?'

'The day after the show it was a bit puffy . . . but once I get back to daily classes that should disappear. Evie's discharged me now. I'm a free agent again.'

Too free, she thought to herself.

'Hmm, yes,' he said sombrely, bringing his forefingers together. 'Which brings us to business. It is a worry that you danced only one act,' he said abruptly.

Pia stared at him. 'Oh, but that had nothing to do with my stamina! I didn't stop because I was in pain.'

'So you were just . . . unprofessional, then?' he asked, raising a crooked eyebrow.

'Well, n-no . . .' Pia stammered.

'Then what? What could have made you walk out on the Royal Ballet?'

'It was complicated.'

Alvisio said nothing but his face showed that that answer wasn't going to cut it.

'I received some news that made it untenable for me to stay,' Pia enlarged, looking at her hands.

'News? When?'

'During the interval. I went back to change and . . . I learnt some things that changed everything for me.' She took a big breath and looked up at him. She was clearly going to have to tell him all of it.

'You have to understand it had been very difficult for me, during my convalescence. I wasn't allowed to go home to Chicago. I had to stay in England in a place where I didn't know anybody. I was frightened and lonely and in pain. I really thought I would never be able to dance fully again.' She shrugged. 'And then when I learnt that Ava was going to dance *The Songbird*, I became very depressed as well. I could feel my whole world slipping away from me.'

She paused.

'Go on.'

'But I started working with Evie and she said she could make me even better than I had been before, so I began to feel hopeful again. I began to settle in.'

'Good.'

'Well, yes, it was. Until the competition with the ChiCi was sprung on me and then everything sped up. It was all too much too soon. I was frightened about going on *pointe* again; frightened of jumping; frightened of spinning; frightened of . . . everything!' she said, throwing her hands in the air. 'But nobody would listen. They all kept saying I would be fine on the night and that it was a great opportunity to launch me back into the spotlight. And what could I do? I was indebted to them for what they'd done for me.'

'But they were right – you *were* great on the night,' Alvisio said.

Pia shook her head. 'No, I was lucky. It was too soon. I knew it but I went out there anyway because I felt *obliged*.' She held up an index finger. 'Just one wrong step or slight twist could have taken me straight back to surgery again. I was risking my future on a sense of honour.'

Alvisio was silent for a long moment. 'So then what happened to change that?'

'I found out that I wasn't the one indebted to them. *They* were indebted to me. I owed them nothing, after all.' She nodded to herself and sat back in the chair. 'And so I ran. I had to.'

'And you came here?'

Pia nodded. 'I haven't left my room since I got here. I've been waiting for you. I wanted to get things sorted out with you first before showing my face in public again. I thought that if we could sign contracts, I could hold a press conference and answer questions then. It would help keep things a bit more controlled.'

'A press conference?'

'Yes,' she smiled. 'Telling them that I'm joining La Scala.'

Alvisio stared at her. 'I think . . .' he said finally, 'that things are moving too fast for you again.'

'No, no,' she said. 'I'm fine now. I just need to get back in class and work with a regular partner again. Work with *you*,' she smiled, stretching her back. 'I'm just aching to dance again.'

'It is not that easy, I'm afraid, Pia.'

'What do you mean?'

'It is a problem that you did not finish the ballet. There are still questions about your performance strength. The powers-that-be need to see that you can still dance for three hours at the highest level, night after night.'

'But that's fine. I can show them that once I'm there,' Pia shrugged. 'There's really no issue at all about my fitness.'

Alvisio sighed. 'You are not our only consideration any more, Pia. Things have changed.'

Pia grew pale. 'What do you mean?' she said slowly.

There was a brief pause as Alvisio considered his words.

'For the past few weeks, we have been in talks with other people,' he said mildly.

'*Other* people?'

He nodded.

'I don't dance like *other* people, *signore*,' Pia said quietly. '*Other* people don't compare to me.'

The man shrugged noncommittally and a tense silence fell.

Pia watched him. She realized he couldn't meet her eyes on this, that his body language was evasive.

She leant in towards him.

'Is it other people, *signore*? Or another *person*?'

Signore Alvisio sighed heavily and stared at his lap, before looking slowly back up at her. He didn't need to say it.

'Ava,' she spat, throwing herself back in her chair.

Alvisio absorbed the enmity.

'She is very keen to dance for us too.' He held his hands up, showing her his dilemma.

'Oh yes? Since when?'

Alvisio said nothing. Petrova's sudden desire to sign to La Scala had been news to him too, but his bosses liked the promise of investment in some new studios that came with her signing. It was a better financial package, and in terms of international profile and box-office draw, they kept saying there wasn't much between the two primas now anyway.

'You wrote *The Songbird* for me, *signore*,' Pia whispered. 'You've always wanted *me*. I'm the best dancer to interpret your vision. We both know that.'

The old man coughed. 'Yes, but Ava danced it beautifully too. I didn't expect her to dance it so . . . poetically.' He looked in her eyes. 'It was how I imagined you dancing it when I wrote it.'

'That's because she copied my style. She was like my clone,

up there. It had nothing to do with her own interpretation at all. She doesn't feel your choreography the way I do. She's just making it up.'

Alvisio sighed. It was no use arguing. His hands were tied. 'I would have agreed with you two months ago. I used to find her dancing very punchy. But she has changed since dancing in Chicago. She has broadened her technique and artistry. And if I ignore her development, I do so at my peril.' He shrugged. 'I have to do what is right for the prestige of La Scala.'

Pia's eyes scanned his frantically, like a laser. This couldn't be the end. It couldn't. Ava couldn't take this away from her too. Why did she even want La Scala anyway? Why not the Royal or the Paris Opera? They were both better suited to her technique.

She got up and started pacing the room, her hands to her mouth.

'Pia, I'm sorry it has to be like this. If there was any other way . . . But we both know *The Songbird* was your exam for us.'

She turned on her heel to face him. 'What if I beat her?'

'*Scusilo?*' An image of the two of them in boxing gloves popped up in his head.

'If I compete against her again? Go the full distance this time, no matter what, and show you that I'm back to my best.'

The choreographer looked confused.

'You mean another dance-off?'

'No.' Pia shook her head. 'Better than that. We'll enter the International Ballet Competition in Varna in July. What better setting than the most prestigious ballet event in the world? We'll have to compete against the best of the rest, as well as against each other, and we'll have to do it over three rounds, so you know I will have had to hit form.'

Alvisio tilted his head, intrigued and impressed. She didn't know what she was really up against, that his bosses were already drawing up the contracts for Ava to sign, but it was clear she wouldn't give up. It was clear that this mattered terribly to her.

It was what he'd always liked about her – her fire, her spirit. It was what informed her dancing, and what shaped his ballets. And at the end of the day, it was written in his contract that he had the final say on who they signed, regardless of whatever pressure the board brought to bear on him. He nodded slowly at the vision of Pia, so defiant, wearing a too-old tweed suit, eyes glimmering, and he knew they'd cope fine in the old studios if they had to. Pia Soto would be recompense enough.

He stood up arthritically and pursed his lips.

'I'm going to sweep the board clean and give you another chance to show me what you can do. If Ava wins, I'll sign her. But if you do, I'll sign you instead.'

Pia gasped and clapped her hands together at the reprieve, before suddenly rushing forward and giving the choreographer an exuberant hug. 'Thank you, *signore*,' she whispered.

'You haven't won yet,' he grinned in spite of himself.

'No, but I will,' she replied.

'I hope so,' he said. And meant it.

Mrs Bremar put the teapot onto the tray and looked out of the kitchen window as the last lorry, kitted out with lighting rigs and stage sets, rumbled down the drive. The dancers, the guests, the stage crew, the television companies and the reporters had all gone, and every last helicopter had buzzed into the air. Only the flattened yellow grass and a stray torch still burning across the lawn gave any clue to the fact that any of them had ever been there.

Mrs Bremar knew precious little about the worlds of showbiz, celebrity or finance, but she knew well enough that her employer had been humiliated. The papers were already painting him as a figure of ridicule: the impresario who had fallen short. And Pia? Pundits were predicting that she'd rise like a phoenix from the ashes, with some sexy scanty cover shoot and a woebegone tale of the pressures of perfection.

She heard a knock at the back door and looked around. Violet was waving at her. The housekeeper indicated for her to come in.

'Hi, Mrs Bremar,' Violet smiled, panting slightly from her brisk walk through the dividing woods. Her cheeks were flushed pink and her eyes bright.

'How are you, Violet?'

'Well, thanks,' Violet said, leaning a hand on the worktop. 'I just wondered whether Will was around? I need to have a chat with him,' she said, blowing out her cheeks. 'About the horses, you know,' she added unnecessarily.

'Yes, of course. He's in the study. I was just taking this through to him.' She put another cup and saucer on the tray. 'Follow me.'

Violet held the door open for her and they walked down the wide hallway.

Will's voice – tense – could be heard as they reached the closed door. Violet knocked once for Mrs Bremar.

'Let me just tell him you're here. One second,' she said, pushing the door open with her ample hips.

Will looked up as Mrs Bremar silently crossed the room.

'. . . yes, I appreciate that . . . but there's hardly a connection between the two . . . We're expecting to see a twelve per cent return on the fund by the end of this quarter . . . Well, that's a hysterical overreaction . . . I'm surprised you're . . . I see, right . . . fine.'

He dropped the phone onto the desk and vigorously rubbed his face with his hands. He looked worn out. He'd locked himself away in here for the past two days and nights.

'Violet's here to see you,' she said quietly.

'Violet?'

The housekeeper nodded. 'Shall I send her in?'

He sighed wearily. She was no doubt here to beg for his business back on Tanner's behalf. Christ. That was the least of his worries right now. 'I guess you'd better.'

Mrs Bremar brought Violet in. He got up to shut the door behind her.

'Violet, what a nice surprise,' he said politely, getting a waft of her fruit-shampooed hair as she passed.

'Hi, Will, hope you don't mind me popping in like this.' She looked around the study, impressed. She'd never been in here before. The walls were hung with a broad-striped celery-coloured paper, and one wall – opposite the two floor-to-ceiling windows – was covered with cherry-wood shelving with a library ladder to access the upper reaches.

The Napoleonic desk had three computer screens popping up through it and was covered with papers. He leant against it, his ankles crossed, while he watched her admire the room. He knew she could feel the power in here, the hub of his empire.

'Not at all. It's always a pleasure to see you.' He put a little pressure on the last word, and she looked back at him and gave a small smile. She wandered over to the window.

A couple of peahens were perambulating over the lawn like Victorian ladies.

'I heard about Pia,' she said quietly. 'I'm sorry . . .'

'Don't be,' he shrugged. 'I've always believed good things come to those who wait.'

'What do you mean?' she asked, baffled. Did he mean he thought Pia would come back to him? Surely he could see her disappearance was a categorical rebuttal.

'Just that,' he said simply, clearly feeling no need to elaborate. 'Some tea?'

She nodded and watched him as he poured, one hand still in his trouser pocket. He radiated power like pheromones. Minky had been right about approaching him directly after all. It was better to sidestep around Tanner altogether and just take matters into her own hands. She'd given Tanner every opportunity to shrug off his sulk but there was clearly way too much testosterone between the two men for them to ever act like grown-ups, and they'd parry insults and jabs till the cows came home. Besides, Tanner had spent the past two days deep in consolation with Jonty, the two of them talking late into the night. They'd barely noticed her.

Will handed her a cup.

'You're probably wondering why I'm here,' she said.

'Yes, I was rather,' he smiled.

She took a deep breath. 'It's about Tanner.'

There was a pause. 'That's a shame.'

'I think he's making a mistake,' Violet said. 'Getting rid of you, I mean.'

'Seems to be all the rage these days,' he quipped. 'Looks like he was ahead of the trend. He should come and work for me as an analyst.'

Violet chuckled at his self-deprecation and bit the rim of

her cup. 'You and I both know how stubborn he can be,' she said. 'He's readily cutting off his nose to spite his face. But this time he's threatening the livelihood of the yard. Seven other people could lose their jobs if we let him carry on like this.'

'We?'

'You and I both know he's not going to back down,' she said. 'I thought maybe you could be the bigger man. Initiate talks. Go to him with a revised deal.'

Will's eyes narrowed. 'Revised how?'

She shrugged casually. 'A thirty per cent mark-up should make him reconsider.'

'I should think it would,' he laughed, as amused by her naivety as by her boldness. 'But why would I want to do that?' he asked.

'The convenience of having your horses stabled next door.'

'For thirty per cent more? That's a high premium just for that privilege. Besides, I've already made alternative arrangements. The horses are leaving tomorrow and it would be very inconvenient to change my plans again.'

Violet took another sip of her drink, trying to think of another reason he should pay more, but Business wasn't her thing.

'But what about the people from the village we employ? You can't let them lose their jobs.'

Will shrugged. 'Their jobs aren't my concern, Violet. Ludgrove's told me to sling my hook and so I am. It's his lookout to secure alternative business to keep them in work. Not mine.'

Violet swallowed hard at the flat rebuttals. She realized she had picked her time badly. What with Pia's abandonment, and whatever that phone call had been about, he was clearly full of anger. Right now, he didn't give a stuff about being the bigger man. She was going to have to play dirty.

'Well, there's also the small fact of Pia stealing my horse,' she said slyly. 'Ebony hasn't been right since that ride. She won't jump any of the hedges now and I haven't been able to hunt with her since. It's only been my pleas that have stopped Tanner from reporting the incident to the police.'

Will looked at her, thoroughly amused. 'You wouldn't be trying to blackmail me, would you, Violet?'

She hated the way he kept saying her name. So patronizing. She took a large gulp of her tea and shrugged carelessly.

'Because I admire the sentiment, really I do, but I don't see what it's got to do with me. Pia was merely a house guest. And now she's gone, God only knows where.' He watched the indignation build in her eyes and he put his drink down on his desk. 'But if you do report her to the police and they find her, would you be so kind as to ask them to let me know of her whereabouts? She and I have some unfinished business as well.'

Violet moved towards him and put her cup down hard, next to his. 'This was a mistake. I shouldn't have come,' she said, eyes flashing. 'I thought I could come here and appeal to your better nature. Clearly I was wrong.'

She went to storm past him, but he grabbed her wrist and swung her to him.

'Violet,' he said in a low voice, 'you and I have long known that it's not my *better* nature you appeal to.'

Chapter Forty-two

'Sophie, are you coming or not?' Esther called from the bottom of the stairs.

Sophie stayed sitting on the end of the bed. It was still covered with the patchwork quilt she'd had as a child. 'I'll be right down,' she called, staring blankly at the damp stain on the chimney breast. It had been there for as long as she could remember, the ancient beige Laura Ashley trellis wallpaper peeling away from the plaster.

Her mobile lay on the bed behind her, Adam's text as yet undeleted.

> So sorry you had to find out like that. Pls call.

'Come on, Soph!' Esther hollered up again. 'They'll stop serving at half past.'

Sophie sighed and stood up, staring at herself in the triple mirror on her dressing table. Her hair was still effortlessly sleek, thanks to the Brazilian perm she'd had put in, in Chicago, and she knew her family were intimidated by the changes in her. Her mother was convinced her weight loss was down to spending too much time round 'these anorexic ballerinas – everyone knows they don't eat'. And her father kept staring disapprovingly at the gold coat that was left hanging at the bottom of the stairs, as though it was a symbol of the decadence – for which read corruption – of big city life. Her eleven-year-old twin sisters, Eilidh and Marie, on the other hand, had been overjoyed by her haul of designer make-up, and Esther, just turned nineteen, had been trying for days to get her to come out to the pub so that she could show off her glamorous big sister. 'Everyone's talking about you coming home,' she kept saying. 'They're desperate to see you.'

She walked down the stairs and into the sitting room. Her father was sitting in his usual armchair, reading the paper. He looked at her briefly as she came in, then went back to it in silence. When her mother had brought her home that first day back, he'd neither smiled, embraced nor kissed her, simply looked her up and down like she'd just returned from getting bread at the village shop, and then walked out of the kitchen to his vegetable patch. He hadn't looked her in the eye once since her return. Though no one had brought it up – preferring to pretend it had never happened – there was an implicit understanding of what she'd done.

'We won't be long, Father,' Esther said, buttoning her coat.

Sophie picked an old bottle-green cord blazer out of the under-stairs cupboard. She'd not worn it since she was fifteen, but it still fitted and looked good against her new hair tone. Her jeans were a battered pair of 501s dragged out from the back of her drawers. They were too short in the legs, grazing the top of her ankles, but they looked fine with the oxblood penny loafers she'd worn at school. She seriously needed to do some shopping.

The sisters walked up the lane, arms linked. 'I still can't believe you're back,' Esther sighed excitedly. 'Even more than that, I can't believe that it's taken over a week to get you out of the house where I can speak to you alone and get all the *real* gossip.'

Sophie shook her head. 'You'll only be disappointed, I'm afraid. My life wasn't half as glamorous as you'd like to think.' She watched a cat creep towards an unsuspecting rabbit that was nibbling on some dock leaves and catching the last of the day's sun. She clapped her hands and sent both scarpering.

'Oh yeah? Well, who's this Adam, then?' Esther grinned.

Sophie stopped, startled. 'How'd you know about him?'

Esther shrugged. 'I saw your mobile lying on the bed earlier. I think you've forgotten there are no secrets when you share a room,' she grinned.

Sophie sighed and started walking again.

'So tell me – who is he?'

'Nobody. Just someone I knew in Chicago.'

'A boyfriend?'

Sophie watched her feet walking. 'For a bit. It was never serious.'

'Not like you and Jerry, then?'

Sophie pulled her arm away, suddenly angry. 'Jerry? Jesus! What made you bring him up?'

'Nothing, I . . . I . . .' Esther stammered, taken aback by Sophie's vehemence. 'I'm sorry. I didn't mean to upset you. I guess I was just trying to find out whether or not you still thought about him.'

Sophie stared at her, shaking. 'Well, I don't, okay?'

'Okay,' Esther said quietly.

'Is he going to be here tonight? Is that why you've been so desperate to drag me out?'

Esther shook her head. 'No. No, he moved away not long after you left. He's living in Waterford now.'

Sophie took a deep breath and looked up the lane at the little thatched pub that was sitting fatly on the corner. 'Well, okay, then. That's all right.'

She started walking slowly. Esther, shaken by the conversation, walked a couple of steps behind her. After a minute's silence, Sophie turned round. 'Look, I'm sorry if I overreacted,' she said softly. 'But all that's bygones, see? My life has moved on. I don't want to think about any of it any more.'

Esther smiled, relieved to have been forgiven, and caught her up. 'Well, I can't say as I blame you. I never did get what you saw in him.'

Chuckling, they went up the steps together, opening the door and releasing a burst of warmth, light and laughter into the street.

Esther went straight to the bar and ordered them a cider each. Sophie felt the stares settle on her like a blanket. She smiled nervously, managing to avoid making direct eye contact with anyone.

'Come on, we'll sit over there,' Esther said, taking their drinks and heading towards a table in the corner.

'Hey, Esther,' people murmured as they passed, shuffling their chairs out of the way as an excuse to look closer at Sophie. She was scarcely recognizable as the little girl who'd run away seven years before.

'I've never been so popular,' Esther said under her breath as they sat down.

Sophie took her drink. 'Cheers,' she said nervously and took a noisy sip.

'Hey, Esther, how's it going?' a black-haired blue-eyed guy asked, coming over from the bar. 'Hey, Sophie. It's been a while.'

Sophie looked up and instantly recognized Finn O'Connor

from her Irish dancing classes. They'd been pretty good for a while back in the day, before she'd suddenly shot up at fourteen, towering over not just Finn but all the boys in the year and finding it all but impossible to keep her long back stiff and straight.

He'd caught her up now, though.

'Finn,' she gasped, delighted to see him. She stood up and kissed him on each cheek.

'Hoh!' Finn laughed, unaccustomed to these sophisticated social mores. 'Doubly good to see you too.'

Sophie laughed. 'Won't you join us?' she asked, pulling out a chair for him.

'Well, I'd love to, but I'm with that rowdy bunch at the bar,' he said, rolling his eyes towards a group of guys all clutching their pints and looking over expectantly.

Sophie caught Esther's eye. 'They're good lads,' she shrugged.

'What the hell? The more the merrier,' Sophie smiled.

'Right you are, then. Hey, lads!' Finn shouted, indicating for them all to come over.

They each grabbed a chair on the way over, and much shuffling of the surrounding tables ensued. They thrust out friendly hands as they sat down.

'Tom Driscoll,' beamed the ginger-haired one with the bright blue, naughty eyes.

'Joe Scanlan,' grinned the tall one, with shaggy brown hair and a face full of freckles.

'Tony Byrne,' said the last one, with pitch-black hair and green-flecked eyes. He was wearing a chunky white cable-knit jumper, even though it was May.

'Sophie,' she said, even though they all knew perfectly

well who she was. 'Don't tell me you're cold?' she said to Tony as he sat down next to her.

'Ach, he's always bothering about the cold,' Tom joshed, digging him in the ribs.

'Well, you were worth the wait,' Finn said, watching Sophie as she settled back to her drink, her fingers tracing the rim of her glass.

Sophie looked up. 'What do you mean?'

Finn shrugged. 'Well, it's been the talk of the village you coming home. We've been coming here every night hoping to see you. Fair spent a month's wages in here waiting for you to come in.'

'Sorry to have kept you waiting. What can I say? Jet lag,' she lied.

'Where did you come in from?' Joe asked, a slug of foam on his top lip.

'America.'

'Really? Whereabouts?' Tom asked.

'Chicago.'

'Is it as windy as they say over there, then?' Finn asked.

'Well, they do sell a lot of kites,' she nodded.

'What did you do over there?' Joe asked.

Esther smiled, leaning forward. 'See if you can guess.'

The guys tipped their heads in consideration.

'Banking.'

'Doctor.'

'No, advertising.'

'I reckon it was scaffolding,' Finn grinned.

'What?' Sophie said, bursting out laughing and smacking him on the arm.

'You're all way off the mark, the lot of you,' Esther said proudly, taking an impressive swig of cider.

KAREN SWAN

'What was it, then?'

'Sophie's an artist. She had an exhibition out there and everything.'

'Seriously?' Joe said. 'You must be pretty good. What kind of art?'

Sophie paused. 'Portraits, mainly.'

'Hey! Would you do mine?' Joe grinned, pushing a napkin towards her. 'Emer, have you got a pen?' he called over to the woman behind the bar.

She pushed a biro over the counter and he got up to get it.

'Ah well, seeing as you're up, you can get another round in, Joe,' Tom laughed.

Joe dropped his head in his hands, and Sophie and Esther laughed as he threw a peanut at Tom – before dutifully ordering another round.

Sophie picked up the pen. 'Okay, who's first, then?' she said boldly, looking at them all in turn. 'Tom.'

'How d'you want me?' he asked, turning his head to the side and puckering up.

'Oh nice, nice,' Sophie laughed, getting a handle on the shape of his eyes, in spite of his best efforts to manipulate and distort his face. She drew quickly and effortlessly, the months spent sitting in the studio capturing split-second movements as Adam and Ava whipped past her, finally paying off.

'God, you're fast,' Finn said, watching her hand expertly reproduce his mate's features.

'How's that?' she asked, pushing the napkin towards Tom and sitting back in her chair. She took a large, proud swig of her drink.

'Jesus, you're good,' Tom said, laughing. 'Although I don't

394

think you've *quite* captured exactly how handsome I really am.'

Joe cuffed his shoulder. 'You'd look like that in your dreams, mate.'

'Who's next?' Sophie asked, handing her empty glass to Emer as she came over with the fresh drinks. 'Tony?' She smiled at the quietest member of the group. He'd said scarcely a word since sitting down but she sensed he'd been watching her closely all the while. 'You've been suspiciously quiet,' she teased.

He sat back in his chair, his arms resting languidly on the table. He seemed to say more with his silence than the rest of the guys managed in full banter.

'Ach, not for long,' Finn said finally. 'You'll be sick of the sound of him two minutes into his set.'

'His set? What do you mean?' Sophie asked, intrigued.

'No, no. I'm not doing that tonight,' Tony protested, batting the suggestion away with an idle hand.

'Tony here's our resident star,' Finn grinned. 'At least, he was till you came back.'

Sophie looked at him, her interest piqued. 'What do you do?' she asked, leaning her arms on the table. 'Tell me.'

He looked at her, a glimmer of amusement in his eyes. 'I'm a carpenter,' he said, before taking a defensive gulp of his beer.

The guys roared at his evasiveness.

Sophie looked at them all and at Esther. 'And when you're not doing that for a living, what are you really?' she asked, refusing to be deterred.

He stared at her with a smouldering defiance and she knew in a flash he'd judged her as the big city girl with the glitzy career, flirting with the locals as she passed through on her way to bigger and brighter things. He refused to compete.

There was a sudden piercing whine and she saw Finn had got up and was standing on a small stage in the opposite corner by the fireplace. 'Ahem, ladies and gentlemen,' he drawled suavely into the microphone. 'In honour of the return of one of Fennor's finest womenfolk, Tony Byrne is going to play a small set for you all tonight.'

A massive cheer went up through the pub and, groaning, Tony slapped his hand across his forehead.

Sophie raised her eyebrows in amusement as he reluctantly stood up. 'Good luck.'

He walked between the tables and sat down at the piano, the top of which was covered with half-full pints. 'Emer, do you mind?' he asked blandly, sending the barmaid running over with a tray. 'It's just I wouldn't want them to fall off while I'm playing,' he added apologetically as she hurried to clear them.

'For sure, Tony,' the woman smiled. 'You're always so thoughtful like that.'

He stared at the keys for a moment, then began to play, his fingers teasing out a haunting ballad. Sophie sat back in the chair, watching him as his voice – low and steady – filled the room.

Everyone had fallen silent now. He was sitting facing her but his eyes were pinned to the ivory keys. Sophie took the opportunity to examine him – how his hair flopped across his forehead as he moved, the hollow of his cheeks as he sang, how his eyelashes cast shadows when he looked down. He really was . . . not handsome, but beautiful, like some medieval angel.

Slowly, she drew a clean napkin across the table and began

to sketch again, her hands moving while her eyes remained upon him. Not that he would notice. His absorption was mesmerizing as he segued easily from one song to the next. She'd never heard of any of them.

'What are these songs?' she whispered to Esther. 'I don't remember any of them.'

'You wouldn't,' her sister shrugged. 'He wrote them all. This is a rare thing nowadays, him playing impromptu like this, let me tell you. Usually, Emer has to put tickets on the door to control numbers when he does a gig.'

'I'm not surprised. He's amazing.'

Esther rolled her eyes and put a hand on her arm. 'Join the queue, sis. Half of Cork's already madly in love with him.'

Sophie tutted, annoyed. 'As if,' she whispered. 'I just mean that I like his music.'

'Yeah, well, I think he's going to be going places anyway. He won't be hanging around here for much longer. The bright city lights are already beckoning.'

'What do you mean?'

'A talent scout came all the way from Dublin a few weeks ago to come and listen to him. He's going to go and do some gigs there.'

'Oh. Well, that's . . . great,' Sophie said, looking back and catching him watching her after all, his eyes steady as his fingers flew. She swallowed and tried to smile as everyone broke into applause.

The boys stood up, whistling and cheering. 'See what I mean?' Finn grinned, sitting down and turning back to her. 'Our resident star.'

'He certainly is,' Sophie agreed, clapping so hard her hands burnt.

Finn saw the sketch of Tony on the napkin. 'Hey, let's have a look,' he said, turning it around.

Tony came back over, a shy smile on his face. He was flushed slightly and he pulled off his jumper, his grey T-shirt lifting to reveal a slice of brown, rock-hard stomach.

Sophie looked back at Esther and found her already grinning at her.

Finn pushed the napkin over to Tony. 'You should use that for your first album cover,' he said.

Tony lifted an eyebrow. Sophie looked away, embarrassed, feeling she'd overdrawn. She'd flattered him.

'Not bad,' he said, looking down at it but leaving it on the table.

'Not bad yourself,' she countered, taking a sip of her drink and fixing her eyes on the bottom of the glass.

There was an awkward silence as Esther and the guys all shot each other amused looks.

'Right, well, I think we'd better be off,' Sophie said, suddenly desperate to get out of there.

'Sure,' Esther murmured.

'Yup, us too,' Joe said, draining his drink. 'I've an early start in the morning.'

They all drank the dregs and stood up to go.

'It was good to see you, Finn,' Sophie said, feeling awkward again as she put on her jacket. 'And to meet all of you guys,' she added, looking at Tom and Joe but not quite able to meet Tony's eyes. She could feel his scorn that she was patronizing them with her presence.

'Likewise,' Tom smiled. 'We'll see you in here again soon, I hope.'

She shrugged noncommittally. 'Yes. Maybe.'

'How long are you back for?' Tony asked casually, pulling his jumper back on. Sophie couldn't help looking down at his stomach again as his head disappeared inside it.

'I'm not sure,' she replied.

His head emerged through the neck of his jumper and he raked a hand through his hair to pull it back off his face. They stared at each other for a moment.

There was a pause. 'Well, if we don't see you again, have a nice trip,' he said blandly.

Sophie swallowed, feeling suddenly crushed. 'Thanks,' she said finally. 'I will.'

'Come on, then,' Esther said, pulling her sister away by the arm.

They walked out together into the night, Esther getting out a torch from her pocket. Sophie grabbed her arm, having forgotten exactly how dark it gets in the countryside without street lights.

'Are y'on Florence Nightingale duty tomorrow, Esther?' Joe called after her.

'What do you think?'

'Great,' he called back and she could hear him grinning in the darkness. 'I'll make sure to get in the way when Tom gets the ball. That should guarantee a whacked shin as he fluffs his pass!'

'Oi!' Tom protested, giving him a shove.

Esther giggled delightedly and squeezed Sophie's arm tighter. Sophie smiled back. Esther had done a lot of growing up in her absence and she felt a sharp pain when she thought about exactly how much of her family's life she must have missed out on.

Inside the pub, Emer started clearing away the empties. She picked up the sketch of Tom that had been left, forgotten, on the table. She admired it for a moment and then stuffed it into a glass with the empty crisp packets.

The door opened again, and Tony suddenly ran back in. 'Sorry, Emer,' he said, flashing her a smile and picking up the napkin Sophie had drawn on for him. He folded it carefully into his back pocket. 'I just forgot something.'

Chapter Forty-three

Sophie sat on the picnic blanket and helped herself to another sandwich. It was a glorious day in May – mild and bright – and even the gulls seemed to be enjoying the high pressure, gliding to ever-loftier heights until they became nothing more than black dots in the sky.

She sighed happily and looked around her. It was a typical Saturday afternoon, exactly as she remembered them – just as she'd left them: the men of the village playing a to-the-death hurling match against the men of the next village, the womenfolk of both sitting round the sides, blethering and sewing, and not taking a blind bit of notice.

The twins were running around, playing Forty Forty It with their friends in the silver birches – just as she had – and Esther was chopping up oranges for half-time.

'You've really grown up, Ess,' Sophie said, watching her slice her way through the bag. 'That always used to be Mam's job.'

'Ay, well, it's not so good for her hands to hold such a small knife nowadays,' she said. 'They get ever so stiff.'

Sophie nodded. The shame she was so used to wrapped around her like cling film – accusing her, reminding her that she never should have gone, that her family had needed her.

She watched her mother sitting with the other women on the deck chairs around the pitch. She was knitting an Aran jumper – her speciality – for Eilidh, and laughing as Eithne Finlay regaled the group with a story about her husband backing his tractor into the slurry tank and how she'd made him sleep downstairs for a month.

She watched the way her mother put her knitting in her lap when she laughed hard – to save from dropping stitches – and how she tilted her head to the right when she was listening, how she rested her knitting needles on her tummy (a habit from childhood) rather than letting them waggle in the air in the traditional fashion, and how a sheen of fear flickered over her face every time her eyes sought out her children – not the youngest two but her eldest daughters, who were sitting with their long slender legs stretched out before them, their matching red hair blowing behind them like pennants in the breeze.

She met her mother's gaze and smiled – apologetically, encouragingly, willing her to believe that she wouldn't run again.

The ref – her father, dressed in his customary top-to-toe black – blew the half-time whistle shrilly. Fifteen–nine to the visitors. He was notorious for his by-the-book refereeing and everyone knew not to bother trying to get anything past him. The man had eyes in the back of his head.

All thirty players dropped to the ground like dead ducks, thankful for a reprieve, and Sophie tittered as she watched the collective green-and-red-clad beer bellies heave up and down on the grass.

Esther ran on with the orange quarters and they wearily rolled themselves back up to sitting, plastering the segments to their teeth like gum shields and sucking the juice frantically. Finn stuck one in his mouth and gave her a great orange grin.

Sophie rolled her eyes and he motioned for her to come over. Tom, Joe and Tony lay scattered like shrapnel around him.

'Hi,' she said, standing over them all. 'You look like you've got your work cut out for you today. They're thrashing y'all. What've you been doing all match? Painting your toenails?'

'Whisht! You've no idea,' Joe panted. 'It's man's work.'

'Is it 'cos you forgot to strap your bellies on? Is that it?' she teased, settling herself into a gangly cross-legged heap. 'Because the old boys are doing a better job than you lot. Y'ought to be ashamed of yourselves!'

'It's your fault, actually,' Finn grinned. 'Keeping us in the pub till all hours. You city girls with your twenty-four-seven living. You forget that we country boys go to bed with the sun.'

'Well, it's certainly all you go to bed with,' Tom teased, ducking out the way as Finn skimmed his wizened orange quarter at him.

Sophie slid her eyes over to Tony. He was lying on his back enjoying the sun, one arm thrown carelessly over his face, and, judging by the slow rise and fall of his stomach, he'd got his breath back.

'Age sure isn't mellowing your father,' Finn said.

You're telling me, Sophie thought to herself. She just smiled.

'Did you see how he picked me up on that five-step? Sure, I was only a step over. You'd think he'd have just let it go. Anyone would think he didn't want Fennor to win the league. Aglish are all over us now. You're going to have to have a word with him for us, Soph. The man's a tartar.'

She shrugged and began making a daisy chain. 'I'm the last person who's got any kind of influence over him,' she said mildly.

Tony, picking up the finality in her voice, stared at her from beneath his elbow. 'What does that mean?' he asked, breaking his customary silence.

'Nothing more than that. He's just his own man, that's all. He would never be swayed by what I think.'

'What? Not his newly returned prodigal daughter? I'd have thought he'd be treading on eggshells in his desire to keep you happy and stop you from running again.' She couldn't miss the sarcastic note in his voice.

Sophie swallowed. 'If I go again, it won't be because I'm running.'

'Why did you run?' Tom asked cheekily, sucking on a blade of grass.

'To get away from fellas like you,' she retorted, managing a half-smile.

Tony sighed and obscured his face again, and she felt belittled by the gesture. He clearly didn't want her there. She took a deep breath of defiance. Well tough. These were her friends.

'I can't believe how big your brother's grown, Finn,' she said, changing the subject, as a lanky half-forward jogged past. 'I scarcely recognized him when I got here. How old's he now?'

'Fifteen.'

Sophie shook her head. 'God! And to think I used to babysit for him.'

'He's not my only baby brother now, either. Stephen's nearly six – he was born soon after you left.'

'Really? So – what? You're one of . . .' she counted in her head. 'Seven now?'

'Ay. Da's got his seven-a-side team, after all.'

'Your poor mam! Seven burly boys to cook and feed and clean up after. It's beyond imagination what your bathroom must be like in the mornings.'

'She loves it, really,' he chuckled. 'Family's what it's all about at the end of the day, isn't it?'

'Ach, don't talk such rot,' Tony mumbled, his eyes still closed.

Sophie arched her eyebrows and looked back at Finn. He shrugged, nonplussed, and she looked away, watching the way all the families intertwined with each other, the bigger children looking after the little ones, the mothers burping each other's babies, pulling spare rattles and biscuits out of their bags.

She wondered what they would have thought about her self-imposed exile in the big cities – first London, then Chicago – where she lived anonymously, not knowing the faces, much less the names of her neighbours in the apartments above and below hers (Greg didn't count; he was more like a stalker than a neighbour). Here, the families could trace their ancestors back for generations, and crumbling old bothies and strips of land that had long since been abandoned were still known as 'Maggie's house' or 'Paddy's field', and they all knew and told each other's family stories as well as their own.

Fennor nurtured and protected its sense of community as its most valuable asset, and if she tried to describe what it had been like to live as one among millions in a big city, the people here would have felt only horror and pity. They wouldn't understand that there's a certain comfort in being anonymous; in living where no one knows your secrets but you; in being taken at face value and not with the burden of reputation and village standing and heritage on your shoulders. Getting lost had been the only way she knew to find herself and it had been exactly what she needed. It was how she had learnt to live with her ghosts.

But now that she had returned, back to the bosom of her family, she wasn't sure she had come home. Her father's silent anger threw a glass wall around everyone and everything. She felt she occupied a purgatory, hovering between two worlds, and she had no idea which she belonged to any more.

'So which is your family, Tony?' she asked, looking around. She knew all the older faces here. Only the babies and small children were strangers to her.

'I don't have one,' he said curtly. 'Thank God.'

'What do you mean?' she asked, shocked.

'What – that I don't have a family?'

'The "thank God" bit. How can you say that?'

'Quite easily actually,' he said, rolling himself up and resting his elbows on his knees. His voice was calm but his eyes were blazing. He looked straight at her, and she shrank a little beneath his gaze. 'You're making the classic mistake of assuming everyone grew up in a perfect family like yours.'

'My family's *not* perfect,' she retorted.

'Yeah, right,' Tony snorted.

'You've got no right to assume anything about my family. You don't know anything about me.'

'I don't know you, no. But I know them and I know that, compared to my family, they come pretty damn close to being perfect.'

Only because I left, Sophie fumed silently. If I'd stayed, it would have been a different matter entirely.

'So what was so terrible about them, then? Why is life so much better without them?'

He shrugged and watched some of the players begin to get up. 'My pa was okay. Strict, but . . . I couldn't blame him after what he had to put up with from my mother.'

'What? She had an affair?' she asked casually, her ever-so-slightly mocking tone betraying the world-weariness that came from city living. It might not happen much here, but all the rest of the world was at it, and it would hardly classify his family as the house of horrors he was insistent upon.

He looked directly at her, stung by her nonchalance. 'She was a drug addict and she abandoned us,' he said peremptorily.

There was a horrified silence. Sophie noticed the other guys were looking away, their bodies stiff.

'Oh,' she said in a tiny voice, her cheeks burning from his scorn. 'I'm sorry.'

'Don't be. I'm not,' he said tersely. 'It's been a valuable lesson. Life is better lived alone, without ties or attachments.'

'By which you mean . . . family? You want to be *all alone*? Forever?'

Tony nodded.

'You don't seriously mean that,' she scoffed.

He raised his eyebrows at her as her father marched briskly past, the Pied Piper of Fennor, with all the players in his wake.

'You want me to believe that you *never* want to settle down and have a family of your own?'

'That's right.'

'All because of your mother?'

He nodded, looking away. His jaw was set.

'But if she was an addict, then—'

'Don't tell me addiction's a disease. She was no victim and there are no excuses for it,' he said, cutting her off as he got to his feet. 'She doesn't deserve explanations. And I'm not sure why you should be so keen to find one for her. I'd have thought you'd have understood more than anybody.'

'What do you mean by that?'

'Well, you walked out on your family, abandoned them. You know as well as I do how easily people can turn their backs on the ones they love.'

'There's nothing *easy* about it!' How dare he judge her! He knew nothing about her reasons for leaving or how she'd suffered out there on her own – a fifteen-year-old girl with no money and no contacts, but just a talent and a desire to hide.

'Well, you could have fooled everyone here,' he said, picking up his hurley stick and jogging off, taking his position in the midfield.

Sophie watched him go, stunned by the verbal attack, tears pricking her eyes.

'Don't let him upset you,' Finn said awkwardly. 'It's a prickly subject at the best of times.'

'Best of times?' she muttered, her voice thick.

'Well, he was unnecessarily harsh with you. He's not usually so aggressive.'

'He despises me. He thinks I'm too big for my boots, coming back here.'

He stood up and held his hand out for her. 'Well, *I'm* glad you're back. Don't take it too bad. He's all right when you get to know him.'

She let him pull her up to standing. 'I don't think I'll bother, thanks,' she said sulkily, watching Tony jog on the spot, his cheeks swarthy and stubbled. 'Seems more effort than it's worth.'

Finn shrugged and ran back onto the pitch, just as the whistle blew and the ball flew through the air towards Tom. He went to hit it, but missed, whacking Joe on the shins instead.

'Ow! Ya basta'd!' Joe hollered, hopping around on one foot, before a great smile broke out across his face as Esther ran towards him with the ice bucket.

Chapter Forty-four

Sophie let the elderly couple get off the bus before her, worried she might hold them up with her wide load. She climbed down the steps sideways, hoisting the bags under her arms, but one got jammed as the doors closed.

She gave it a pull. Nothing happened. 'Excuse me! Driver!' she called out. But he couldn't hear her. She tugged it forcefully again and this time it came free, but not before the bag ripped and the contents flew out all over the pavement.

'Bugger,' she hissed as the bus pulled away and its wheels left tyre tracks on a new T-shirt. She fell to her knees to start picking it all up.

'I see you're single-handedly reviving the Irish economy,' said a deadpan voice across the way. 'What's your plan? To shop us out of bankruptcy?'

Sophie looked up. Tony was standing outside the newsagent's on the other side of the street. He was wearing jeans and a faded red T-shirt that had ripped slightly at the neck.

Oh great.

'I've got no clothes,' she shrugged, embarrassed by the bulging bags all around her. They'd no doubt confirm the rich-city-girl image he'd formed of her.

He crossed the road and picked up a six-pack of knickers.

'You say that like it's a bad thing,' he said, handing them to her.

She took them, wishing he'd just go. Instead, he bent down and helped her. 'It looks like you're intending to stay for a bit, at least,' he said, as he gathered up stray tights, jeans and pyjamas.

'Looks like it,' she said tersely, reaching to grab a T-shirt that was threatening to blow away.

He picked up a primrose-yellow bra. 'Well,' he grinned, 'apparently you really *don't* have any clothes.' He handed the bra back to her and stood up.

Sophie stuffed the bra to the bottom of a bag and stood up too.

His eyes glittered. 'It raises the question: *why*'ve you got no clothes?'

Sophie paused. 'I just left in a bit of a hurry.'

He nodded, staring at her intently. 'So having run *away* from here, something sent you running *back* again. What could that have been, I wonder?' he mused.

She didn't bother to answer. It was none of his damned business. 'Thanks for the help,' she said, starting to walk away.

Tony watched her go for a moment, her satiny hair swinging around her shoulders.

'I wanted to apologize, by the way,' he said, catching her up.

'For what? You don't owe me an apology,' she said shortly, not stopping.

'But I do. I was very rude to you the other day. Making all sorts of assumptions about you and your family.' God, she was walking fast, her eyes dead ahead. He grabbed her by the elbow and forced her to stop. 'Finn gave me a right bollocking after the match. And he was right. I shouldn't have said what I said to you.'

She stared at him for a moment. 'Fine,' she said finally. 'Apology accepted.'

She turned and went to walk away again.

'Wait,' he said, holding her by the arm again, chuckling at her determination to leave. 'I want to make it up to you. Let me give you a ride home,' he said.

'My house is two hundred yards down the road,' she said drily. 'I'm fine.'

'No, you're not,' he said, with a conviction that had nothing to do with her bag-carrying ability.

She stared at him, at that beautiful face with its dancing green eyes and contoured cheekbones, and she suddenly felt like he could see right inside her and read all her secrets. She swallowed hard. Esther must have told Joe, who'd told him all about Adam.

'Come on,' he said, taking the bags from her hands and tilting his head. 'I'm just parked over there.'

Reluctantly she followed him over to where an ancient burgundy Morris Minor was sitting. Sophie noticed that moss was growing on the window ledges. Tony threw her bags in the back and opened the door for her. She curled herself into the passenger seat and felt a bit of the roof interior pressing against her head.

'Mmm, sorry about that,' he said, reaching into the back footwell and grabbing some tacks and a hammer. He leant over and pinned it back up again. 'There,' he smiled.

Sophie burst out laughing at the gesture.

'I guess they don't have cars like this in Chicago,' he said, resting his arm on the back of her seat and looking out of the back windscreen as he put the car into reverse.

'No,' she smiled. 'More's the pity.'

Tony raised an eyebrow. 'What? You mean you don't go in for bigger, faster, glossier? Cadillacs and Chevrolets?'

Sophie shook her head. 'Nope. Why would you think I would?'

He shrugged. 'You just . . . you just look the type.'

'What does that mean?'

'I don't know. The perfect hair, the flawless figure . . .'

'Oh my God! You have got to be joking!' she mumbled. He obviously couldn't read anything about her at all. She was as far from that glossy image he'd just painted as it was possible to get.

Tony cast a glance at her. She was staring out of the window.

'I hear you've got some interest from Dublin,' she said finally, embarrassed as they lapsed into silence.

'Yes.' He didn't elaborate. He obviously didn't want to talk to her about it. He probably thought she was patronizing him again.

She sighed, frustrated by his chippiness. 'Well, it doesn't surprise me. You were really good the other night,' she said politely, opening her bag and looking for the keys. They were approaching her parents' house. She couldn't wait to jump out.

'Yeah? You think so?' He looked across at her.

She nodded as he slowly parked.

Tony cleared his throat. 'I don't suppose . . .' he began. Then changed his mind. 'No, forget it.'

'No, what is it?' Sophie asked absently, leaning over the back seat to get her bags.

'Well, I was just wondering whether you'd like to come back to my place,' he said, staring fixedly ahead. 'To hear what I'm working on, I mean.'

Sophie sat back down and stared at him, baffled. One minute he acted like she was a nuisance, in the way of him having a good time with his mates. The next he was helping her with her bags and wanting her opinion.

He gave a small smile and shrugged. 'I could do with a fresh ear. The guys can only offer so much.'

She looked out of the car and saw her father standing behind the curtain, watching them both, and she felt the familiar claustrophobia wash over her.

'Why not?' she said, giving a small smile and putting her seatbelt back on.

'Great.' Tony gave her a sheepish grin and pulled away. He took a left and a right out of the village and idled past Murphy's farm. Friesians were lying down in the field, occasional rabbits flashing their cottontails on the fringes of the pasture. Tony hooked a right down by the fisheries onto an unmade track Sophie didn't remember from her childhood. They bumped down the lane, the Morris Minor's suspension barely up to the job of crossing a gravel drive, much less this cratered landscape. He stopped a perilous half mile later outside a stone cottage that overlooked the lake.

'God, it's beautiful,' Sophie gasped, stepping out of the car and staring at the view. 'I've not seen it down this way before. How long have you lived here?'

Tony shrugged. 'Coming up to four years now.'

'Have you always lived round here? I don't remember you.'

'I grew up in Tregarnon,' he said, opening the front door, which he'd just left on the latch. 'South Mayo.'

'So what made you come to Fennor?' she asked, walking round the car.

'My father died and I decided to take off around the

country. When I got here, I couldn't think of a good enough reason to leave. So I stayed.' He stood back to let her in.

She stepped into the cottage. It was a single room with a huge inglenook fireplace to the right and a black stove that appeared to pre-date an Aga on the far wall. The bed was built into a huge cupboard in the corner, with heart-shaped cut-out wooden doors. A grand piano sat, rather conspicuously, in the middle of the room.

Sophie walked round the little cottage with undisguised delight. 'God, I just . . . I just love it!' she exclaimed.

Tony grinned. 'Me too.' He walked over to the fire. 'Are you warm enough?' he asked. 'Shall I set the fire?'

Sophie nodded, and seeing there was nowhere else to sit she plonked herself down on the piano stool. It might be May but the evenings were still chilly. She watched as he set to getting the fire going, the muscles in his back clearly visible beneath his T-shirt.

'You don't like the cold, do you?' she smiled.

He shook his head. 'I can't ever seem to get used to it.' He got up and walked over to the fridge. He pulled out a bunch of grapes and took a huge wedge of Brie down from the slate larder shelf.

'Merlot okay?' he asked, holding up a New World bottle.

'Lovely.'

He grabbed two glasses and brought them over to the piano. He poured the wine and sat next to her, their legs not quite touching and yet she could feel the warmth of his, so close to hers.

'Cheers,' he said. 'To new friends.'

She raised an eyebrow and clinked his glass. 'So that's what we are, are we?' she asked, taking a sip.

'You sound surprised.'

'Can you blame me? You haven't exactly been welcoming up till now.'

Tony looked down at the ivory keys. 'It wasn't that,' he said quietly, beginning to press down on them softly. Sophie wanted to ask him what it was, then; but he was letting his fingers do the talking, a mournful melody beginning to swirl like mist around them.

Sophie watched the tendons in his forearms as his fingers skated across the keys, the hairs on the back of his hand, the way his bicep bulged softly as he ran up the octaves. Slowly, she dragged her eyes up to his shoulders, his neck and throat, his face. Staring at his profile she saw that his eyes were shut. He was lost to her, immersed in the music. God, he was so beautiful. She wanted to reach out and touch him, run her fingers over his face like a sculptor, commit his contours to her own touch.

Quietly, she slid off the stool and padded over to the worktop. A Stanley knife-sharpened HB pencil was sitting on top of some sketches of a barn. She took it and a clean piece of paper and looked around for somewhere to sit. The bed was the only other place and it gave her a good angle of him.

She pushed her shoes off and sat down cross-legged, hurriedly sketching him in vignettes – the long lashes sweeping down and back up off his cheekbones, his straight nose, the full lips, the black curls at the nape of his neck. Over the paper her pencil flew, drafting his passion, his tenderness, his joy.

When she finally looked up again, she realized he'd stopped. His eyes were roaming over her face, intrigued by her own absorption. He got up and walked over to her.

'Let me see,' he said, standing above her and holding his hand out.

She held it up slowly. 'I'm sorry. I know I should have asked,' she said awkwardly. 'You asked me here to listen to your music, not so that I could . . .' As the paper left her hand, she caught sight of what she had drawn and she realized suddenly how much she had exposed herself, her hunger for him leaping off the paper as she tried to capture him, to get to the heart of him.

He looked at it for a long moment, and she felt her cheeks flame from embarrassment. How could she have been so unguarded? She saw the paper waft from his hands to the floor. He hated it!

She looked up at him and found him staring at her. Time stopped.

Without saying anything, he propped a knee on the bed, between hers, and bent down over her, forcing her backwards until the mattress spread out under her and there was nowhere left to go. Her hair fanned out beneath her and she felt her heart flip as finally, blissfully, he covered her mouth with his.

She untangled her long legs, wrapping them around him, gasps escaping her as his hot breath covered her neck. She wound her fingers in his hair, keeping him close to her as she felt his fingers unbutton her shirt. He had it off in an instant, his brown hands caressing her pale waist, his scarlet lips on her pink nipples.

She rolled on top of him, pulling his T-shirt off in one fluid movement, and wriggling down him, covering his chest with hungry kisses while she pushed his jeans off with her legs, desperate to get to him. She wriggled out of hers and ran her fingers up the length of him, hearing him moan as she

KAREN SWAN

increased the pressure and pace. She felt the tension build in him, his breathing change, and she sprang up like a cat, straddling him. Her knickers were still on but neither could wait. She pulled them to the side, lifting herself on to him and falling into a rhythm that had them both panting within seconds. His hands grabbed hers, their fingers entwined, and he pulled her body down to his, every part of them touching as they succumbed together to an unworldly, unstoppable climax.

The fire crackled across the room, sending out stray sparks which hissed into cold oblivion on the stone floor. The Brie began to ooze on the plate.

Sophie lay in his arms, feeling the heat emanating from him, hearing his heart hammer under her cheek.

'Why weren't we friends the other times?' she whispered.

She felt him pause before he let the words out. He tipped her chin up with his hand and kissed her sweetly between her eyes. He rolled over, pinning her beneath him. 'Because I thought I was going to lose you,' he said. 'The very night I'd finally found you.'

Chapter Forty-five

Tanner folded his arms as he watched the horses being brought in from the outer fields. It was four in the afternoon and he'd come straight from the airport to the farm, his bags still in the car. Velasquez wasn't due back at the estate until after six, and he'd taken the opportunity to come and check out the horses' fitness and temperaments for the journey that lay ahead.

All around him, cicadas were ticking in the trees, the mosquitoes rising up from the grasses, and he admired the stately mountain range that fanned out below the estate, as though it had been parked there by Velasquez's own decree.

He wiped his forehead with the back of his hand, dripping in sweat. It was the middle of June and the humidity was oppressive. His chinos were clinging to his thighs and a dark sweat patch was slowly spreading between his shoulders. His ironing wasn't going to stand up to much out here. Since Jonty had returned to his MLitt at Cambridge – paparazzi pictures of Harry and Lulie at Cannes together finally convincing him that she wasn't coming back – and Violet had gone, he had had to do a crash course in household maintenance.

His nostrils flared at the memory of walking in on them – Violet on her knees in Silk's office – when he'd gone to chase up the outstanding invoice that Pia, of course, had failed to pass on to him. He hadn't been hurt by the infidelity, though his pride had, as, yet again, Will Silk pulled a number on the Ludgrove family.

But he was determined to have the last laugh. Velasquez had not only paid the yard's entire liveries a year upfront, but he'd paid them at double the rate Silk had negotiated. His fortunes were on the up and things were better without Violet, even if he did keep pulling pink shirts from the washing machine.

'Ha!' cried the groom, rounding the horses easily into the pen and shutting the gate behind the last of them.

Tanner crossed his arms again and walked slowly round, appraising them. They were fresh and skippy, but a couple were looking a bit too frisky for such a long journey – he'd have to check the feed they were on and make sure they weren't on oats.

He jumped over the fencing and moved between the horses, talking to them gently. 'Are they supplemented with vitamins?' he asked, running his hand down one mare's flank and lifting the hoof.

The groom sat on his horse, arms crossed on the back of the horse's neck. '*Si, senhor*. Very good.'

Tanner nodded, weaving through the horses like a snake through water. His Portuguese was about as good as this guy's English. He'd have to wait for Velasquez's return before he could get any level of detail on them.

'Right,' he said, completing his check and vaulting back out. 'Well, that'll do for today. They look fit enough. I'll check them against their vet records tomorrow.'

'*Si, senhor*,' the groom replied, clearly not understanding a word.

He and Tanner stared at each other. 'Shall we go up to the house, then?' Tanner asked finally.

'House? *Si, senhor,*' the groom replied, cantering over to the jeep and speaking to the driver in rapid-fire Portuguese.

Tanner rolled his eyes wearily. He was going to be here only three days but he had a feeling it was going to be a long trip.

Velasquez was sitting on the verandah, a fan spinning above him, when Tanner finally came downstairs. He had succumbed to a fitful sleep on top of the bed and awoken only when the sound of parrots screeching in the imperial palm trees pierced his dreams.

'Welcome, my friend,' Velasquez said, rising and pumping Tanner's hand.

'Vittorio,' he said warmly, appreciative of the large cold rum his host immediately set to pouring. 'It's good to be here.'

'I am sorry I could not be here when you arrived. I had urgent business in Santiago that could not be put off.'

'It was no problem,' Tanner demurred. 'I took the opportunity to go and check out the horses.'

Velasquez smiled at him. 'Yes, I heard that you had wasted no time seeing them. And what did you think?' He handed Tanner his drink and leant on the verandah rail.

'Every bit as glossy as your portfolio suggested. It looks like a winning team.'

'I hope so, my friend,' Velasquez laughed, throwing his hands in the air. 'What it is costing me to bankroll, I hope so.'

Tanner laughed. They both knew that the cost of running

a polo team – around a million dollars per annum – was but buttons in the Velasquez fortune. They also both knew that the true extent of Velasquez's wealth was indubitably far greater than the $180 million figure which was officially published. He had inherited the coffee plantation from his father and been one of the first owners to predict the rise of the speciality coffee market, leaving behind the poor-quality, high-volume blended business, to carve a niche supplying purer strains, before diversifying into eucalyptus forestry, buying up vast swathes of land in the south and supplying wood pulp to the States.

'I'd like to go round with the vet tomorrow. The mare with the blaze had weepy eyes and a bit of a wheeze. And I've asked for all of them to be taken off oats with immediate effect. I don't want them hyperactive on the plane.'

Velsaquez shrugged. 'My resources are at your disposal. You must do whatever you believe to be in the best interests of the horses. It has taken several years and a lot of money to cherry-pick a team of this calibre. I do not want to lose any of them on the plane to something as avoidable as high spirits.'

'Thank you.'

'Ah! Here she is,' Vittorio exclaimed, walking over to greet a dark-haired woman even hairier and stockier than he. 'My wife, Izadora.'

Tanner put his drink down and walked over to her. 'It's a pleasure to meet you, Senhora Velasquez. Your home is beautiful.' He betrayed no evidence of having seen Velasquez leaving Claridge's with his Russian mistress, en route to Paris.

'*Gracias*, Senhor Ludgrove,' the woman smiled. She was wearing a fuchsia-pink jacquard suit that hung like a box, with matching shoes, and on her finger the most atrociously enormous pink diamond Tanner had ever seen. 'This is your first time to Brazil?'

Tanner nodded. 'Not my last, I hope. It's a beautiful country. I won't have time on this trip, obviously, but I'm intrigued to come back and explore it properly,' he lied. He was a sucker through and through for the green, green fields of England.

'Well, our doors are always open to you. You are welcome here any time.'

'Thank you, *senhora*.'

'Brazil is a country of great extremes, Tanner, from the mountains,' Vittorio said, sweeping his arms out expansively, 'to the beaches. From the *carnivale* to the religious festas. It is a country that defies categorization. It wants to be everything. And why shouldn't it be?' he laughed.

Tanner laughed along. A maid in a black and white uniform came silently onto the verandah and tipped her head.

'Come, let us eat,' Velasquez said, shepherding the group into the house.

'You know, Tanner,' he continued as they took their places around a vast round dining table. 'Tomorrow you shall see for yourself the contradiction at the heart of Brazil.'

Tanner cocked an eyebrow. 'How so?'

'It is the culmination of the Festo do Divino Espirito Santo. All day we observe God's love and beneficence. But by night we throw a party and then – then huh?' He laughed. 'Well . . . then you see how we have a good time.'

'I look forward to it,' Tanner replied, inwardly groaning at the prospect of travelling the following morning with thirty-six horses and a hangover.

'Do not worry. You do not have to observe the *festa* in the day,' Velasquez pooh-poohed the thought. 'It is very dull,' he whispered jocularly. 'No, I have arranged a trek for you tomorrow to a very special place. So that you can see some more of Brazil before you go.'

'A ride? Not on the polo ponies, though?'

'Of course not,' Velasquez cried. 'What do you take me for? These are my trekkers. You will like them, you'll see.'

Tanner nodded. 'Will you be coming too?'

'Sadly, no,' Velasquez said, throwing out his hands apologetically. 'I do not have the stamina that I used to have for such a trek.' He patted his portly tummy. 'But my son, Paolo, will join you. He's flying in with his new girlfriend in the morning. He will take you to all the best places.'

Tanner's smile remained rigid. He was well acquainted with Paolo's reputation on the polo circuit and the last thing he needed was a playboy for a guide. He was here to work, not play, but he knew there'd be no way out without offending his host. He raised his glass to his toast. 'Well, here's to an adventure, then,' he smiled.

Chapter Forty-six

Tanner slapped his thigh, irritated, and turned over, twisting himself in the sheets.

The mosquito whined in his ear again and this time he sat bolt upright, shaking his head like a horse. Bloody little buggers. He reluctantly opened his eyes and looked down at his chest. He was covered with bites.

He sighed – exhausted from a night of broken sleep – and looked around. The room reeked of musk and colonial splendour. There was a rococo mahogany mirror on the wall, a heavy four-poster, glossy floors and painted grey shutters. He kicked his way out of the mosquito nets – fat lot of good they'd been – and walked to the windows, feeling the breeze tickle over his bare skin. He stretched his arms above his head and yawned noisily, feeling the impressive weight of his morning glory.

Outside his window, Brazil fell away in undulating folds, the green coffee plants dotting the hills in long rows, threaded like cornrows all the way to the horizon. He heard a giggle and looked down. A maid was crossing the path in the garden, a pile of sheets in her arms. She looked up again and found him staring back at her.

Tanner smiled, amused and unembarrassed, as she boldly held his gaze, and he suddenly hoped she'd be coming up to change his sheets. He hadn't been with anyone since Violet had left and he was beginning to feel desperate. He watched her as she walked into the hacienda, a mini-me of the main house, with the same grey-blue painted shutters and a clock tower on the roof.

He turned away, disappointed, and walked across to the bathroom. That was probably going to be the highlight of his day – being eyed up by the maid.

His hosts were already eating out on the verandah when he came downstairs, a banquet masquerading as breakfast laid out on the table. He helped himself to the full English, which Velasquez had ordered the kitchens to cook up for him, and joined them.

'Did you sleep well?' Senhora Velasquez enquired.

'Like a baby,' he lied, resisting the urge to scratch a particularly bothersome bite under his arm.

'Earl Grey?' asked a maid.

Tanner looked at her and was pleased to note she was the same one from the garden. Her eyes sparkled provocatively.

'Thanks,' he grinned as she poured.

'So. You will make an early start today,' Velasquez said, sitting back in his chair and dabbing his upper lip effetely with his napkin. 'There is much for you to see.'

Tanner nodded, a forkful of bacon in his mouth. He was far more concerned with checking the horses for the journey than going on some glorified tour of the grounds. 'Has your son arrived, then?' he asked, spearing a sausage and watching the maid move around the table.

Velasquez looked out into the cloudless sky. 'Not yet. But any moment,' he said, picking up a small pair of binoculars and scouring the horizon. 'The pilot radioed to say they'd left Joinville fifty minutes ago.'

As if by his command, a dot appeared in the endless blue, growing steadily larger until eventually the distinctive pucker of propellers could be made out and the plane circled over-head.

They all watched from the table as the plane descended, landing bumpily on a tarmac strip that connected to the far end of the lawns. The propellers slowed into distinction, and the fuselage door opened, a small staircase dropping down to the ground below.

There was a few minutes' pause and Tanner sensed his hosts' escalating tension, before a man finally emerged, waving, at the top of the steps. Tanner put down his fork and watched as the lean figure – black-haired, in a cream suit and golden aviators – gambolled down. The girlfriend emerged a moment later, wearing matching aviators and white shorts, her hair swinging lustrously in a high ponytail. Even from a distance, she was stunning.

Senhora Velasquez rose up from the table and started walking down the garden to meet them. 'My boy,' she cried proudly. 'My boy.' She embraced him tightly and he bent down patiently as she clasped his head in her hands, kissing him on both cheeks and his forehead.

The girlfriend hung back, slouching coolly, her long smooth legs gleaming in the morning sun. Velasquez narrowed his eyes and picked up the binoculars. He burst out laughing.

'I don't believe it! It's true what they say,' he roared, smacking the table and handing the binoculars over. 'What goes around, comes around.'

Tanner looked through the eyeglasses, baffled by his host's amusement.

'It looks like she is going after my millions, after all, Tanner, but still with the man thirty years younger.'

Tanner watched the unlikely trio move up to the house, hardly able to believe his eyes.

'Father,' Paolo said, bounding up the steps, arms wide. 'It is so good to see you.'

The two men embraced.

'I want you to meet Pia,' he beamed, drawing her forward.

Velasquez's grin widened. 'It is a very great honour to meet you, young lady,' he said, clasping her slim hand in his great bear paws. 'I have long been an admirer of yours.'

Pia pushed her glasses to the top of her head and smiled knowingly back. She only had to take one look at his wife to know what *that* meant.

'Come,' Velasquez beamed, turning towards Tanner. 'Paolo, Pia. Let me introduce Tanner Ludgrove. He has agreed to be our new manager for the polo team.'

Paolo looked at Tanner like a lizard at a fly. 'Paolo Almerida,' he said, offering a weak handshake. 'My father has told me much about you,' he said slowly. 'We are lucky to have you.'

Tanner disliked his slimy manners immediately. 'Likewise. I understand you're eight-goal.' Paolo nodded. 'Sorry, you said Paolo *Almerida*? Not Velasquez?'

'Well observed, Tanner,' Velasquez laughed. 'No. It is custom in Brazil for the children to take their mother's surname.'

'Oh,' Tanner replied. 'I never knew that.'

'And why should you?' Paolo smiled, without it ever reaching his eyes.

Tanner looked across at Pia.

'Pia,' he said stiffly. 'How are you?' he asked, bitterly regretting their last meeting and how he'd stormed around her in a whisky-fuelled rage, determined to hold her responsible for his brother's misery.

'Tanner,' she nodded back, her smile equally thin. For a split second she wondered whether he would betray her location to Will – it was still a well-kept secret, even though she had been back in Brazil for a few weeks now, hiding out at her old academy until she could resurface in Bulgaria at the ballet competition. But from the look on his face, he was as surprised as she was to be meeting again here. Besides, as much as he hated her, she was sure he hated Will more. Why would he do him the favour of giving up her hiding place?

'Come! You must change. The horses are saddled up and Tanner is waiting,' Velasquez said, bundling the newcomers back down the steps. 'Maria has everything unpacked for you in the hacienda. You will find all you need in there.'

Maria? Tanner wondered if that was the maid's name. He made a mental note to try to find her later. They all watched as Paolo took Pia's hand and led her towards the hacienda, Pia's ponytail bouncing, her legs swishing.

'I think I'll go down to the stables and get ready, then,' Tanner said, breaking up the Pia Soto fan club. 'Thanks for breakfast. Very much appreciated.'

He jogged down the steps and turned in the opposite direction, towards the front of the house. Fountains spurted bountifully every fifty feet, interconnected by a lacework of paths that criss-crossed the lawns.

He followed the one down to the stables, grateful to be getting back to what he'd come over for. He passed a field of ponies and they trotted over to the fence as he walked by, eager for carrots or a sugar cube. He stopped and dug in his pockets. They were the equivalent of most women's handbags, with all bar the kitchen sink in them. He fished out a battered tube of Polos and handed them out, enjoying the horses' whiskers tickling his palm and the heat of the sun on his back.

The trek horses were tethered in the shade, their heads in nosebags, when he sauntered into the yard. A gaucho was working on *doma* (saddle work) in the manege, with two grooms sitting on the fence, watching.

'Mind if I join you?' he asked, resting a foot on the railing.

The grooms shrugged and looked back at the action. The horse looked promising – changing legs easily mid-canter, stopping quickly and riding off hard. He watched as the gaucho spoke softly, encouraging him on, building up trust between them.

'He looks good,' a voice said after a while, over his shoulder.

The grooms immediately jumped off the fence and started sweeping.

Tanner looked round at Pia. Paolo was in the corner, talking loudly on his mobile as he checked the girth strap on one of the tethered ponies. Tanner looked her over, aghast. She was wearing boots, fawn jodhpurs and a pale pink shirt that made her skin look like caramel.

'What are you doing dressed like that?' he demanded in a low voice.

'Well, what would you prefer to see me ride in?' she demanded, hands on hips. 'A bikini?' she smiled, knowing full well that that image would make it hard for the grooms to do their jobs.

'You're not coming out for this ride too,' he said, more of a statement than a question.

'Oh yes, I am,' she countered, her head to the side. 'Is that a problem?'

Tanner's eyes flickered over to Paolo, who had moved on to fiddling with his horse's bit. They both knew it wasn't his call.

'Don't you think I'm up to it?' she said archly, evoking the memory of their chase after she'd stolen Violet's horse.

Tanner snorted. 'Talking of which, you never did explain how you came to be such a good rider,' he said.

'You never asked,' she quipped, offering nothing more.

Tanner sighed, frustrated. 'Okay, so I'm asking now. How did you come to be such a good rider?'

'Growing up here, we rode bareback all the time, catching the wild horses on the *cerrado*,' she shrugged. 'My brother and I did it all the time. I almost rode before I could walk.'

'And certainly before you could dance,' he said. 'I thought ballerinas made terrible riders.'

'Well, that's true. We use exactly the opposite sets of muscles.' She turned her hip out absent-mindedly and lifted it in *attitude*. 'But I rode long before I danced. And by the time I escaped to ballet school, I was far away from horses, so . . .' she dropped her leg down. 'The two never overlapped.'

'Except today.'

'I guess I'll pay for it tomorrow, then,' Pia quipped.

They mounted the horses and left the yard quickly. Water had been packed into panniers on the saddles but that was all they had need for – lunch was apparently being helicoptered in to a picnic spot on the far side of the plantation.

Paolo led the trek – alternately pointing out the vast extent of his family's estate, which, from what Tanner could tell, stretched as far as the eye could see, and pulling back to ostentatiously kiss Pia and make the heavy-handed point that she was his. Tanner left them to it, dropping back to the rear; but with nothing else to look at – one coffee plant looked the same as all the rest after two miles – his eyes settled on the narrow span of her shoulders, the cinch of her waist, the fan of her hips and those wisps of baby hair that tickled the back of her neck, not yet long enough for her ponytail.

After ninety minutes of trekking and heavy petting, Tanner was relieved when they stopped for water and to give the horses a rest. He jumped down, keen to stretch out his legs and get away from the lovebirds for a minute. He sat on a rock overlooking the valley and wondered what Will would say if he knew Tanner was riding with Pia and her new lover in the Brazilian highlands. The thought of Will's ire pleased him, although with Violet now sleeping in Will's bed, the revenge scenario would be even more appealing without Paolo in it.

After a while, they got back on the horses again, and the landscape began to change as they moved away from the plantation into the bordering rainforest, the shrubs shooting up into skyscraping trees, the big sky being replaced with scrappy patches glimpsed through the leaves, the steady drone of reaping machinery giving way to intermittent trills and squawks of unseen birds and monkeys. The vegetation grew thick and disorienting, and the humidity rose with the tree height, but Paolo knew his way through it as though there were big red arrows painted on the trunks.

'Paolo,' Pia whined eventually, massaging her thighs. 'This is dull. I want to stop now.'

'We're nearly there, baby. Listen,' he said, cupping his ear. 'Can't you hear it?'

Pia frowned and strained to hear. In the distance, the constant sound of a rushing river asserted itself over the noises of animal life.

'That's where we're headed? But it's miles off.'

'Not as far as you think,' he contradicted, clicking his horse forward. 'Come on. They're dropping lunch at one.' He checked his watch. 'It's half past twelve now. If we don't keep up, it'll start getting cold.'

He broke into a gentle trot and the others followed him, Tanner aware of a slackening of Pia's form. She looked tired and he noticed she kept flexing her right foot in the stirrup.

'You okay?' he asked, drawing up alongside.

Pia looked at him and nodded. Paolo turned at the sound of his voice and Tanner quickly let his horse fall back again.

Gradually the forest began to open up a bit into tracts of flat land. The sound of the river was getting louder, and as they rounded an outcrop of rocks it suddenly exploded into a roar.

Pia and Tanner gasped at the sight of a massive waterfall plunging from two hundred feet above them into a large pool, the water shimmering turquoise, wet rocks glistening like sleeping seals all around. The river continued along its path another hundred yards further on, but more delicately, tumbling down boulders and skipping down rock pools as it recovered from its dramatic dive.

On a huge dry stone by the side of the pool, Tanner's eyes fastened on several hampers. Lunch! He realized he was starving. He jumped off and tied his horse to a nearby tree. Both Pia and Paolo left theirs loose.

'Hadn't you better secure them?' he frowned, rolling up his sleeves.

'You British, so uptight,' Paolo said dismissively. 'Besides, there is nowhere for them to go here.'

Tanner raised a sceptical eyebrow and looked round at the rather large rainforest that surrounded them on all sides.

Paolo noted the question mark. 'I have been coming here since I was a boy and there has never been a problem,' he said, somewhat testily.

'Well, that's all right, then,' Tanner muttered under his breath.

The chefs had prepared a lunch as sumptuous as breakfast had been, with lobster thermidor, a ripe avocado salad and passion-fruit pavlova. They ate in silence, ravenous from the trek, and Tanner was surprised by Pia's hearty appetite – she looked as though she inhaled rice cakes. Afterwards they all lay down on the rocks in the sun. The break in the trees made for a perfect suntrap and their bodies steamed like puddings.

Tanner let himself doze. The jet lag, last night's sleeplessness and now this trek were taking it out of him. He didn't hear the splashes in the water as Pia titillated Paolo with a frisky water fight. He just drifted off, hands behind his head, as occasional droplets flecked his cheeks and wet his hair.

He awoke an hour later to silence. Sleepily, he rubbed his eyes and rolled his head to the side. The horses were nodding quietly by the trees. Paolo was asleep in just his jeans on a giant flat rock that looked like it could have been used for prehistoric sacrifices.

He looked in the other direction and was startled to find Pia sitting close by, watching him. He brought himself up on his elbows, embarrassed. 'What are you looking at?' he muttered.

She smiled. 'You look like you're seven when you sleep,' she whispered.

Tanner frowned. 'What's that supposed to mean? That I dribble?'

She smiled and shifted slightly. She was wearing Paolo's shirt, he noticed. Out of the corner of his eye, he could see a pink thong dangling on a bush in the breeze. She carried on staring at him.

'What?' he said, irritated by her scrutiny.

'Sssh,' she said, putting a finger to her lips. 'You'll wake him.'

'So?'

She said nothing.

'So what makes him so much better than Silk, then?' he asked finally, before immediately wondering why he'd asked.

'He's not really. But at least he's my choice.'

Tanner squinted at her. A shaft of sunlight was piercing straight through a giant eucalyptus and bouncing off her hair to create a halo mirage. She looked deceptively angelic. 'So, you don't really rate him but that's fine because you're calling the shots, is that right?'

'Something like that.'

'Women,' he muttered, shaking his head and staring down at his feet.

'How's Violet?'

'What is this? A coffee morning?'

'I'm just interested to know.'

'Well, I wouldn't know,' he sighed. 'She's with Will now.' He lay back down, resting his hands behind his head again.

Pia digested the revelation. It didn't surprise her. Violet

had always felt like a competitor to her. Pia had assumed it might be because she was worried about Pia going after Tanner. She should have realized that Violet had set her own sights on Pia's supposed prize.

She looked back at Tanner, pretending to doze and clearly uncomfortable with her company. 'You don't seem upset.'

'I'm not. It was over anyway. I'm just pissed off she went off with that tosser.'

Pia rested her chin on her hands. 'Why do you hate him so much?' she asked.

There was a long silence. He wasn't going to answer.

'Come on. I bet it can't be that bad,' she cajoled.

'Really? Because you know precisely *what* about me?'

'Tell me – what did he do?' she persisted.

'Look, what's with the sudden interest in my feelings and my history? I don't want to talk about it – and especially not with you.'

'Why not? There's nothing else to do,' she sighed, looking away and resting her cheek on her knees.

Tanner watched her. She seemed very small, sitting huddled on that rock. Small and lonely, he realized. For some reason, he felt sorry for her.

'My mother died when I was six,' he said reluctantly. 'My father fell into a depression and began to drink. He got into debt and had to start leveraging against the estate.'

'What estate?'

'Plumbridge.'

Pia's eyebrows shot up. 'It was yours?'

'I was born there. So was my father and his before him. Our family had owned it for six generations. It was our home, not the fucking mausoleum he's turned it into.'

Pia tipped her head to the side at his temper.

He took a deep breath. 'My father was introduced to Silk by an acquaintance at his club, White's. They don't let just anyone in. It's unbelievably select and Silk was touting for a seconder for membership.'

'Why?'

'Most of his business is done in places like that. His USP has been to gather a few – but astronomic – sources of under-achieving capital and put a rocket beneath them. He realized that the old boys sleeping off lunch in the White's library are generally living off the interest on their investments, but most of them have colossal amounts tied up in hibernating trusts that were established fifty, eighty, a hundred years ago and aren't performing anywhere near their potential. They were an untapped market and he knew that if he could just get in, then he could get to them from the inside. It also meant he was able to steer clear of the dodgy sources of ultra-wealth that you get with the mafia and Russian oligarchs.'

'So he was clever about who he did business with. So what?'

'Well, it wasn't looking good for him. Behind the flashy headlines and all the charity work he shouts about, Silk has a pretty shady reputation in finance and some of the more senior figures at the club were out to blackball him. So after they were introduced, he did some digging around on my father. He found out about our financial troubles and struck a deal: he would bail out my father's debts if my father seconded his proposal.

'My father couldn't refuse. He was on the cusp of losing his family's heritage and his children's home. He'd already lost his wife. The thought of it was more than he could bear. All he had to do was lend his good name to the membership proposal, and Silk would put up the cash. So they shook on it.'

'They *shook* on it? You mean – they didn't have a contract?'

'It was a gentleman's agreement. My father was from a different generation. It was how he always did business. But, as I told you once before, Silk's no gentleman. He reneged on the deal. My father kept his end of the bargain and got him in, but Silk kept delaying and delaying until the bank foreclosed. Then, and only then, Silk stepped in and snapped up the estate at a fraction of its value. My father never recovered from the shock. He believed in honour. He'd never dealt with someone like Silk before, and after everything he'd already been through it was too much for him.'

'Why did you work with him, then, if you despised him so much?'

'I had no choice.' He paused, his jaw set. 'My father's health deteriorated sharply following Silk's deception and I spent the next couple of years dashing up from Ciren to look after him. After he died and I finally looked around me, the only thing that was left that I could make a go of was the yard. And Silk was the only owner big enough locally to make it commercially viable.'

'So you drank from the poisoned chalice,' Pia murmured.

'You could say that.' He cocked an eyebrow and stared at her. 'And you thought you had it bad? It was Silk's total *absence* of chivalry that screwed my family over.'

'And now he's screwing Violet,' she replied testily. She didn't like him making light of Will's manipulation of her. Her freedom was the thing she prized more than anything in the world. 'Don't tell me it's not killing you, the thought of what he could be doing to her right now.'

Tanner swung himself up into sitting, his eyes blazing. She couldn't rile him. 'Not half as much as it would kill him to know that I'm here in Brazil with you.'

'You're not *with* me,' she countered. 'I'm with Paolo.'

Tanner shrugged but his eyes were dark and unreadable. 'Yes. But he doesn't know that.'

There was a long silence as the forbidden image of the two of them together hovered in the air. 'He'd never believe it,' she said finally. 'He knows you despise me.'

Tanner stared at her for a moment, then lay back down again. He stretched languidly in the sun. 'That's true. He'd never buy it.'

Pia looked down at the rock, stung by Tanner's casual dismissal of the very idea of the two of them as lovers. '*Do* you still despise me?'

'Yes.'

'But why? I'm not with Will any more.'

He rolled his head to the side and looked up at her, a frown across his face. 'I didn't hate you because you were *with him*,' he said, almost amused by the suggestion.

Pia stared down at him, baffled. 'Then why do you hate me? What's so wrong with me?'

Tanner laughed shortly.

'What? What is so funny?'

Tanner propped himself back up on his elbows. 'You really don't know?'

'Know what?'

'It's your godforsaken manners.'

'My manners? Oh God, what is this – some English thing? Some code of honour I've missed? Lost in translation?'

Tanner narrowed his eyes. 'Generally speaking, when

439

someone saves your life – whatever your culture – it's considered polite to say thank you.'

Now it was Pia's turn to laugh. 'When someone saves your . . . ?' She shrugged, baffled.

Tanner continued to stare at her, resolutely unamused.

'Oh my God, you are such an egomaniac! Are you implying . . . are you trying to say you saved my life?' she giggled. '*You*?'

There was a stiff silence and the smile gradually slid off Pia's face. 'You? You saved me?' His face blurred out of sight as the jumble of images and sounds from that day, which she had tried so hard not to revisit, rushed back at her.

The sound of the dog barking.

She realized suddenly that even the British, with their love of irony, don't call a black Labrador Custard. It had to have been Biscuit. That was why she was always so excitable around Pia . . . And his hands . . . when he'd been carrying her back through the wood – she remembered they'd felt big, but rough. Will's hands were smooth from a life spent brokering deals on the phone.

Pia grabbed his hand. She rubbed her fingers over the long fingers that were every bit as worked and calloused as her feet. But that didn't mean anything. He worked with horses; anyone who worked with animals would have the same.

Tanner watched her. She was staring at him, but he knew she wasn't seeing him. Her mind was racing, her eyes darting as her subconscious allowed the memories to surface. She remembered . . . that day when he'd chased her across the fields. She'd caught a trace of it when he'd been standing in front of her, chastising her, but then he'd gone to knock on the door and . . . She lurched forward and pressed her nose to his neck, inhaling his scent. She breathed in deeply. There it was! Not Trumper's Lime cologne that Will slathered on, but the smell that had been her first conscious sense as he'd brought her back to life.

She drew back fractionally and saw that he'd caught his breath. Her face was just inches from his. 'It was you,' she said. Tanner didn't reply. He realized that she'd never known. That Will had spun her yet another lie.

'And I never even said thank you,' she whispered, her voice cracking. 'No wonder you hate me.'

His eyes wandered over her face, finally allowing the thought to intrude that – in spite of being an absolute nightmare – she was still the most gorgeous thing he had ever laid eyes on.

'It's probably just as well that I did,' he said quietly, his eyes falling to her lips. Her hair was tickling his jaw and she smelt as sweet as vanilla – so sweet that he wanted to lick her like ice cream.

'*Punto da filha!*' Paolo suddenly exclaimed, and Pia sprang back from him like a feral cat, her eyes wild at the prospect that Paolo had caught them. But his back was to them as he scanned the forest edge. He was staring at the horses. Or rather, the lack of them.

'Why are there only two horses there?' he demanded, as though it was their fault that one of the horses had wandered off during his sleep. Pia and Tanner scanned the clearing, looking for a tail swish, or the sound of a hoof on a rock to identify the missing horse's whereabouts. But it had gone.

'Maybe someone stole it,' Tanner quipped, expecting Pia to shoot him a look. But she was staring into the pool, trying to process what she'd just discovered.

Paolo looked at Pia standing on the rock in just his shirt. 'Pia, put your clothes on,' he ordered, casting a nervous glance at Tanner. Pia snapped out of her trance and glared at him, not liking the tone of his voice. Tanner kept his eyes on the forest, sensing a domestic brewing.

'Well, it's not a catastrophe,' Paolo said casually. 'You can stay here, Pia, and the helicopter will be back in a while to pick up the baskets. They can take you to the house with them.'

'What?' Pia cried, grabbing her knickers and stepping into them. 'You're going to leave me here on my own?' She stepped behind a boulder and started getting changed, worried he might actually go without her.

'You'll be fine,' Paolo shrugged. 'There's no one about. You'll be safe.'

'Why can't you stay with me till the chopper comes?'

'Because it's a three-hour trek back to the house. We need to start moving again before the sun goes down.'

Pia peered out from behind the boulder. 'I don't think so,' she said in a dangerous voice. 'If you were any kind of gentleman you'd give me your horse.' She threw his shirt at him.

Paolo sighed and put it on. 'I can't. I have to lead Tanner back out of here. He'd never find his way out alone and we need to get the horses back. I don't see what the problem is.'

'Well, why can't I ride on your horse with you?' she demanded, zipping up her jodhpurs and pulling on her boots.

'Because my horse isn't big enough.'

Pia looked at the two horses standing in the glade. There was a visible discrepancy in the size of them, as there was a visible discrepancy in the size of the two men.

'Fine,' she said. 'I'll ride on Tanner's, then.'

'What?' Tanner said, finding himself drawn into the dispute, after all.

'That's okay, isn't it?' she demanded. 'Your horse is perfectly capable of carrying us both.' She looked back at Paolo. 'Unlike *his* runty donkey.'

Tanner tried not to laugh at her furious description. One look at Paolo's face told him it was definitely not the time to laugh.

'Well . . . if it helps,' he said blankly, shrugging at Paolo like there were a million other things he'd prefer.

'Okay, so that's sorted, then,' Pia said, tucking her shirt into her tiny waistband.

Tanner rolled his eyes to heaven, and walked over to untie his horse. He put his foot in the stirrup and climbed up. Then he took his foot out of the stirrup and she put hers in. He saw how effortlessly her leg reached up to it. It was like she was made of elastic.

'Duck,' she ordered, and he moved his head out of the way just in time as she swung her leg over him, before sliding her back down his chest.

He felt a jolt of desire course through his body at the feel of her skimming down him. He swallowed hard, trying to get a grip. Paolo was standing with his hands on his hips, frowning at them.

Tanner pulled a face as her ponytail tickled his nose. 'Shove forward,' he grumbled noisily. 'You're taking all the room.'

Pia shifted forward an inch.

'Oh great. Thanks,' he drawled sarcastically. 'Bet you're a treat with the duvet.'

'Wouldn't you like to know,' she quipped.

Tanner gave an exaggerated sigh. 'Come on, then,' he said

to Paolo, shaking the reins. 'Let's get this over and done with.'

The horses picked their way faithfully back through the forest, an innate contrary sense telling them that heading deeper into the forest was the best way out of it. Tanner tipped his head to the side to see round Pia, his arms circling her waist as he held the reins.

Paolo kept turning around suspiciously every few minutes to check on them, but Tanner kept his face resolutely grim and martyred, and as the miles clocked up, Paolo stopped bothering.

The trio rode on in silence, letting the scenery do all the talking as deep velvety creeks folded into the mountainside. The scale of them was unlike anything found in the British Isles. Why did everything seem to be bigger, wilder, more dramatic and flamboyant here, he wondered, watching a wisp of baby hair flutter on the nape of Pia's neck.

Eventually, though, the epic landscape hit a different scale and the lofty, bosky forest yielded to the orderly dwarf rows of the coffee plantations. They had been going for nearly two hours now and were all tired, but they were nearly there. Tanner couldn't even bear to think about finding the energy to party at the festa tonight and still cope with a transatlantic journey in the morning. He'd scarcely be able to move after this. He'd need a cortisone injection just to get on the plane.

Pia began to lean into him.

'Sorry,' she mumbled, correcting herself and drawing up again. But when she sank back for the fifth time, he put a hand on her shoulder and kept her there. 'It's fine,' he said quietly. He well remembered how fragile she'd been after the accident. 'Just rest.'

444

She rested her head back against his chest, but after a few minutes he became aware of her breath on his jaw.

'You're staring at me again,' he muttered.

'I just can't help wondering . . .' she said in a soft voice.

'What?'

'What it's like to save someone's life.'

There was a long silence and she thought he wasn't going to answer, again.

'Bloody awful,' he said in a tight voice eventually. 'I thought I was too late. You weren't breathing.' Pia took in his words and saw in the set of his jaw the full extent of the drama he had gone through.

'Thank you,' she whispered.

Tanner flickered his eyes down to her and the sight of her resting against his chest, doe-eyes staring back up at him, her hair floating in the breeze, made his heart skip a beat.

'You're welcome,' he replied gruffly, looking back up again and praying for the house to heave into view. He needed to get off this horse and away from her. It had been weeks since he'd had a woman, and the sight of her, grateful and gorgeous, pressed up against him, was beginning to be more than he could bear. He clenched his jaw and looked grimly ahead.

'I guess this means I'm indebted to *you* now.'

'No, you're not.'

'Yes, I am. That Chinese proverb says that when someone saves your life, your soul belongs to them'

'Stuff the Chinese proverb.'

'But what if I *want* to make it up to you?' she whispered and he felt her hips tilt back fractionally, her buttocks pushing up against him.

'I've already told you, you don't owe me anything,' he

said, trying to move away, but he was already jammed on the back of the saddle. Short of jumping off the horse altogether, there was nowhere to go.

The horse's tempo rocked their bodies together, and as much as Tanner recited the Periodic Table, trying to keep himself from growing hard, it was no good. His brain wouldn't fool his body this time. It had stored the images of her knockout curves for just such a moment as this. 'Just stop it,' he hissed. 'I'm not Silk.'

'Precisely,' she murmured. He felt her legs widen – that impressive turn out easily able to press her thighs back to his – and it took all the control he had not to drop the reins and slide a hand into her jodhpurs to feel her own excitement.

Slowly Pia turned her face upwards and, softly, so that he could barely feel it, kissed his throat. A treasonous moan of desire escaped him. She took his idle hand off his thigh and brought it up to her breast. He felt the weight of it sink into his hand with each trot and instinctively he squeezed it lightly, wondrously, utterly unable to stop himself. She sighed with pleasure, her butt pushing into his groin, the horse's rhythm rubbing her against him.

Every fibre in his body was straining to swivel her around and have her there and then on the horse, but Paolo was only a few yards ahead and the house was in sight. Plantation workers were walking up the path fifty feet away, finished for another day. Tanner dropped his hand from her glorious, weighty breast and took up the rein, trying to steady his breathing.

Pia, sensing his change, pulled herself back up, just as Paolo turned round to them.

'Well, we did it,' he smiled, winking at Pia, already forgetful of their argument. 'It was good, no?'

She shrugged noncommittally, putting on her best stroppy face.

Tanner nodded stiffly. 'Thank you, Paolo.'

'There aren't many places in the world that can boast picnic spots like that,' Paolo replied. 'Even if it does take a super-human effort to get there.'

Sod the ride. It's taken superhuman effort not to sleep with your girlfriend, Tanner thought to himself, staring hatefully at Paolo's slight spoilt back. They trotted into the yard, and the grooms rushed forward.

Paolo jumped off, and held his arms up to Pia. She slid down into them. 'Time to go back for a rest now, hmm?' he said to her, bending down and planting a kiss on her neck. Pia looked up at Tanner and for a second he saw panic in her eyes.

He looked away angrily – frustrated with desire, furious that she was with Paolo, his boss's son, half demented that there was nothing he could do about it. He couldn't afford to lose Velasquez's patronage. It was precisely this relationship that had freed him from Silk. The yard's survival depended on the business from one of those two men, and having to choose between honouring his father's memory or getting the girl of his dreams was an unbearable quandary. So much for living life on his terms.

He dismounted to the other side, away from the two lovers, and handed the reins to a groom, patting the horse and buying himself some recovery time.

'Well, thanks again, Paolo,' he said finally, shaking his hand quickly. 'That was a great trek. Really impressive. Great, uh . . . great views.' He ran his hand through his hair, unable to meet Pia's eyes.

KAREN SWAN

'Yes, it always goes down well with our guests,' Paolo boasted half-heartedly. He was clearly eager to get Pia back to the hacienda. 'Okay, so we'll see you later, at the festa,' he said dismissively.

Tanner shook his head. 'No. Sorry. I'm beat. I'll have to give it a miss. Besides, I need to prepare for the journey back tomorrow.'

'You're leaving?' Pia asked, shocked.

'Nonsense!' Paolo said, thumping him on the back. 'My father won't hear of such a thing. Anyway, the yard manager will have everything sorted for the journey. It's his job. You go and rest and shower now before dinner. We'll meet you back at the house at eight.'

Tanner nodded wearily. He knew Velasquez would never let him wriggle out of the occasion. He watched Paolo lead Pia back up the path, his hand wandering casually over her butt. He let them round the corner before he kicked the ground furiously, startling and then amusing the grooms in turn. They hadn't missed Pia's looks to him and a blind man could see his frustrations. He turned abruptly and strode up the path to the house, hoping to God that he'd find Maria turning down the sheets.

Chapter Forty-seven

Pia lay on the bed, ankles firmly crossed.

'Hey, baby,' Paolo cooed at her, his hand tracing circles on her tummy. He'd only managed to get as far as unbuttoning her shirt. 'Don't be like this. We get so little time together as it is.'

Pia flashed her eyes at him. 'I told you I'm still cross with you, Paolo. You were going to abandon me out there.'

'But, baby, I simply thought it would be easier for you to go back in the chopper.'

'No. You were prepared to leave me behind in the middle of the rainforest so that you wouldn't be late back and risk angering your dear papa. The prodigal son has returned, after all. He needs to show off his heir to all Brazil's glitterati tonight. He probably wants to introduce you to your future wife, the meek ugly daughter of some shipping magnate,' she said cruelly. It was well known how Velasquez Senior controlled his son through the purse strings.

'Now you're being crazy. He knows I could never look at another woman. He can see I'm mad about you.'

'I think we both know what your father can see you're mad about.'

Paolo took his hand off her and jumped off the bed. This was proving to be more hassle than it was worth. He shouldn't have broken off his flirtation with that Venezuelan model, Irina. He thought both he and Pia had gone into the relationship knowing it was nothing more than sex. Why was she giving him a hard time about their affair now? They'd been having fun. What was with the guilt trip? Why was she being so uptight today?

He pulled on his clean trousers, irritated. He was tired and horny. Why couldn't she just put out, help him relax before tonight? 'I need to help my parents greet the guests,' he said, shrugging on his jacket and checking his hair in the mirror. He picked up his shades from the table and looked down at her. She stayed staring at her feet.

'I'll see you up there, then,' he said tetchily.

Pia heard the door slam behind him and closed her eyes with relief. She needed time alone. Time to think.

She'd done nothing but dance since coming back to Brazil. Her tutors had been delighted when she'd sought refuge with them, and in return she had allowed nothing to impinge upon her thoughts beyond training for Varna. Every day she was going to class and making rehearsals, feeling increasingly confident that she was finally making the full recovery – both physical and emotional – that only time could provide and that Will had denied her. The date of her showdown with Ava was fast approaching and she knew she needed to be in the best condition of her life. There were no more second chances.

Which was why Paolo had fitted into the plan nicely. It was an easy, thoughtless, uncomplicated affair – a little light relief in the evenings – and took up absolutely no headspace at all. Just what she had thought she needed. Going back to her old ways, being wild and free like she had been in the good old days – the days before the accident, before Will and

Tanner had entered her life and Sophie had left it – was supposed to have proved to her that she'd got her life back, after all, the one she'd been wrenched from.

Except that now she had it back, it didn't seem enough somehow. She didn't feel free, like she'd expected. She felt lost and bored and lonely. Something had changed. *She* had changed. The old fall-backs weren't working.

It was Tanner's fault, she knew. He kept knocking her off balance. Every single time he opened his mouth, he revealed another truth that sent her world spinning off its axis – Will's lies, Sophie's innocence, and now the small fact that he'd saved her life . . .

It was her reaction to that that bothered her most of all. When she'd thought it was Will who'd saved her, she'd felt crippled by the debt. He'd wanted her body, soul and trademark. But Tanner? Well, a plain thank you would have sufficed. He didn't make her feel beholden to him in any way, and yet as they'd trekked back on the horse together and the real story of the past few months settled in her brain, she'd felt desperate to *be* beholden to him. She could have risen a man from the dead doing what she'd done to him today, and although he hadn't entirely succeeded in stopping her seduction, she knew he was determined to resist her.

She locked her arms behind her head as she watched the ceiling fan rotate, trying to remember what she'd loved to hate about him – his uppishness, his arrogance, his oh-so-British stiff upper lip – but her head kept reminding her of the ingratitude and the insults that she'd thrown at him following his heroics . . . And, well, why on earth *wouldn't* he have acted like that towards her? He'd been quite right to hate her.

It left just one question going round and round in her head: now that they both knew the truth about each other's actions, did he hate her still?

Pia walked up the path through the resplendent gardens. Coloured paper lanterns swung from every tree and hundreds of floating lanterns were weighted down on the grass, ready to be lit and cast up into the night sky. A band was playing on the verandah of the house and the sound of laughter and dancing met her ears before the spectacle reached her eyes.

She stopped and stared. This was the Brazil she loved. The Brazil of her childhood. Colour, music, laughter, vivacity, life, celebration. Brazilians were always thankful, even those who had nothing – like her family. This family, though? They had everything: land, wealth, status. All of São Paolo's finest were here. Many were international jet-setters, and acquaintances from the yacht-hopping scene off Cannes every August.

'Pia! You are here!' squealed a thin brunette in leopard-print Cavalli.

Pia winced and fixed her smile.

'Seems so. How are you, Alegria?' Pia smiled, kissing the air next to her, her eyes expertly sweeping the grounds for familiar faces. She clocked Paolo, in his pale blue suit, flirting with a group of teenage girls.

'Is there a reward for finding you?'

'Why? Are things that difficult for Eduardo now?' Pia teased, taking a mojito from a waitress.

'*Aaiiee!*' Alegria sighed, rolling her eyes. 'You joke but . . . the hedge-fund market now? Not going to keep me in Manolos for more than a month, I can tell you.' She narrowed her eyes and appraised Pia more closely. 'But you look different. What have you had done?'

'You mean apart from my ankle?'

Alegria screeched with laughter. 'You always are so funny. Seriously, though, you look good. Relaxed, I think.'

Pia shrugged. 'Thanks. I guess that's what skipping the international-tour circuit does for a girl.'

Alegria sipped her drink. 'So who are you here with? Or should we all be keeping closer watch on our husbands tonight?'

Pia looked back at her sharply, but Alegria was smiling. 'I'm only joking, Pia. It's my way of saying you look sensational. No one can compare.'

'Actually I'm here with Paolo.'

There was a brief pause. 'Paolo Almerida?' Alegria's eyes flitted briefly in the direction of Paolo and the girls.

'Yes. Why?' Pia asked, completely unfazed.

Alegria shook her head quickly. 'Nothing, nothing.' She took another sip of her drink. 'Is it serious?'

'Not remotely. It's just sex.' She liked to be blunt at 'society dos'. It stopped her getting bored.

Alegria lifted an eyebrow as much as her Botox would allow.

'Oh, there's Paolo's mother,' Pia said, putting a hand lightly on her arm. 'Look, I'd better go and talk to her. I've scarcely said more than two words to her since getting here. I'll catch you later.'

'Sure, Pia, see you later,' Alegria nodded, watching her go and coveting the vintage Alaia broderie anglaise dress, which was scarcely up to the job of containing Pia's curves.

Pia moved through the crowd, acknowledging the admiring stares – which were as much for the excitement of being present at her first public appearance since the dance-off, as for her bombshell figure.

'*Senhora*,' Pia smiled. 'I'm so sorry I have not had a chance to thank you yet for your great kindness in inviting me here this weekend.'

'The pleasure is all ours,' Izadora replied, taking Pia's hands in hers. 'It makes us so happy to see our son so contented.' Pia knew full well that Paolo's current contentment was in his mother's direct line of sight. Pia smiled.

'Well, you've created a wonderful setting for the festa. Everything looks so beautiful. And there're so many people here. There must be three hundred at least.'

'Well, this was always Paolo's favourite festival. He was such a . . . pious boy in his youth.' She paused, and her eyes twinkled. 'Pity it didn't last.'

Both women laughed at the playboy's incongruous past and Pia realized the older woman was more clued up about her son's – and no doubt her husband's – wayward antics than she let on.

'Ah, here comes our guest of honour. Senhor Ludgrove,' Izadora smiled, reaching up to kiss him on each cheek. 'My son said you were tired from the trek today, but you look especially handsome this evening.'

Tanner nodded awkwardly at the compliment, shooting a furtive look at Pia. She took in the sight of him in his cream linen suit and pink linen shirt. He'd caught a bit of sun too.

'You certainly know how to throw a party, Senhora Velasquez,' he said politely.

'How do you say it?' Izadora replied, shrugging her shoulders modestly. 'High days and holidays, no?'

Tanner nodded. 'So what does this festival celebrate, then?'

'The Festa do Divino Espirito Santo is one of the highlights of our year. It reminds us all to help those less fortunate than ourselves and to remember that we show God's love through serving others.'

There was a brief pause. 'I see,' Tanner said. 'Does that mean the waiters will beat us all to St Peter's gates?'

The two women laughed. He clearly wasn't Catholic. 'There's a very sweet story attached to it,' Pia smiled. 'Would you like to hear it?'

Tanner reluctantly looked at her. He most certainly did not want to hear it. Manners would dictate that he'd have to look at her and, frankly, the sight of her in that tiny flippy dress, with all those cut-out bits . . .

'Go ahead,' he said, gripping his drink and looking casually around the gardens.

'It's based on the legend of Queen Saint Isabel.'

'A queen and a saint? Isn't that a bit greedy?' Tanner said archly.

Pia tipped her head to the side patiently. She was determined to win him over and show him there was more to her than tantrums and tutus.

'Go on, then,' he said finally. Izadora tapped his arm lightly and left them while she went to greet her other guests.

'She was a very kind queen. So kind, in fact, that she used to save bread from her own table and give it to the poor.'

'Would she approve, then, this benevolent queen, of the excesses of tonight?' He looked around at the scene of opulence. The paths and lawns were strewn with petals and huge antique urns were filled with thick, tumescent sprays of orchids. 'The flower bill for tonight alone could probably feed a village for a year.'

'It's symbolic.'

'And I expect you know why,' Tanner said, taking in the change from horseback seducer to devout convent girl.

'Of course. Every good Catholic girl knows the story.'

Tanner stared at her steadily, biting back the obvious riposte.

'Please enlighten me.'

'Well, good Queen Saint Isabel would hide her food in her cloak, which enraged the king. One day he demanded to see what she was hiding in her cloak so she offered up a prayer and when she opened her cloak, red roses tumbled out.'

Tanner smiled at the fable. 'Nice story,' he said, defying the gravity that was dragging his eyes to her uplifted cleavage. Goddam peripheral vision. It was obvious what tumbled out when she opened *her* cloak. 'But since when did you become a good Catholic girl?'

She bit her lip. 'You really do think very poorly of me, don't you?'

Tanner paused, then shrugged. He knew he was being unnecessarily defensive. He just couldn't stop thinking about their unfinished seduction. It was almost more than he could bear not to reach out and touch her. He was desperately holding on – waiting for her usual arrogance to assert itself, to pique his anger and subvert the urge to kiss her. Where the hell was it?

'I guess old habits die hard,' he sniffed. 'I apologize.'

'Hmm, that sounds suspiciously like a truce. Does this mean we're going to be friends, then?' she asked lightly.

He hoped to God not. If he couldn't hate her . . .

'I don't know . . . does it?' he replied casually.

There was a weighty silence. 'Well, I guess unless we can think of any other reasons to keep hating each other, we'll have to be.' She took a sip of her drink and looked around the party. Paolo's posse had swelled impressively.

'I guess so,' he replied, tracing her profile with his eyes. She eclipsed every woman there. She turned back to face him and caught him out. He gave a short, bland smile and looked away.

'So when did you find God?' he asked sarcastically, determined to get them back into their old habits, after all. This playing nice was too difficult.

She stiffened at his tone. He clearly couldn't do it – couldn't treat her with anything other than disdain. Whatever the reasons they'd had for hating each other to begin with, it had become a habit that he just couldn't break now. Or didn't want to. 'When did I lose him, you mean,' she said quietly.

Tanner frowned at her. 'Okay, when did you lose him?' he echoed. 'Bottom of one of your handbags?'

'Actually it was the day my family was stolen from me,' she said flatly. She kept her eyes on Paolo's back.

Jesus! 'What do you m—'

'I was ten. My father was a violent alcoholic,' she said. 'He used to beat my mother . . . He'd begun to hit us too – my brother and me. We all knew it was going to get worse. But we were poor. We had nothing, no money, nowhere to go. We lived in a tiny *favela* outside Salvador. My mother would work out in the *cerrados* for fourteen hours a day in the blazing sun while he sat around, drinking. So she started saving to get us out of there, to take us to Rio. She thought we would be safer there, away from him. But it was taking too long. The beatings were happening every day. He was going to kill her if we stayed there much longer. So I came up with another idea.'

Tanner noticed her knuckles had whitened around her drink.

'The Bolshoi Ballet in Russia announced it was going to open an academy in Santa Catarina and they were giving full scholarships. I knew it was a way out for us – an education, a home, a career – so I stole a book showing ballet steps and copied them. Then I taught them to my little brother on the way home from school.

'We couldn't afford for all three of us to go, so my mother gave me all her money so that we could take the train to the auditions. She was going to join us as soon as she'd saved up enough for her train ticket. We didn't tell my brother that we wouldn't be going back, regardless of whether we got in or not. We couldn't go back.' She paused for a moment, and Tanner saw that her eyes had misted. 'But I can't imagine what my father must have done to my mother when he found out we'd gone. It was so bad that she was forced to tell him exactly where we were, and she never would . . . she never would have done that unless he'd really . . .' Her voice trailed away and she took a long, slow gulp of her drink. He noticed her hand was trembling.

'Pia, you don't have to tell me this if you don't want to.'

'But I do!' she said sharply, her eyes bright with tears. 'I want you to know why I'm the way I am, to know that I wasn't always such a bitch.'

'God! I don't think you're a—'

'Yes, you do! You despise me. You can't help yourself. You just said it. But I used to be different. I used to be a better person than I am now.' She took a deep breath and looked back at the party but she wasn't seeing anything.

Tanner watched her. 'So what happened?' he asked quietly.

'My father came to the academy and snatched my brother while I was in the audition. He was only eight. He just took him – he wasn't interested in me – and I never saw him again. Actually, I never saw any of them again.'

'But what happened to them? Surely you can trace them?'

Pia shook her head lightly, determined to keep her composure in front of everybody, in front of him. 'No. I already tried that. My father never returned to the village where we grew up. My mother thought he'd gone to Rio so she went there, but . . .' Her voice cracked and she fell silent for a long moment. 'I discovered later that she couldn't get a job so she ended up working for one of the cartels, anything to get some money together to find us. One day there was a shoot-out with the police and she got caught in the crossfire. It's pretty commonplace.'

'Jesus!' Tanner spluttered. 'And your brother?'

'I never managed to get a trace on him, but the odds were slim. Did you know that a child's chance of dying in the drug areas of the *favelas* is nine times greater than in the Middle East?'

Tanner shook his head. 'I . . . uh . . . God, no. I had no idea.'

'No? Well, did you know that drug gangs account for half of all child murders here?'

Tanner shook his head.

'Mmm. Up to ten million children live on the streets and seventy per cent of those are boys. What about this: in São Paolo, twenty per cent of homicides committed by the *police* are against minors. Did you know that?'

Tanner looked down at her anxiously. 'You know an awful lot about this, Pia.'

'Well, I have to. It's because of me that these statistics are the odds my little brother will have had to battle.'

'But how can you say that? How on earth can you think you're responsible?'

'Because in going to the audition I forced my father's hand. It's because of what *I* did that my brother was taken away, and then my mother went to find him and was killed herself. It's because of me that my family was sacrificed.'

'But you'd found a way out for you and your brother.'

She shook her head. 'I wasn't being selfless,' she snapped. 'I was being selfish. There were other ways we could have escaped him, but I *wanted* to dance,' she said in a disgusted tone. 'I wanted to. So, yes, I make it my business to know the horror of what I put my family through, to never forget for an instant the price they paid for my freedom and my desires.'

Tanner saw the tears begin to stream down her cheeks and reached into his pocket. She turned away from the other guests. He pulled out a clean hanky and passed it to her, but she didn't respond. Gently, he lifted her chin with his hand and began dabbing under her eyes.

'Do you know for a fact that your brother is dead?' he asked.

'No. But I've hired the very best investigators to look for him and there's been no trace. He had . . . he had this birthmark on his arm, a port wine stain in the shape of a sickle. It's quite distinctive, the kind of thing people would remember, but there's been nothing, no reports of him at all.'

He stroked her cheek with his thumb. 'And your father?'

She shrugged. 'I neither know nor care.'

There was a long silence as Tanner absorbed her revelations. It put Silk's duplicity into perspective. It also explained a lot about her – never staying in one place too long, the lack of close friends or family, her distrust of people, keeping everyone at arms' length, always being the aggressor, her ferocious ambition, her obsessive desire to remain independent and unbeholden. He hadn't quite been able to reconcile her frigid resistance to Will with her promiscuous, party-loving reputation, but now he clearly saw why she needed to remain in control. She would never again give anyone any power over her destiny.

'If it's so painful for you, why do you dance?' he asked quietly.

'Because I have to. It's my punishment, the price of my freedom – all the pain, the hours, the injuries . . . I welcome it. The suffering makes me feel better. Why shouldn't I suffer? My family did.'

She stared into the distance at the sooty mountains backlit by the orange sky.

'But it means you're . . . you're torturing yourself with it.'

She shook her head. 'No, not all the time. It is different on the stage to in the studio. It's not punishment then. It's a release. When there's an audience and the orchestra just keeps on playing, when they don't stop every time I make a mistake or miss a beat, but just keep going and take me along with them, that's when I feel at peace. I can just . . . disappear into the music and forget what I did for a while.' She stared at her drink. 'It's exhausting for me *not* to dance, actually.'

He thought back to her agitation with Violet during her convalescence. 'That must have made your recuperation doubly hard.'

She shrugged.

'Have you ever told anyone this before?'

KAREN SWAN

'No,' she said, meeting his eyes. 'Why do you think I've told you?'

'I don't know,' he said haplessly. 'Maybe because you're never going to see me again?'

'Aren't I?' she asked.

'Well, I'm going back to England tomorrow and you're – what? Where will you go? Off into the sunset with Paolo?' He thought he'd choke on the words.

'I'll go back to the Bolshoi.'

'To Russia?'

'No. To the academy here. I'm in training.'

'For what?'

'Varna. It's an international dancing competition. I have to win it. It's the only way I'll make Assoluta now.'

'What's Assoluta?' he asked, baffled.

'Prima Ballerina Assoluta. The untouchable status every ballerina aspires to. Only a few ballerinas in every generation are awarded the honour.'

'And you've got to win this competition to get the title?'

'Well, I've got to win the competition in order to get to La Scala, to get to the choreographer who'll have the power and the desire to give me the title.' Tanner looked lost. 'It's a long story,' she sighed.

'Right. And once you've made Assoluta – what then? Carry on touring the world? You can't keep running, you know.' His eyes roamed her face and the sight of his concern made her want to fall into his arms.

'I may retire,' she said. Then shrugged. 'Or I may not. But it will mean that I've gone as far as I possibly can, and . . . while I can never justify the decision I made, at least I can live in the knowledge that I took the opportunity ballet gave me to its fullest potential. My family's suffering won't have been *completely* for nothing. One of us got away. I'll never be free of my past, but I think this will be the best way for me to learn to live with it. It's my redemption.'

Tanner stared at her, recognizing the weight of the history she carried about on those tiny shoulders. She was a fugitive from her own past, always on the run. He couldn't bear to think of her living with the burden of guilt, day after day, wrongly blaming herself for the sins of her father, as unable to stop dancing as the ballerina in that film, the one with the red shoes. He desperately wanted to take her in his arms and slough the guilt off her, but he feared that if he started touching her he'd never be able to stop. All the feelings for her he'd tried to deny were refusing to stay in their box. It had been so much easier when they hated each other, when he could transpose the passion into aggression. But now, with the barriers down . . .

He shook his head, conflicted. He couldn't get involved with her. She was his boss's son's girlfriend now. That made her toxic. If he claimed her for his own, he'd lose the client that was going to save his business. It would force him to go begging back to Silk, the man he held responsible for his father's death, and he'd end up hating them both if he did that.

And yet the thought of never seeing her again, of losing all contact with her . . .

He noticed Paolo approaching from the flank and felt panic rise up inside him, like bile. They were running out of time.

'You know, seeing as we're friends now,' he began, 'we should stay in touch. That is what friends do, after all.'

Her spirits slumped at his platonic tone. 'It's not much of a friendship,' she said flatly.

'It could be.'

'We've been friends for only ten minutes.'

'Half a day, actually. We started being friends when you thanked me earlier. And this time tomorrow, it'll be a day and a half.'

'This time tomorrow you'll be halfway across the world, remember?'

'Well, you know where I live,' he shrugged. 'At least I've *got* an address.'

Pia cracked a weary smile. 'That is true.'

'You should try getting one of those instead of a new boyfriend.'

'You think so?'

'Definitely,' he said as Paolo reached her, running an arm round her waist and kissing her on the shoulder.

'Hey, baby,' he slurred. 'Why are you standing here talking to him all night? You've been driving me crazy standing here and ignoring me. I give in, you win.'

Pia raised her eyebrows, unimpressed. She'd forgotten all about him.

'Look, they're lighting the candles. Quick, take one and make a wish.' He reached down and picked up a couple of the floating lanterns. 'Go on,' he grinned. 'Make a wish.'

He lit his candle and closed his eyes, releasing it into the night sky, like a dove. 'Can you guess what I wished for?'

Tanner had to fight the urge to deck him.

'Go on, your turn.'

Pia closed her eyes and made her wish. Tanner watched her lips move, like a little girl learning to read. She opened her hand and the lantern floated dreamily away, along with the thousands of others that were heading for the vaulted star-studded sky. She looked over at Tanner.

'Come on, baby, let's go make up,' Paolo whispered not very quietly in her ear.

Tanner swallowed hard, but he gave away nothing. How could he? There was nothing he could do. He coughed and looked away.

'Why not?' she said, looking at his set jaw.

Tanner looked back at her. 'Pia, are you sure you . . . uh . . . ?' His voice trailed off. He glanced at Paolo, who had screwed his eyes into lasers and was staring at him hatefully, full of drink and just gunning for an excuse to lay into the man who'd been chatting up his girlfriend all night.

'Nothing,' he said finally. 'It was good chatting with you.'

'Chatting,' she echoed blankly, and he thought he saw a dullness come into her eyes. 'Yes. It was.' She looked at him for a long moment. 'Well . . . if I'm ever in England, I'll be sure to look you up,' she said lightly.

If.

Tanner nodded and watched her go, the folds of her skirt bouncing jauntily around the butt she'd so insistently pressed into his groin that very afternoon. He felt his heart plummet to his boots at the prospect of never seeing her again. Suddenly that two-letter word – 'If' – seemed like the biggest word in the English language.

Chapter Forty-eight

'Are y'awake?' Tony whispered into her ear, sliding under the blankets and wrapping his cold body around hers. There was no central heating in the old cottage but, even though it was the middle of July, the fire still crackled brightly across the room.

'Well, I am now,' Sophie mumbled into the wall, flinching beneath his cool touch. 'What time is it?'

'Late,' he murmured, feeling her warmth seep into him, inhaling the smell of her hair on his pillow. 'But I've got something to tell you,' he said, nuzzling into the crook of her shoulder, his hand beginning to roam up her taut tummy towards her breasts. He liked the feel of them, the way they moulded to his touch, responded to his mouth. He rolled her onto her back.

She looked up at him sleepily. 'It went well, then?' she smiled, corkscrews of hair obscuring her vision. The Brazilian perm had almost given up the fight now and her ringlets were asserting themselves more strongly each day. He preferred her hair like that anyway. He could imagine how she'd looked as a little girl growing up here. That super-sleek city look she'd been wearing when she arrived was too groomed for walks in the fields and sex in the hay. It was like someone coming for dinner but keeping their coat

466

on; he thought she might just get up one day, and leave – good to go.

'Better than well. I've been offered a contract,' he said, walking his fingers back down, down, all the way down between her legs.

Sophie gasped with delight on both counts. 'Oh my God,' she whispered, instantly awake, lacing her arms around his neck, pulling him down to kiss her. He tasted salty, of beer and peanuts, but she liked it. 'It's a two-album deal –' he said, in between kisses – 'I've got to record it . . . in Dublin . . . But if that does all right . . . who knows? . . . Madison Square Garden, here I come . . .'

'Here you come indeed,' she said, moving his hand and guiding him into her. She closed herself around him and rocked him gently, in no hurry, as he lowered his head to her breasts. 'God, I'm so proud of you,' she sighed, her back arched gymnastically, her hands gripping his buttocks and holding him into her, keeping him as close to her as she could get him.

'It means I'll be needing a groupie, though,' he murmured. 'Someone who's got all the tricks for keeping me satisfied on the road.' She grinned in the dark and hitched her ankles up, keeping her knees parallel, and she heard his breath catch as the change in angle quickened his lust.

She matched his stride.

'Don't know anyone, do you . . . ?'

'Maybe,' she smiled.

She looked around in the darkness. The embers in the fire smouldered silently now, only stray puffs of ash occasionally lifting off the hearth as the breeze got trapped and blew down the chimney.

She smiled sadly. There hadn't been a night that they hadn't made love in front of that fire. He'd have it lit all year round, she knew. She watched him sleep and felt the first cracks split through her heart. But there was nothing to be done. She had to go now, before it was too late.

The first chinks of dawn were hitting the trees, throwing out pale vanilla shoots that would water down the night's inky blackness, and she knew it wouldn't be long before he began to stir. He was an early riser, even with a hangover.

In the distance she heard the engine of the car rumbling slowly down the track. She had asked the driver to wait by the trees. She looked back and allowed herself to drink him in for the final time; she knew the images she stored now would have to nourish her for the rest of her life. She watched the rise and fall of his chest, the contours of his profile, the dark stubble, the pink flush in his cheeks that he only ever got after sex or during sleep.

And then, with a burst of courage, she stepped out of the cottage and closed the door behind her. The lake shimmered, viscous with cold, and she saw a grey heron standing motionless on one leg, hoping for an early morning catch. She tiptoed up the track to the waiting cab.

'Morning, Padraig,' she mumbled as she tossed her overnight bag along the seat and fell in after it.

'Y'all right, Sophie?' the driver asked, concerned. She was pinched white.

'Ay,' she gasped, like a drowning woman reaching for breath. 'Just take me to Dublin. Please.'

Sitting down at her usual seat, Esther opened her bag and pulled out her iPod. She flicked listlessly through the menu, wholly unable to decide whether she fancied the new Black Eyed Peas album or Lily Allen. Truth be told, what she really fancied was another three hours in bed. She felt gopping. She was going to have to cut back on those nights out with the lads down the pub. If nothing else, her bank balance was as battered as her liver. And besides, she was fed up with her parents' disapproving looks when she staggered in each night and had to pretend she wasn't nearly as drunk as she actually was.

She plumped for the Black Eyed Peas – they'd wake her up – and put in the earplugs. She was checking her texts when the woman next to her tapped her on the shoulder.

'Oh God, am I playing my music too loud? I'm so sorry,' she blustered, fumbling for the volume control before the woman could get a word out.

'It's not that,' the woman said. 'It's just that I think the man over there's trying to get your attention.'

'Huh?' Esther looked out of the window, baffled. She saw the driver of a burgundy Morris Minor honking his horn and driving like a lunatic, swerving round parked cars and trying to get as close as possible to the bus. 'Holy mother of God! What are y'doin', Tony?' she screeched through the window, jumping to her feet and knocking the contents of her bag all over the floor. 'Shit, shit, shit!' she cried, crouching down to pick it all up before standing up again and trying to gesticulate to him that she was picking things up from the floor, not hiding from him.

The woman kindly rang the bell for the bus to stop, and helped her pick up her things.

'Thanks, oh thanks so much,' Esther blustered. 'That's my sister's boyfriend out there. Oh God, something must have happened.' Her voice quavered.

The bus came to a stop. Tony abandoned his car in the middle of the road and jumped out.

'Where is she?' he shouted, running towards her.

'Who? Sophie?'

'Who else?'

'Well, why would I know? I thought she was with you. She's *always* with you,' she said, not quite able to keep the jealousy out of her voice.

'She was gone when I woke up this morning.'

'Gone? Gone where?'

'*That*'s what I'm trying to find out, Esther,' he said, exasperated. 'Do you mean to say you have no idea where she is?'

'No,' Esther said, shaking her head. 'None.'

'She didn't confide in you about anything? Was she unhappy about anything? Had I done something to upset her?'

Esther shook her head, her bottom lip beginning to tremble. 'Nothing. She seemed absolutely fine when I saw her last. Oh God! Don't say she's gone again. She's only just come back.'

'Please don't cry, Esther. I'll find her. You just need to help me. When did you see her last?'

'The day before yesterday. She wanted to have lunch with me.'

'You guys don't normally meet for lunch.'

'Well, no . . . but only because she's always with you. I guess she felt she'd been neglecting the rest of us and was trying to make it up a little.'

'So the lunch was her idea.'

'Uh-huh.'

'Did she say anything that struck you as odd?'

Esther thought for a moment, then shook her head. 'No, she . . .'

'What?'

'Well, it's . . . no, it was probably nothing.'

'What was? Tell me what was nothing.'

'Well, it's just that I was moaning about Mam and Dad giving me a rough time recently, and she told me not to be so hard on them. She said they were going to need me, that I'm their rock.'

'She said that?'

Esther nodded. 'I thought it was an odd thing to say at the time, because she's the eldest. That means she's the rock, doesn't it?'

'It does. Unless she knew she wasn't going to be around,' Tony said, staring into space. His colour was ashen, his clothes rumpled. He clearly hadn't shaved, probably hadn't eaten. He looked like he'd jumped out of bed and straight into the car.

'Oh God, how am I going to tell Mam? I can't believe she'd do this again,' Esther said, beginning to cry. 'Not after all the heartache it caused last time.'

Tony looked at her. 'Why *did* she leave last time? Whenever I asked about it, she would never say.'

Esther shook her head. 'No. Please don't ask me. I can't talk about it. Mam and Dad made me swear that I never would.'

'Well, you're going to have to tell me, Esther,' he said grimly. 'Because I'm not going anywhere until you have. I'm going to get to the bottom of this once and for all.'

Chapter Forty-nine

Sophie shifted position. She took a deep breath and tried again, but she felt distracted, disengaged.

She checked her watch. Three o'clock.

A black-clad assistant came over, crouched down and tried to make herself as small as possible in the darkened wings. 'Would you like a coffee?' she whispered, handing over a polystyrene cup.

Sophie smiled and took it, though she couldn't think of anything worse. It was like drinking mud.

'Thanks. How much longer are rehearsals going on for today?'

'Just another hour. The main performances start at seven.'

Sophie nodded and found herself hunching down at the thought. It was the first round tonight – the classical chore-ography section – and she knew Pia was here. Everyone did. She and Ava were the headline acts, the Varna ballet organizers having spotted a dream opportunity to market the event as the ultimate and defining encounter between the two primas, following the truncated Chicago–London dance-off.

It had infused the competition – usually a rarefied, elitist date – with the kind of glitzy mass-market appeal of *The X Factor*, and press attendance had quadrupled. Every hotel in the city was booked and if you wanted to leave it would have to be by foot or by bus.

Sophie felt drained by it all and regretted agreeing to take part – she wasn't sure she wanted to confine her career to just ballet portraiture anyway – but she needed the money.

Still, the buzz backstage alone was enough to give her pins and needles. It was like playing hide and seek as she avoided the larger-than-life characters – Adam, Ava, Pia – who had contributed to her misery, and if she wasn't hiding in the dark behind her easel, she was sequestered in her hotel room.

She put down her chalk and switched to charcoals, trying to focus on José Cabrera as he rehearsed his adagio variation on James, the groom hero in *La Sylphide*. Sophie watched him refine his *grand pas de chat* time after time and tried not to feel bored.

Adam. She hadn't seen him yet either. She suspected he was trying to keep away from Ava, who – she had heard from Lucy – had ruthlessly discarded him straight after the gala.

And Sophie knew for a fact that the two women hadn't met up yet. Ava's strikes had been long-range, and she and Pia hadn't been face to face in over two years. It was the moment everyone was waiting for. Junior dancers had taken up strategic positions backstage, keeping the balletomaniacs updated via Twitter; the stage crew was running a book, with three-to-one odds on a catfight.

So far, they'd been rehearsing in private studios but, with the first round tonight, they wouldn't be able to avoid seeing each other any longer.

Sophie shook her head and made her hand move across the paper again, but she knew she was producing dross. She felt wiped out. There was no point in continuing. She'd be better off going back to the room for a couple of hours' sleep before the real performances began.

Clicking the easel shut, she tiptoed off the stage – no mean feat in squeaky Converse trainers – and left it propped up against the wall by the backstage door. With her folio under her arm she opened the door and stepped out into the balmy sunshine, stopping to admire the view over Varna Bay. It felt so good to her to be here. Most tourists came for the ancient spa qualities of the Black Sea, and there were mud and water therapy complexes on the beach. But Sophie just liked the smell of the salt on the wind. It felt exfoliating, cleansing.

'Knock, knock,' said a voice to her left.

Sophie whirled round, startled.

'What . . . ?'

'You say: "Who's there?"' a redhead said. She was sitting on the wall opposite, grinning at Sophie, dressed bewilderingly in pale pink towelling hot pants, oatmeal-coloured long johns and a yellow vest. There was only one person Sophie knew who would pull together an ensemble like that.

'P—' she began, incredulously.

Pia held her finger up to her lips and jumped down. Boldly walking past the photographers grouped around the back-stage exit, she came up to Sophie and winked at her. 'Hiding in plain sight only works if you don't say my name,' she whispered. She playfully bobbed her wig with her hands. 'Like it?'

Sophie cocked an eyebrow. 'If that's supposed to be in homage to me . . .' she said darkly.

'As if. There's no perm strong enough that could rival those curls,' she grinned.

'Tell me about it,' Sophie groaned, before stiffening. 'What are you doing here anyway?'

'Waiting for you. I've been sitting here for two hours actually. It's been quite an education, I can tell you. Did you know they think I'm sleeping with four of the jurors – one of whom's a woman!' Her eyes twinkled.

Sophie's didn't. There was a loaded silence.

'But that's not why I came here,' Pia said, picking up Sophie's resistance. 'We need to talk.'

'You think so?' Sophie replied off-handedly.

'Yes,' Pia said. 'Come back to my hotel with me.'

'No, thanks.' If Pia thought she could just charge back into her life and start calling the shots, after the way she'd treated her . . . She wasn't her boss any more.

There was a pause.

'Please.'

Sophie's eyebrows shot up. She wasn't sure she'd ever heard that word fall from Pia's lips before.

'There are some things I really need to say to you.'

Sophie hesitated. It was disconcerting being so close to Pia again. She'd forgotten how dazzling her beauty was.

'Look, I'd say it here if those guys weren't hanging around,' Pia jerked her head towards the paparazzi off to the side. 'But I think I've pushed my luck enough for one day. If one of them begins to twig . . . Let's just get out of here.'

'Oh fine,' Sophie said resignedly. 'Where's your car?'

Pia shook her head. 'I'm not using one. That's what *they're* looking out for. Let them chase Ava around town. I'm getting about on that.' She stepped back so that Sophie could see the gleaming red Vespa propped up behind her.

Sophie shook her head. 'Oh no. I'm not getting on that

thing with *you*. I think I can probably imagine what your driving's like.'

'I'm a changed woman,' Pia grinned, handing her a helmet. It was Ferrari red with two thick racing stripes down the middle. 'Hop on.'

Sophie perched precariously on the back, holding on to the handrail behind her seat, and closed her eyes, willing herself to be strong. She mustn't let Pia back in.

They wove like skiers out of the Sea Gardens, past the strolling families and necking teenagers, and onto the open boulevards. The roads were wide and pale, with thick-canopied trees lining the pavements, like fur trims. Parasols dotted the streets, and though the shops boasted none of the glitzy brands of northern Europe, it could only be a matter of time – cafe culture was already alive and kicking, with internet cafes everywhere.

Pia knew her way around the city intimately, whizzing down backstreets, and Sophie let herself relax as the mid-summer sun beat down upon her. She knew that she looked pale, ghostly even, and spending her days cooped up in rehearsal studios didn't help. Still she hadn't come here to top up her tan.

Pia came to a stop outside a concrete lump that rose inelegantly among the ice-cream-coloured Italianate villas that so characterized the Bulgarian city. Sophie raised her eyebrows at the insalubrious address and looked around, wondering where the deluxe boutique hotel must be hiding. After all, the organizers had put *her* up in the five-star Musala Palace Hotel and she was only the competition artist.

'Well, I never thought I'd say this but you're a surprisingly good driver,' Sophie said, climbing off the back of the bike.

'See? I told you. Formal tuition's overrated,' Pia shrugged, pulling off her helmet and the wig with it. Her hair fell like snow, settling in thick clouds around her shoulders.

'What?' Sophie shrieked. 'You mean you *haven't* had any lessons? Are you even insured?'

A group of teenage boys across the street stopped and stared. They had recognized Pia – her hair alone signalled that she was a star. She saw them get out their mobiles.

'Quick. This way,' Pia said, tucking her helmet under her arm and breaking into a trot, heading down the street away from the hotel. Sophie followed, struggling with her folio and the helmet.

They went two hundred yards before Pia darted into a side alley. She ran down it and then shot left again, doubling back on herself. They had come round to the back of the hotel. A tradesmen's entrance was there, and the door was open as crates of beer were being unloaded.

Pia shoved her helmet back on her head. Sophie followed suit, convinced they looked like something out of *The Italian Job*. The men stopped unloading as the girls trotted past, Pia holding her hand up cheerily, and Sophie was unable to stop herself from bursting into laughter at the sight of Pia, in baby pink shorts and long johns, pretending to be a courier.

They found a stairwell and bounded up it. Sophie expected they'd have to climb to the top, but Pia stopped at the second floor. Poking her helmeted head round the corner into the corridor, she checked the coast was clear.

'It's okay,' she said, taking off the helmet and shaking herself out again. 'There's no one around.'

Pia opened the door to her room and Sophie gasped at the sight. The view from her window was . . . a brick wall.

She turned around, aghast. 'What the hell are you doing in here?' she whispered, taking in the ply headboard and blue polyester eiderdown. 'Why aren't you in the penthouse? In fact, this hotel can't even have a penthouse. What is it? Three-star?'

'If that! But no one will think to look for me here,' she said gleefully. 'They all think I'm at the Musala Palace. I doubt anyone staying there has had a full night's sleep for a week there're so many journalists camped outside. I certainly hope Ava hasn't,' she sniggered. 'Besides, I'm here to dance. What does it matter what the view is outside the window? I only come back here to sleep.'

'Christ, you really have changed,' Sophie said, shaking her head.

'More than you know,' Pia mumbled, grabbing two cans of Diet Coke from her tote. She held one up for Sophie. 'Want one?'

Sophie's stomach turned at the thought. She clapped her hand over it. 'No, thanks. Big night last night.'

'Water, then? There's no minibar here so it'll have to be from the tap, I'm afraid.'

Sophie scrunched her face at the thought of that too and shook her head. 'I'm good.'

Pia flopped down on the bed. 'That's always been your problem,' she said, opening the can. But their run through the alleys had shaken up the contents, and as she released the ring pull Coke spurted out, as from a hydrant, and drenched her.

Sophie burst out laughing again, smacking her thighs with hilarity. Pia sat up spluttering and looking . . . well, looking just like Sophie usually did. For once, the boot was on the other foot, and the more Sophie tried to stop giggling the harder she laughed. She collapsed onto the bed while Pia looked at her and blinked hard several times – Coke dripping off the end of her nose – before she burst out laughing too.

The sound of their shrieks echoed down the corridors, and no one would ever have guessed that they belonged to the diva Pia Soto and the acclaimed new artist Sophie O'Farrell. It just sounded like two friends on a city break.

Sophie clutched her sides as her giggles abated. 'Oh God,' she gasped. 'I can't remember the last time I laughed like that.'

'Me neither,' Pia said, getting the hiccups. 'In fact, I'm not sure I've *ever* laughed like that.'

'Well, that's just sad,' Sophie said, looking across at her.

'Yes, it is, isn't it?' Pia said quietly.

They lapsed into silence and Pia took a sip from the almost-empty can.

'How's your ankle?' Sophie asked, looking at Pia's feet.

Pia waggled it carelessly. 'Great. I've been lucky.'

'I doubt it's come down to luck,' Sophie countered. 'I can well imagine how hard you must have worked to get yourself back. I bet you were a nightmare patient while the cast was on. Glad I wasn't around to see it,' she added sardonically.

Pia turned to her, as if to say something.

'Thank God for Will Silk, hey?' Sophie continued. 'Didn't he turn out to be a knight in shining armour?'

Pia sat back and hesitated before answering. 'Not really.'

'Oh?' Sophie frowned and looked at her. 'Oh no! Tell me you've at least thanked him for what he did for you,' she said sternly.

Pia didn't answer. She was lost in another memory of withheld thanks.

'Pia?'

'Huh?' She glanced up. Sophie was sitting up, looking cross. 'I said, did you thank him for what he did for you?'

'Not in the way that he wanted, no,' Pia said slowly. 'He wasn't quite the hero that he seemed, you know.'

'Oh don't tell me. He secretly wanted to go to bed with you,' Sophie said sarcastically. 'That can hardly have been a surprise, Pia.'

'That wasn't, no,' Pia said, staring at her feet. 'The fact that the accident was his fault was, though.'

'Huh? What do you mean?'

'Oh it's a long story,' Pia sighed, not wanting to let Sophie know that Alonso's seduction of her had been on the boss's orders. That would hardly boost her ego. 'I'm not saying it was entirely his fault. It wasn't like he pushed me in front of the horse, but he wasn't blameless either. Tanner was right: there was a clear thread of culpability.'

'Who's Tanner?'

Pia looked up, startled to realize that Sophie hadn't met him, nor even heard of him.

'Just a guy,' she said quietly, biting back that he was the real hero. What did it matter now? 'But forget about Will's role in the fiasco. It doesn't excuse the fact that I completely overreacted. I was jealous of you with Alonso, and then when I . . . I thought I'd never dance again, I was frightened and I took it out on you. I was a total bitch.'

Sophie's mouth dropped open.

'In fact, I'm amazed you're even talking to me.'

Sophie stared at her for a moment, then reached over and pinched her arm. 'Who are you?' she asked. 'Which planet have you come from?'

Pia giggled, thankful for the light relief. 'I'm trying to say I'm sorry.'

Sophie clapped her hand to her forehead and slid down the bed. 'Oh God, now I know I'm having an extra-terrestrial experience!'

Pia giggled harder as she watched Sophie goof about. She looked different somehow. Her hair had lost the frizz and she'd put on a bit of weight, but it wasn't that. Her demeanour was different. She'd lost that meek docility that had made her seem perpetually on the point of apologizing, and in its place there was a quiet resolve. Success had been good for her. Pia realized suddenly that Sophie had thrived in her absence, while Pia had floundered in Sophie's.

'So you forgive me, then?'

'I suppose so. But I'm not coming back to work for you,' Sophie replied flatly.

'I wasn't going to ask you to,' Pia countered. 'I think we're far better off as friends.'

There was a brief pause. 'Did you just say the f-word?' Sophie gasped in mock surprise.

'Besides, the art world's need is greater than mine. I heard your exhibition did well,' she said lightly, making no reference to the dance-off that had accompanied it.

Sophie looked up in surprise. 'Uh, yes. It did okay, thanks,' she replied modestly.

'I heard it did better than that,' Pia smiled. 'I even shelled out myself.'

'You did?' Sophie gasped.

'Of course,' she shrugged. 'As soon as I saw what you'd been doing all that time, I had to have something.'

'Which one did you get?'

'I bought seven.'

'Seven?'

'All of me, of course,' Pia said, arching her eyebrows, a twinkle in her eyes.

'Of course,' Sophie grinned.

'My favourite is that one showing me before curtain-up . . .' She looked at Sophie. 'Did you change the tutu?'

Sophie nodded. 'I thought it had a more . . . romantic feeling to it.'

'Thought so . . . You were right.'

'Why'd you like that one so much? I'd have thought you'd prefer the one of you in *penché* in *Giselle*.'

Pia shrugged. 'Yes, but . . . the other one makes me think of my brother.'

There was a short pause. 'I didn't know you have a brother,' Sophie said.

Pia kept her eyes down. 'Used to. He's . . . he's . . . well, you know . . . dead.' She fiddled with her fingers. 'I always feel most connected to him in those few minutes before curtain-up. I dance for him. He's the reason I do it. He's the reason I *can* do it.'

Sophie sat back against the headboard. So there was the answer to the question she'd been asking herself, and which Ava had correctly guessed: '. . . she is like that because she is haunted by something, and she only ever gets away from it when she dances . . .'

Pia broke the silence first. 'And to think I used to assume you were just hanging around with my bowl, waiting for me to throw up,' Pia said mocking herself. 'How self-absorbed was I not to notice the masterpieces in front of me?'

'They're not . . . they're just . . . You weren't self-absorbed. You were preparing to perform. Blocking out the rest of the world is how you get up on that stage.'

There was a pause. 'No. I was just self-absorbed,' Pia said.

Sophie chuckled lightly at Pia's new self-awareness. Pia picked up a bulging suit carrier. 'Come on. We'd better get back. The performances start in an hour and I'm fourth on.'

'Why've you got your costume here?' Sophie asked, spying some frothy wisps through the carrier's plastic window. 'Shouldn't it be left in your dressing room?' she frowned.

'With Ava Petrova lurking about?' she asked, opening the door. 'Not likely. I wouldn't trust her not to cover it with jam.'

'Or drop maggots into it . . .' Sophie giggled as they stepped into the hallway.

'Or stick pins in the crotch . . .'

Pia locked the door and linked her arm through Sophie's as they walked down the corridor, giggling like schoolgirls. 'Or sprinkle it with itching powder . . .'

Chapter Fifty

'No wig?' Sophie asked, as they approached the theatre. Pia had put her shades on, even though the sun had set.

Pia shook her head. 'No. I have to be me now,' she said, stiffening as the photographers caught sight of her and turned as one, like a shoal of fish. 'It's time to face the music.'

Flashbulbs popped like flares in their faces and as Sophie froze, unable to see where to go, Pia calmly grabbed her elbow and pushed her through the scrum. A security man held the door open for them, and they fell in together.

The atmosphere backstage instantly felt different to the usual curtain-up vibe.

'What's different?' she asked, looking around. Ladders and old set boards were propped up against the walls, as usual. Stage crew, dressed all in black and looking like roadies, dashed behind the scenes, refilling the rosin trays and shimmying across the lighting rigs overhead.

'No orchestra,' Pia said, leading the way to her dressing room. Junior dancers pressed themselves to the wall as she passed. 'All the music's on disc. Everyone has to bring their own.'

They descended a stone staircase into the basement. Dancers were standing in pairs, catching up on the previous night's exploits, and they stopped talking as Pia approached.

A contracted hush fell over the corridor and Pia turned back to Sophie knowingly.

'I guess that means Ava's already here,' she said loudly. She knew full well that everyone was expecting her to fly at the rival who was so stealthily eclipsing her.

They stepped into the dressing room and Sophie shut the door behind her. It was small and airless, with only a ventilation grille in the wall, and was harshly lit by the bulbs framing the mirror. Though Pia had been wily enough to keep her costumes with her, her maquillage was already positioned across the dressing table and her dozens of shoes – mostly pink, a few white and some black – were lined up in a row on a shelf.

Sophie looked around, astonished. The lack of flowers was stark. There was no ballet company behind Pia, no family, no friends, clearly no lover either. She was the competition's wild card, and was here alone, with just her ghosts for company.

She felt a sudden rush of protectiveness for her friend. For all her prima donna behaviour, Pia had been but a pawn in a bigger game. Ava, Baudrand, and seemingly even Will, had all played her, exploiting her injury, her talent, her fame, to their own advantage.

She watched as Pia settled into her familiar rituals, lighting some Diptyque Figue candles before applying her make-up – the heavy base that caked her skin, the elongated eye shape of Maria Callas – and spraying her lustrous mane into rigid sleekness.

'What are you dancing tonight?' Sophie asked, perching on a tub chair and fishing in her bag for a mint. She had a terrible metallic taste in her mouth that she couldn't shift.

'Variation of Odette, Act II first; then variation of Aurora Act I.'

'Can I see your costumes?'

'Sure, they're in the bag,' Pia said.

Sophie unzipped the hanging bag and let the frothy meringues spill out. The *Swan Lake* costume for the first solo was breathtaking. It was stiffly starched with the tulle layers so precisely cut and moulded that they fanned out like an open umbrella, bobbing gently as one skin, the perimeter as sharp as a shell. But it was the bodice that made Sophie gasp: the usual design of velvet embroidered with Swarovski crystals had been replaced by scissored feathers, and the traditional sculpted headdress had been replaced by a neck collar of softest swan down.

'Oh my godfathers, this is exquisite,' Sophie whispered, her fingers as soft as breath.

'Do you like it?' Pia smiled, wearing nothing but a thong as she stepped into her white tights. 'Karl designed it for me.'

'Lagerfeld?' Sophie gulped. It was just like something out of the Chanel couture.

At that moment there was a knock at the door.

'Come in,' Pia said, rolling up her tights.

She looked up casually. 'Adam!'

Dismayed, Sophie dropped the tutu, and it billowed down like a parachute, landing with a soft sigh on the ground. She looked over at Pia, panicking. The contrast of her peachy skin against the marble-white veneer of the tights was startling, and Sophie knew Pia wouldn't bother to cover herself. She wasn't being provocative. Aside from the fact that she'd never considered Adam as a lover, her body was just a tool here. Not a weapon.

'Pia . . .' Adam faltered. He'd spotted Sophie and was clearly wrong-footed to see them allied again. 'I . . . I came to wish you luck.' He stepped into the room and placed a spray of lilies in her arms, kissing her lightly on the cheek.

'Thanks,' Pia said. 'I appreciate it. You're dancing?'

'Yes. *Pas de deux* of *The Nutcracker*, with Ingrid.'

Pia's understudy, Sophie recalled, shocked to hear that he wasn't partnering Ava.

'How are you, Sophie?' he asked, turning his gaze to her.

Sophie nodded curtly. She didn't dare to test her voice, afraid it might betray her. He continued to stare at her. She knew she looked different and she wondered if he could guess the reason.

'Have you seen Ava yet?' Pia asked quickly, sensing Sophie's discomfort. 'Have you taken flowers to her too?' she added wickedly as she stepped into the tutu.

'No,' Adam said, tearing his eyes off Sophie and standing to attention. He knew he deserved the barbs and scepticism – from both of them. He'd betrayed them both in different ways. 'No, I've no interest in how she does,' he added, looking at Sophie.

'What's she dancing, do you know?'

'Variation of Odette, and variation of Aurora, I believe,' Adam replied.

Sophie's eyes met Pia's.

'Well,' Pia said finally. 'What are the chances of that? There are – what? Nearly forty options on the repertoire, and she chooses the exact same ones as me?' Pia shook her head. 'Why am I not surprised?'

'You're not dancing a *pas de deux*?'

'And who would I dance with, Adam?' Pia said, suddenly

sharp. 'I'm on my own, remember? I'm the lone ranger of the ballet world now.' She raised her arm in a whipping motion. 'Yee-hah,' she said sarcastically.

Adam nodded. He knew it better than anyone. He was a great dancer, but he'd needed her in order to be world class. 'Well, good luck anyway,' he said, walking backwards to the door. 'I'm rooting for you.'

The door shut behind him and Pia whirled round to Sophie, her eyes wild and the flush in her cheeks beating past even the heavy layer of make-up.

'That bitch has got someone on the jury,' she whispered. 'The chances of us choosing the same variations are minuscule.' Pia's eyes narrowed. 'She's rigging this.'

'But she can't! You're just being paranoid. The voting's electronic,' Sophie soothed.

The organizers had been boasting to all the press about their world-first mathematically encrypted voting system.

'Maybe, but it takes only one person to max her votes and crunch mine to make the difference between gold and silver.' She shook her head and pursed her lips. 'She's definitely got someone on the inside. I don't believe for one moment that it's a coincidence.'

Sophie nodded bleakly. It did seem unlikely. 'Look, I can't stay. I've got to go and set up. The first dancer's on in ten minutes. Try to stay calm,' she said, walking over and giving Pia a hug. 'Just be amazing. I'll give you extra long legs!'

'And Ava three heads?'

'Of course!'

She shut the door and turned down the corridor.

'Sophie,' a voice called behind her, and she felt a hand on her arm.

'Adam? What are you still doing here?' she whispered,

worried that someone might come out and catch them – someone like Ava.

'I need to talk to you.' He stared down at her, every inch the dashing prince, looking magnificent in a bottle-green velvet jacket, his legs heavily contoured in navy tights, his stage make-up adding to the strength of his already striking face – the swell of his lips, the carve of his cheek, the cut of his jaw . . .

'There's nothing to talk about, Adam,' she said, turning away.

'Please, Sophie,' he said, squeezing her arm. 'I made a mistake. Can't we at least talk?'

She looked up at him, the man she'd adored from afar for so long, and realized that she felt curiously unmoved. Once upon a time she'd thought he was her Happy Ever After. How much of her infatuation with him had been habit, she wondered. Or loneliness?

'There's really nothing to talk about.'

'You know there is. There was always something between us.'

Sophie snorted. 'Forgive me for not realizing that you'd noticed.'

'Of course I noticed! But I was so stressed about Ava and all her games and then when I saw you with that journalist—'

'Oh, so it's my fault, is it?' she flashed back. 'You didn't notice me for three months, Adam! Three months of seeing you every day and watching you fly out through the door at the end of each one before I could even get my easel folded. And then the very day someone else shows a bit of interest and I have some fun, suddenly you're on my doorstep and

I'm supposed to believe *that* revelation propelled you into Ava's bed?' She shook her head angrily.

He held out his hands appeasingly. 'She was all over me suddenly.'

'Oh, well, in that case . . .' Sophie retorted sarcastically. 'God forbid that you would have turned her down.'

Adam's hands fell to his sides. He had no defence.

'Do you want to know why she was all over you, Adam?' Sophie asked, resting her trembling hands on her hips. 'Because *I* asked her to make an effort with you. I told her how I felt about you and she – being the prize bitch that she is – took that as reason enough to seduce you.'

She was aware of heads beginning to peer around doorways. Adam shifted his weight uneasily.

'She seduced you to score a point against me. And, by extension, against Pia. Because, at the end of the day, that's all any of this has ever been about. You, me – we've both just been ammunition in her war against Pia. But don't worry, it's not personal. She's had what she needed from both of us. She'll leave us alone now.' She looked at Adam's pale face. He looked as sick as she felt. 'And I'd appreciate it if you'd do the same.'

Ava's dressing-room door – two down from Pia's – suddenly opened, and a man came out carrying a cane. He was remarkably short and broad. As he approached and passed them, he nodded his head in greeting.

'Adam, Miss O'Farrell,' he said in a thick accent.

'Mr Alekseev,' Adam said quietly.

Sophie stared at the man's retreating back. She'd met him before, she was certain.

'Who is that man?' she whispered fiercely. 'I know him.'

'I'm sure you do. That's Mikhail Alekseev.'

Russian name. Russian . . .

'I know that. You just said that. But who *is* he?' she repeated.

And then it came back to her – where she'd met him. The Russian she'd met at the snow polo in St Moritz. He'd said he . . .

'He's a broker,' she said. 'What's *he* doing here?'

'No, you must be mixing him up with someone else, Sophie. He's no city boy. That's Ava's manager.'

Sophie climbed back up the stairs and into the warren of backstage passages. Yelena Maritsuva, the Belarusian prodigy and first to dance, spun past in *pirouette*.

Sophie walked on, her heart hammering with what she'd just learnt, and mindful of the stares that followed her. She wasn't just recognizable for being the official competition artist. Thanks to Russell's lead article, which had then spawned a hundred others, everyone knew she'd been caught between the primas – first as Pia's ally; latterly as Ava's – and already rumours were circulating that she'd been seen out with Pia again. This would only add yet another level of intrigue for the bystanders watching the famous rivalry; it was something else for the balletomaniacs to Tweet about.

A security guard let her out of the backstage area, and as she walked out towards her easel and chair in the open-air theatre her feet faltered at the sight of the night-time extravaganza. The semi-circular stage, which was offset by ivy-decked classical columns and had looked like a hanging garden by day, was now dramatically spotlit, looking romantic and haunting, mystical and pagan all at once. She couldn't imagine a more fitting setting for a ballet competition, and she fiercely wished its beauty was the only reason she was here.

She sat down at her easel and began to flick through the sketches she'd made of Yelena during rehearsal the day before. She was performing a variation of the Mistress of the Driads in *Don Quixote* and Sophie had particularly liked her *developpés*. They were silky, and lambent. She decided to go with that and started arranging her pastels so that she wouldn't need to rummage around once the lights dipped, but her mind was on other things.

The revelation that the spooky Russian was Ava's manager had unnerved her. She realized now that he was the same man she'd seen speaking to Baudrand – upsetting him – on the night of the exhibition. But it was the fact that they'd first met in St Moritz that weighed upon her mind. What had he been doing there? It was too much of a stretch to believe that it was just coincidence, surely? St Moritz was where everything had gone wrong for Pia and where everything had gone right for Ava.

Okay, it wasn't Ava's fault that Pia had been suspended, or injured, or even that Baudrand had come knocking at *her* door. And the Cartier campaign had only come to Ava because Pia was indisposed. But it was in St Moritz, in the Cartier tent, that Pia lost her coveted contract with Patek Philippe. It was obvious that Alekseev must have been the one who alerted them to her flirtation with Cartier. Managers were notorious for their ruthlessness when it came to promoting their clients. Sophie wondered how much Ava had been involved in the sabotage. Probably fully, she thought, as Ava's cruel adulterous smile flashed before her eyes again.

But, losing the Patek Philippe contract had ended up being small fry compared to everything else that had happened to

Pia subsequently. Sophie shook her head and sighed, unable to make a connection. He and Ava probably weren't guilty of anything other than profiteering from Pia's bad luck.

Maybe he hadn't been there to spy on Pia, after all. Maybe it *was* just a coincidence. He may have been there to meet someone else entirely.

Still, one thing just didn't make sense: *why* had he called himself a broker? It was such a strange term for a manager to use about himself.

She felt the atmosphere shift, and looked around her easel to see the judges – all twelve – coming in. Sophie politely joined in with the clapping as they took their seats directly behind her. She recognized Madame Faure, Directrice of the Paris Opera; she saw Terence Duff, choreographer for the New York Met; a Korean man she didn't know; Carlos Acosta, the international dancer; Ichiro Takahashi, the avant-garde composer; Irina Nowak, the Polish principal dancer and former laureate of Varna; Mary Stoppes-Wade, the dance critic; Ivan Topalov, the secretary of the competition and . . . Baudrand.

Her hands stopped their automatic clapping and she heard her pastels clatter to the floor. *The Songbird* dance-off may have come and gone, but Baudrand had a direct interest in making sure that Ava, as his new star, always came out on top. Pia had been right, after all. Dancing wasn't going to be enough.

Slowly, not wanting him to spot her, she slid down her seat to pick up the colours from the floor. The clapping continued all around her.

She sat back up and tried to make herself like a statue, but to no avail. She felt a finger tap her on the shoulder.

Oh God! It was pointless trying to hide. As one of the

judges he must have known she was here, and it figured that he would want an explanation. She hadn't seen him since the night of the exhibition and he had left countless messages asking where she was. How could she tell him she'd fled because Ava had seduced Adam? It was hardly professional behaviour. And after the break he'd given her . . .

She turned around with a fixed smile in position.

But it wasn't Baudrand who was smiling back.

Chapter Fifty-one

The dancers followed each other in quick succession, and there was no time between performances to get backstage to warn Pia. She counted them down, hoping to catch Pia's eye from the wings, but the lights shining up onto the stage meant Pia couldn't see her, the judges or anyone else in the front four rows. Sophie took a scant comfort in the knowledge that ignorance was bliss.

As it was, she needn't have worried. Not yet anyway. Pia gave a faultless performance that no judge – even a bent one – would have been able to mark down without arousing suspicion. Her arms looked so fluid, fluttering delicately, that Sophie began to question whether she actually had any bones in them, and her feet shimmered lightly in the pinpoint *bourrées* that made her glide across the floor.

The audience gave her a standing ovation, but Sophie remained sitting. She preferred to stay out of sight for the moment, pretending to put the final flourishes to her depiction of Pia.

Adam and Ingrid put on a less stellar performance. Ingrid's timing was off, meaning she could only perform two *pirouettes* instead of three and Adam was left desperately trying to bring her up to tempo around the stage. But it wasn't marked against him. His stylish recovery and exuberant *entrechats* garnered points with the judges. Like all the dancers performing a *pas de deux*, they were being scored individually.

It was nearly forty minutes later that Ava came on. The lots she had drawn meant she was on last, and the audience was restless to compare the two primas.

Sophie heard the first strains of Tchaikovsky's score drift over the theatre and she squinted appraisingly as Ava came out in a tutu so historic and tiny it could have belonged to Dame Margot Fonteyn. Silk feathers wrapped around her ears in the classical style, the tulle layers of the skirt as frothy as foam.

Talk about variations on a theme, Sophie thought to herself as Ava danced the steps with more exactitude and power than Pia, her feet pattering across the floor in tiny staccatos, her arms beating and stately, her neck extended majestically. The audience loved it, rising to their feet yet again and apparently forgetting that they'd done the very same for Pia's quite different, more sparkling interpretation just an hour previously.

She realized Ava had been right that day at their first lunch, when she said that every champion needs a rival. The audience loves to see the gods do battle, Sophie mused, watching them all clap and call excitedly. Pia's joyous etherealism or Ava's steely classicism? Who cares, so long as they promise to duel to the death?

Everybody knew there was no way either of them would be going out before the third round. The organizers would have a riot on their hands.

Sophie casually let the judges file out, before she jumped up from her seat and darted backstage. She needed to alert Pia to what she was up against. Sophie strode down the corridor. Pools of light from open communal dressing rooms dotted the concrete floor but most of the rooms were empty as the dancers had moved off in secretive pairs to discuss the other performances, or hung around in the wings, soaking up the vibe. Many were outside for cigarette breaks, relieving the tension with some much-needed flirtation. The competition gathered together all the greatest luminaries in the ballet world and the combination of talent, ambition, physical perfection and adrenalin meant it was like the Olympic village: seduction was rife.

But Pia wasn't among them. She had already changed into her *Sleeping Beauty* costume when Sophie walked in. Her back was turned to the door but Sophie could clearly see her reflection in the mirror.

'Pia, what's wrong? What is it?' she asked, astonished to see Pia look so . . . forlorn.

Pia wiped her cheeks hurriedly. 'Oh,' she said turning away. 'It's nothing.'

Sophie hesitated. 'It doesn't look like nothing.'

'I'm just tired,' Pia shrugged. 'I've not been sleeping well.'

Sophie stared at her. She didn't look tired. She looked like Sophie felt. Broken-hearted; broken. It looked like Sophie wasn't the only one with a secret.

'Because of the wall?' Sophie said lightly, knowing when not to push. She sat down in the tub chair.

Pia laughed. 'Yes, exactly. It's that bloody wall keeping me awake at night. I might need to go five-star, after all.' She looked back into the mirror and began to fix her make-up, which had smudged under the eyes.

They sat in easy silence together.

'So tell me,' Pia said, gathering her voice. 'How did Ava dance it?'

'You didn't see?'

Pia shook her head. 'No. I'm not going to give them all the satisfaction of spying on her like some peeping Tom.'

'You're determined to confound expectations, aren't you?' Sophie said. 'Have you come across her yet?'

Pia shook her head. 'Don't intend to, either. There're a hundred and forty dancers here. That's more than enough to separate us – at least until the third round.'

'Mmm,' Sophie sighed.

'So come on, tell me. Don't keep me hanging.'

'Well . . . she gave it more attack. Her *fouettés* were sharp and her extensions were . . . acrobatic, I guess you'd say, but her arms were stiff, and as for her *épaulement* – well, she was just vertical, like she was being pulled up by strings. Personally, I thought she played it more Odile than Odette.'

Pia considered for a moment, then continued reapplying her maquillage.

'Well, at least she's not copying how I'm dancing,' she muttered. 'Although it's hard to know whether that's a good or bad thing.'

Sophie gave a small cough. 'Have you seen who's on the panel, Pia?'

Something in Sophie's voice caught her attention and she spun round to face her.

'A few. They were still confirming names when I asked. I know Carlos is here and Ivan, of course, Mary—'

'It's Baudrand. He's here.'

Pia paled. 'As a judge?'

Sophie nodded.

Pia blew out slowly through her cheeks. 'Well,' she said finally, in a low voice, 'at least we know who it is Ava's got in her camp.' She shook her head despondently. 'I can't believe they'd allow it. She's in his company. She's his prima. And everybody knows *our* history. He has a clear bias.'

Sophie chewed her lip for a moment. 'Well, there may be some light on the horizon.'

Pia looked at her. 'What do you mean?'

'I saw Will. He's on the jury too.'

'Will is?' Pia asked, incredulous.

Sophie nodded, leaning forward. 'That's what I thought. I don't understand how he can be. He's a banker, isn't he?'

There was a long pause. Pia was deep in concentration. 'Yes,' she said slowly. 'Although you could be forgiven for thinking he's the chief executive of the Royal Ballet, he spends so much time there. Time and money. '

'But why? Does he *really* love ballet that much?'

Pia shrugged. 'He probably secretly prefers just looking at pretty girls in tutus, but once these men get to a certain level of wealth they like to be seen to be influential in the right circles. It's a snobbery thing. Ballet is high culture and becoming a patron puts a stamp of old-money credibility on their self-made millions. He's not unusual by any means. Hedge-funders are the biggest private benefactors to ballet and opera now. They're the ones with all the money. The grand old families simply can't compete any more.'

'He just didn't seem the type to try so hard,' Sophie mused.

'Oh, trust me – he is! Tanner told me some things about him and he's a desperate social climber, trying to get into all the right clubs. It's just the kind of thing he *would* do.'

Sophie's ears pricked at the mention of Tanner again, but she let it pass. 'I thought he was just feigning an interest in it to get to you.'

'Oh no, he's serious about ballet all right. He's one of the

Royal's biggest patrons. That's how he managed to get them to dance with me for the premiere of *The Songbird*. Rudie told me he donated a good few million for a new wing and he developed their Young Artist's Programme.'

She nodded suddenly and sat bolt upright. '*That*'s probably why he's here – to lure the cream of the crop in the senior events and cherry-pick the up-comers in the juniors.'

Sophie tipped her head in assent. 'Or that's his *official* reason, at least,' she said slyly.

'What do you mean?'

'He went out of his way to say hello to me. He would have known I'd come straight to you.' She sighed and raised her eyebrows. 'I bet he's here to win you back.'

There was a long silence.

Pia collapsed her head onto her elbows. 'Oh God, probably. He doesn't like to lose – ever. I made it impossible for him to find me after I left. I changed my phone, left the country . . . But with all the headlines about me and Ava going head-to-head again . . . He must have realized this would be his first opportunity to catch up with me.'

Sophie raised her eyebrows thoughtfully. 'Well, I guess his being here doesn't have to be all bad news,' she said slowly.

'You think?' Pia snorted. 'I don't know what it's going to take to get rid of the man. He just never gives up.'

'Maybe, but perhaps you should play that to your advantage for the time being.'

'What do you mean?'

'Well, if Ava *has* got someone in her pocket, it surely wouldn't hurt for you to have someone in yours . . .'

Pia looked at her. Aside from the fact that it hadn't occurred to her to win on anything other than merit, the thought of allowing Will close to her made her skin creep. She despised him for taking the credit for saving her life and letting her rant against Tanner. And in the light of what he'd done to Tanner's family as well it would be a double betrayal. And yet . . .

She sighed heavily. Tanner wasn't interested in who she did or didn't go to bed with. He'd made that plain in Brazil. And if Ava was manipulating the scores, she couldn't afford to be naive. This was her last chance to get to La Scala and make Assoluta. She had to win here. Only then could she truly be free.

She was going to have to do whatever it took.

Chapter Fifty-two

'Right, well, that's the loos done and the floors. I'll come back on Thursday and do the bedrooms and I'll try to make a start on those windows. They're a disgrace. And I've left a pie on the side for you. Just slide it into the baking oven for forty-five minutes.'

Tanner smiled patiently. Mrs Cooper might be a battleaxe, but she was a damned fine housekeeper, and he'd quickly grown tired of running out of milk and scorching his shirts. Besides, she'd been his father's housekeeper when they'd lived in the big house and, to her credit, she'd refused to stay on when Silk took up residence, and she had continued to drop in twice a week to help his father, even though he couldn't afford to pay her.

'Thanks, Coop,' he grinned. 'You're a star. I don't know what I'd do without you. '

'No,' the old woman said, knotting her headscarf. 'Nor do I. If only you'd married that girl, you wouldn't be in this mess.'

'Well, I hardly think marrying a girl for her housekeeping abilities is a sound basis for a happy marriage,' he laughed.

'No?' Mrs Cooper said, sending her eyebrows heavenwards. 'It never did me and Len any harm.'

Tanner hastily readjusted his features. 'Well, that's true.

Maybe I . . . uh . . . maybe I have been looking at everything the wrong way round.'

'Mark my words. A clean home is a happy home. Find a girl to keep house and you'll be a contented man.'

An image of Pia with a pinny and duster wafted in front of his eyes and he tried not to let his mirth reach his eyes. 'Right. Got it. You know, you should look at going into the dating business, Coop. You could make your fortune.'

She cuffed him round the ear. 'Don't mock me, my lad,' she said, before winking and opening the door. 'Thursday, then.'

'Thursday.' Tanner peered out into the evening sky. He didn't like the look of the clouds. 'Think I'd better bring the horses in. Thanks, Coop,' he called after her as he loped across the yard, Biscuit scampering at his heels.

Velasquez's ponies had made a good transition to the British soil and climate, and their journey over had been seamless (his had been less so, as he was tormented by the retreating vision of Pia and Paolo and with a planeful of horses in his charge he'd been unable to plumb the depths of Velasquez's in-flight hospitality). Still, they wouldn't appreciate the kind of storm only the British summer could conjure up. There had been flood warnings in force for days.

He gathered them in from the paddocks and stabled them all, scattering fresh sweet hay for them. By the time he came in two hours later it was dusk and fat raindrops were beginning to scattergun the ground.

He tried to remember what Coop had said about the pie. Thirty minutes in the roasting oven, was it? He poured himself a whisky and noticed a piece of paper she'd wisely pinned to the top of the pie: 'Baking oven, forty-five minutes.'

He duly obliged and wandered aimlessly round the house.

He'd come to dread the evenings. During the day he could busy himself with the horses – some of them had come down with laminitis on the lush Dorset grass, a few others had a sweet-itch problem that had been aggravated by the English weather – and with Cowdray this weekend and Cartier the week after, he was rushed off his feet, medicating and training them up in time for the highlights of the polo year.

So the days had passed in a much-welcomed blur since getting home, but come the evenings . . . well, Rob was always off with Jessy now – things had started to get pretty serious between them – and Jonty was incommunicado, buried somewhere deep in the bowels of Cambridge's Squire Law Library. Usually it took half a bottle of one of his father's single malts to get the memories from Brazil out of his head.

He ambled into the drawing room – which, even after Coop's expert attention, was really far too shabby for such a grand name – and stared out of the window. He could just make out the gleam of lights shining from the big house through the trees and he briefly imagined Violet over there with Will. He was amazed at how little he cared. She wasn't the one in his thoughts these days.

He turned away from the window and picked up a copy of some magazine Coop had left behind. She was an absolute workhorse and took great pride in her work, but it didn't matter what she was doing: every afternoon, come four o'clock, she would down tools, make herself a weak coffee (she kept a jar of Marvel in her bag) and read a magazine for exactly thirty minutes. Usually it was *Woman* or *Woman's Digest*, something like that.

But today it was *OK!* and today it was not okay, because there, on the front cover, looking sensational and subdued, was Pia. She was surrounded by grubby-faced children in T-shirts, all climbing over her, so that all that could really be seen of her was one thin, finely muscled arm, that gleaming ponytail and her ripe, laughing mouth.

Tanner sank into the nearest chair and stared at the image. It felt almost impossible to believe that he had ever been in her orbit. Minutes passed before it occurred to him to flick through the magazine to the article, which ran for six pages from the centre spread. Every page was crammed with pictures of her with the children. In most she was laughing with them, but some – where she was standing apart, being shown their living conditions – showed her crying.

His eyes scanned the saccharine text. UNICEF had appointed her as one of their goodwill ambassadors and she was in Rio, bringing the international spotlight onto the appalling misery endured by the street children there.

He remembered, word for word, the statistics she had thrown at him that night in Brazil during their *chat* – Christ, he hated himself for having said that to her. He knew how personal this crusade was for her. Did anyone else? Did Paolo? He scrutinized the pictures, trying to locate him in the background, but he could find no trace of the weasel. There was no mention of him in the copy either.

He got up angrily and threw the magazine in the bin. Why was he putting himself through this? What was the point of looking at it? Of looking at her? He was never going to see her again. He'd made his decision. He'd chosen the business and his employees and his father's honour over her. They were good reasons, sound reasons, for letting her go. He had to live with it.

He stalked around the room a few times, eyeing the trashed magazine like an unexploded bomb. He stopped and stared at it, hands on hips, then reached down and pulled it back out. He unrolled it and smoothed the pages flat, just as the first wafts of blackening pastry floated into the room.

'Shit!' he said, dropping it onto the ottoman and racing back through to the kitchen. Forgetting to grab a teacloth, he snatched the pie from the jaws of doom and threw it across the table. 'Ow! Bugger! Goddamn!' he cried as his fingers burnt on the baking tray. He darted over to the sink and ran cold water over them.

Biscuit watched his agitation quietly from her favourite corner of the room. 'That's all *her* fault,' Tanner muttered darkly to her, as his fingers went numb. 'She's not even here and she's causing trouble.'

Biscuit gave a sympathetic whine and rested her head on her paws, her eyes fixed faithfully on her doleful master.

There was a quick rap at the kitchen door and Tanner looked up in surprise. He wasn't expecting anyone. He opened the door.

'Yes?'

'Hello,' said a voice with an Irish brogue. 'I'm looking for Sophie O'Farrell.'

Tanner peered more closely into the gloom. The thunderclouds had knocked out all the vestigial sunset and it was black as pitch out there, the rain stinging like barbs.

Slowly his eyes adjusted and he saw a man standing there, in just jeans, a T-shirt and a thin jersey.

'God, man, you'll catch your death!' Tanner exclaimed, sounding just like his father.

'There wasn't a bus service from the town,' the man shrugged nonchalantly.

'Well, no, there wouldn't be,' Tanner replied. 'Have you just walked three miles in this rain dressed like that?'

The man nodded, not interested in talking about the weather. 'Is she here?'

Tanner shook his head. 'No, sorry. There's no one of that name here. I've never even heard of her.'

The man's shoulders slumped and he looked away. 'I see.'

'What made you think she was here?'

'She used to work for a woman called Pia Soto.'

'Pia?'

'Yes. You know her, then?'

'Well, yes, sort of . . .' He trailed off. It was a long story and he couldn't leave the poor fellow out in the rain while he told it. Besides, his curiosity had been pricked. Even just the opportunity to talk about Pia was too tempting to pass up. 'Look, you'd better come in. You can't stand out there in this weather,' Tanner said, opening the door wide.

'Thanks.'

The man came in and Tanner instantly saw he was drenched.

'Christ, you're really soaked. You'll get pneumonia. You'd better get warm by the Aga. I'll go and get a towel.'

He went up the back stairs and grabbed a towel from the airing cupboard. The man pulled it tightly round his shoulders but he was still shivering uncontrollably.

'Take a seat,' Tanner said, pulling his chair nearer the Aga. The man flopped down gratefully. 'What's your name?' Tanner asked, leaning against the dresser. He was intrigued to know this stranger's connection to Pia.

'Tony. Tony Byrne. Thanks for all this.'

Tanner shrugged. 'Can't leave a fellow to drown,' he smiled. 'I'm Tanner Ludgrove.' The chap nodded politely but he looked devastated. 'So tell me why you're walking around the Dorset countryside looking for some girl in the driving rain.'

'Sophie's my girlfriend.'

'She Irish too?'

'Yes, but she'd been away for a long time. She's been home only a few months.'

'And you say she knew Pia?'

'She worked for her for a few years, until about six months ago.'

'Around the time of Pia's accident?'

'I think so. I don't know if they lost touch with each other but I've got no other leads at all on Sophie's whereabouts – no other clues about her life outside Ireland. All I know is that the village cabbie took her to Dublin airport, a three-hour drive away. Her sister said she'd worked with Pia, so I thought she might know where she is. She's my last chance.'

Tanner nodded. Poor bloke. He really was clutching at straws, playing detective like this.

'But who told you to look for Pia here? I hardly know the woman,' Tanner said, realizing even as he uttered the words that quite possibly he was one of the only people in the world who did.

'I read in some press clippings online that she lived here while she was recovering from an injury.'

'Ah, well, that explains it,' Tanner nodded grimly. 'You've come to the wrong house. She was next door, at Plumbridge House. This is the farm. She was involved with Will Silk at the time, but they've split now. I don't think he's been in touch with her for several months. I doubt he'd know her whereabouts.'

Tony slumped further back into the chair, despondent at

the bad news. Tanner watched him. His lips were bluish and he was still shivering.

'Listen, have you eaten?' Tanner asked, walking over to the table and picking up the cooling pie. 'I was just about to eat.'

'Oh no, really, I should get out of your way,' Tony said, standing up and shrugging the towel off his shoulders. 'I'd better head off.'

'Well, wait a minute. Don't tell me you're going to walk back to the village in that rain. Have you even got anywhere to stay?'

'It's fine.'

Tanner was unconvinced. 'No. I don't think it is,' he said. 'Your colour's bad. Sit down and eat with me. You can stay here tonight.'

Tony opened his mouth but Tanner held his hand up. 'Don't argue. You'll end up with double pneumonia if you go back out in this, and there's no hotel for miles. I don't want to be responsible for you being found collapsed in the lane tomorrow morning. You're not going to find her tonight in these conditions anyway.'

Tony hesitated, then sank back down again. He knew Tanner was right. 'Okay. Well, thanks. I really appreciate it.'

'No worries. Go upstairs and in the bedroom directly opposite at the top you'll find some of my brother's clothes in the wardrobe there. They should fit you. You look around the same build. Change into something dry while I plate up.'

'Thanks.'

Biscuit assumed the position around the Aga, hoovering

up stray crumbs as Tanner served up the pie. Tony came down a few minutes later in dry jeans and a T-shirt.

'Thanks so much again for all this. I feel better already,' he said, pulling a chunky ribbed fisherman's jersey over his head.

Tanner put the plates on the table and straightened up. He froze.

'What?' Tony asked, stalling, as his head poked through the top. 'What's wrong? Have I taken the wrong things? Shit, did I go into the wrong room?'

There was a long silence, and Tony immediately wondered what he'd walked into here.

'It's not that,' Tanner mumbled, shaking his head slowly. He blinked and chewed his lip. 'I think I'd better pour us both a drink.'

Chapter Fifty-three

Sophie dropped her bag heavily on the floor, wincing as she heard the coffee cup she'd bought (she couldn't deal with any more polystyrene) break into two. She felt drained.

She yawned noisily, wishing to goodness she could stomach a coffee. Hot Ribena was going to be scant help today. The night before she'd been working past midnight at the super-gala of former laureates, and now she could scarcely keep her eyes open – not, she knew, that sleeping would provide any rest. Every night she woke up, breathless and sweating, as the memories of Tony joined the other ghosts of her past.

Sinking into her seat, she offered up a silent prayer of thanks that they were now in the second round and the lowest-scoring hundred dancers had been culled from the competition. Her job was going to get easier with every passing day now and by Wednesday night she could finally get out of here.

'Hey!' a low voice said, and she looked up to find Pia vaulting off the stage towards her. The early birds in the audience gasped with excitement. She was still dressed in her off-duty kit – a cranberry toga-tunic and black leggings – even though she was due onstage in half an hour, just before Ava. The organizers had locked on to the two primas' game of behaving like adults – although everyone knew it was just a game of course – and skirting around each other with frustrating success, and Sophie wouldn't have been surprised if the judges had eliminated the rest of the field between them in order to place their performances together. They were determined to get them face to face.

'Shouldn't you be getting ready?' Sophie whispered, just as her phone rang. 'Oh hang on a sec.' She pressed the connect button. 'Hello?'

Pia watched her grow pale and turn away slightly.

'Well, is there no other time available? . . . Yes, I understand that but I organized this a fortnight ago . . . No, I can't do that!' she said, getting agitated. She took a deep breath. 'I'm flying out the day after . . . But my schedule is . . . Uh-huh . . . I see . . . Well, I guess I'll have to, then . . . All right, yes, thank you.' She hung up and gave Pia a tiny smile.

'Everything okay?' Pia asked, her head tipped to the side in concern. She realized suddenly, as she took in Sophie's appearance, how dreadful she looked. Her skin looked grey and she had dark circles beneath her eyes. She clearly wasn't sleeping well. Probably the stress of covering such a prestigious event, Pia mused. Alongside the actual competition, there was a whole raft of cultural events, including an international symposium with members of the jury, distinguished ballet figures and VIPs; a photo exhibition; a sculpture exhibition; and Sophie's big exhibition: 'Ballet in Fine Art'. Following the sell-out success of the Chicago exhibition, she was headlining it and Pia knew she was securing her professional reputation out here.

'Absolutely,' Sophie said, scribbling some details down on a Post-it hidden beneath the paper on her easel. 'Just the . . . uh, airline messing me about.' She let the paper obscure the

Post-it again and sat back in her chair. She gave a heavy sigh and tried to smile. 'Why aren't you getting ready anyway?'

Pia shrugged. 'Just wanted to let you know the eagle has landed.'

'Oh? You got hold of him, then.'

'We're meeting tonight for dinner.'

Will had proved to be a surprisingly elusive catch. Unlike Ava's dressing room, with the festival of flowers spilling from it, Pia's room had remained starkly barren. Not a bouquet, nor magnum, nor even a congratulatory note had arrived from him or anyone (not even Signore Alvisio, she'd fretted) and she had begun to seriously doubt that he was in Varna to win her back. Her calls to his hotel suite had gone unreturned, and of course she couldn't approach him in front of the judges. It had been almost impossible to catch him alone and the days were beginning to rack up.

It had been only when he had dropped in to watch one of the master classes at the academy – which ran concurrently with the competition – that she had had a chance to speak to him. Everything had gone well from there. It was clear from the defiance in his eyes that he had been deliberately playing a different game to their previous encounters, but she had only needed to stand three feet from him – sweating and breathless – to intoxicate him and make his pride fall away. He'd readily agreed to her suggestion of dinner.

'That's great! I told you he was just trying not to be desperate. He knows you well enough to know that's the kiss-of-death with you.'

Pia shrugged. 'I guess.'

'Where are you meeting him?'

'He's going to pick me up from my dressing room later.

We obviously can't be seen together so he's going to come back after everyone's gone.'

'Have you worked out what you're going to say to him yet?'

'Not really. I'll just play it by ear.' She looked around and saw that the auditorium was filling up quickly. 'Anyway, I'll keep you posted. I'd better go before the autograph hunters get me. Wish me luck.'

'Good luck,' Sophie said. 'Not that you need it.'

'We all need luck, Sophie,' Pia called over her shoulder as she skittered away like a gazelle.

Pia watched from the wings and felt the familiar ice creep up her bones. She shook her arms and legs like a rag doll, trying to keep warm and soft, and stretched her neck, pressing each ear down to her shoulders. It was the start of the second week of the competition and it was from here that things really began to hot up. She couldn't afford any mistakes now.

It was too late to secure Will's support for this, the second round, but so long as she danced her sublime best it would be almost impossible for Baudrand to mark her down without raising eyebrows. She couldn't give him – or Ava – any ammunition.

The dancer on stage before her ran off, giving her a cursory nod of luck as she passed. Pia bent down and rolled off her red leg warmers. She was on the countdown now. Two minutes . . .

'Yes, you wouldn't want to make that mistake twice,' a reed-thin voice piped behind her. 'Looking back, that was the beginning of the end, wasn't it?'

Pia stiffened but didn't turn around. She didn't need to.

'Why are you out of your cage?' she said quietly, fixing a benign look upon her face. 'You're not on for another twenty minutes.'

'I felt it was time to come and say hello. I'm actually really very excited you're here. It's been somewhat . . . frustrating having to keep beating you from afar.'

Slowly Pia turned to face her. Ava was fractionally shorter and much thinner, with snow-white papery skin barely covering her muscles of steel. Pia looked voluptuous by comparison, and fresh off the beach. Again, their choice of variations matched and they were both wearing their peasant costumes. Ava's Giselle was in the classical brown, like Cinderella before the ball; Pia's a more Romantic-period pale blue.

'You're not winning this one, Ava. We were both on twenty-two points, last time I looked.'

'I guess this next round will be do or die, then,' the Russian smiled but her eyes were as cold as the snow in Moscow. 'Here,' she said loudly, offering her hand.

Pia stared at it, the insincere civility an insult to everything Ava had stolen from her – *The Songbird*, the ChiCi, Adam, Sophie – and everything she had sabotaged: her Patek Philippe contract, the Cartier campaign.

'What? You won't look me in the eye and shake my hand?' Ava said, loudly enough to enable the loitering crew, who'd been too scared to stare outright, to turn and watch.

Pia shook it, perfectly aware of the lighting guy filming the scene on his iPhone and transmitting it to YouTube. 'Don't think I don't know it was you who detached the ribbons on my shoes,' she said, her face a mask. When she'd reached her dressing room twenty minutes previously, she'd found every single pair bar one had had their ribbons – which she sewed on herself to ensure the perfect fit – unpicked. There'd been no time to fix them.

'I have no idea what you're talking about, Pia. I've come straight from my hotel room. The dressing rooms here aren't to my taste,' she added preciously. 'It must have been some of the other dancers messing with you. You're not the most popular person here, you know.'

'But you are?'

Ava shrugged. 'There's only one person's popularity contest I want to win.' She tipped her head to the side. 'Weren't the flowers he sent just *divine*?'

Pia's eyes narrowed but her stomach lurched. She was lying. She had to be. There was no way Dimitri Alvisio would have sent Ava flowers and not her. She'd been the front runner, his favourite, for so long. Surely Ava hadn't stolen the march to that extent?

She pulled her hand away and turned around. She had to keep focus, but Ava saw that the damage was done. Her confidence was shaken.

The music started up and Pia closed her eyes, blocking out Ava from her thoughts. She knew Ava was deliberately trying to break her concentration. The very fact that she had chosen now to make her approach . . . everybody knew how sacrosanct these final golden minutes before curtain-up were, and for her most of all.

But there was no time to think now. Her cue was coming up. She opened her eyes again and looked out past the lights, not even needing to count the beats. This was it.

She launched into her *ballottées*, springing lightly like a hopping robin. Her head filled with the music and the story, and she felt Ava's insidious poison begin to roll off her. Her rival was irrelevant out here, insignificant. Dancing in front of the spotlights was where it mattered. She would show the Russian exactly what she could do. Ava's plans of sabotage, this time at least, had been gauche and naive. Pia thanked God she had gone backstage when she had. This stage was where justice would be served.

Pia felt untouchable as the dance enveloped her and she swept down into an *arabesque penchée*, then defiantly up! –

– an agonizing sharpness rocketed up from her right foot as she stood on *pointe* and she felt the white glare of the lights begin to spread with the blinding spasms. Her body kept moving, years of discipline drilling her forward through the pain, but every step took a tungsten strength of will to block out the pain and she felt her mime begin to falter.

She knew that her leg was over-extending in the *fondues* for a true Romantic line, that her neck had stiffened and her fingers were getting spiky, but these were details beyond her reach now. It was all she could do just to keep going.

As Pia *pirouetted* past the wings, she saw Ava watching, gloating. The cut ribbons hadn't been a threat, a prank, naive or gauche, after all. They'd been strategic. They'd forced her into the one pair of shoes she had left – the pair with the tacks sprinkled inside.

Pia was still soaking her feet in a bowl of salted water when there was a knock at the door. Everyone had long since gone, but as usual she'd been left alone the second she shut her dressing-room door. Her only visitor was Sophie and she wouldn't be coming tonight now she knew Will was taking Pia to dinner.

'Come in,' she said. The sobs had abated as the water had cooled, but the hot angry tears had left their mark, pulling her make-up down with them.

Will's eyebrow cocked at the sight of her. She looked tiny sitting there in her dressing gown, her feet in a bowl of red water. 'It wasn't that bad,' he said, shutting the door behind him. 'You're still through.'

Pia felt the tears well up instantly. It wasn't enough to be through, limping over the finish line. Alvisio wasn't going to just *settle*.

She watched him shrug off his dinner jacket and settle into the tub chair that Sophie had claimed as her own.

'What did they give me?' she asked, not able to look at him.

'Nineteen.'

'Nineteen?' She half screeched, half hiccuped. Nineteen was the minimum pass mark.

'Well, what did you expect? Your legs were all over the place. I half expected you to go into the cancan . . . Your *retirés* were floppy . . . Your—'

'What did *she* get?'

'Who?'

'Who do you think, Will?' she snapped. 'We haven't been apart that long.'

There was a pause. 'Twenty-four.' One mark off flawless. 'And actually it feels like an age since you left. To me anyway.'

'Oh please don't ask me to believe that you've missed me,' she said. 'Last I heard you'd taken up with Violet.'

Will looked up at her sharply and she recoiled from his stare. 'And who told you that?' he asked quietly, pulling off his bow tie and folding it into his pocket. He sat back and rested one ankle on his knee.

'Just gossip I picked up,' she replied, suddenly worried about bringing up Tanner's name. 'Is it true?'

'Do you even care?' he countered casually.

Pia looked at him. He wasn't going to capitulate quickly. She'd obviously hurt his pride walking out on him so publicly, and if she wanted him to counterbalance Ava's inside man she was going to have to change tack. This wasn't the time to act up, especially now she was trailing so badly.

'I wouldn't be asking if I didn't,' she said, more mildly.

He shrugged his eyebrows but didn't answer her question.

'So are you – together, I mean?'

'That depends,' he said, looking straight at her, and she felt a sudden chill at the prospect of having to get close to this man again, of having to bring him back into her life when she'd done everything she could to keep him out of it. But it was different here. It wasn't his arrogant control that repelled her now, not his puppet-master routine that was so determined to break her and have her dancing to his tune, but the thought of Tanner's reaction when he found out. And she had no doubt he would. The universe had a way of making sure that the worst secrets were always let out.

The water was chilly around her feet. She gave a little shiver and pulled them out. She pulled her right leg up over her left thigh – the dressing gown falling open over her legs as she did – and examined her foot. The deepest cut was over the bridge of her toes, where a pin had embedded itself as she rested her body weight upon that narrow five-inch span.

She waited for him to question her about it, to open up the discussion about Ava's dirty tricks.

'Ow,' she said quietly.

He said nothing.

'See this?' she asked finally.

Will didn't bother to examine it. 'Just another day at the office, surely,' he replied. 'Bleeding feet are par for the course.'

'Bleeding, yes; haemorrhaging, no.'

'You always were overdramatic,' he said, with a hint of a grin.

'I would hardly call an open wound overdramatic,' she replied. 'I'd call it sabotage.'

Will raised an eyebrow, bemused rather than aghast. 'Are you making an allegation against a fellow dancer?'

'Formally, no. But off the record . . . you know what I'm saying.'

'I don't think I do.'

Pia sighed. He was being deliberately naive. 'Ava's responsible. She put tacks in my shoes.'

Will stared at her for a long time, clearly not believing a word of it.

'She did!'

'Okay,' he shrugged. 'So report her.'

'No.'

'Why not?'

'Because I can't prove it. And, besides, I'm going to show her I'm the better dancer. I'll beat her even with pins in my shoes.'

'You didn't in this round.'

'The competition's not over yet.'

His shrug was loquacious. 'She's going through to the final with the highest mean score.'

Her eyes narrowed. 'Whose side are you on anyway?'

'Depends,' he said again.

Pia swallowed, surprised by the sudden intimation that

he was a floating voter. She'd just assumed she had his support, that he'd do anything to get her back. But, when she thought about it, he had good reason to vote against her. It would no doubt be a satisfying revenge for the way she'd humiliated him. 'Do you hate me?'

He hesitated for a moment, clearly torn between pride and desire. 'Why would I hate you?' he echoed.

'Because of what I did . . . running out on you like that.'

There was a long silence and he had to look away. 'Why did you go?' he asked eventually.

'Stage fright,' she lied.

'I don't think so,' he countered, looking back at her.

Pia didn't say anything, just shrugged a little. There was no way she was going to tell him that Tanner had blown the whistle on him – both about his orders in St Moritz and about having rescued her.

The gesture angered him. 'Aside from the compensation I had to pay out – to the television companies, the advertisers, the travel companies and the ticket-holders – do you have any idea what it was like for me to have to get up on that stage and tell everyone that you'd done a runner?' he asked.

'I'm so sorry, Will,' she said, startled by his anger. 'I didn't realize. I never thought for a moment . . . It was just too soon for me. I didn't have . . . I didn't have my nerve back. I was so frightened of landing badly on it. Doing further damage.' It was half the truth at least.

Will looked away, his eyes taking in the lack of flowers and good-luck cards. 'So where did you go?'

'Back to Brazil.'

'To Paolo Almerida.'

'No!' she said, shocked that he knew. 'That was just the

papers screwing me over – as usual.' She swallowed hard. 'I went back to the Bolshoi. My teachers there have been training me, getting me ready for this.'

He watched her rub her foot. She seemed to have forgotten how small the polo circuit was. She stood up and put her weight on her foot. The bleeding had stopped now. Most of the damage was across the top of it, meaning it was fine to walk on, but completely raw up on *pointe*. It had four days to heal before the final round.

'It was a surprise to find out *you* were here,' she said in a quiet voice, pressing down on the ball of her foot.

'I'll bet it was.'

'I'm sorry, Will. You only ever showed me kindness and I repaid you with—'

'As far as I'm aware, you haven't repaid me yet,' he said quietly, a slow smile beginning to cross his lips.

She looked up at him, startled, as he came and stood next to her. Instinctively she held her breath. She heard the buzz of the light bulbs from her mirror and caught sight of her own frozen reflection.

Casually, he hooked a finger into the belt of her dressing gown. The bow untied easily, the weight of the loose ends pulling the edges away from each other. He looked down at her, at the revealed peach-skin dip between her breasts, the silken run of her abdomen.

'Why did you really ask me back here tonight?' he asked.

'I wanted your help,' she said in a tiny voice.

'Oh so *now* you want my help,' he drawled, his eyes still heavy upon her.

She nodded almost imperceptibly, trying to ignore the sarcasm in his voice. 'I think Ava's bribing one of the judges.'

He paused at the accusation. Sabotage and now bribery?
'Only one?' he asked.

'I don't know,' she whispered. She felt his eyes travel down
her again and tried not to shudder.

'She's beating you fair and square at the moment.'

'Not fair and square,' Pia said, daring herself to meet his
eyes. 'She disabled my second-round performance.'

He drew his breath in slowly and she heard it whistle
round his teeth. 'The finals are in four days' time,' he said.
'What do you think I can possibly do?'

'Counteract the vote,' she said quietly. 'Give me a top score
– just to neutralize her advantage.'

He shook his head doubtfully. 'Tricky, without raising
suspicion. She's going to go out there and dance the dance
of her life.'

'So am I,' she said, pleading with her eyes. 'I'm not asking
you to get anyone else involved. I just want it brought back
to a level playing field.'

There was a long silence, his breath still hot against her
ear.

'And if I do it? What do I get in return?'

Her throat tightened. 'What do you want?'

'Oh I think we both know what I want, Pia,' he said,
flicking the fabric off her shoulders so that the robe slipped
off her like oil.

She felt her skin prickle as his eyes probed her like fingers.
She'd never been shy about nudity, but standing there before
him she felt utterly exposed. Violated. She could feel his
breath on her shoulder as he moved slightly, and she tensed,
the adrenalin beginning to pump around her.

She squeezed her eyes shut.

'You don't look wholly sold on the arrangement,' he said,

watching her in the mirror. 'And on your past track record, how do I know you won't just cut and run again?'

She shook her head. 'I won't,' she said, her voice cracking.

'Then you've got my vote, Miss Soto,' he said, lowering his head to kiss her neck, one hand brushing across her belly.

She shivered and caught his arm.

'We can't tonight,' she said quietly. 'I'm not ready.'

'Not *ready*?'

'Timing's wrong,' she said mildly. He caught her meaning.

'Well, I'm not waiting till after the competition – *timing* or not. I'm not taking any chances on you disappearing again. Once bitten and all that,' he chuckled softly, kissing her shoulder and inhaling her warmth.

He drew himself up and blew out his cheeks. It was dangerous standing too close to her.

'I'll come here – and show you exactly what I want – an hour before curtain-up on Wednesday,' he said. 'That way I get peace of mind that your end of the bargain is upheld before I cast my vote.'

Pia nodded. She felt she had turned to ice, from her heart all the way out to the ends of her lashes.

He walked across the room and opened the door. He looked back at her. 'I'm so glad you asked for my help, Pia. You know I'd do anything for you.'

The door closed and a voice inside her began to scream. She listened to the sound of his footsteps disappearing down the corridor. Then she ran to the toilet and threw up in it.

Chapter Fifty-four

Tanner walked around the paddock in his now-customary black mood, alternately double-checking the girth straps and looking at his watch. Where the hell was Paolo? They were due on in half an hour and he was the team's star player. God knows, they couldn't rely on Velasquez Senior to bring anything more to the game than his money.

He sighed and hollered to Jessy to try him on his mobile again. She came running out of the horsebox looking flustered. Tanner put his hands on his hips impatiently and waited. Sure enough, Rob followed nonchalantly a minute later.

'Ah . . . busted!' he said with a rueful grin, seeing Tanner was wise to their tricks.

Tanner shook his head, exasperated and suffering a sense of humour failure. 'For fuck's sake . . .' he muttered. Their relentless happiness was driving him to the edge of despair. 'I'm going to check on the competition,' he said grimly. It appeared he was the only one taking this tournament seriously. Didn't anyone else realize that their livelihoods depended upon Velasquez doing well and keeping his business with them?

He stalked out of the paddock in a fury, heading up to Smith's Lawn. Picnickers were lounging around everywhere, with small children playing chase around the blankets and making the dogs bark excitedly. It was a blisteringly hot day and he felt the sweat trickle down the dip between the muscles on either side of his spine. He pulled his baseball cap out of his back pocket and put it on, wishing he could take off the red and black Velasquez team jersey instead.

He walked towards the stands and flashed up his team badge. The security man waved him in and he leant against the barrier, watching Zegna thrash it out with Black Harbour in the semi-finals.

'You all right?'

He turned and saw Rob next to him. Tanner shrugged.

'Thought you looked a bit upset,' Rob said with quiet understatement. He was worried about him. Tanner had been alternately morose and agitated for weeks now – ever since he'd brought the new ponies back from Velasquez's estate, in fact. He wondered whether Tanner had jumped from the frying pan into the fire when he'd insisted on swapping Silk's business for the Brazilian's. Certainly the son couldn't be relied upon. 'Wanna talk about it?'

'Nope.' Talking about it wasn't going to change anything. Pia was dating the boss's son; he needed the boss's money. End of. He gulped down some air and looked away. 'I'm just pissed off everyone seems to think this is a day trip,' he deflected.

They watched the action on the pitch, Tanner's eyes trained like guns on the Black Harbour number three player. It was the first time he'd seen Silk for months – since that day in the library.

'Zegna are looking strong,' Rob said. 'Their number two's attacking like a panther.'

'Looks like they're using Quarter breeds, instead of Argentines,' Tanner mused.

'Mmm. They seem quite skippy, though. I don't like the pressure they're putting on the front legs. They'll have knees like Nadal if they carry on playing that hard.'

Tanner surveyed the glossy crowd. He could hear a helicopter nearby. 'I suppose it would be too much to hope that that's Paolo arriving?'

Rob turned back towards the stick-and-ball field, and caught sight of a black helicopter landing in a neighbouring field.

'You're in luck,' he said, squinting into his binoculars. 'That's him now.'

Tanner turned and watched as the Velasquez chopper cut its engines. He raised his eyebrows. 'So good of him to join us,' he muttered, pushing himself off the barriers. 'Come on, then. Let's go to scrape and bow. I couldn't bear to spend another minute looking at Silk's gut in that shirt anyway. Christ, he's packed on some weight, hasn't he?'

Rob looked at him. 'But that's not Silk playing,' he said, standing stock still and staring at his friend. 'Surely you've heard?'

They marched back to the paddock, Tanner conflicted by his response. A month ago, he'd have expected to feel delight at the news. Instead he felt flat. He didn't care what went on in Silk's world any more – he was utterly absorbed by the misery in his own.

He watched as Paolo jumped down, already dressed in his kit, thankfully, followed by . . . a stunning tawny blonde. Tanner blinked hard, his mouth drying up as he watched them run across the field. She couldn't be here. She was supposed to be in Bulgaria. The ballet competition she'd told him about didn't finish till tomorrow. He'd checked online.

She couldn't have been knocked out. She was going to win it – she *had* to win it. It was her ticket to freedom.

He felt his chest tighten at the thought of seeing her again and hurriedly turned his back to them, pretending to check on the bridles.

'Paolo! You made it,' Rob said jovially, with a sarcastic undercurrent only Tanner would pick up. 'It's *great* to see you.'

'Roberto! Are the ponies ready?' Paolo grinned, clapping his hands and rolling his Rs extravagantly.

'As ever.'

'And where is Tan . . . Ah! There you are,' he said to Tanner's back. 'Tell me, did you sort out this one's diet? She felt heavy last week.' Tanner heard him smack the horse's flank. 'Heavy and sluggish.'

Tanner took a deep breath and turned round. 'Yes. She's off the sugarbee—' His voice trailed away.

Paolo clocked Tanner's response and burst out laughing. 'I know!' he said conspiratorially. 'She is a beauty, no? She makes me speechless too . . . Luckily, we don't spend much of our time talking,' he said, smacking her on the bottom.

Tanner offered a hand. His day was just getting better and better. 'Tanner Ludgrove.'

'Irina,' the supermodel replied.

An infectious grin spread from one side of Tanner's face to the other. 'You can have absolutely no idea how thrilled I am to meet you.'

Sophie walked towards the lifts, her bag packed, the red-carpeted corridor stretching before her, seemingly endless and elastic, like in some warped dream. Her feet shuffled along slowly but she knew it was pointless. Pigeon steps wouldn't halt the relentless march of time. They'd just make her late. The finale was starting in just over an hour.

She stopped at the cubbyhole where the drinks and ice machines were hidden. Her mouth felt dry, metallic. She rummaged in her jeans for some change and pressed a button. A polystyrene cup popped out – more bloody polystyrene! – filled with tepid water.

She eyed it suspiciously before taking a tentative sip, and almost spat it straight back out again. She swore it was just desalinated water. Her stomach heaved and she leant over the bin, just in case.

Further down the corridor, a door opened. Great! she thought. What's the betting that they need ice and I'm standing here retching like a drunk?

'. . . a job well done,' she heard a man say. 'The money will be wired through immediately afterwards.'

'Okay,' another man replied, and the accent made Sophie's stomach perform a double-pike dive. 'I'll wait here for your instructions.'

She edged closer to the machines, like a very bad spy, just as the door shut with a soft 'toc' sound. She waited a moment, before slowly peering round the corridor, down towards the lifts. The man was standing there, staring at his reflection in the bronzed doors and fiddling with his cuffs. He stood there a minute before the doors pinged open and he stepped out of sight.

Sophie leant against the wall for support, her anger with the polystyrene cups all forgotten. She had to get hold of Pia.

Chapter Fifty-five

Pia sat in her dressing room, and watched her legs shake. There was no way she would be able to dance like this. She could barely stand. She hadn't slept for the last four nights and the weight was falling off her again, becoming a topic of heated debate: the pressure had got to her, she couldn't match Ava's professionalism and stamina, it was still too soon after her injury, she was trying to get down to Ava's weight . . . What the hell did they know?

She looked at herself in the mirror. Her cheeks were hollow, her eyes haunted, and she felt faint whenever she stood up. She dropped her head in her hands. Her dream was slipping away. Why was she going through with this? Everything was against her. Everything and everybody. Earlier that day someone had even put glycerine in her rosin tray, and she'd slipped her way through rehearsals, giving everyone a good laugh, knocking her confidence still further.

Short of Ava dancing like a clown or falling off the stage, there was no way Pia could catch her up in points now anyway. Even Will wasn't going to be able to save her this time. It was too late. She had lost again.

She listened to her knees knock and it was a moment before she realized it was coming from the door.

'Yes?' she said in a quiet voice.

Pavel, the security guard, poked his head round. She'd paid him to stand outside and guard her room for the day because, as much as it would delight Ava to see her paranoia, she was taking no chances. 'There is a man here to see you.'

Will. Oh God. Her stomach lurched and she clapped her hand over her mouth until the threat died down.

'Are you okay, Miss Soto? You want me to get a doctor?'

Pia put her hands on her knees and tried to smile. She took a deep breath and shook her head. There was still this chance, slim though it was. She had to take it. It was the only way left to win, to make Assoluta, to avenge her family.

'Send him in, please.' She closed her eyes and prayed for strength.

When she opened them, a tall, dark man was standing in front of her, looking more scared than even she felt.

She smiled and he smiled back with an innate gentleness that calmed her. She didn't usually let fans into her dressing room; they had to wait for autographs by the backstage door.

'Oh, hello,' she managed, a massive wave of relief washing over her. A stay of execution – for five minutes, at least. 'Would you like me to sign something for you?' she asked, holding out her hands for a programme.

The man paused. He seemed taken aback by the question. Maybe he'd thought he wouldn't get this far. 'Uh, yes, okay,' he said.

His voice surprised her.

'You're Irish?' she asked, dropping her hands to her hips.

He nodded. 'Like you.'

'I'm Brazilian,' she corrected.

He hesitated. 'Yes . . . but your father was Irish, wasn't he?'

His face was open, benign, non-challenging.

'That's right,' she said eventually. 'You must be a big fan. Not a lot of people know that about me.'

The man shrugged. 'I probably know a whole lot more about you than most people . . . Priscilla.'

Pia burst out laughing. It had been years since anyone had called her by her full name. 'Oh my goodness, you really do,' she said, shaking her head. 'I didn't think anybody knew that about me . . . These journalists, they dig up everything . . .' A thought suddenly occurred to her, and she looked up at him harshly. '*You're* not a journalist, are you?'

He shook his head, surprised by the sudden aggression.

She nodded, relieved. No, he didn't look like a press hound. He didn't have that furtive savvy they all wore. 'Well, this Priscilla business . . . keep it under your hat, will you?' she said conspiratorially.

The man looked tentatively around the room. He seemed at a loss to know what to say.

'This is where the magic happens,' she shrugged. 'I know it's not much to look at, is it?'

He smiled. It looked like a cell. He'd expected more flowers. 'Well . . . I don't know what I was expecting, really. Something grander, probably. More ostentatious.'

There was a knock on the door and Pavel put his head round. Pia caught her breath again.

'There's another gentleman out here for you, Miss Soto. Says he has an appointment?'

Pia felt herself pale.

'Right, yes,' she said quietly, looking down.

The fan coughed again and Pia looked back at him. She

wished he could stay instead. He seemed sweet. 'I'm sorry I . . . I have to see him,' she said. 'What was it you wanted me to sign for you?'

He looked at her for a long moment, then a light flickered in his eyes. 'This – if you would,' he said, rolling up his sleeve and proffering his arm.

Pia looked down and felt something in her break – a golden thread, a metaphysical tension that had held her together for all these years. The bonds of the pain that had trussed her up burst open, and she felt a giddying lightness eddy through her heart.

Slowly, she looked up into the eyes that matched hers, and saw her childhood reflected back at her.

'Pavel,' she said, unable to look away from her brother. 'Tell Mr Silk to leave, please. I'm busy.'

Sophie overpaid the driver – though why, she didn't know, she'd have been faster hopping – and ran into the theatre. She caught a glimpse as she sped through. Bums were already on seats and the water glasses on the judges' table were being freshly filled.

Without bothering to dump her bags, she ran along the backstage corridors, bumping into ballerinas and stepping on those precious toes. Adam was leaning against a wall, chatting intensely to Ingrid, losing his flow as she streamed past.

'Hey, Soph!' he called after her.

Sophie stopped and turned. 'Yes?'

Adam stared at her. He hadn't expected her to stop.

'Uh, I . . . I . . .' he stammered, desperate for something to say to keep her here. 'Have you . . . uh – have you heard about Ava?'

'What about her?' Sophie sighed.

'She's leaving the ChiCi. Going to Europe. Her manager announced it this afternoon.'

'Where?'

Adam shrugged. 'Wouldn't confirm. Milan, I'd guess.'

Sophie's eyes narrowed. She wouldn't. She knew exactly where Ava was gunning for next. 'Does Baudrand know?'

'Apparently he's known for months. All the suits have. It's all just been embargoed from the press until today.'

'Uh-huh,' Sophie said slowly. It made sense of a lot of things. She remembered Baudrand's agitated conversation with Alekseev after the dance-off – the manager must have been telling him then. It also explained why the Varna committee had allowed Baudrand to serve as a judge. Ava wasn't his employee any more. In effect, he was non-partisan about both her and Pia.

But if that was the case, it also meant one more thing: if Ava wasn't Baudrand's pet any more, then it also meant he wasn't the judge in her pocket.

But then, Sophie already knew that.

She flew down the concrete steps three at a time, her Converse trainers squeaking madly, like a mouse being tortured, before coming to a bewildered, flailing stop outside Pia's door.

What was with the bouncer? Had things really got so bad with Ava?

'Hi, can I, uh . . .' she started, sidestepping around him like an inconvenient boulder.

Pavel stepped with her.

'I'm just here to see Pia. I'm a friend of hers.'

Pavel shook his head and remained staring at a fixed point behind her, like one of the Queen's guards.

'No one's allowed in, miss,' he said automatically, like a robot.

'Yes, but I'm her friend . . . her best friend. I'm not just anyone.'

Pavel shrugged. 'Orders are orders.'

'Well, can you tell her I'm here, then, please?'

He shook his head. 'She says she's not to be disturbed *at all*, under *any* circumstances.' She could hear Pia's intonation in his repetition.

Sophie narrowed her eyes. 'I've got a really important message for her. You have *got* to let me through.'

Pavel widened his stance as though getting ready to wrestle with her. 'Can't do that,' he replied, staring above her head again.

'Then what do you suggest we do?' she said, folding her arms like a stern headmistress. 'Because I can tell you now that she'll fire your arse when she finds out you've barred me from getting in to see her.'

'I'm only hired for the day,' he shrugged.

Sophie heard the music from *La Bayadère* start upstairs. Shit! The first performance had begun. She had to get to her seat. She couldn't stand out here waiting for Pia.

'I can pass on a message for you, if you like,' he said, clocking her genuine panic, and softening a little.

'No, that's no good,' Sophie muttered. 'It's confidential.'

An idea struck her. She rummaged around in her bag and found a birthday card she'd been intending to send to her little sisters. Hurriedly she wrote in it in purple pencil.

'Just make sure she gets that, will you?' she said, sealing the envelope. The gum almost made her retch again.

'Sure,' Pavel said, holding it in his hands like she'd given him her shopping list. She walked back up the corridor, anxiety rising in her throat like bile.

'You'll be sure to see that she gets it?' she called, turning around at the steps.

Pavel nodded.

'Because I can't get back here again . . . I have to go . . . But it's important. She needs to read it.'

'Yes, yes,' Pavel said, shooing her away with his hands.

Sophie reluctantly climbed the stairs and made her way to the auditorium, crawling on all fours to get to her seat. She gave a heavy sigh and started to draw, but she couldn't shake the feeling that her help had come too late.

Chapter Fifty-six

The music filled the air like steam, billowing and expansive, making the audience sit forward and gasp for breath as they watched the vision on stage. History was being made – no, rewritten – as Pia's variation of *Façade* infused Ashton's debutante with a glamour and wit that even the great choreographer himself couldn't have imagined.

Her technical and lyrical brilliance had always been apparent, but now she was dancing with a transparent joy that transcended any mere physical ability. For the first time since her very first audition – before her family had been taken from her – she hadn't frozen up. Her lungs hadn't compressed to the size of raisins; acid hadn't drip-fed into her stomach. She was free at last, and as she traced the ballet's story with her sinuous limbs she proved categorically that for a discipline that is based on supreme physical mastery, it is the heart that is the most powerful muscle of all. There was nuance and anima in every part of her. She could tell a story with her back, a poem with her arms. She seemed to be as light as the wind and just as elusive to catch.

The audience watched, thunderstruck, as she attacked her *jetés* with abandon, her back curving sculpturally and seeming to almost rest on her back leg; they gasped as one during her *assemblés*; and they forgot to exhale as she *pirouetted* across the stage like a flicked whip, her lean limbs slicing through the air. But when, at the end of a dazzling and bravura *enchainement* of *piqué* and *chaîné* turns, she pulled off a virtuoso *double tour en l'air* – which had never been attempted in *pointe* shoes in modern times – they rose to their feet before the music had even come to a stop.

Their cheers and roars rose into the sky like balloons, falling back down and sprinkling over the traffic and pedestrians outside, and Pia let the tears stream forth. Nothing she could have done would have stopped them. In the wings she could see Tony clapping hardest of all, dumbstruck by his sister's talent and the love that was washing over her from the crowd.

She ran off into his arms and they cried and laughed. And cried again. She'd done it! Ava stood silently in the opposite wing, watching. Pia met her eyes but she didn't need to say anything. They both knew that nothing Ava did could match that. It had been the performance of a lifetime.

'That was incredible,' Tony said, as they staggered backstage, hardly able to move for congratulations. 'Is it always like this?'

'No!' Pia laughed, amused – and thrilled – by her fellow dancers' admiration. She realized it was the first time in her life she'd ever felt popular.

There was an hour to go till the prize-giving and they fell into her dressing room to celebrate. Pavel – thinking he'd signed on to an easy job with this lonely ballerina – suddenly found himself earning his pay as he struggled to contain the hordes of fans rushing backstage with champagne and flowers. Ava must have been dancing to an empty auditorium.

Tony opened a bottle of Dom as Pia unwound her ballet

shoes and wiggled her toes. He gasped at the sight of the bloodstains.

'Jesus! Could you not break them in first?' he exclaimed.

Pia smiled. 'It's okay,' she soothed. 'It looks worse than it is . . . I'm used to it.'

Tony raised his eyebrows dubiously, and poured them each a glass. He held one up for a toast. 'To us.'

Pia blinked hard. She'd never thought she'd be part of an 'us' again.

'To us,' she said, laughing happily and letting the tears plop into her flute. She drained it in one gulp and he poured her another.

'I can't believe what you did out there tonight,' he said, shaking his head.

'I did it for you,' she said, clasping his hand. 'Because of you. I always have. I've never once gone on that stage and not done it for you. It's important you know that.'

'You thought I was dead,' he said simply.

Pia nodded.

'And I thought you were dead,' he said, shrugging. 'Dad told me you'd been killed in an accident.'

Pia's face tightened at the mention of their father. She looked away. She didn't want to ask, and yet the agony of not knowing . . .

'Is he dead?'

Tony nodded. 'Cancer, four years ago.'

'Good.' She looked into the distance and they were silent for a few minutes, lost in the memories of their ruptured childhood, thinking of what could have been, what *should* have been. 'So what did he do . . . after . . .'

'We slept rough for a few weeks after he came and found me; he pretended to try to get a job, but we went for days without food. Then one day he came back in tears, drunk, of course. He told me that you'd been killed – hit by a motorbike outside the academy. He said that there was nothing left for us in Brazil and he asked my – sorry, our – grandfather to bring us back to Ireland.'

Pia looked at him. She obviously hadn't been the only one with survivor's guilt. 'That must have been hard. You were only eight.'

'Aye. I couldn't speak any English . . . I didn't know what was going on,' he said quietly. 'I couldn't get used to the cold. And it never bloody stopped raining.'

'But what about Mamma?'

His mouth set into a grim line at the mention of her. He was still digesting the new truth. Everything he'd thought about the villains and saviours of his childhood had been turned upside down in the past few days. He felt a deep ache in his chest at the thought of the hatred and resentment he'd harboured against his mother all these years; a gnawing sickness at the love and care he'd given his father, the man he had now learnt had tricked, cheated and stolen him.

'She never came . . . well, so *he* said. He told me she was packing up the house and was going to join us in Rio, but the weeks went by and . . . nothing. He said he left a plane ticket for her with a friend so that she could join us . . .' His voice trailed off and he looked away. 'He said she got involved with the cartels instead. That she chose drugs over me.' He shook his head. 'But there never was a plane ticket. I know now that it was all lies.'

'Who told you it was lies? Not Dad, surely? I can't believe he'd confess to his crimes against his family, even on his deathbed.'

'No. No, he didn't.'

'So – what happened then? How did you find out I was alive?'

'It was by accident, really. I went over to England looking for my girlfriend, Sophie – Sophie O'Farrell.'

'Sophie?' Pia repeated, shocked. She'd never mentioned a boyfriend but . . . there'd been a distance in their friendship that Pia hadn't been able to bridge. Pia had put it down to lingering mistrust between them still, but a broken heart made a whole lot more sense.

'Yes,' he said, anxiously scanning her face, relieved that Pia so clearly knew her after all. 'She ran away last week. I found out she'd worked for you, so I came looking for you to see if you'd heard from her. I read that you were recovering from an injury in Dorset, so I went to track you down there.'

Pia went very still. The thought of Tony meeting Will made her feel sick.

'Luckily, I went to the wrong house. I ended up at the farm by mistake and it was your friend Tanner who made the connection between us. He was the one who told me you were my sister.'

Her friend Tanner? How mild the words sounded, completely unlike the reaction his name elicited in her.

'Tanner? But how did he know?'

'He saw my birthmark,' he shrugged.

'He did?' Pia shook her head in disbelief. She had mentioned it in passing. It had only been an off-the-cuff detail; but it was one that he had remembered, and it had changed her life.

'I couldn't believe it at first. I'd heard of you of course, but shortening your name to Pia and using Mamma's surname – it just never crossed my mind that you could be my sister.

Dad told me you had died and I just accepted it without question. Why would I have doubted him – especially about something like that?' He looked at his drink.

'I understand,' Pia replied. 'It certainly explains why I never had any leads in Brazil. I never . . . I never thought to look in Ireland.'

There was a heavy silence.

'Look, about Sophie . . .' Tony said. 'I don't want to draw our celebrations short at all, but it's really important that I find her. I'm running out of time. Have you heard from her? Do you know where she is?'

Pia snapped back into focus. 'Sophie? God, yes! Of course I have.'

Tony's face lit up. 'Where is she? Has she gone back to America?'

'No!' she beamed excitedly. 'She's here!'

'Here?' He looked like he was going to fall over.

'Right here. In Varna. Sitting in front of the stage. She's the official artist for the competition. Between you and me, I asked them to secure her for the competition – it was one of my demands for agreeing to appear. The advantages of being a prima donna!' she laughed, mocking herself. 'But quick! You must go to her,' she said, jumping up and taking his glass from him. 'The performance after mine was the last one. It'll be finishing any moment. Go to her. Go and get her.'

She opened the door and found Pavel arguing with the crowd of people who were trying to get through.

'Pavel, do you think you could move everyone to the backstage door?' she asked, smiling sweetly. 'I think this door will cave in if there's any more pushing against it and I'd just hate for Ava to be unable to get into her dressing room.'

A titter of laughter swept through the horde of fans as the

burly security guard started bunching them all out of the corridor. 'I promise I'll sign everything you put in front of me after the prize-giving,' she said to them all.

She shut the door and closed her eyes, thankful for the sudden peace. She needed some quiet, a little time on her own to absorb the enormity of the past hour's events. It was scarcely credible that she wasn't alone any more, that Antonio was alive and returned to her after all these years!

She sank down at the dressing table and rubbed her face in her hands. She stared at herself in the mirror. The ghosts had left her, like shadows. She could stop running now. The nightmare was over, but she knew it was going to be weeks – months, even – before she fully woke up.

She noticed an envelope in front of her and opened it absent-mindedly. She was frowning at the 'I Am Twelve' badge as the door opened.

She read the message inside and it was a few moments before she saw the shiny black tips of his shoes. Instinctively she stood up.

'We had an agreement,' Will said, walking slowly towards her. 'Surely you didn't think hiring a bodyguard was going to stop me from cashing in my chips?'

She stared at him, the colour in her cheeks building. She refused to step back.

'I'm sorry,' she said in a low, dangerous voice. 'But I think you'll find that agreement's null and void. Not worth the paper it was written on.'

Will stared at her, and knew that she knew.

'Did you really think I wouldn't find out?' she hissed, tossing the card at him.

He opened it and read Sophie's purple scrawl. He looked back at her, smiling.

'Does this mean I'm not going to get the little bonus I was all set to award myself, then?' he drawled chillingly, combing his eyes up and down her.

'*Bonus?*' she cried.

'Sure, why not? You've certainly tried my patience over the past six months. I figure I deserve some kind of reward.'

'You deserve nothing but contempt,' she spat. 'I see you exactly for what you are. A spoilt, indulged child out for revenge. And all because I didn't dance a second act? You're pathetic.'

'Revenge?' he repeated, nodding his head slowly.

'Yes, revenge. Don't try to deny it. Why else would you be doing Ava's dirty work here?'

'*Am* I doing her dirty work?' he mused, pursing his lips. 'Or is she doing mine?'

She stopped short.

'What do you mean?' she asked, her voice smaller. The threat that he was masterminding something bigger than Ava's ambition hung in the air. 'What's going on, then? Why did you spend all those months trying to get my career back on track, just so that you could derail it out here? It doesn't make sense.'

'That's because you're looking at it from the wrong viewpoint,' he said contemptuously. 'As usual, your ego is taking up all the room and you can't possibly conceive that I had any reason for caring about your recovery, other than being desperately in love with you.'

Pia stared at him. He was bluffing, trying to salvage some pride. Of course he'd done it because he wanted her. There was no other explanation for it. Why else would he have looked after her, kept her close – too close – for all those months? He wasn't a Samaritan.

'I don't believe you,' she snapped. 'You told me lie after lie to try to make me beholden to you, because you knew that you had no other chance of having me. But I would *never* have slept with you – no matter how many times you pretended to save my life, or how many galas you threw. I would never have been grateful enough for *that*. You repulse me.' She sneered at him. 'Your seedy little rendezvous at the boathouse? It was never going to happen. It never will.'

A slow smile crept across Will's face. 'On the contrary, Pia. Tonight you're going to give me everything I've ever wanted from you.'

Pia let out a cry of distress and raised a hand to slap him, but he caught her wrist and held it firm. He kissed her hard and their teeth clashed. She tried to pull away but he easily overpowered her, ripping at her tutu with one hand, the other jammed between her legs. She started to cry as he began carrying her back to the wall, slamming her against it so violently that she felt the breath knocked out of her. She closed her eyes instinctively and felt a strong pressure building against her chest.

'And we'll start with this,' he snarled. 'Sign it!'

Pia opened her eyes and looked at him. What? She glanced down. He was holding a piece of paper against her.

'What? What's this?' she whispered, incredulous.

'I bet I can guess,' said a low voice to the side of them, as clear as a bell.

Will turned in shock, dropping her carelessly as he clocked their intruder.

'It's a contract, isn't that right, Silk?' Tanner said, sauntering lazily into the room as though he'd just come in to make some tea.

Will said nothing. He watched as Pia hastily scrambled back up to standing, trying to read the piece of paper.

'A contract? For what?' she asked, but her hands were shaking too much to read it.

'Can't you guess?' Will growled. 'Is your brain really so tiny that you haven't joined up the dots yet?' he said, flicking her temple contemptuously with his fingers.

Tanner advanced rapidly and hurled Will against the wall. 'You don't speak to her like that. You don't touch her. Period.'

'She's got you hook, line and sinker, I see,' Will said calmly, unperturbed by Tanner's temper. 'Well, you'll live to regret it. She's just a prick-te—'

Tanner delivered a solid punch to his left cheek, followed by a swift uppercut that caught him just below the ribs. Silk fell to his knees with a groan. Tanner raised his fist to hit him again – after years of suppressing his rage against this man, it felt good, so good, to let it all out now.

'Don't, Tanner! Stop. He's not worth it,' Pia cried, rushing forward.

There was a pause. Tanner squatted down to his heels, looking closely at his old enemy.

'You're right there,' he said. 'You're really not worth much at all, are you?'

The comment stunned Silk more than any punch. 'I don't know what you're on about,' he muttered, but Tanner saw the fear in his eyes.

'I think you do,' he smiled, standing up again.

Will dropped his head.

'That aborted gala really cost you, didn't it? You lost far

more than your pride when Pia ran out on you. Such a high-profile failure really scarred your brand; people lost confidence in you overnight and that's when the *first* run of investors redeemed their positions. You've had to liquidate assets – fast. Selling the polo team, for example?'

'I was bored of it,' Will snarled, getting up and dusting himself down.

Tanner ignored his bravado. 'But it would all still have been okay as long as you delivered on your terms to Perry Everleigh. That was the one that really mattered.'

'Everleigh?' Pia repeated. 'You mean Lord Everleigh? The Royal Ballet's—'

'Chief executive?' Tanner nodded, turning to face her. 'Yes. He was Black Harbour's principal investor. He invested over half a billion and launched Silk into the big time a year ago. It was one hell of a coup landing him. Silk had had to get extra-creative to succeed where the others failed. But all it took was a little lateral thinking, isn't that right, Silk? Once my father got you into White's and you were in the club – well, he listened to you then.'

'I don't understand,' Pia said quietly, trying to keep up.

'Ever since Everleigh sold the family publishing empire to Herald News Inc. he was the big fish to reel in. All the financiers wanted his money, but Everleigh's old school. He had no interest in exposing his portfolio to a high-risk area like hedge funds. So our friend here thought outside the box.'

'He did?' Pia asked nervously.

'He became a patron of the Royal Ballet – a big one – and went straight to the top of the tree. He homed in on Everleigh's big passion and made it his own, then pitched him with a proposal – the only one – that didn't cap performance fees. He brought something else to the table instead.'

Pia shook her head. 'And what was that?'

'Can't you guess?'

She looked at him, puzzled. 'No,' she shrugged.

'Everleigh wanted something even *his* money couldn't buy,' he smiled. 'He wanted—'

'Me!' Pia gasped, her eyes suddenly wide as she remembered the countless offers, the ridiculous pay deals far and above what anyone else was being given. She realized now that they must have been coming from Will's private resources. There was no way the Royal had access to the funds he'd been offering.

She looked down at the crumpled paper in her hand. She saw now that it was a contract formalizing her position as principal dancer at the Royal Ballet in London. She looked back at Will, aghast.

'*That*'s what it's all been about? Getting me to sign to the Royal Ballet?'

Will shrugged. 'What can I say? Rich men and their foibles. They do pride themselves on having what no one else can buy. It was the condition attached to the bond.'

'So you used me. I was just a commodity to you . . . part of a trade,' she whispered. She looked up at him. 'And *everything* you did – paying to meet me in New York, rescuing me in Switzerland, my rehabilitation, the gala – it was all just for a deal . . .'

'Oh I've done so much more than that, Pia,' he snapped tersely. 'Behind the scenes I've been hard at work, I can assure you. I've been manoeuvring you for months now. I had Ava lined up in the wings for weeks, just waiting for you to make a wrong move. Luckily for me, you make a lot of those –

double-dating with Victoria's Secret? That was perfect ammunition for getting you suspended and bringing her in. Flirting with Cartier when you were under contract to Patek Philippe. Dating a married man . . .'

'So you've been . . . what? Dismantling my life?' she asked, horrified.

'I guess you could put it like that. I've thought of it more as shepherding you. Shutting down your exit routes. Forcing you into position. And I've tried to do it nicely,' he said, walking towards her. He looked down. 'I flattered you, looked after you, played your games. I suggested the right move to you, even arranged meetings for you – *that* was the purpose of the boathouse by the way – but you're such a prima donna. You just won't do as you're told, will you?'

Pia didn't respond. She felt chilled to the bone by the level of deception he had kept up around her, all these months.

'You look upset, Pia. Tell me, did you prefer it when you thought I was just doing these things because I was trying to get between your legs?' he mocked. 'You should be flattered really. I've spent far more time, money and effort just trying to corral you to the Royal than I have ever spent on any other woman before.'

She bit her lip. 'So Ava's been working for you all along? You've been using her to block me?'

'Now you're getting it,' he smiled. 'She's the only one good enough to compete with you. Whatever you want, she's the only one who can feasibly stop you from getting it.'

'And her sudden desire to go to La Scala . . . ?'

'Purely to stop you going there. She likes to piss you off but her real desire is to please her manager.'

'Her manager?'

'Well, he's been more of a broker to me, but he's actually

her husband. Daft girl's only gone and fallen in love with him. And to think she only married him in the first place to be emancipated from her parents and leave Russia.' He shook his head pityingly.

'But *he's* Russian.' Sophie had told her that he'd been the balletomaniac she'd met in St Moritz.

'No,' Will said, blinking slowly. 'He's Polish. Europe? Access all areas.'

She shook her head, appalled by his tactics. 'All of this just so that I would be left with no option but to sign with the Royal.'

'Well, he had a six-hundred-million pound investment riding on the back of it,' Tanner interjected, almost chuckling. 'You've got to feel sorry for him actually, Pia. He must have thought he'd done all the hard work getting Everleigh to commit. How could he ever have known that his company, with such massive resources at its disposal, would come unstuck by something as *innocuous* as a pretty ballerina refusing to sign on the dotted line? You were just the small print to him, a postscript at the end of the contract. But it's all unravelled now. You're the mouse that roared, Pia.'

'Maybe,' Will said tersely. 'But it doesn't change the fact that you're all out of options now. You're never going to win here. I'll be seeing to that myself. Face it – La Scala's gone, Pia. Even if you had won, I'd have given them a sweetener that they wouldn't be able to *afford* to turn down. You can't win.' He took a pen from his pocket and held it out to her. 'Just sign it. You know I won't stop until you do. I'll just keep blocking you, humiliating you. I don't lose, Pia.'

Tanner stepped forward. 'Don't do it,' he said, seeing the confusion cross her features. The shock was too much. He had been stalking her, coercing her all this time . . .

'It's hardly as though she's being asked to dance in Timbuktu!' Will snapped back at him. 'They're one of the top three ballet companies in the world,' he said, turning back to her. 'You'll enjoy all the prestige, the profile, the tours, the roles that you would in Milan. More so, in fact.'

'But not the rank. I'll never get it there,' Pia replied flatly.

'Fuck that!' Will growled. 'It's a title. Get over it.'

'No. It's so much more than that,' Pia said quietly. Will inhaled sharply. He had no idea what she was on about and he didn't care. 'Just sign it, Pia. There's still time.'

'Not for you, Silk. You're the one who's out of time – isn't that right? She doesn't need to sign anything.' Tanner looked straight at her. 'You've already got your redemption, Pia. You've got him back.'

'Who? Who's she got back?' Will asked.

Pia stared at Tanner. His eyes were burning brightly with righteous indignation.

'He can't force you into anything, no matter what he says,' Tanner said. 'Because either way, this all ends tonight. He needed you to lose here so that La Scala took Ava and he could step in with a counter-offer from the Royal. And it might well have worked too. But he didn't factor in Tony . . .'

Will looked on, his brain frantically trying to make connections. Who the hell was Tony?

'It doesn't *matter* whether you win or lose now. You told me in Brazil that once you had redemption you might retire – or not. So the decision facing you now is not where, but *if*, you dance. And you've got all the time in the world for that. Unlike him.' He nodded his head casually towards Will. 'Everleigh's tired of waiting. If you don't sign by tonight, he's pulling his investment. The Black Harbour fund will go under.'

'You don't know what you're gabbling on about,' Will sneered, scarcely able to believe that Tanner had cottoned on to his scheme. 'High finance is above and beyond the brain-power of a country boy like you,' he bluffed.

'You're quite right. Thank heavens Mrs Bremar was able to fill in all the gaps for me,' he said casually. 'You know, you really ought to be careful what you say when your tea's being brought in.'

Pia's hands flew up to her mouth and Will saw she was stifling a shriek of delight. She just loved that woman!

'You won't be laughing when she finds she can't get another job this side of Dublin,' Will managed.

'On the contrary, I've decided to keep her on.'

Will stared at him, trying to guess his meaning. Only his accountants knew that the house had been seized.

'You've what?' His skin had turned grey.

'I've bought Plumbridge back, thanks to Velasquez's very generous patronage. You might recall there's a clause in the contract that says the bank had to give me first refusal if the house was sold on again within five years.' Tanner smiled and shrugged. 'It's been four.'

There was a brusque knock on the door and Pavel came in.

'I've been asked to check whether Mr Silk is in here,' he said, looking at both Tanner and Will blankly – either would do as far as he was concerned. 'The judges are going back into the auditorium.'

Pia looked at Will, and felt her elation ebb away. Tanner's revelations meant one thing was startlingly clear at least: her competition was over.

There was a long silence as she accepted her loss, and she saw the hope fade from Will's eyes. His competition was over too.

'Goodbye, Will,' she said flatly.

Will's cat-like eyes, always so sharp and sure, deadened. He straightened his jacket and walked past without another word. There really was nothing more to be said. No one had won.

'And you too, Miss Soto,' Pavel added. 'They're announcing the winners in five minutes. Everyone has to go back on stage.'

Pia looked at Tanner in panic. Her tutu was torn, her tiara broken.

'But I can't go back out like this,' she said, aghast.

'Yes, you can,' he said, grabbing a red *Firebird* tutu that was hanging behind the door. 'Wear that.'

'But I didn't wear it tonight,' she panicked. There was no point in going out there anyway.

'Nobody cares about what you're wearing. They just want to see you,' he said, walking to the door. 'Now get changed. Your public awaits.'

She came out ninety seconds later, a small smile playing on her lips.

'Still think its *carnivale*?' she said archly, pushing a red feathered headdress into her hair as she fluttered past him. Tanner's eyes tickled the length of her.

'Bloody fantastic,' he murmured, as she ran ahead of him, almost colliding with Tony as he hurtled round the corner.

'Antonio!' Pia exclaimed, brightening up instantly. 'Great timing. They're just doing the prize-giving. Come with us and then we'll all go out for dinner afterwards. How was Sophie?'

Tony nodded at Tanner, but he looked frantic. 'She wasn't there.'

'Really?' Pia replied. 'Oh, well, don't worry. She probably just got nobbled by the judges. We'll catch her later.'

'No,' he said urgently. 'I've checked everywhere. One of the security guards said he saw her leave right after the last performance.'

Pia frowned. 'But that can't be right. She's got to stay till the prize-giving. She must be around.'

Tony shook his head. 'She's not. I know she's not.' He dug into his jeans pocket. 'She's gone here.'

He held out a Post-it. It had Sophie's writing on it, in the same purple as she'd used to write the card earlier. 'Tregov Klinik.'

'Where did you find this?'

'On her easel. Beneath the papers.'

'Beneath . . . ?' Pia murmured, remembering the call Sophie had taken the day of the second round and how it seemed to have disturbed her. She handed it back to him. 'That call really upset her,' she mumbled. 'She played it down but I could tell it had bothered her.' She looked back at the address. 'But why does she need to go to a clinic? Is she sick?'

As the words came out, a jumble of images and memories flashed through her brain – the grey pallor, the exhaustion, off her customary coffee, this weird obsession about polystyrene cups. I mean, polystyr— Her eyes widened. Sophie's heightened sense of smell . . .

'Oh my God! She's pregnant!' she cried.

'I know,' Tony said, looking anxiously at the Post-it, seeming to turn grey in front of her. 'And I think she's come here to have an abortion.'

Chapter Fifty-seven

Tony ran through the streets, trying to keep up with Pavel, who was surprisingly nimble and parting the sea of pedestrians in his path, like Moses. Pavel had known the address instantly, it was only four blocks away, and Tony felt his throat burn as he tore through the air to get to Sophie. They careered to a halt outside a tall sand-coloured building with balconies stepped all the way up. Pavel checked the lettering on the plastic sign before nodding to Tony. 'This is it.'

They shook hands briefly and Tony bounded up the steps.

A severe-looking woman in glasses was sitting behind a curved reception desk, tapping into a computer.

'May I help you?' she asked.

'Yes, please. I'm looking for the Tregov Klinik,' he panted.

'Third floor,' the woman said, looking back down at her screen.

He ran towards the stairs. 'Uh . . . we have lifts,' she said, motioning in the opposite direction.

'These are quicker, thanks,' he said, sprinting up two at a time.

He rounded the corner on the third floor and came out

into an open-plan waiting area. A bold blue carpet patterned with a yellow lattice covered the floors, and fluorescent lights hanging from the plastic ceiling tiles buzzed overhead. There was no sign of Sophie.

Frantically, he scanned the area again. Maybe she'd gone to the loo . . . 'Oh please, God!' he prayed. 'Don't let me be too late.' He couldn't have tracked her down all this way only to be ten minutes too late.

He saw a grey-haired man with a clipboard coming out of a side room. He ran over.

'Please . . . I'm looking for Sophie O'Farrell,' he said urgently. 'Is she here?'

The man looked at him. 'I'm sorry Mr . . . ?'

'Byrne. Tony Byrne.'

'I'm afraid our client list is strictly confidential.'

'But I'm the father,' Tony pleaded. 'I have a right to be here. I have to see her.'

He scanned the room again, his line of sight curtailed by the rows of shut doors.

'Sophie!' he hollered. 'Sophie!'

'Please, sir,' the doctor said nervously, glancing at one of the doors. It was enough for Tony. He darted over.

'Sophie?' he shouted, bursting in.

She was leaning, fully dressed, against the bed, her arms folded around her, her chin dropped down, like a lonely swan's. She looked deathly pale and her eyes were red from crying.

'Sophie! Oh God, Soph!' he cried. 'Don't say you've done it.'

She stared at him, bewildered. She couldn't work out what he was doing here, how he had found her . . . He put his arms round her, whispering into her hair.

'Am I too late? Please tell me,' he begged, clamping his hands over her ears and pleading into her eyes.

She shook her head.

'Oh thank God,' he said, burying his face in her hair, and beginning to cry with her. 'Why did you disappear? Why didn't you talk to me about it?' he asked, standing up straight.

'I ruined it for us,' she said, her voice breaking. 'I forgot to take my pill the morning after our first night together. I got home the next morning and I have to hide them, see, from my parents, and I just forgot 'cos I always take it before bed and I could only think about you, and then when I realized . . . we've only been together a few months.'

'So? It's *us*, Sophie. You and me. We both know we're forever.'

She cried harder at his confidence.

'I panicked,' she sobbed. 'I don't deserve to have a baby.'

'How can you even think that?' Tony asked, aghast.

'Because of . . . because of . . .' she hiccuped.

'When you were fifteen?'

She stopped. 'How did you know?' she whispered.

'Esther told me. Don't be mad – I made her. She told me what happened.' He shrugged. 'I can see why it would have been so difficult for you. Why you felt you had to go.'

'I had no choice. I couldn't stay! It would have humiliated my father. How could he have remained in his post if everyone in the village knew I'd had an abortion? It would have made him a laughing stock. It's so traditional there, still . . .' Her sobs grew deeper at the memory and he muffled her head in his chest. She clasped her arms around his waist, gratefully. 'I was too young. Barely fifteen. And Jerry . . .

God, Jerry. He was going to stand by me, you know? He wanted to get married and settle down.' She gave a joyless laugh. 'I hadn't even *started* my life by then but he was already trying to shackle me down with a kid a year and a pinny.'

She shook her head sadly. 'I just knew there was more for me out there. That I had a life to live first.' She looked up at him, her owlish eyes filling up. 'I'm disgusting, aren't I? For putting my life before my baby's?' Her shoulders shook as the tears began to spill again. 'I'm disgusting!'

Tony looked at her, horrified by her vehemence. 'Stop it, Soph! Don't talk like that! Of course you're not disgusting. You were a child, for God's sake. You've got to forgive yourself.'

'I can't!' she cried, shaking her head. 'I've tried, really I have. After I had the abortion in London. I tried but I . . . I just couldn't cope with what I'd done. I had nightmares about it every night for years.' She bit her lip, trying to keep the hysteria at bay. 'Sleeping with you in the cottage was the first time I *didn't* have the nightmares. But then, when I found out I was pregnant again, they came back and I realized . . . well, how could I choose one baby over another? How could I let one baby die and the other live? What right do I have to any happiness after I did such a terrible thing?' She started to shake and Tony hugged her tightly.

'You were a child, Sophie. Anyone would understand. God knows, I wouldn't have been able to become a parent at fifteen. I wouldn't even have been capable last Christmas! I spent my childhood so filled with rage and hate for my mother that I grew up just despising the idea of family. It was the absolute opposite of what I knew. I couldn't imagine a time when I would ever be free of those feelings, when I would ever *dare* to try to break that cycle and hope for anything good to come out of it.'

He raised her chin with his finger and stared into her eyes. 'Not until I met you, anyway.'

Sophie swallowed. 'But . . . but . . . you said . . .'

'I know what I said. And I was wrong – about everything. About my father; but about my mother, most of all.' He shook his head, the sediment of the past week's revelations still trying to settle. 'She didn't abandon me; she didn't give me up for drugs. She died trying to save me . . . When I think of all the curses I threw at her memory . . . I thought she was the worst mother in the world. Literally the worst . . .' He swallowed and nodded sombrely, his own eyes wet. 'But I found out last week that she died for me. She died in Rio trying to find me and my sister.'

'You've got a sister?'

His eyes widened as he remembered she didn't know the final piece of the puzzle yet. 'Yes. I thought she was dead but it turns out she's been right in front of me, for years.'

'She has?'

'It's because of her that I found you actually.' He stopped and considered. 'Or is it the other way round?'

Sophie shook her head, baffled. 'You've lost me.'

'It's Pia,' he smiled. 'She's my sister.'

Sophie gasped and her hands flew to her mouth as the connections began to link up. She scrutinized his face – the one she adored and which she had recognized at a spiritual level that first night in the pub. She matched up the Irish eyes, the caramel skin, and their cameo-perfect profiles. How could she not have seen it before?

'She's the one who told me where to find you. She's worried

sick about you.' He shrugged. 'And she really wants to be an aunty, you know.'

Sophie gave a small hysterical giggle. 'Oh God! Pia, my baby's aunt? Can you imagine a mini-her with the terrible twos? I'm not sure I can cope with her DNA in my kids!'

Tony grinned and leant down to kiss her. 'Tough.'

She sighed and looked up at him. 'So we're doing this, then? You, me and –' she placed her hands over her tummy – 'Bump?'

Tony nodded. She bit her lip anxiously. 'But how am I going to tell my father? The abortion's like the elephant in the room at home. He knows what I did – they all do – but we don't talk about it. How can I go back again and say I'm now having your baby *out of wedlock*? You don't know my father,' she said, shaking her fists in the air. 'Hellfire and brimstones!'

'Actually, he already knows,' Tony shrugged. 'I went over to your house after Esther told me what happened – and I told him why you'd run away again.'

'You did not!' she whispered.

He nodded.

'How *did* you know?' she asked, curious.

He shrugged. 'You stopped drinking coffee every hour on the hour, for a start. And the Brie went untouched.' He stroked her cheek. 'And you *love* Brie. And you never finished your glass of wine in the evenings . . . shall I go on?'

She shook her head.

'Anyway, I told your father it was my fault because I'd made it categorically clear to you that I never wanted a family. I explained about my messed-up background. I didn't even know the truth by then about Pia and my parents – even though it's changed everything for me anyway – but getting you and our baby back was all that mattered. It was all I wanted. When I found you gone that morning, I was out of my mind . . .' He swallowed nervously. 'It made me realize I don't ever want to be without you. So I asked him a question.'

'You asked my father *a question*?' she echoed, as horrified as if he'd just said he'd asked him to share a spliff.

Tony nodded. He took her hand and sank gallantly to his knee.

'Will you marry me, Sophie O'Farrell?' he asked, his eyes shining as he looked up at her.

She gasped. 'You asked him for my hand?' she breathed.

'Kind of.'

'What does that mean?' she frowned.

His eyes twinkled. 'I'm not telling until you give me an answer.'

'Yes! Yes! Of course, it's yes!' she cried, and he sprang up and kissed her passionately.

'Thank God,' he murmured, clasping her head in his hands, their foreheads pressed together.

'So what was the question?' she said, impatient to know, nuzzling his nose with hers.

Tony grinned.

'I asked him to marry us. And he's got a space – a week on Saturday.'

All the dancers were standing on the stage and the prize-giving had already begun. The gold, silver and bronze had been awarded to the juniors and they'd started on the bounty prizes for the seniors as Pia delicately ran to join them.

Tanner stood watching from the wings, and he smiled at the audible sigh of relief that greeted her late arrival. She made him feel that way too.

He saw one particularly thin ballerina appraise Pia in the line-up – eyeing up the new tutu, the beatific smile – and, from the spite written all over her face, he knew instantly she was Ava. He saw that Silk had returned to the judging panel, but nothing could disguise the bruising on his face. He was swelling up like a pufferfish.

He tuned back in to the secretary of the competition who was handing out the prizes.

'. . . And in third position, with an arithmetic mean of sixty-three points, is Miss Yelena Maritsuva.'

The Belarusian girl skittered forward, beaming brightly as she was handed a bronze statuette and a spray of roses.

A polite round of applause swayed around the theatre. Bronze was nowhere. This tournament was all about – and always had been – Pia and Ava. Only one could come out on top.

'In second position,' the secretary said, raising his eyebrows teasingly, 'with a mean of sixty-seven points . . .' He took his time; he knew exactly how hotly anticipated this announcement was.

'Miss Pia Soto!'

The stunned audience took a collective gasp of breath, sucking the air from the star-canopied auditorium like a vacuum cleaner. Tanner saw Pia stiffen and the smile fix more rigidly to her beautiful face, as she glided forward.

He looked over at Ava and saw the gloat in her eyes, the way her chin rose in the air triumphantly.

Pia slid forward graciously, easily able to keep the tears at bay. Will was sitting right in front of her and she wouldn't give him the satisfaction of crying. Besides, their showdown had given her time to prepare for this. She knew now she never would have won, no matter what she'd done.

It wasn't that she wasn't devastated. She was. After all, it was the final destination of her lifelong journey, ever since that first day at the Bolshoi when she'd pulled on those satin ballet slippers for the first time. From barefoot ballerina leaping across the *cerrados* to prima ballerina, her race from her past was at an end now, regardless of whether she made Assoluta or not. She was free from her debt of honour. Antonio was alive. If she continued to dance from here on, it would be only because she wanted to.

Ava and Will had stripped her of the right to a fair contest, but she knew in her heart that the trophy and the audience were hers. They proved it the way they roared as she took possession of her statuette. The hairs on the back of her neck stood on end as they rose to their feet and stamped loudly, partly as support, partly in protest at the wrong call.

Ava swallowed nervously and looked around, baffled by the response. She was second! Why all the fuss?

The secretary tried to call the audience to order, waving his hands and pleading with them to return to their seats. Slowly, they sat back down, but catcalls of 'Wrong!' and 'Disgusting!' whistled through the darkness.

'And in first place, the gold medal for the Thirtieth Varna International Ballet Competition goes to . . .' He paused dramatically, but the atmosphere had dissipated like a slow puncture. Everybody knew perfectly well who it was going to: 'Miss Ava Petrova.'

A polite round of applause – damning with its faint praise – scattered around the gallery as Ava skipped forward and was handed the torch with which to light the flame of the

Varna Olympiad, but a few low boos were distinguishable and the clapping ended before she had finished her curtsey.

Murmurs of discord began to rumble from the audience as they waited restlessly for the flame to catch. No one was interested in indulging Ava's moment of glory. Pia Soto's third-round performance had been epic and career-defining. It was inconceivable that she hadn't won.

'A travesty!'

They began to stand up to leave, making their displeasure known by voting with their feet. There would be no encore for the winner this year.

'Ladies and gentlemen,' the secretary said, waving his arms to encourage the audience to stay sitting down. 'Please stay in your seats. We still have one prize remaining.'

The audience looked around at each other, puzzled. The bounty awards had already been presented. They always finished with the top three last.

They sank back down again, perplexed, but still disgruntled.

'This year we have a very special prize to present . . .' The news blanketed the last remaining protests and a curious silence fell.

'It is one that has been presented only *once* in the esteemed thirty-year history of the competition. But in honour of the definitive and flawless variation that we witnessed tonight, and which few of us will ever see equalled again in our lifetime –' a rumbling roar like thunder suddenly gathered in anticipation in the darkness – 'it is the judges' very great honour to present the Varna Grand Prix . . . to Miss Pia Soto!'

A cheer that could have lifted the roof – had there been one – heaved forth and Tanner looked across at Pia to find her covering her face with her hands, her shoulders shaking. Her shock and awe only pleased the crowd more and it was three minutes before she could compose herself enough to step forward and receive the prize.

Tanner hollered and stamped his feet, sure that wasn't quite etiquette at a ballet competition, but everyone else was doing the same. They gave her a standing ovation that lasted sixteen minutes, so long that Tanner began to despair of her ever being returned to him again.

When she did finally come off stage, she ran straight to him, led by instinct, not sight. Her eyes were blinded with tears.

Tanner grabbed her by the waist and swung her into him.

'You did it,' he said, eyes glittering. 'You're free.'

'Actually, I'm very expensive,' she giggled, impressing herself with her ability to be contrary even at a time like this.

Tanner chuckled, equally impressed and not remotely surprised. 'I meant you're free from your ghosts. *And* a free agent. You're not with Paolo any more.'

'Never was, not once you turned up,' she blinked.

'But that night in Brazil—'

'He passed out. Not that that was the point – you were supposed to fight for me.' She gave him a soft punch in the stomach.

He looked down at her, hypnotized. She was impossibly lovely.

'Does today count instead?'

Pia nodded. 'But you know – you have to stop rescuing me.'

'Do I?' he shrugged. 'It seems to be such a tough habit to break.'

'I mean, you even found Tony!' she said, throwing her arms out hopelessly. 'What's a girl to do?'

'Yes . . . about that,' he said, sighing forbiddingly. 'I'm afraid we're going to have to talk.'

'Why? What's wrong?' She felt cold suddenly.

'Well, you see, it was one thing saving your life. That was free, *gratis*, on the house. But bringing your brother back from the dead too?' He shook his head. 'I'm going to have to charge you for that. I know what a song and dance you make about being independent, that you don't like to be beholden and all that jazz, but . . . it's a pretty big debt.'

'I see,' she said, unable to fight back a smile. 'And how long am I going to be beholden to you for?' she said, wriggling closer to him so that he nearly lost the power of speech.

He shrugged and tried to look casual.

'It's looking like life.'

'Thank God for that,' she mumbled, pulling his head down to hers and pushing the sweet spring of her lips against his.

Players

by

KAREN SWAN

ISBN: 978-1-4472-2373-3

Friendships are strong. Lust is stronger . . .

*Harry Hunter was everywhere you looked – bearing down
from bus billboards, beaming out from the society pages,
falling out of nightclubs in the gossip columns, and
flirting up a storm on the telly chat show circuit.*

Harry Hunter is the new golden boy of the literary scene.
With his books selling by the millions, the paparazzi on his
tail, and a supermodel on each arm, he seems to have the
world at his feet. Women all over the globe adore him but
few suspect that his angelic looks hide a darker side, a side
that conceals a lifetime of lies and deceit.

Tor, Cress and Kate have been best friends for as long as they
can remember. Through all the challenges of marriage, raising children and maintaining their high-flying careers, they
have stuck together as a powerful and loyal force to be reckoned with – living proof that twenty-first-century women
can have it all, and do. It is only when the captivating Harry
comes into their lives that things begin to get complicated, as
Tor, Cress and Kate are drawn into Harry's dangerous games.

Christmas at Tiffany's

by

KAREN SWAN

ISBN: 978-0-330-53272-3

**Three cities, three seasons,
one chance to find the life that fits**

Cassie settled down too young, marrying her first serious boyfriend. Now, ten years later, she is betrayed and broken. With her marriage in tatters and no career or home of her own, she needs to work out where she belongs in the world and who she really is.

So begins a year-long trial as Cassie leaves her sheltered life in rural Scotland to stay with each of her best friends in the most glamorous cities in the world: New York, Paris and London. Exchanging the grouse moor and mousy hair for low-carb diets and high-end highlights, Cassie tries on each city for size as she attempts to track down the life she was supposed to have been leading, and with it, the man who was supposed to love her all along.

The Perfect Present

by

KAREN SWAN

ISBN: 978-0-330-53273-0

Memories are a gift . . .

Haunted by a past she can't escape, Laura Cunningham desires nothing more than to keep her world small and precise – her quiet relationship and growing jewellery business are all she needs to get by. Until the day when Rob Blake walks into her studio and commissions a necklace that will tell his enigmatic wife Cat's life in charms.

As Laura interviews Cat's family, friends and former lovers, she steps out of her world and into theirs – a charmed world where weekends are spent in Verbier and the air is lavender-scented, where friends are wild, extravagant and jealous, and a big love has to compete with grand passions.

Hearts are opened, secrets revealed and as the necklace begins to fill up with trinkets, Cat's intoxicating life envelops Laura's own. By the time she has to identify the final charm, Laura's metamorphosis is almost complete. But the last story left to tell has the power to change all of their lives forever, and Laura is forced to choose between who she really is and who it is she wants to be.

Christmas at Claridge's

by

KAREN SWAN

ISBN: 978-1-4472-1969-9

The best presents can't be wrapped

Portobello – home to the world-famous street market, Notting Hill Carnival . . . and Clem Alderton. She's the queen of the scene, the girl everyone wants to be or be with. But beneath the morning-after make-up, Clem is keeping a secret, and when she goes too far one reckless night she endangers everything – her home, her job and even her adored brother's love.

Portofino – a place of wild beauty and old-school glamour. Clem has been here once before and vowed never to return. But when a handsome stranger asks Clem to restore a neglected villa, it seems like the answer to her problems – if she can just face up to her past.

Claridge's – at Christmas, Clem is back in London working on a special commission for London's grandest hotel. But is this where her heart really lies?